Death by Stealth
(A Mike Cannon jumps racing mystery)

# Eric Horridge

# DEDICATION

This book is dedicated to all the NHS and other Health Professionals around the world who have put themselves at the forefront of the Covid-19 Pandemic in 2020, in order to save the lives of many.

Death by Stealth

# Prologue

The three of them were soaked to the skin, the rain hammered down unrelentingly. They trudged through the darkness, occasionally slipping and scratching themselves on the branches of the trees, cuts to their hands and faces. They were barely able to see in front of them as they shuffled through the carpet of leaves that covered the forest floor. The spiky fingers of the trees, darkened even more by the moonless night, seemed to reach out towards them like monsters from a horror film, their jagged branches acting like hands with razors attached.

The man at the front had his hands tied behind his back, the man directly behind him held a gun, a *Sig Sauer P938* an inch from the back of the neck, and with the other hand, held the first man's collar.

They had entered the area after having driven off the A34 and down a side road towards Roundhill Wood. They were miles from the closest motorway and they had seen no houses anywhere for the past 15 minutes of the drive. Eventually, they had turned off the side road and onto a dirt path before stopping about half a mile along it. It was just as well they had a 4 x 4 which allowed them access and an ability to drive without becoming stuck in the mud.

"Keep going," the gunman said, pushing the first in the back, making him fall to the ground with a grunt. Slowly the man stood up. His jacket was covered in dead leaves, his face muddied and his hair matted with dirt, rivulets of rainwater running down his neck. He staggered as he stood, finding his balance difficult in the soft ground which undulated upwards, then dropped towards a swollen stream that they could just about hear gushing along, the sound muted by the continuous heavy rain.

After a couple of minutes, the gunman pulled at the arms of the man ahead, stopping him. They were standing in a small copse of trees within the woods themselves. The third individual watched, staying a few metres behind the others, saying nothing, but caressing their own weapon hidden in the palm of a hand.

The man with the handgun placed it directly behind the head of his prisoner and without any hesitation, pulled the trigger.

# CHAPTER 1

There was no sound.

Darkness enveloped the figure dressed all in black as it took off the lid. The sky was an inky black, the few clouds above the course hung like cotton balls, there being no breeze at all to move them on. A cold front had arrived during the afternoon but had now stalled half-way across the country, leaving the sky almost clear and temperatures low. Across to the right was the outline of the grandstand, a lone light attached to its side shone towards the ground illuminating the cold concrete of the public viewing area. It was too far away to have any impact on the figure. Beyond the empty building, the road led through Esher and on to Cobham. Directly ahead of the trespasser lay the back straight of the track, over a kilometre long, with both hurdle and steeplechase fences spaced out along its length. The figure poured the liquid from the container it held onto the birch of the jump, moving from left to right and back again ensuring that the whole barrier received a soaking. The strong smell of petrol permeated the still air, invading the nostrils of the dark shadow, a smile of satisfaction creased the face. Putting the cap back onto the container the trespasser reached into a jacket pocket and placed the device into the birch of the jump, then turned away and walked casually towards the hole in the fence that had been the entry point onto the course. Once through the fence, the figure clambered up the bank that hid the train line from the racetrack. At the top of the bank, the figure turned and waited.

It took seven minutes, exactly as expected, before the steeplechase fence ignited in a ball of flame as the device left there did what it was designed to do. The petrol-soaked birch burned rapidly, and within less than a minute the whole fence including the base and wings were ablaze, flames licking upwards with sparks and embers shooting off into the night sky.

The figure smiled, then turned away, the red glow of the burning birch, wood, and plastic danced on the back of the individual's jacket as it drifted silently away into the cold and dark of the night.

# CHAPTER 2

"If I gave you one hundred thousand pounds, would you be able to find me something decent?" the man asked.

Cannon took a silent intake of breath. One hundred thousand pounds was a lot of money.

The two men were sitting in the bar of the Old Swan Hotel, in Minster Lovell, Witney, about 15 miles from Cannon's stables in Woodstock, not far from Blenheim Palace in Oxfordshire. The meeting was at the behest of a potential benefactor, a new owner into Cannon's stables, James Formrobe.

Formrobe was a partner in a software firm, situated on the road between Asthall and the tiny hamlet of Swinbrook not far from the river Windrush in West Oxfordshire. The company had done exceptionally well through the development of various applications used in its own business and for those of others who had the ideas but were willing to pay to have someone create and maintain them. The 'apps' sat on all the platforms, Apple, Google, and Microsoft. Formrobe was a very wealthy man, young, 34, and with lots of energy. He was tall, just over six feet, with medium length blond hair. He had a small scar on his left cheek from a stud accidentally scraped across his face in a school rugby match. His eyes were blue and were often described by others as *deep*. He wore glasses that seemed too thick and accentuated the perception. He had a longish face matched by a slimline nose. With broad shoulders and similar waist size, he was looked upon as having a solid build.

Cannon wasn't sure if it was a case of the man had too much money and it was burning a hole in his pocket or that he had a genuine interest in racing, especially jumps racing. There were no guarantees in the business, except perhaps hard work and disappointment.

"Can I ask why you are so keen on the racing game?" Cannon said. "It's not for the faint-hearted, and no amount of money can ever guarantee success."

Formrobe took a swig of his beer then placed the near-empty glass on the small wooden table that sat between them.

"Redrum," he said.

Cannon had an inkling of what Formrobe was referring to. Nearly everyone knew the story of how Ginger McCain, a used car salesman and former taxi driver, bought Redrum for 6000 guineas and trained the horse on Southport's beaches. The horse became a household name, a superstar by winning the Grand National three times and running second twice. What was even more remarkable was the fact that despite running in over 100 races, the horse never fell.

"That was a long time ago," Cannon replied. "It's not something that happens every day, you know. Very rarely will you find a horse like Redrum, in fact, he was a once in a lifetime animal."

"Yes, before I was even born."

Cannon contemplated this last comment before acknowledging it with a nod of his head.

"So, what is the fascination then, James?" Cannon asked, trying to get a better understanding of Formrobe's motivation. Cannon was happy to help his potential client, and in some ruthless way was happy to take his money, but he needed to know the younger man's expectations and they both needed to agree on them. Falling out with your owners when things weren't going as expected was not good for business, nor indeed was it good for one's self-esteem.

"Ever since I heard the story and watched the film of the 1973 *National* I always wanted to own a racehorse," Formrobe answered. "It was one of those moments that has stayed with me. A point in time that will forever be etched in history and it's something I want to experience myself. I've been thinking about it for nearly ten years now. I would have done it ages ago if the business had not taken up most of my time."

Cannon smiled. He knew of thousands of people who would have had the same wish, the same dream of owning their own Redrum. However, he also knew, as did most others, that it was exactly that, a dream. To be brutally frank, a pipedream. A horse like Redrum came along once in a lifetime, and it wasn't going to be in Cannon's lifetime.

"Look James, I don't want to be negative but if you are serious about buying a horse, could we please agree on something?"

"Sure, what is it?"

"That whatever happens, you accept upfront that we are going for a ride, if you'll pardon the pun, and that you are happy to go wherever it leads us? Without that kind of acceptance, I'm not sure I want to accept your patronage. Besides, I am keen to understand why you chose me as your potential trainer. Can you shed some light on that as well for me?"

Formrobe looked a little downcast. It wasn't often that people said no to his money.

"Okay," he said eventually.

"Good," Cannon replied, looking forward to hearing more. "But before we get into more detail about options regarding buying you a horse, tell me a little bit more about yourself. What I read on the internet after I *googled* you was a little vague. So please, tell me more."

Formrobe looked around, seemingly satisfied that no one else was listening to what he and Cannon were discussing. To Cannon, he looked embarrassed, his *geeky* appearance almost mirroring his personality.

"I was never any good at sport," Formrobe began. "I think it's probably a cliché but I spent most of my time in my bedroom when I was growing up, surfing the net, watching YouTube, Skyping, and sharing stuff with my friends. Eventually, after I finished school I went to university in Manchester and did a degree in IT Security and Networking."

Cannon wasn't sure what all this meant but he had a rough idea about where it was all going.

"In my final year, my friend, Alan Smerdon, who I had met during my second year, and I, decided to build a couple of applications for mobile phones around data-protection. We didn't really expect them to be as successful as they were, but before we knew it, our apps sort of took off and we were suddenly making more money than we could ever have imagined."

"And that formed the basis of your company?" Cannon asked.

"Yes, *SecureTwo*."

"How long ago did you start the business?"

"As I said, we started with the products, our *apps*, fifteen years ago now and we haven't looked back since."

"And you are both still the sole owners of the business?" Cannon asked realizing that he was slipping back into his old habit of questioning almost everything. His life as a policeman, a Detective Inspector, was well behind him now, however it never seemed to leave him fully. "Once a cop always a cop" was an adage he never seemed to be able to dislodge from himself.

Formrobe reached for the last of his drink and he and Cannon emptied their glasses simultaneously. To any observer, it looked like they had coordinated their movements as they did so.

"No, Alan and I no longer speak. We parted ways a few years ago."

Cannon was surprised, and it showed on his face. It wasn't something he had anticipated nor was the information in the public domain. When he had searched for information about Formrobe and his company, there was nothing mentioned anywhere that would have indicated a rift between Formrobe and his business partner.

"We kept the personal things between us very quiet," Formrobe said, anticipating Cannon's questions. "When we went to the market to raise funds for the business we worked through proxies, lawyers, and one of the larger accounting firms. Both of us were naïve, we were predominantly *geeks* who had ideas, but little business knowledge. Eventually, the naivety caught up with us and our relationship fell apart."

Cannon sat quietly for a short while, watching Formrobe's face as he ruminated about the past. As he looked at the young man, Cannon thought he saw a sadness in the man's eyes, with lines creasing his face. Something in the past still sat uncomfortably within Formrobe's memory.

"What happened?" Cannon asked, "If you don't mind sharing it with me?" he went on sympathetically.

The young man considered Cannon's request. For a few seconds, it looked like he intended to decline the invitation. After what seemed like an age, but was merely seconds, he nodded in Cannon's direction, indicating a willingness to carry on the conversation. Then remembering that their glasses were empty he called the barman over for another drink. He asked if Cannon would like another, Cannon declined.

"It was a woman," Formrobe said, a sad smile on his face.

Cannon had half expected the answer. Wasn't it often the case, he thought, that long term friends and women, don't always mix? Especially when there is money around.

"Oh," Cannon replied, feigning surprise.

"Yes, but it isn't what you think?"

"I'm not sure what to think, to be honest. But as you know it's none of my business why you and your business partner decided to go separate ways," he said. "I'm just keen to understand if I can do a job for you that we can both benefit from. It's all about mutual respect."

"Understood," replied Formrobe.

"Okay, I'm glad we sorted that out. So please, carry on."

"Well the woman we fell out over was his mother,"

"His mother?" repeated Cannon.

"Yes, she was, is, a very strong woman," Formrobe said, his voice and manner indicating something unpleasant about the lady concerned. "When we were looking to expand, we needed more capital, more funds. Alan's family, well his mother, is very well-off and we had hoped to borrow money from her."

"And let me guess, she said 'no'?"

Formrobe's face reflected how he felt. To Cannon, it seemed the man was reliving all that had happened in his mind. He waited for Formrobe to speak.

"Yes," he said eventually. "We were both surprised as we knew we had a good product, a great future, but she just decided to be difficult."

"So, what happened?"

"She wanted us to sell the business. We were way past the start-up phase. She felt that we had some great clients, an annuity business, and we were developing new solutions that the market wanted, so it was a great time to sell."

"Take the money and run?" asked Cannon.

"I guess so."

It wouldn't have been the first time that a *start-up* had been sold by its owners, founders, for a large sum, Cannon thought. The past twenty years had been littered with such stories. Some businesses had been sold for huge sums, making many people instant millionaires. Many businesses had been absorbed by larger companies and never heard of again and many others had grown exponentially through such acquisitions. Globalization was inherent in how the market worked. Size, scale, reach, profits, and valuations were endemic in how business now operated.

Cannon was pleased that his own world didn't stretch to such extremes anymore. In his past, he had seen greed lead to anger, and anger lead to murder....

"And?" Cannon asked. He wasn't sure why, but he felt he needed to encourage Formrobe to continue, to get the issue on the table. Looking into his potential client's face, he noticed an air of disappointment. The man's eyes glazed over, remembering what must have been a difficult time for him.

Formrobe shook his head, apologizing for seeming to be so far away.

"Sorry," he continued, "was miles away."

Cannon just smiled.

"To make a long story short, Alan and I eventually came to an agreement, which his mother finally, but reluctantly, accepted. He sold fifty percent of his shares to an investor, twenty-five percent to me, fifteen percent to his mother and he kept the remaining ten percent for himself."

"Which means that if you each had a half share initially, he still has a five percent stake in the business and his mother seven and a half percent?"

"Yes."

"And you have the major stake with an investor owning twenty-five percent of the business," responded Cannon.

"That was the position initially. Since then our investor has bought some more shares," he smiled. "I sold nearly all of what I bought from Alan to them a year or so later and made an even bigger profit than Alan had made. His mother was very annoyed with me."

"So why didn't Alan and his mother just sell out completely if it was all about the money?"

"It's quite simple really. Alan had sold his stake to our investor at quite a premium to what we had put in ourselves. He made a huge amount of money and his mother could see the potential to make even more money over time without much risk," Formrobe continued. "Now *he* has a small stake but doesn't need to worry about how the company performs. He's a very wealthy man now. His mother has the greater risk but given how well we have done to date she now realizes that the business is worth so much more than she ever imagined. Her share has quadrupled in value since she bought Alan's stake. She can sell anytime she wants to, but since she became a stakeholder in the business and has seen how well we have done, she wants to hold on to her stake for a while longer yet."

Greed, Cannon thought.

"That's surprising from what you said earlier. I thought she wanted *out?*" he said.

"She did, but she changed her mind. I think she'll sell at some point. In the meantime, it seems she's happy to wear the risk if something went wrong. After all, she's already wealthy, keeping her share has been nothing but positive for her."

"While you wear most of the risk?" Cannon interrupted.

"That's true, yes," Formrobe said, "although our investor has to accept that they have to bear some of the risks as well."

"Sounds a bit too complicated for me," Cannon continued. "I'm assuming that you know where your business is heading so I wish you luck with it to be honest."

"Thanks, Mike, I appreciate your understanding."

Cannon didn't fully understand the intricacies of trusts, start-ups, buy-outs, share swops etcetera but he knew enough to know that within a business, of any type, there would always be tension whenever money and people were part of the equation.

Having heard the story, Cannon decided it was time to move the conversation on. He was satisfied that Formrobe wasn't getting into horse ownership on a whim. It seemed to Cannon that despite his obvious wealth, Formrobe still appeared to be *grounded* and that the desire to get involved with the game had been something he had not decided upon lightly. It appeared to be something that had been smouldering within him for quite some time.

"Okay, let's talk about the options," Cannon said, picking up an envelope and removing the contents. "As you can see there are various ways of becoming an owner," he continued, holding up a couple of pieces of paper that included information about rights, obligations, and responsibilities regarding the ownership of a racehorse that would run under National Hunt Rules.

"Sorry Mike," chimed in Formrobe, interrupting Cannon's flow, "I don't wish to appear rude, but for your information, I don't want to buy into a syndicate, a partnership or even lease a horse, I'm looking to buy one *outright*," the emphasis on the last word was obvious. "I just wanted to make that clear," he continued.

Cannon took a couple of seconds before responding. "Sorry James, I forgot. I was considering your risk. I should have realised from what you told me just now that it wasn't an issue. Most people understand that jumps racing is a risky business, that their investment can be a very short one, in fact so short as their horse may never reach the track. Because of that, I always want my clients to know what they could be facing."

Formrobe nodded. "I get it, Mike, I really do. One Hundred Thousand pounds is a lot of money, even to me, but it's what I'm prepared to spend. I know that whatever a horse costs, it doesn't guarantee success."

"Glad you understand that," Cannon said.

"So that's why the 100K. I *could* spend a lot more but I'd prefer to put my toe in the water first, rather than jump in with both feet."

"And you chose me to be your trainer because….?"

"I saw what happened a few years ago at Aintree. That issue with *RockGod* and its owner. Ever since then I have had you in mind."

Cannon acknowledged the sentiment then said, "OK, can I make a suggestion?"

"Sure," replied Formrobe, sitting slightly forward on his seat, glad that they were no longer talking about his business.

"We have a few options," Cannon said, his mind now focused on the next steps. "If we are buying outright, we can look to see if there is anything reasonable for sale currently. There are always horses on the market, but not all of them are worth what some pay for them," he said. "You can find lots of people selling racehorses on-line but I suggest I make a few enquiries with those that I know and trust and see if we can find something available now that could be worth considering? The alternate is to look at some of the horses available at one of the upcoming Goffs sales or even wait until their sales later in the year…"

"I wouldn't want to wait too long," Formrobe interrupted, "I'd really like to find something asap. Now that I've made my mind up, I'm keen to get going."

Cannon looked at the man opposite. Even though Cannon had a good feeling about him, it was obvious that Formrobe was ambitious and had a bit of a steel streak within him. It would suggest that they *could* still clash in the future, despite what they had discussed earlier. Formrobe clearly knew what he wanted.

"Okay," Cannon said eventually. "With the season's start just a couple of weeks away, let me see what I can do. I think for 100,000 pounds there is very likely going to be something worth considering out there, but we just have to find it."

"Thanks, Mike,"

"No problem," Cannon said, standing up and offering his hand. "I'll be in touch."

# CHAPTER 3

"Bloody vandals!" the man wearing the tie said. "What's the world coming to?" he opined out-loud to no one in particular.

There were three of them standing at the fence. The twisted plastic of the wing of the jump spread out in different directions, congealed like jelly but shaped like a weed that had suddenly infected the landscape and attached itself like a protuberance on a dead tree. The birch that had previously stood tall atop the base of the jump had now been turned to ash. During the early hours, a soft rain had begun, leaving a cold and misty morning. The smoke from the slightly smouldering remains merged with the mist and the rain.

"Just as well we've got a couple of weeks before our first meeting," said the man wearing the brown overalls. "It would be a bugger if we weren't able to fix it in time."

"You can say that again," acknowledged the man with the tie, thinking about the cost of replacing the jump. "How long do you think it will take?"

The Clerk of the course, William Stark, looked at his colleague, jumping in to answer the Chairman's question before Edward Billingsgate, his course manager, was able to reply.

"I think Ed and his team, should be able to sort this out by tomorrow afternoon, Mr. Chairman," he stated with authority, "Isn't that right Edward?" he continued.

Billingsgate's eyes reflected how he felt when asked the question. If looks could kill….

Stark knew that Billingsgate had limited staff at the moment due to illness and the redundancies that had been made recently. He was aware that there was only Billingsgate and one other to do all the work needed on the track. Times were tough. The smaller racetracks were no longer able to compete with the larger ones. Very few punters attended the smaller racetracks anymore. Most people bet on-line nowadays so the money from entrance fees, tote betting, and the few concession stands had dwindled considerably over the years. Survival was the name of the game now. Extra costs like fixing fences that had been vandalized only added to the pressure on the bottom line.

-----------------------------------------

"How much?!" asked the Chairman.

"About four thousand quid," said Billingsgate.

They were sitting in the boardroom at the back of the course grandstand. It was just the two of them. Stark had gone to call his GM Commercial Operations to see if their insurance policy covered the cost of repairs for the fire-damaged fence.

"Four thousand pounds?" repeated the Chairman.

"Yes, Frank. These things are not cheap. And by the way that's only the cost of materials. It doesn't cover my time or that of my other staff."

Frank Mallick sat back in his chair and looked around. The walls were filled with photographs from the past. Great racehorses that had raced on the track that he could see through a picture window to his right. The mist had lifted slightly but specks of rain still caressed the glass. He sighed audibly. Billingsgate stayed quiet.

Mallick stood, walked over to the window, and peered out. "Winter's coming," he said nodding at the scene outside. "It may be a while yet, but already I'm feeling the cold." Turning back towards Billingsgate, he said, "Must be my age," a sad smile spread across his face. Sixty-seven and retired, Mallick was beginning to feel the years. "Not sure how you do it, Ed, you're only a few years younger than me."

"Probably it's about movement," Billingsgate replied. "If I stop, it'll be permanently," he continued good-naturedly. "So, I don't…I've been at this course for over thirty years now, so I just have to keep going I suppose, though I think I've only a couple of years left in me."

"Fair enough," Mallick replied, "fair enough. That's the problem isn't it?" he continued, "time, it just catches up with us all eventually."

As Billingsgate was about to answer, Mallick's mobile phone that he had placed on the boardroom table, began to ring. Billingsgate recognized the tune, *Fly me to the moon.*

Mallick looked at the number on the phone's screen. It was unknown. He decided to answer anyway.

"Hello?"

"Mr. Mallick?" the voice replied.

"Yes, who is this please?"

"Inspector Timothy Bayman, from the Nottinghamshire police,"

"Oh, hello Inspector, how can I help you?"

"Firstly, I hope you don't mind but your Clerk of the Course, Mr. William Stark gave me your mobile number."

Mallick had no objections. "No problem at all Inspector," he said. "Is this to do with the recent vandalism we've experienced?"

Bayman responded in the affirmative. "I would like to come and see you, if I may?" he answered. "Would two o'clock this afternoon work for you?"

"Yes, that would be no problem at all."

"Perfect," replied the policeman.

Before Bayman had the chance to end the call, Mallick jumped in with a question.

"Umm, Inspector, could I ask you something?"

"Of course, Sir. What is it?"

"I was just wondering why such a high-profile member of the police would be interested in discussing a random act of vandalism with us? I would have thought a normal PC would come down, had a look at the damage, and made his report based on those findings? After all, we have no idea who did it and it's pretty obvious there was nothing else damaged."

Bayman didn't respond initially. He wanted to be careful with his response.

"I think it best Mr. Mallick that we discuss it face to face," he replied. "I am happy to share what we know and provide you any appropriate detail then. I hope you understand?"

"Absolutely."

"Thank you, Sir," Bayman continued, "I will see you at two then."

# CHAPTER 4

"What do you think?" he asked.

Rich Telside, Cannon's assistant, thought for a second before responding. One hundred thousand pounds to buy a horse didn't come along very often.

"I could think of other ways to spend it," he replied smiling. "How old is he again?"

"Thirty-four," answered Cannon.

"Bloody hell, thirty-four! Some people have all the luck."

"I'm not sure if it's luck, Rich, but it certainly suggests that we are in the wrong game."

The two men laughed. They wouldn't change what they did for the world, but every day, every week, was a struggle. The racing game had been kind to them and they loved what they did. However, it wasn't a game for the weak-hearted, especially with regards to finances.

One year could bring success, the next could bring ruin. Injuries, loss of form, or worse, the loss of a horse, could be disastrous for a stable. The thought of new blood, a new owner, and a potential new equine athlete was exciting. Despite Cannon's stables now having some excellent charges and the prospect of another being added, the season ahead held no guarantees.

The two men were standing in the yard of Cannon's stable. The sky had lightened already, though a cold wind blew from the west. Rain had fallen overnight and while the summer had been reasonable overall, the coming autumn was beginning to show its face.

Around them, the staff continued with their duties. Washing and cleaning the horses after the morning's exercise and schooling, the *mucking out* of stables, the preparation of food, and the replacement of a horse's bedding within the stall was paramount to the successful and organized running of a racing stable.

Fortunately, Rich was excellent at ensuring things were done properly. Unfortunately doing things *properly* was expensive. It was why they needed the likes of James Formrobe and his money. Cannon wasn't mercenary, he was pragmatic. Life as a Detective Inspector had made him realise what was important to him. It wasn't money. It was about being happy, settled, doing what you loved. He was grateful for what he had. However, he was saddened when the past sometimes came calling. While it happened less and less nowadays, he knew that sometimes through no fault of his own he was compelled to face it, to confront matters that flowed from those he found around him, sometimes to face the very lowest acts of human nature. If only those ghosts would leave him alone.

Telside raised the issue of stable maintenance, it was a never-ending problem. Despite Cannon having built up the stables over the years, including the addition of new equipment, a walking machine, and a small operating facility to manage an injury, there were always the basics to stay on top of. Leaky roofs, stable door replacements (when horses kicked them down), storage barn repairs, security. It never seemed to end.

"Oh, I wanted to tell you," Telside said, "remember the leak we had a few weeks ago in the tack room, during that hailstorm?"

"Yes," replied Cannon, aware of the storm that Telside was referring to. It caused a bit of damage to the area, ripping down trees and some power lines., causing a localised blackout for a few hours.

"You remember the outage we had?"

"Yes, of course, what about it?" he answered.

"Well, it seems we may have had a power surge as a result of water leaking into the electrics and no one noticed that it must have shorted out the CCTV recorder. It seems to have gone on the blink."

"How do you mean?" enquired Cannon.

"I was looking at the footage yesterday afternoon as I wanted to check on something."

"Check on what Rich?" Cannon asked.

"Nothing serious, but I have a feeling that someone is stealing feed and some of our drugs and I wanted to see if I could see anything on the recordings."

Cannon was not happy. He believed that he was a fair employer and given he had the responsibility and trust of every owner who gave him horses to train and look after, he expected the same level of trust from his staff. So far, he had been very lucky. He hadn't experienced any problems with anyone in recent years. If Rich was right, and he had no reason to doubt him, he would be very disappointed.

"And did you?"

"No, I didn't. It looks like the cameras are working, so you can see what's going on in real-time, but the recorder isn't recording anything. The latest vision on the card inside the recorder is from the same day of the storm."

"Which was two weeks ago now."

"Yes, so over the past couple of weeks nothing was recorded."

"That's great!" replied Cannon annoyed at the situation. Apart from the cost to repair the recording device, the fact that one of his team could be a thief was more concerning.

To placate Cannon, Telside said, "I'll try and get it fixed asap Mike, but it may take a few days. I'm not sure what's needed to repair the damn thing, but I suggest we stay quiet about it. We don't want anyone to think that we don't have security."

"Agreed, just keep me informed," Cannon replied. "By the way do you have any idea as to who it could be…stealing?" he added.

"I have an idea but can't prove anything yet. Once I'm sure, I'll let you know."

"Okay," Cannon replied.

He had started off the conversation in a very positive mood, now he wasn't as chirpy. Telside noticed Cannon's demeanour and decided to change the subject.

"Have you spoken to Henry?" he asked.

Henry Bronton was an equine agent who recently and quite unexpectedly had made contact with Cannon and several other trainers in the Woodstock area offering his services. Whilst Cannon had not yet met the man, he had spoken to him on the phone and they had shared a Skype call where Bronton had formally introduced himself.

From what Cannon had been able to gather, Bronton's business had been around for nearly eight years and had become extremely successful. He operated from Doncaster, not too far from the racecourse there, just off South Parade. It didn't seem far from Oxfordshire when Bronton had advised where he operated from, however, it was at least a two and a half-hour drive one way, and a round trip of about three hundred miles. Not something one would do lightly unless the man had something special to show you, Cannon had thought when they had first talked on the phone. He had also wondered at the time why Bronton was now stretching his wings into Cannon's area? Perhaps success had bred success and Bronton was widening his market? It was something that Cannon would ask about later.

"No, not yet," Cannon eventually answered Telside, "but I intend to give him a call later."

"Okay," replied Telside. "I'm sure he'll know if there is anything reasonable available, particularly now, with the season starting shortly."

"Maybe," replied Cannon. "I've had a look on the web already and there isn't much available that I can see. I'm guessing from what he told me a few weeks ago that he has contacts and insight into some of the larger stables and perhaps knows a few owners that could be in the market to sell."

Telside nodded. Buying horse flesh wasn't his game. Looking after a horse once in his possession was what he was good at. The prospect of working with a new animal, one that was talented and could potentially win a big race that would enhance the stables standing, would be fantastic. A few years prior, the stable had an extremely talented horse called *Rockgod* that very nearly won the Grand National at Aintree. Unfortunately, the horse owner caused the race to be abandoned just as *Rockgod* hit the lead at the last fence. The owner was killed after running onto the track.

"Well," said Telside, "I hope he knows what he's doing. Even if 50K is small change to Formrobe, I'm sure he won't be very pleased with you if you buy him a donkey. Even millionaires don't like to waste their money."

Cannon laughed.

"Agreed, Rich," he said, and with that, he started to walk away towards the house where he kept his office. As he crossed the thirty-odd yards he turned to see Rich asking one of the staff, which was mostly female, to spray down the yard with a hose. Cleanliness was a big part of the stable regime. Keeping the place neat and tidy was something Rich was extremely keen on. Cannon realized how lucky he was to have worked with Rich over the years since he had earned his license as a trainer. People like Rich Telside didn't come along every day. As he walked through the front door into the house he could hear the phone ringing in his office. He called out to Michelle to answer it for him if she could, however by the time she got to the receiver the caller had ended the call.

------------------------------------------------

Night had fallen but Cannon was still working in his office. Michelle was in the kitchen making dinner. He had no idea what she was cooking but he could smell some interesting aromas. In the lounge the TV was on, Cannon could hear the murmur of people talking. It sounded to him like an *Escape to the Country* or an *Antique Roadshow* type program. He could never remember which was on at this time of day, but he knew that Michelle liked to watch both programs.

After he had finished talking to Rich, Cannon had spent the past couple of hours looking at the upcoming race meetings and updating a spreadsheet containing the names of the horses in his stable, their training regimes, and the meetings and races they could potentially compete in over the first few months of the season, once it started.

Telside had provided updates on those horses with injuries and the vet Cannon used had provided the necessary information about treatments, diagnoses, and likely dates by which those with longer-term problems would be ready to recommence training.

The admin that Cannon had to do was a necessary evil. The paperwork needing to be completed when horses transferred trainer, or retired or worse, died, was never-ending. Even a name change, which the animal itself didn't care about, needed *paperwork* to be completed. Fortunately, *paper* per se was no longer required, most activities were now done on-line.

Cannon sat back in his chair. The past few hours seemed to have flown by as he had worked through everything he needed to do. He stretched his back and was just about to stand up from his chair when Michelle called him to come through to the dining room to eat.

"Coming," he called back.

He stood up and stretched again as he looked out into the darkness knocking silently against his office window that looked out at the stable car park. An orange sodium light from the lane that ran alongside the stable provided an eerie glow directly below itself, the light barely making it across the stone wall that separated the stable yard from the road. The sky was now clear of cloud. The watery sunshine of the day had been erased only to be replaced by the deep dark carpet of a moonless evening. Cannon would do a final inspection of the stables before he was done for the day. The staff had all left for their homes and Rich, having ensured that he was satisfied with things, had also left for home. If Telside had seen anything to concern Cannon, he would have dropped by his office before leaving. The fact that he hadn't, gave Cannon a good feeling. He shut down his computer. It would be turned on by six am, an hour after Cannon and his team would have started the new day. When one day ended, it wasn't long before another began.

He walked towards his office door. As he reached it, the office phone rang. He was in two minds as to whether he should answer it, particularly given that Michelle had already called him to eat.

He decided to answer it.

He crossed the floor in three strides and picked up the receiver.

"Hello?" he said into the mouthpiece.

"Mr. Cannon?" a voice asked.

"Yes. Who is this?"

"Oh, sorry, my name is Samuel Jacobsen. I hope I haven't called you at an inconvenient time?"

Cannon sighed. Yes, it was inconvenient, but he didn't want to say so. Not just yet. He had no idea who the caller was. He sat back down in his chair.

"I'm sorry if it is a bit late in the day, but I did try to call you earlier," Jacobsen continued, "however the phone wasn't answered so I rang off."

The *earlier* caller, Cannon thought, putting two and two together.

"Well, Mr. Jacobsen, I'm sorry I missed you earlier, but how can I help you now?" Cannon said.

Jacobsen didn't respond immediately. Cannon thought he could hear papers being shuffled, almost as if Jacobsen needed to consult a prop before he continued. Finally, he said. "Mr. Cannon, I represent *SecureTwo* in a legal capacity, as Chief Legal Officer but I also represent Mr. James Formrobe in a personal capacity as his Solicitor."

Cannon didn't respond. He remained silent as he had no idea what Jacobsen wanted from him. James Formrobe's legal matters had nothing to do with him.

Jacobsen continued. "The reason I am calling you Mr. Cannon is that I believe James has been discussing with you the possible acquisition of a racehorse. Is that correct?"

Cannon noted the lack of formality by Jacobsen when referring to Formrobe. Was there something behind it he thought?

"Yes, Mr. Jacobsen, *James*, and I have discussed the matter. I'm not sure of the relevance to yourself, other than you being his lawyer, perhaps you could enlighten me?" Cannon asked.

"The term we use in the UK is Solicitor, Mr. Cannon. The use of Americanisms nowadays is somewhat off-putting don't you think?"

Cannon didn't respond. He wasn't sure if Jacobsen was having a laugh at his expense or if he was serious. He waited for his caller to speak. Eventually, Cannon heard Jacobsen clear his throat before saying. "To put it simply, when *SecureTwo* restructured its ownership when Mr. Alan Smerdon, one of the founders of the company, effectively *sold out,* an investor bought into the company, later buying an increased stake by acquiring shares from James. At that point James asked me to establish a Trust fund to ensure that his cash was safe, so to speak."

Cannon nodded silently. Not quite understanding everything but he knew enough about Trust funds. In his past life, he recalled incidents including violence and assaults when families literally fought over Trust monies. He had no idea how or if Formrobe had any family that would seek monies from him.

"I understand Mr. Jacobsen," he replied, "I guess it makes sense if you have the odd million to protect," he continued jokingly.

"I think Mr. Cannon, when there are several millions of pounds involved, there is no better way…" Jacobsen replied. While Cannon could not see the man, he imagined a very taciturn figure at the end of the line. He allowed the Solicitor to continue.

"So, Mr. Cannon, getting to the point. The reason for the call is quite simple. If James wishes to spend any of his money, the Trust deed requires that James and the Executor, that is me in this case, need to sign any purchase agreement over fifty thousand pounds, together. Anything below that James may sign and purchase himself, without my involvement."

"Okay," Cannon said, "*James* talked about 100 K, way over his limit. I'm not sure why he has suggested that amount, but I guess you would need to speak with him directly about that, Mr. Jacobsen. However, at this stage, I can assure you that I have no intention of buying him *any* horse, at *any* amount until I have done a thorough check of the market."

"That's good to hear, Mr. Cannon. Horseflesh and the value thereof, is to my mind very subjective, especially those in the jumping game. If they are not mares then most horses are geldings and the latter only have value when racing."

Cannon was surprised to hear Jacobsen's observations.

"You know something about the game?" he asked.

"I used to own a few horses in the past," came the reply. "My late wife loved the races and we travelled the length and breadth of the country over the years. Sadly, she passed away nearly seven years ago now."

"I'm sorry to hear that," interjected Cannon.

"Thank you," replied Jacobsen, "that's kind of you to say so. Anyway, after her passing, I sold our horses," he continued, his voice tinged with a sense of melancholy. "Yes, I sold our horses and life has moved on. But I still have the memories and that's what counts."

Cannon felt a stirring within himself as Jacobsen's words changed from being sad to being philosophical. Cannon himself had lost his wife to cancer a few years back. While he missed her terribly, like Jacobsen he had also moved on. He was grateful to have Michelle in his life.

There was a pause between the two men, both living a memory, both thinking of the past. Cannon eventually broke the silence.

"Mr. Jacobsen, thank you for sharing the information you have. I appreciate it. It makes my job much easier and I can promise you that should I find James a suitable horse to buy, if the purchase price exceeds the limit you have detailed then I will make sure that James complies with his obligations."

Jacobsen was happy with Cannon's response. The two men then said their goodbyes and ended the call.

Cannon sat back in his chair, his mind thinking, his eyes fixed on his reflection in the office window.

Michelle put her head around the door, saying "Mike?"

He didn't move, he hadn't heard her.

A ghost from the past appeared in his mind's eye, Sally, his late wife. *Why was he thinking about her?*

"Mike?" Michelle said again, crossing the room and touching him on the shoulder.

The pressure of Michelle's hand brought Cannon back to the present.

"Sorry love," he said, "I didn't hear you. I've just had a phone call with James Formrobe's solicitor, and I lost track of time."

"I understand," she said. "Anyway, dinner's ready, in fact it's getting cold, so I thought it better to come and get you," she smiled, bending down to kiss him on the cheek.

Cannon stood up. "Let's go," he said, "I'm starving."

He followed her out of the room.

As he did so, he felt a chill in his bones.

# CHAPTER 5

"Have you received such a letter yourselves?" he asked.

Inspector Tim Bayman waited while Frank Mallick looked at the letter again.

"No, definitely not Inspector," came the reply.

They were sitting in the boardroom again after the Inspector had arrived. The Southwell racecourse in the East Midlands was the first track to be subject to an arson attack outside of the greater London area. Only the police were aware of this, the attack on Sandown had been kept from the public.

Mallick passed the letter back to Bayman. The detail within it had been quite a simple message. *Stop racing over the jumps or horses and jockeys will be hurt, if not killed.*

There had been no other detail provided. No one knew who had sent the letter, there were no demands for monies, just the threat.

Even the document itself was just a plain A4 page, printed on an Epson printer using a plain Arial font at size 20. The police had established that the document was printed at an internet café and then photocopied but they had no idea where.

Also, the document had been sent through the mail, on pre-addressed, prepaid stamped envelopes so there was no stamp with any possible saliva or another way of extracting any DNA. The person who had sent the letter had been extremely meticulous.

"Which other course has received such a letter?" asked Mallick.

"At the risk of opening up a can of worms, there have been two others so far," he said. "I need to make it clear Mr. Mallick that the police are taking this very seriously and we have advised the courses concerned *not* to make these incidents public. We don't want the wider public to be scared of such threats, nor indeed anyone directly involved in the industry. If anything, we hoped that by not reacting, we can potentially flush out the person or persons involved."

"Thank you, Inspector, I understand."

"Good. Two other courses have received the letter. It's good that you haven't, so far, but following the MO of the perpetrator, we expect that you will receive one shortly. The two courses concerned are Sandown and Kempton Park."

Mallick whistled through his teeth. Both tracks mentioned were significant in size, stature, and importance to the racing game, jumps, or otherwise.

"And they both had fences burnt? Like ours?"

"Yes Sir," replied Bayman, "then both received a letter. The one that I have shown you is an exact copy of that received by the management of both tracks."

"Do you expect more courses like ours to be targeted?"

"We are not sure, but we have informed other jurisdictions of the possibility. For example, the South Yorkshire and Gloucestershire police, where courses such as Doncaster and Cheltenham could be targeted."

"That's quite a range and distance from each other, do you believe this is a coordinated effort by a particular group of people, a group of *activists* maybe, or just the work of an individual?"

"We are not sure yet, Mr. Mallick. What we do know is that three separate courses, including here at Southwell, have been subject to an arson attack. We are taking them, and the implied threat, very seriously and we need your help."

"Of course, Inspector, anything at all that we can do, we will."

"Thank you. What we need you to do is to look at any CCTV footage you may have as part of your security and to see if you have anything useful that we can use."

Mallick nodded.

"In addition," Bayman continued, "if you receive such a letter," he pointed at the copy sitting on the boardroom table between them, "please contact me straight away."

Bayman took out his wallet and placed a card on the table, with the necessary details already printed on it.

"Finally," he went on, "as I mentioned before, please could you keep the incident with the fence out of the public domain for now? Should we need to make any public announcements we would like it to come from the police liaison department. Effectively to issue a measured message rather than one which the public may misconstrue."

Mallick wasn't totally convinced. Three attacks to date, including large metropolitan tracks but only issuing statements concerning small regional courses, seemed a little like a cover-up. He decided to take the easy route and just acquiesce *for now*.

"Just as a matter of interest," he asked, "did the other courses manage to get any vision of who could have been involved in these incidents?"

"Unfortunately, not. The burning of the jumps at the other two tracks was at spots furthest away from the grandstands and well away from where the CCTV was focused on."

"A bit like here then?"

"I guess so," replied the Inspector. "We were just hoping that being a smaller track your CCTV may have vision that those with larger boundaries may not have."

"Well we will review what we have Inspector, but I'm not confident. Being a country racecourse, our budget doesn't stretch to having an unlimited set of cameras to cover the entire area. The main focus of our security is on the stables, the betting ring, and the inside of our Grandstand, not of the track itself."

"I understand. But if you can review what you have, particularly over the past twenty-four to forty-eight hours that would be good."

"We will certainly do that for you Inspector."

With that, the two men stood up, shook hands, and walked from the boardroom down to the Inspectors' car.

As Bayman began to drive off, Stark's car turned into the car park. Bayman waved goodbye. Mallick waited until Stark was out of his car and then both men walked back towards the boardroom.

"Well, any joy?" asked the Chairman, eager to learn what Stark had to say.

"We're in luck Frank," he said, "it seems like our Insurance policy *does* cover acts of vandalism, but not arson. So, what we need to do is claim the former not the latter."

"Which is what Bayman is requiring us to do. Keep the issue as low key as possible, say it was vandalism and let the police manage things should the issue worsen or escalate. They will issue any necessary communications once they see fit to do so."

"Then let's get the claim in immediately," replied Stark.

"Agreed William. Thank Christ that we can hopefully recover our outlay. It's not something I want to be stuck with. It's already likely to impact our cash flow in the short term. It's the last thing we need."

# CHAPTER 6

The moonless night made it easy for the figure to leap the perimeter fence. It had been quite a long trip. The journey to Cheltenham was never going to be quick, it had taken over two hours. Roadworks, traffic snarl-ups due to an accident on the M4 on the south side of Swindon had made the trip a challenge.

The figure had parked the car in the Pittville Student Village, part of the University of Gloucester's grounds. It was not a very long walk to the track. The figure had not invoked any unnecessary attention. The backpack that it carried contained the necessary materials to set fire to one of the racecourse fences but did not seem out of place sitting on the shoulder of the figure. Wearing a dark jacket and a dark grey hoodie and black jeans the figure attracted no attention from the few individuals and groups that passed by. While it was dark, it wasn't too late, the last of the Summer months meant that darkness fell around 7 pm. With luck, the figure would be back home before 11 pm.

The figure walked away as the fence erupted in flame. It had taken only half an hour to place the device inside the birch and then pour the liquid onto and across the entire width of the jump.

It was a pleasing night's work.

# CHAPTER 7

They had agreed to meet halfway.

Henry Bronton had booked a lunchtime table at the EFES Mangal BBQ restaurant on Braunstone Gate in Leicester, a Turkish and Mediterranean eatery not far from Leicester Castle.

Cannon had arrived a little later than planned and Bronton was already snacking on some *cold meze* and *warm halloumi* sitting next to a glass of beer that occupied part of the table for two.

He apologized for being late, which was duly accepted, and after he had sat down he ordered a beer for himself.

Not having met Bronton other than via the Skype calls they shared, Cannon assessed the man more closely. He was bigger than he imagined, taller, and wider. The man's bulk seemed to make him appear uncomfortable in his chair. He was just over six feet tall but he appeared to weigh well above 100kgs. He had a waistline that seemed a little unhealthy to Cannon and a complexion not noticeable on a PC screen, but ruddier when seen in the flesh. He wore dark blue chino trousers, with a casual light blue shirt under a beige lightweight cotton bomber jacket. In his late forties, he seemed to be trying to remain a decade younger. His Vans casual shoes completed the ensemble.

"So pleased to meet you, Mike," Bronton said, "I'm glad you could make it, I know it's a bit of a drive for you. Do you know Leicester at all?"

Cannon wasn't sure if he should reveal his past to any significant degree, so he decided to be a little vague. Sometimes talking about the past as a Detective Inspector put people off.

"I used to be in the police several years ago. Sometimes I would come to the city if an investigation warranted it, but mainly, if I needed to discuss things with the local teams, I would call them, fax or whatever," he said.

The use of the word *fax* indicated to Bronton that Cannon's time in the police force had been several years prior. Bronton took solace in that.

"I haven't been to Leicester for a while now," Cannon continued. "If it wasn't for the GPS I don't think I would have ever found this place."

"Well I'm glad you did, Mike, and I hope our meeting proves successful. It would be good if we can do some business together."

Cannon nodded.

"So tell me Henry, when you contacted me and other trainers in the Oxfordshire area a short while ago, you said you were looking to enter new markets, offering your services across the country. How is that going?"

"To be honest Mike, not as well as I would have liked. It seems like some of the folk *down south* are not so keen to deal in horseflesh with a *Northerner*. You are one of the first that I have been able to meet with formally."

Cannon was surprised, but he kept his thoughts to himself. He wondered why it would be the case that some were not as receptive to Bronton as he was. Did they know something he didn't? He had tried to find out as much as he could about Bronton and his services. From the online detail he had been able to gather, everything the man was involved in appeared legitimate.

"I'm sorry to hear that you are having difficulty," Cannon went on, "perhaps if things work out between us, I could be a catalyst for you?"

Bronton smiled, "That would be nice."

With a waiter hovering near their table, the two men decided to order lunch. Cannon ordered an Adana Kofte Kebab and Bronton ordered a Lamb Beyti. While they waited for their food to arrive, they started to discuss the reason why they were meeting.

Cannon wanted to keep his powder dry about how much money he had available at his disposal on behalf of James Formrobe, so decided to ask Bronton how he may be able to help find a suitable horse.

"I have a client," he said, "who has sufficient funds to buy himself a reasonable National Hunt horse. He is looking to me to find such an animal and train it for him. I understand from our previous conversation that you may be able to find him something that would be worth acquiring?"

"When you say, *worth* acquiring, are we talking about a horse with a Class 1 potential or something a little lower in expectation?"

"We are talking about a top-quality animal. Yes, one that could reach the highest level," Cannon responded. "I was fortunate, as you may know, to have had the privilege of training such a horse myself. *RockGod* was an amazing horse. Sadly, I lost him. Sold off as part of an estate when his owner was killed at Aintree."

"Yes, I recall that," responded Bronton.

"So, you'll understand why my potential owner is looking for a good horse that he would like me to train for him."

"I do indeed."

"So, do you think you can assist?"

"I'm sure I can," Bronton replied.

Before they could get into detail, their food arrived. The aroma from the cooked meat quite intoxicating. Both men eagerly tucked into their meals. As they ate, Bronton raised the possible next steps, should Cannon want to proceed on behalf of his buyer.

"Absolutely I do," Cannon said in response to Bronton's offer.

"That's good to hear Mike. So, as I said, there are three options. One, I send you some detail via email about the few owners I represent along with the detail of the horses they want to sell. That way you can check pedigree, their career to date etcetera. Secondly, we can arrange to meet and go to a couple of the stables where the horses I am helping owners to sell are housed and trained, to see them at work and discuss with their current trainers what each animal is like. Finally, we can go to some of the sales where I am the representative for the seller and possibly try the auction route. What do you think?"

Cannon knew this was coming. He had already prepared his answer.

"To be honest Henry, my preference is what you have called option two. I want to see a horse in work, I want to check how well it has been treated, stabled and I want to see the general conformation and health of the animal."

"Fair enough," replied Bronton, "and I assume you want to move quickly?"

"My client certainly appears to, yes. With the season starting soon, I'd like to think that we could find something that would almost be ready to race within the first month or so. Obviously, that depends on the horse itself."

"Excellent," Bronton replied, wiping his mouth on a napkin and then finishing his lunch with a large swallow of his remaining beer. He commented on the food noticing that Cannon likewise had just finished eating.

"I really enjoyed that," he said, "highly recommended."

Cannon concurred, rejecting however the notion of a dessert that Bronton offered.

"No thanks," he said, "I'm pretty full after all that. I need to concentrate on the drive back to Woodstock. If I eat anymore, I'm likely to get drowsy. It's a long drive home."

"I understand, Mike," replied his host.

The two men agreed to speak again once Bronton had contacted the applicable owners and trainers about the horses that he had on his books. Cannon could then decide which he wanted to see and which he would not be interested in. It was expected that Cannon would receive the necessary information within the following 72 hours. Thereafter it was likely a two-day trip to view the various animals. Cannon realized that Michelle may not be totally happy about him being away for a couple of days, but he knew she did understand that it was part of the job.

With the school holidays about to end, Cannon rationalised that Michelle was already preparing for her return to class anyway, so she would be kept busy and would likely not miss him too much.

Cannon thanked Bronton for lunch.

"My pleasure," his host replied. "I'm glad you enjoyed it."

# CHAPTER 8

The letter arrived the following day.
It was the same as the one that Mallick had been shown by Bayman.
The threat was simple.

*Stop jumps racing at your track, otherwise, horses and jockeys could be injured or killed.*
*We make no apology for this request.*
*You have five days to comply.*
*Insert a postponement on your website of upcoming events to confirm compliance with this request.*

The letter unsigned, undated.
Who are these people? Mallick thought.
He picked up the phone in his office and called Bayman.
He relayed to him his thoughts.
"We can't comply with such a request," he complained, "the course is already struggling to stay open. We need the income, we need the custom," he argued.
Bayman listened attentively, thanking Mallick for contacting him immediately once the letter had arrived.
"I agree, Mr. Mallick. We don't want to allow ourselves to be impacted negatively by such threats, however, we do need to ensure the safety of the public and that of the horses, trainers, and most importantly the jockeys."
"Do you have any idea who is behind this and what their motives are?"
"Not at this stage. However, I have been informed this morning that overnight one of the fences at Cheltenham was also attacked and damaged."
"In the same way?" interrupted Mallick.
"It would appear so, although no letter has yet been received," Bayman continued, "however if the MO is the same, then the course authorities should expect to receive one tomorrow or the following day, at worst."
"My God! Is no one safe from these people?"
"At this stage, I'd have to say unfortunately not."
Mallick didn't know what to think. He waited for Bayman to speak, hoping for an answer. What steps to take. Finally, the Inspector responded.
"I know this will be difficult Mr. Mallick, but I'd strongly suggest that we attempt to minimize the threat concerning this matter, by *appearing* to comply with the request made."
"Appearing?"
"Yes Sir. I notice that your first meeting of the season is still another few

weeks away. What I would like to suggest is that you formally arrange a postponement of that meeting by a couple of weeks, lets' say until the first week of October. I suggest that you advise the Owners and Trainers Association through the alternate channels you have, for example, your own databases, about the postponement, and emphasize that it is because of necessary track maintenance or something like that so that they would understand, or accept it as normal. If you do it that way but update the website as per the letter then this *group or individual* who has issued the threat will hopefully believe they have succeeded in shutting you and the other courses down. That way, I hope it will give us time to find out who is behind this."

Mallick wasn't fully convinced. "But we can't shut the entire industry down just like that. Surely the media, the public will get wind of what's going on very quickly? Social media will soon see to that."

"I agree, but we need to be vigilant, sensible. If we can keep the letter away from the wider public then we may be able to find out who is behind this *before* it's too late. The last thing we need is the public thinking that every racecourse in the country holds a risk."

"I think that's a big ask, Inspector. If these people are serious it wouldn't surprise me if they are already planning to engage with the press and others directly."

"And that could be their undoing," Bayman said. "If they do go public, especially online then we may be able to track them down. While they continue using printed and copied letters such as the one you received, it will be much harder for us."

Mallick needed to ask Bayman a further question. He would verify the answer later. "One final question Inspector. What have the other courses that have been attacked decided to do about racing?"

"Sandown and Kempton have agreed to a postponement as well. We are not sure yet about Cheltenham, but given their first meeting is some time away, we think that they will agree to the request in the letter through their website but will do the same as yourself in the background. It's all about the *optics,* unfortunately."

"What a sad world we live in!" Mallick responded.

"Sad *and* unfortunately, a dangerous one as well," replied Bayman.

# CHAPTER 9

"I think it's working," said the man with the dreadlocks.

He and two other men sat in a corner of the Angel Inn pub, on Market Square, in Witney. It was just after 9 pm. The men had been sitting in the same spot for the past couple of hours. On the small table were at least five empty pint glasses. The landlord sent a young waitress over to where the men were sitting to collect the empties. While she did so the men remained silent. After she had wiped the table with a damp cloth, she carried the discarded glasses back to the bar for washing. The man with the dreadlocks reached for a sixth glass, downed the remaining beer, and placed the empty glass back on the table with a bang.

The young waitress turned around to see what was going on. She then looked at the landlord who was standing at the bar pouring another patron a drink from a bottle. He shook his head imperceptibly, advising her to ignore what was going on. She took the hint and decided to leave the empty glass where it was. She would collect it later.

# CHAPTER 10

Formrobe sat in his office. It was well past 8 pm. The building was quiet, but he knew that some of his team were still busy working.

The development of new applications never seemed to end. There were always those who looked to copy what you were doing. Steal your IP, take things to market that didn't work but sucked people in, and stole their money. Scams, phishing, hacking, identity theft were all part of the modern world. Being online meant that it was possible to be tricked in so many more ways than was ever possible previously.

It was this that drove him. He and Alan Smerdon had become successful because the skill and drive that they had in creating *SecureTwo* was something both were passionate about. They wanted to trade wits and beat those who tried to break into *secure* personal databases just for fun or to destroy businesses just because they could. Formrobe had been very upset when Smerdon bowed out of the business. They had been good friends. Formrobe wasn't sure how much of an influence Smerdon's mother had been at the time Alan left, but with hindsight, it had become much clearer. She had wanted Alan to buy Formrobe out. Alan had refused, their friendship and history of developing *SecureTwo* together meant a lot to him. Eventually, Smerdon's mother forced her son out of the business almost entirely. He was now really just a silent partner, having no involvement with the business at all. While he held the title of Director, he never attended meetings. He was a bit of a misnomer now.

Formrobe sighed, it was time to go home. He logged off from his laptop computer, packed it away into a shoulder bag, and left his office, entering the general work area. He could see about six or seven heads, all face down typing away, writing code. The various projects they were busy with was enhancing the company's name in the market. Revenue was increasing, profits growing.

He was about to say goodnight to the team leader responsible for those still working when he was interrupted.

"Fuck!" said the voice.

It was one of the developers sitting furthest away from the team leader. The man in his early twenties took off a set of headphones he was wearing and threw them onto his desk.

"Are you okay, Paul?" Formrobe asked.

Paul Alblom, Lead Security Consultant in *SecureTwo* stood up from his chair, shaking his head.

"Sorry James, but no, I'm not."

"What's the matter?" asked the team leader, now standing up from his desk.

"It's this email I just received, Barry," said Alblom to the team leader. "Come and have a look."

Both men walked across to where Alblom was standing.

He pointed to the email that was open on his screen.

Sender: *Unknown*

Addressee: *All @ SecureTwo*

Message: *All your systems have been compromised.*

*Your business servers and cloud computing access will be shut down by midnight.*

*097/01010011/116/01100101/083/0101011*

"That's not possible," said Formrobe. "It must be some kind of scam. Can we find out where this has come from?" he asked.

Barry Sincaid called over to the rest of the team still busy working at their desks.

"Did any of you receive an email just now from an unknown sender?" he asked, "suggesting that our systems had been compromised?"

None of those assembled had received the mail.

"Thank God, for that," said Formrobe.

"Agreed," replied Sincaid. "I think it's a hoax anyway. Our firewalls and other protections seem to be intact, and we've had no alerts from any of our systems. It just seems to be another attempt at hacking us," he said.

Formrobe turned to Alblom. "What do you think Paul?"

"Barry may be right," Alblom said, "but I think we need to be vigilant. It seems that someone is starting a bit of a crusade. This is not the first time this has happened this week, or indeed the last couple of weeks."

Formrobe was surprised. He hadn't heard of any such attacks.

Was he being kept out of the loop or was it something that was just being handled by the team? After all, his business was about being subtle, handling possible breaches into computer systems with the minimum of fuss.

"I'll see what I can find out," Alblom continued. "I'll get the mail deleted out of everyone's in-boxes who have received it and then I'll do some investigation as to who could have sent it."

"In addition," Sincaid jumped in, "I'll check with our other service partners to see if there are any issues with our cloud services. I doubt, though, that our servers will have been impacted. I'll let you know, James, if I find anything."

"Thanks Barry,"

"No worries," replied Sincaid.

Formrobe thanked Alblom again. He then left the office. He had an uneasy

feeling in his stomach as he climbed into his car.
Was it possible somebody had started a vendetta against the company?
If so, why?
And who was behind it?
And what did the numbers mean?
He wasn't yet sure, but he thought they meant something.

# CHAPTER 11

The attacker was happy with the test. From what they could see, the mail had reached the intended audience.

With a few keystrokes, it was clear that the message had got through.

Looking at one of the three screens in front of them, the pathway for the *hack* was unable to be followed or traced. No matter how they investigated the email, *SecureTwo* staff would not be able to find out who had sent it.

The attacker, however, did acknowledge that they had been unable to pierce *SecureTwo's* firewalls and bring down the network, or indeed get access to any data. It was something of a challenge and one the attacker was keen to take up.

It was just a matter of time…

# CHAPTER 12

The day had broken with bright sunshine. With no racing yet, the stable had been much quieter than during the week. Saturday would normally have meant the stable was a hive of activity, especially if there were any runners on that day. As it was, with the season to start soon, some of the horses in the stable had needed further exercise and schooling, while those with more long-term plans for the season, had only light exercise. Even equine athletes needed rest at times. Training wasn't all about fitness. Getting a horse's mind right to race, despite its natural instinct to run, was a big part of being a successful trainer.

Most of the work each day was managed by Rich, and Cannon was eternally grateful for it. Their relationship, partnership, and friendship had developed over the years to the extent that Cannon was more than happy nowadays to take time to enhance the *relationship* side of the business. Working with new clients was just as important as working with new horses.

The trip up from Woodstock to Crabapple Farm near Brodsworth, just off the Secondary road B6422, had taken them just over two and a half hours and Cannon and Formrobe climbed out of the car just before 11 am. The two men had enjoyed each other's company on the drive. Cannon was fascinated with the detail that Formrobe had shared with him. His past, the relationship with Alan Smerdon and the excitement Formrobe had in finding himself a racehorse. Cannon was beginning to understand the rationale behind his client's thinking. The thought of winning a race with a horse gave Formrobe a rush, something the man had been missing out on, according to Formrobe himself.

From what Cannon had gathered from their conversation during the journey, it appeared that the man had focused so much on his career, his company, that despite his enormous wealth, he had spent little on himself. No wife, no permanent girlfriend or partner, no children and no fancy car or house, nothing….except for some reason, now the money was burning a hole in his pocket.

*No wonder*, Cannon thought, *there was one hundred thousand pounds to throw around.*

Bronton was standing in the sun, the shadow of the stable block behind him splayed itself along the cobbled ground, stopping a foot or so from him. Despite the sunshine, it was still relatively cool. He wore a light jacket over a dark blue jumper to keep himself warm. When they went into the stables there would be a drop in temperature and he knew that it was too soon for the heaters within each stall to be turned on. It was only the start of autumn, but the available daylight was receding each day and he was

feeling the cold. It was still only 11 am, yet it felt much later in the day.
Holding out his hand, he greeted Cannon, and Cannon in turn introduced Formrobe.

"Nice to meet you, Mr. Formrobe," he said, "glad you could make it."

"James, please call me James," replied Formrobe, "and thank you for organizing the visit on my behalf."

"No problem, though I think it's Mr. Cannon here and the trainer Harry Pool who we should be thanking. For setting this up," he continued.

Formrobe nodded his understanding.

"Okay, should we get going?" Bronton asked, turning slightly to allow the visitors to go ahead of him and enter the stable block. Cannon and Formrobe accepted the invitation.

Once through the building door, Cannon noticed that each of the stalls was occupied. Within the boundaries of each were animals of all grades, a total of eighteen horses. Some of them were experienced racehorses, some were novices. On the outside of each stall, a printed name tag with details of the occupant, as well as its ownership, sat within a plastic sheaf.

The men walked between the stalls that sat on either side of a large cement walkway, the remains of sprayed water used in cleaning the building sat in small puddles at various junctures on the ground. Cannon noticed the water buckets and hay nets attached to the inside walls of each stall. It was reminiscent of his own setup.

"Ah, here we are," said Bronton, stopping about two thirds down from the door from which they entered. "Stall ten. *Centaur,*" he said.

Formrobe looked through the bars of the stall that sat on a concrete wall making up the bottom half of the barrier separating the occupant from the visitors. Inside, he could see the hindquarters of a very large horse. It was busy pushing its nose around a feed trough.

"He's enormous," exclaimed Formrobe, somewhat taken aback by what he was seeing.

On TV the horses seemed so much smaller compared to their handlers when they walked around a parade ring, but in the flesh, it was obvious that in both height and length they were very large animals. More so those involved in National Hunt racing.

"Yes, he is big, isn't he?" Bronton acknowledged.

"And it's the reason why we are here," interjected Cannon. "When Henry sent me a summary of his catalogue, *Centaur* here, was a bit of a standout when compared with the others available and I thought it best to come and see him first. We'll then have a reference point when we look at some of the others."

Formrobe seemed a little overwhelmed. It was his first time looking at horseflesh that he had the chance to own.

"He's magnificent," he said, a smile across his face.

Cannon looked at Bronton. He had hoped for a more muted response from his possible client. By showing his excitement it would make Cannon's job in any price negotiations that much harder. If they decided on *Centaur,* or any other horse, Cannon could see that Bronton would try and wring as much money out of the transaction as he could.

"What's his breeding like?" asked Formrobe continuing to study the horse as it turned around and walked the yard or so across the stall and put its nostrils against the bars. Whiskers and air mixed as the horse snorted, Formrobe jumped back in surprise. Cannon smiled.

"Looks like he's happy to see you," he said.

Formrobe steadied himself as Bronton filled them both in on the horse's pedigree. Cannon was aware of the detail, having already done his research on the horse. It was these checks that had brought them to Harry Pool's farm.

"Bred in Ireland, the dam was *New Deal,* the Sire was *The Intellectual.* The horse is now five years old. He's won three of his five starts to date, second in another, and third in his first start. They were all over chase fences," advised Bronton. "As you can see, he's a bay with three white feet, the off-fore is natural and the white mark on his head is in the shape of a diamond. He's a gelding, and he's just shy of seventeen hands in height."

"Gelded?" asked Formrobe. "You mean even if he was successful in his career on the track we couldn't breed with him?"

"That's right James," interrupted Cannon, "under National Hunt rules to minimize health and safety risks, nearly all participating horses are gelded."

"That's a bit sad."

"Well, that's the way it is. Seems to be best for everyone. Horses that are gelded are generally much more compliant, easier to train, and are generally more sociable with other horses."

"Because..?"

"Because they are not fighting for the attention of the females anymore. Once they have been gelded, they seem to focus on being part of the herd, and that means they are easier to engage with. Their temperament improves substantially."

Formrobe nodded. Bronton saw his opportunity to jump in.

"So, what do you think James?" he asked.

Formrobe turned to Cannon. "I'll defer to my *advisor,*" he said. "Mike?"

"Let's see him at work. As I said when we set up this visit, we need to see all potential purchases to show us what they can do."

"Did you look at the races I sent you the links to?" asked Bronton.

"Yes, I did," Cannon replied, "but once I've seen the horse run in the flesh, then I can make a call."

"Understood. Let me go and get Harry to prepare the horse," he said. "I believe his regular work rider will be here to take the horse out, once we give the go-ahead that we want to see more."

"Thanks, Henry."

"Oh, by the way, are there any of the others you may be interested to see?"
Cannon shook his head. "No, only *Centaur* here," he replied. "I've had a
look at the other detail you sent, *Centaur* was the only one of interest."

Bronton's smile belied what he really felt of Cannon's comments. He
nodded again then walked away, searching for Harry Pool.

While they waited on the hill in the slowly fading sun, Cannon repeated to
Formrobe some of the details he looked for in a good National Hunt horse.
Conformation; a good, clear intelligent eye; sound legs; clean wind and huge
hindquarters, the latter being the driving force to run and to jump the large
steeplechase fences. Cannon's preference was to train horses over
steeplechase fences rather than the smaller hurdles, but sometimes a horse
was much better racing over the quicker and smaller obstacles than the
larger ones.

"So, what's your impression of the horse, Mike?" asked his client.

"He looks good, well put together," Cannon replied, "but we need to see if
he has heart."

"But he's won three races already, doesn't that tell you something?"

"It tells me that he's won a few races. It doesn't tell me what the opposition
was like. If they were poor, then all it means is that he won a few poor
races."

"Did I understand that you had a look at the races?"

"Yes."

"And that didn't convince you?"

"No, I need to see more….if you want my honest opinion," he added.

"Okay."

Formrobe stayed silent, the look on his face seemed to suggest the man was
a little deflated, disappointed that Cannon hadn't given a recommendation
already. It was almost like a child that had seen a sweet for the first time but
wasn't allowed to eat it as they hadn't yet seen the full range of sweets
available to them.

Cannon wanted to tell him that he was looking after Formrobe's interest.
He was trying to find Formrobe the best animal he could. Cannon realized,
however, that it wasn't *his* money that was being spent and if his client
wanted to blow his money on an investment that may not bring the return
he expected, then so be it. In the back of his mind, however, Cannon
remembered the conversation he had with Samuel Jacobsen and the
limitation on any monies to be spent without his co-signature to any
agreement of sale. It was an irritant, something Cannon could do without.

*Centaur* raced up the hill alongside his normal running partner *Jasper's Edge*.

The horse was under a stranglehold. He had a big rangy stride and seemed to run across the ground without touching it. He had a grass cutter action, gliding across the surface, which had been made sticky by recent rain. The course was artificial, made of polypropylene, synthetic fibers, recycled rubber, and sand, not grass. A training track about seven metres wide lying between a set of white running rails. The horses ran for about six hundred metres along the track which rose and fell across the undulating hills. They met three steeplechase jumps as they ran. Cannon watched through his binoculars. He had brought Formrobe a set as well, to help him watch the horses exercise. *Centaur* almost flew over each jump, his action not changing as he landed safely on the other side. With each leap, he gained a length on his racing companion. Cannon was impressed.

They watched the horses return the way they had come. The six hundred metre exercise over the same three chase fences back in the direction of the stable block was just as impressive. Cannon had seen enough. He knew that subject to the price he would recommend *Centaur* as a good buy.

The men sat around the kitchen table inside Harry Pool's house. The room was lit by overhead strip lighting. It was just after one-thirty pm. While the sun still shone outside and the sky remained blue, the sun had moved closer to the west, plunging the house, and the kitchen in particular, into cool shadow. A small fire within an open hearth warmed the room.
"So, what do you think, Mike?" Bronton asked.
Harry Pool sat alongside the agent. He had trained *Centaur* ever since the horse had been acquired by his current owner, a businessman who owned a series of furniture shops in Yorkshire, and the north-west and north-east of the country. The horse had been broken in and had come to him as a three-year-old colt. Sadly, the horse had not been quick enough for flat racing and after surgery for a wind issue, which it had now overcome, the horse was put away for a year before it began a new career over fences. The three wins in five races was an excellent return for its first season. The owner had seen the possibility of selling the horse given its results to date and wanted to maximize his return. While Cannon didn't know what the horse had been sold for initially by the breeder, Cannon had been able to find out that the current owner had paid thirty thousand pounds to acquire it.
"Not bad," replied Cannon, a straight face giving nothing away in response to Bronton's question. He sat quietly wanting to keep his powder dry, hoping Formrobe didn't show too much exuberance when it came to a discussion about *making an offer.*
"Not bad!" replied the agent, "I think you are underestimating me, Mike. I can see that Mr. ....sorry James here, appears very interested in the horse."
"That may be so Henry, but despite what we have seen so far, and yes the

horse does look good, if the price is unreasonable then no matter how much we like him, *or not*," Cannon added for emphasis, "we may not be able to do a deal. And besides, this is the first horse we have seen. Over the next thirty -six hours we have another three horses to look at, so let's try and put *Centaur* in perspective."

"Fair enough," replied Bronton, "however, I thought I'd show you the best of the four horses you asked to see, first. That way, if you were happy, we could do a deal and you could get some time back."

Cannon noted this, though doing deals quickly concerning horse flesh was not always sensible. Taking time, doing research, and making observations was the best approach. He wondered why Bronton was so pushy to conclude a deal? Was it the commission he was after or were there others who were interested in the horse and he didn't want to lose the sale? *Agents!* he thought.

Harry Pool had sat at the table watching Cannon and Bronton spar. He noted that Formrobe had likewise remained silent. Pool knew it was part of the game. He had been training officially for nearly twenty-five years, obtaining his license after serving an apprenticeship and learning the training ropes. He knew a good horse when he saw one and *Centaur* was good, very good. "Seventy-five thousand!" Bronton exclaimed without warning.

"What?" replied Cannon. a huge grin across his face. He knew Bronton had set an unrealistic price deliberately so that negotiations on a possible sale could begin. He wanted Bronton to know this and laughed aloud. "I think if that's the price, then James and I should leave for our next stop right now," he said, beginning to rise from his seat.

"Okay Mike, if not seventy-five k, then what are you offering?"

Cannon turned to his client, then faced the agent again.

"What makes you think we want to make an offer now anyway, Henry?" he asked.

Bronton was a little taken aback. While he was an agent, he wasn't necessarily a skilled negotiator and he soon realized that Cannon was. Cannon had been in many situations in his former life where he had needed such skills. Domestic violence situations that had become hostage-taking matters were just one example. Dealing with hardened criminals who had kidnapped or murdered people and hidden them or had dumped bodies were others.

Negotiating with Bronton was going to be much easier compared to what Cannon had been required to do in his past. He smiled inwardly.

The agent took a moment to compose himself.

"I'll tell you what Mike. If you want to keep your options open, and I know you do," he smiled, testing the water to see if Cannon flinched. "Then this is what I propose. Let's go and see the other horses we have already

arranged to see, this afternoon and tomorrow, and once you have done so, I'll give you a week to decide on any of them that you may want to buy….."
Cannon remained stock still, pretending to think about what had been suggested. "Go on," he said eventually.
"If you decide to go ahead with any purchase, just let me know. Alternately if I don't hear from you within a week, then I'll assume that there is no deal with any of the horses we will have seen. If you *do* decide to go ahead then make me a formal offer and I will relay it to the owner."
"Sounds reasonable," responded Cannon. He turned to Formrobe and nodded his acceptance.
"I must warn you however, that given you are not the only potential buyer in the market, you may need to move quickly on some of the horses we are seeing. If you make an offer and it's too low for the seller, I will advise them to accept other offers, should they be made."
Cannon knew that this patter, the warning, was part of Bronton's *spiel*. While it had some merit, it wasn't totally convincing. Cannon began to formulate an offer price in his mind for *Centaur*, he would discuss it with Formrobe later. "I understand," he responded. "Let's park it. Let's move on to the next horse."
"*Valley of Rock*."
"Yes, that's right. I understand he's stabled at a place about fifteen minutes' drive from here?"
Bronton nodded, "Yes, down at Simon Twigg's place."
Cannon stood up from the table and held out his hand to Pool. Formrobe did likewise. Bronton remained seated.
"Thanks Harry, for your time and hospitality, it is much appreciated," Cannon stated.
"No problem at all Mike, anytime…and oh, if you do decide to go with *Centaur*, I don't think you'll be disappointed. I'm sad to see him go, wherever he ends up. He's been a joy to train. I'm just sorry that the owner has decided to sell."
Cannon smiled. "Okay," he said, addressing Bronton. "We'll see you shortly down at Simon's place. In the meantime, James and I will have a chat about a few things," he continued, leaving Bronton to speculate over what.

# CHAPTER 13

She sat across from him, her dyed hair coiffured into a half-moon shape that seemed to defy gravity. It protruded outwards and stood away from her forehead like a wave on the sea that was about to crash down from a dizzy height.

Her face was almost sand in colour, the primer, foundation, and concealer sat atop her skin, making it appear flawless. With the addition of highlighter and mascara on her eyelashes, she looked twenty years younger than her age. To hide the two giveaways, one, the skin around her neck, she wore a light rouge-coloured chiffon scarf, and to hide the other, her hands, she wore a pair of soft white leather gloves. Her ensemble was made complete with a pair of white jeans that hugged her waist and hips, a soft pink top, and bright red mid-height-heeled patent leather shoes.

She was a lady of nearly *seventy* going on forty.

"So, what is this I hear about James being in the market for a racehorse?" she asked.

Samuel Jacobsen had experienced many a conversation with Judy Smerdon. He knew her to be both persistent, nosy, and at times extremely rude. He also knew that no matter what questions she asked him, he was bound by his profession not to disclose personal information that he knew of one party to another. At least *not* without their consent.

"I'm not sure where you are getting your information from Judy, but whoever it is, I'll let them answer your question for you. It's not my place to comment on the personal affairs of another, particularly one of the Directors and the major shareholder of this company."

Judy Smerdon was not to be put off. "Oh, come now Samuel, you know I'll find out in the end."

"That may well be, but not from me. If you want to ask James himself that is your prerogative and I'm sure he'll answer you accordingly. So I think we should make our way to the boardroom now for the meeting, don't you?" he asked.

Judy Smerdon stood up, her face set in a fake smile that was designed to give the right impression, but Jacobsen had seen it too many times. He was able to see right through her. She walked out of the office leaving him in his wake. Jacobsen tutted under his breath and raised his eyes heavenwards. When she was in this mood anything could happen at the meeting.

With the Audit Partner, Clive Winters, responsible for the annual audit of the company as Chair, the quarterly board meeting was kept on a very civil footing. Along with Winters, the attendees included Formrobe as majority shareholder, Judy Smerdon representing herself, and with a proxy for her son. The investor representative Thomas Birtles from Artimediant Investment Company, the CFO of *Securetwo*, Wendy Richards, and Samuel Jacobsen made up the rest.

The meeting followed the usual format, with the major presentation being a series of PowerPoint slides showing the financial status of the business. Richards showed that revenue and profit were increasing each month over the past quarter.

"It's a positive indication of how we are doing. However, we need to ensure that as we continue to grow, we keep a lid on our expenses," she said. She then presented a slide of cashflows and a trendline projection to the end of the financial year. The outlook was extremely positive.

After Richards finished, Jacobsen provided a short overview of the legal matters he was involved in including a dispute with a third party, called BTN, concerning a cloud service that BTN had been supplying. It was a dispute regarding service level breaches. *Securetwo* relied on BTN to ensure that its data centres were maintained with the highest level of integrity. Data breaches or attempts to compromise any data that *Securetwo* placed on those systems, needed to be reported to *Securetwo*. It appeared that this was not happening, and it posed a risk to the business.

"What are our options?" Formrobe asked.

"Well the contract we have with them, does allow us to recover financial penalties, but the main issue I believe we need addressing is their ongoing failure to rectify their breaches. If they don't do that quickly enough, then we do have the right to terminate for breach of contract."

"Which can be very messy, technically" replied Formrobe.

"And legally," Jacobsen said.

Formrobe then advised the rest of the members about the recent attack that the business had been subject to. He let them know that it appeared to be a hoax but that he was conscious that it could be a test as well. That someone was trying to hack into the company's systems, for reasons not yet clear.

Between himself, Wendy Richards, and Jacobsen a discussion ensued about the implication of any possible future attacks. Judy Smerdon became bored, she was only interested in the risk to her investment. Eventually, she stated as such and sought the support of Birtles to ask about the risk to their money.

Formrobe indicated that at this stage there was nothing to be concerned about. The details of the conversation were noted and were to be summarized by Wendy in the minutes.

After the usual *Any other Business?* section of the meeting, the session broke up and Richards and Jacobsen went back to their respective offices. Birtles and Winters said their goodbyes and left together, leaving Judy and Formrobe briefly alone. It was an opportunity too good to miss. Judy asked Formrobe the question she had had not been able to get Jacobsen to answer.

"I hear you are looking to buy a racehorse James?" she enquired.

Like Jacobsen previously Formrobe said, "I'm not sure where you are getting your information from Judy, but to answer your question, yes, I am."

"Any reason?"

He wanted to be reasonable, but he found her questioning a little patronizing.

"To be honest, it's none of your business, but if you must know it's something I have been wanting to do for years."

"And what made you decide now?"

"No specific reason, just seemed like as good a time as any." He was conscious of her questioning and decided to push back at her, trying to find out why the sudden interest in his affairs. "Is there any reason why you ask?" he said.

She stayed quiet for a second, before saying. "I hope it won't take your focus away from the business. I wouldn't like this new *hobby* of yours to take up much of your time such that *my* investment suffers. Especially given what you said in the meeting just now" she said. "If the business is being attacked then I'm sure it will need your 100 percent focus on it."

Formrobe smiled inwardly. *It was all about her, wasn't it?* he thought. It always was. It was the reason why he and Alan's relationship had soured. Sad really. He decided to answer the question then change the subject.

"I'm sure the business is well-positioned to handle any possible attacks, so I wouldn't worry about that," he said, knowing that while he expressed his confidence to her, he needed to ensure that it was well merited throughout the business. The integrity of the systems, procedures, and its people would need to be checked again and again. IT security was not something that could just be looked at once and then ignored. There were always those who wanted to take others down. "How is Alan, by the way?" he asked wanting to move away from her questioning about the business and his own private affairs.

"Oh, I haven't seen him for a little while, but I understand he's formed another small business, but he won't tell me what it is," she said.

Formrobe was surprised, it didn't seem to fit with what he knew of Alan. But if he didn't want to share what the business was about, then he was still pleased for him. Perhaps Alan had developed a stronger backbone? Standing up to his mother was a good sign. He wondered what type of business it could be. Alan, like himself, had been interested in data and information management for as long as he could remember. Formrobe wondered if Alan was back in the game? Perhaps that was where she had obtained the information from about him buying a racehorse? Information and data protection was vital nowadays, but systems couldn't prevent a human being from sharing things by word of mouth. Between himself, Cannon, Bronton, and possibly some of the trainers he had visited, any one of them could have mentioned his name about him being in the market to buy a steeplechaser. Even Jacobsen could have mentioned it, but he doubted it. Nothing nowadays was as easy to keep secret as it should be.

"I'm pleased for him," replied Formrobe with genuine sincerity. "The next time you see or speak to him please pass on my best wishes, if you wouldn't mind? It would be good to catch up with him again at some point. Share a drink maybe?"

Judy Smerdon acknowledged the request with a nod. She picked up the papers she had received as part of the board meeting from off the table, folded them in half, and put them in her handbag. She then shook hands briefly with Formrobe and with a whiff of her perfume remaining behind, she left the room and the building. Formrobe watched through the boardroom window as she climbed into her car, a dark grey Jaguar XE. Darkness was beginning to fall. He watched her tail-lights leave the car park and turn into the road leading away from the offices.

# CHAPTER 14

"Sixty thousand is the most we are prepared to pay," Cannon said.

Bronton stayed quiet for a second. "Mike, you know I can't accept such an offer without first speaking with my client, but I do need to say that for a horse such as *Centaur* anything less than seventy-five thousand pounds is a bargain."

"That may well be Henry but add your commission on top of that and the purchase price can be significant. What is it, by the way?"

"As you know Mike it's normally between 10 and 25 percent, but if you are serious and you want to move quickly, I'll top it at 15 percent this time. As a token of my goodwill."

Cannon smiled inwardly. His view of Bronton, like that of any other agent, was being verified. *Goodwill? Umm…more like simple marketing,* he thought. An easy sale so far. The man had done very little. He let the thought pass. Let's see if he could earn his money by convincing the owner to sell at what Cannon had suggested to Formrobe the offer should be.

"Oh, and besides," Cannon said, "insurance for the horse down to my stable is your responsibility."

Bronton nearly choked.

"Take it out of your commission," Cannon added smiling to himself. He always knew that his negotiation skills would be useful.

Bronton retorted quickly. "Let me see what I can do regarding the price Mike. I'll call my client and get back to you within the next couple of hours or so."

Cannon put down the phone. He sat back in his chair for a few seconds. He had agreed with Formrobe a price range of between fifty-five and seventy thousand pounds for the horse, but thought that the lower end would likely be off-putting to Bronton and would have soured the negotiations a little, so his offer of sixty was a more reasonable one. He doubted it would be successful, but he needed to start the process somewhere. He stood up from his chair, left his office, and walked into the dining room where Michelle was busy with her planning work for the upcoming start of school. Papers were strewn across the table as she tapped away on her laptop.

"How is it going?" he asked.

"Slowly," she said, rubbing a hand on the back of her neck. Cannon stood behind her and put a hand on either side of her head, slowly rubbing his fingers on her temples then began caressing her shoulders.

She closed her eyes enjoying the sensation. "Ahh, that's nice," she said. "I need that."

He continued pressing his fingers into her tired muscles.

"How are the negotiations going?" she asked.

"Interesting," he replied, "I think we'll get there."

"That's good to hear. It seems like the horse is a good one from what you've told me. Won't be a bad first buy for a new owner like Mr. Formrobe."

"As long as the horse stays sound and runs up to his potential," Cannon replied.

"Do you have any doubts?"

"No, not really," he answered almost nonchalantly. "It's just that you can never tell in this game. Look what happened when we were in Australia last year. The horse that had to be euthanized after it broke its leg."

"Yes, I remember," she replied thinking back to their visit down-under.

"Anyway, I need to go and see how Rich is going after this morning's exercise. There are a few horses that I need to check upon. I'll see you later," he said bending down and kissing her on the head. It was a habit he had become familiar with over recent years, perfectly natural to both of them.

He put on a coat as he left the house and walked over to the stables. The weather was beginning to change. The past few days had been clear. A milky blue sky overhead had been the order of the day since he and Formrobe had returned from *up-north,* but a westerly wind was beginning to move the sky around a little. The temperature was dropping, and light rain was forecast overnight. Despite his coat, Cannon shivered as he crossed to the tack room where he knew he would find Rich.

"Anything to tell me?" Cannon asked after he sat down in a chair opposite Telside. His assistant was busy typing into a computer the details of the work done with each of the horses that exercised that morning. The details included times over the measured distances that the horses had run. Whether it was over steeplechase fences or hurdles. Sectionals, such as the last two hundred metres of each session that the horse had run. The quality of the jumping style, too quick, too slow, balanced or not, plus feedback from the riders as to how each of the charges felt *underneath* them. For example, had they laboured, been positive, been reluctant to jump or run? All this information and more was vital nowadays in running a good stable. In addition, medical and veterinary detail was also maintained. The results of blood tests, treatments for injuries were also kept on the computer.

Telside eventually ceased typing. He made a mark on the page attached to a clipboard, indicating where he had stopped.

"Nothing significant to be honest Mike, it looks like everything seems to be on track. Only *Windmill Boy* and *SouthSide Duke* are under treatment still and are likely to be so for a couple more weeks according to the vet. *Sammy's Remote* is over the leg injury he had so he's now going to go onto light work from next week and we'll step that up for his first run that I think he can have in a couple of months. We'll need to get him much fitter than he is now."

Cannon nodded. "That means that we still have plenty to take to the races then, once the season opens."

"Absolutely Mike," Telside replied. "I'm looking forward to this season. I expect it will be a good one."

"Me too."

Telside asked the question that he had been dying to ask since Cannon walked into the room. "Any update on *Centaur?*" he said.

"I've made an offer to Bronton to take back to the owner. I hope to get an answer tonight."

"I hope we can get him, Mike, he's a good prospect that horse."

"I agree, Rich," Cannon replied, "and not a bad first buy for Formrobe either. *If* we can get him," he emphasized.

The two men talked a little while longer. They covered staff issues, feed purchases, and had the usual discussion about the running of the stables. Cannon was pleased that he could focus on his real job, which was about training horses, and not have to worry about his past life, though he knew it was never too far away from his thoughts.

Cannon and Michelle sat at the dining room table. She had pushed the papers she had been working on, along with her laptop, towards one end. They were enjoying the lasagne that she had made during the afternoon. A green salad, now just a few lonely lettuce leaves left in a separate bowl, had supplemented the warm pasta, mince, and cheese. Cannon was on a second helping when his mobile phone pierced the silence between them as they ate. Looking at the number he could see the call was from Bronton. He raised his eyes heavenwards as he looked at Michelle. "Sorry love, I need to take this."

Michelle smiled. "No worries," she said.

Cannon answered.

"Henry," he said politely into the phone, "still working at this time?" he continued while looking at his watch. It was seven forty pm.

"An agent's work is never done," replied Bronton cheerfully. "Anyway, Mike I just wanted to come back to you on the offer you made for *Centaur.*"

"Go ahead," Cannon replied, "I'm all ears."

"I have good news and bad news," Bronton replied. "The good news is that the owner *still* wants to sell. The bad news is not at sixty thousand."

Cannon knew that based on Bronton's comments, a deal was still possible. It was just finding out where the price fell. The owner still willing to sell meant that the offer of sixty-thousand pounds wasn't too far away from the mark.

"What's he looking for?" asked Cannon.

"Sixty-two and a half!"

Cannon smiled, knowing that he had the mandate from Formrobe so he decided to conclude the sale. He would like the horse in his yard as soon as possible. Having found the horse for his client, he didn't want Formrobe to be talked into putting the horse with another trainer. The industry was small enough and competitive enough for the larger stables to *steal* up-and-coming horses from the smaller stables, with promises of better facilities and results. Despite what Formrobe had said earlier about him having chosen Cannon specifically to train for him, anything was possible.

"Done!" Cannon said. A sense of pride stirred within him at the way the transaction had gone. It had been much simpler than he had imagined. "When can you get the paperwork to me?" he asked. "I'll need to get the relevant signatures on it as soon as I can, then we can send you the funds."

"I can get the documents emailed to you tomorrow. I'll get the seller to sign in the morning then send them through. Once you've had them signed, email them back to me and I'll then send you the bank details. I use an encrypted mail service for that to ensure the transaction is kept safe."

"I understand," replied Cannon. "Oh, and thanks for your help here. It's been a pleasure doing business. Finally, when can we expect the horse?"

"Once the money is in the bank. I'll arrange via the new BHA portal for the ownership change details to be processed. It should mean you have the horse in your stables in about three days. I just need to arrange for transport."

"Sounds good," Cannon replied.

The men exchanged pleasantries then rang off. Cannon would make a call to Formrobe once he has finished dinner. He knew that he would need to call Jacobsen as well. He would do so in the morning after he received the paperwork from Bronton.

"Good news?" asked Michelle.

"Looks that way," Cannon replied, putting the last of the lasagne onto his fork.

# CHAPTER 15

It was the fifth course to be attacked. It was hoped that the authorities were beginning to take things seriously now. So far two of the four courses had agreed to postponements of their meetings. It was expected the other two would meet the request as well. Doncaster was next.

The figure leaned over to take out the accelerant from the backpack. As it did so, the barking started. A large dog, a German Shepherd could be heard about two hundred metres away to the left. A figure with the dog shone a torch across the ground and then about ten metres ahead of himself. The exact distance between where the dog was and where the intruder hid was difficult to measure. The silence and darkness around him distorted the sound. The figure decided to make a hasty retreat. They could always come back.

The sound of the barking came closer, the figure could hear the handler straining to hold back the dog, calling its name. The dog barked even louder, the figure began to sweat under the facemask and disguise it was wearing. The animal was getting too close for comfort. The figure crept away from the obstacle that was the intended piece of infrastructure to be set alight, it headed towards the external wall that had been scaled to gain entry onto the track.

The handler saw the movement as the figure reached the wall. They were only fifty metres away. The guard let the dog free. The animal barked louder and with its leash now off, it ran towards the intruder. The guard shouted a command and shone the torch towards the figure. The figure reached the top of the wall, the dog bounding towards it then leaping upwards, its jaws snapping as the figure fell backward on the other side, cracking a shoulder as it landed.

"Fuck!," the figure shouted, the sound giving away where it now lay, prostrate. The guard tried to shimmy up the wall but was unable to do so. The dog continued to bark and growl sensing that the intruder was still on the other side of the wall, that it had not yet got away.

The intruder lay silent for a moment, trying to ease the pain in the shoulder while staying quiet. The backpack that had been thrown over the fence as the intruder had scaled the wall had taken the brunt of the intruders' fall. Fortunately, nothing appeared to have come out from the bottle of accelerant nor had the device been broken. A quick check by the intruder confirmed it. Leaving anything on the ground that could be used by police to track down the intruder was the last thing needed. Everything used in the attack needed to be destroyed in the fire. The device likewise.

Slowly the figure backed away from the wall. The dog could be heard barking and growling as the guard walked away on the other side, back from where they had come. No doubt the incident would be logged and the police informed. The intruder had a feeling that the other racing clubs may have shared information about what had happened to them. It made the figure all the more determined, more pissed off, angrier. Was what was said on the club websites just lies? Were they taking the threat seriously? The figure decided it was time to take the cause to the next level. It may take a few days or weeks to arrange, especially after tonight. The injury to the shoulder would need to heal, but thereafter the figure decided to *up the ante*.

# CHAPTER 16

"We've done the deal," he said. "Sixty-two and a half thousand."

He had finished dinner with Michelle and decided to make the call. It was just after eight pm. Formrobe had answered his mobile almost immediately. He was delighted at the news. "Thank you so much, Mike, I can't wait to see *Centaur* on the track."

"Hey wait a minute, James, there are some things we need to sort out before we can even think about putting the horse in a race."

"I assume you mean all the formalities? The paperwork, etcetera?"

"Yes, we need to get Jacobsen to sign, we need to get the horse down here and we need to register your colours. Also, I want to sit with you at some point to agree on a plan for the coming season. Finally, I'll need to assess the horse's residual fitness since we saw him gallop for us. I don't think he was anywhere near full fitness and we need to get him reasonably close if we want to get him to have a good first-up run."

"When did Bronton say he can get him down to us?"

"If we get the formalities sorted and the money transferred, we can have him in about three to four days."

"Okay," replied Formrobe, "I'll call Jacobsen now, then I'll get the money ready. I'll make the transfer when I've got all the details. Bronton should have it in his bank the day after tomorrow."

"Sounds good," Cannon acknowledged. "Let's catch up again tomorrow once the paperwork arrives. We can go through it over the phone together."

"Thanks again, Mike," Formrobe replied. "I really do appreciate your help. I'm looking forward to having a good relationship with you, I'm sure *Centaur* will be a great addition to your stable."

Cannon was always happy to have good horses sent to him and he believed that *Centaur* was destined to have a good career under his care, but he was always wary that the owner didn't expect too much. A positive start was a good thing, a sound relationship over the longer term was what he preferred. Experience had shown him over the years that what started off well, didn't always end the same way.

"Thanks, James, or should I call you Mr. Formrobe now?" he asked, "seeing as you are now soon to be a client?"

A laugh came down the line. It was good for Cannon to hear the amusement in Formrobe's voice. "James will do, as long as I can keep calling you Mike?"

It was Cannon's turn to acquiesce. "No problem at all *James*," he replied, emphasizing his client's name. "Speak tomorrow. Goodnight."

The two men rang off.

# CHAPTER 17

With the formalities concluded, Cannon looked forward to receiving *Centaur*. The horse was expected that morning, but traffic and the weather had meant a delay. A cold persistent rain had set in from a weather front that had come across the Atlantic bringing low temperatures and blustery winds to the west of the country.

It was early afternoon and despite the rain, work in the stables continued as normal around them, just like most other days.

The horses that had been exercised were now back in their boxes having been washed and groomed. They would be fed their evening meals later. Now it was time to rest or receive any treatment needed.

The charges that had not been able to exercise due to injury were checked over to assess progress. Cannon had made sure that his normal vet would be on-hand to check over *Centaur* once he was unloaded. He wouldn't accept any horse without the vet giving an *all-clear* upon arrival.

The balance of the day would be filled with the appropriate staff cleaning tack, mucking out, painting inside the stables where necessary, and carrying out any maintenance. The staff that rode work had mostly moved on to other stables to do the same for other trainers or alternately went home to rest before being required to do it all again the next day. The cycle never ended, even during the off-season. With a new season due to begin shortly, the general activity around the place had ramped up significantly.

The moment the horse-trailer pulled up in his yard, Cannon had a feeling something was wrong. Rich stood by his side, they both wore overcoats to keep warm. Cannon, as usual, pulled the edges of the coat together with his left hand. Rich wore a flat cap to keep his head dry, Cannon remained hatless, his hair slowly growing more straggly and limp as the rain fell. It ran down his forehead and neck. Puddles were beginning to form on the ground.

"Let's get him out of there," Cannon said. "It's been a long journey. They must have left around six this morning." He walked towards the door at the rear of the horsebox just as the driver arrived from the other side of the vehicle.

"Hi there guv'nor," he said in a gentle black country accent, "Mr. Cannon is it?" he asked.

"Yes," Cannon said, holding out his hand which the driver accepted graciously, "that's me."

"Peter Todd," the man said. "I've got a delivery for you."

"I hope you had a good trip, Mr. Todd?" Cannon asked, before introducing

Rich to the driver.

Todd was about five feet ten tall and was surprisingly young. Cannon estimated that he was in his mid-thirties and appeared in good shape. He had light sandy coloured hair, green eyes, and a nose that seemed too small for his face. He wore jeans, boots, and despite the rain, only wore a traditional brown removalist coat over a blue checked shirt. Cannon thought him a caricature. He showed no sign of fatigue despite the long trip from Yorkshire. Telside shook Todd's hand and then without ceremony began to unlock some of the latches on the left-hand side of the horsebox. He wanted to see the new arrival.

"Hey, let me help you with that," Todd said, walking to the right-hand side of the box to open the latches there. Once all three latches on both sides were unlocked Todd slowly eased down the ramp to create a walkway for the horse to be led down to the ground. *Centaur* had his rump to Cannon so Cannon couldn't see the horse fully as it was dull inside the box, the rain and greyness adding to an inability to properly identify the animal. Protective rubber cups sat on top of each of the horse's hooves to keep them safe from bangs and scrapes as the box was hauled across the country. Likewise, bandages were swathed around the pastern and cannon bones of each leg. Todd walked up the ramp and untied the horse's bridle that had been attached to metal bars within the box. *Centaur* whinnied once he knew that he could move his head around with alacrity. It was so much better than it had been. He had been tied up such that he could only look ahead.

The horse was backed out of the box, then stopped near the base of the ramp, a back-foot landing in a small dark puddle, creating a splash. The horse lifted the foot, it was clear that he didn't like being too wet. It was the first thing Cannon noticed as odd. Only a few days ago when Formrobe and he watched *Centaur* trial, the horse didn't seem to be worried about the wet track. He walked around to the horse's head, holding on to a cheek snaffle at the side of the horse's mouth to be able to look at him fully.

"There's something wrong here," he said, looking towards Todd and pointing at the horse's head. "The marking on the head here, it's not right."

"Sorry?" enquired Todd, "what are you talking about Mr. Cannon?"

"The marking on the head," Cannon repeated, looking towards Telside. "Rich, just take his head, will you?" Cannon asked frustratedly. "Let me see the feet."

Telside did as requested, his face reflecting his lack of understanding about Cannon's concerns.

Todd removed the protective cups and the bandages on *Centaurs'* legs, throwing them into the horsebox after he had removed each one. The horse remained still, its once dry, bay coloured coat slowly darkening as the rain continued.

Finally, once everything had been removed from the horse's legs, Cannon took a couple of steps back and looked the horse up and down.

"I knew it!" he exclaimed. "This isn't *Centaur*, it's not the horse I saw just a few days ago. What the hell is going on?" he asked turning to Todd angrily.

Todd took a step back, Cannon's annoyance evident. As the delivery man, Todd had only done as he was requested. The horse wasn't his. He had not been involved in any transaction, he was just the driver, following instructions.

Telside noted Todd's concern, how uncomfortable he appeared.

"Mike, Mike!" he called, trying to calm Cannon down, "take it easy, will you! What's the problem anyway?"

"The horse, *this* horse, is not what we bought Rich," Cannon stated. "We bought or at least paid for, a very different animal and I need to understand what's going on," he said.

"Perhaps it's just a genuine mistake?" Rich asked. "Maybe they just loaded the wrong horse into the box this morning? It's possible you know."

Cannon nodded, mistakes could be made, but he wasn't convinced.

"Mr. Todd," Cannon said, slowly regaining his composure, "can I ask you a favour?"

"Sure."

"Would you mind putting *this* horse back into the box please?" he said, pointing at the new arrival. "Unfortunately, I can't accept anything as being delivered today," he went on, "so you will need to take it back with you."

"Hang on a minute," Mr. Cannon, replied Todd, "it's been a long trip so before I take anything back with me, could you please check with Mr. Pool who asked me to deliver down here, whether this is the right horse or not?"

Cannon sighed saying, "I know it isn't *Centaur,* but I'll check for you anyway."

"Thank you, Sir."

"Rich?"

"Yes, Mike."

"Could you help Mr. Todd here put the horse back in the box anyway? While I give Pool and Bronton a call?" he asked.

"No worries, Mike," Telside replied and with a clicking of his tongue, he settled the horse down and led him back up the ramp into the box.

They waited while Cannon made his call.

The phone rang interminably. Cannon waited for it to be picked up, his frustration rising with each ring.

He was standing in his office looking out of the window through the growing gloom as the rain and early afternoon darkness began to merge. He watched as Rich and Todd stood talking. He noticed how agitated and animated Todd was. Cannon surmised that the man wanted to get on his way. The horse had been reloaded and the return trip would mean another four or five hours on the road. The man would be exhausted by the time he got back home, Cannon thought.

"C'mon, c'mon," he said out loud to no one but himself, "answer the bloody phone, will you?"

As Cannon was about to slam down the receiver the phone was picked up. "Hello, hello, Harry?" Cannon said.

There was a silence for a few seconds before a voice asked, "Hello?"

Cannon didn't recognize the voice, it was an unusual accent and he thought that perhaps he had dialled the wrong number, the reason why it took so long to be answered.

"Hello," he said again, "Harry? It's Mike, Mike Cannon. Can you hear me?"

There was no response. Cannon could hear breathing at the end of the line. He wondered if the connection was too poor for Pool to hear him. He tried again, shouting into the mouthpiece. "Harry! Harry! It's me, Mike. I need to…"

The phone was suddenly disconnected, Cannon finding himself listening to a series of crackles and pips, then a long slow beep.

He slammed the phone down onto its cradle, an expletive at BT because it was easy to do so, slipped from his lips. "Fuck!" he shouted, pushing a hand through his hair. Michelle came to the office door, her hands wrapped in a tea towel that she had been using in the kitchen.

"Mike? Are you alright?" she asked.

He looked at her face noticing how concerned she seemed. His outburst was somewhat out of character as they had spoken that very morning about the new arrival and how positive things were in the yard. How things were looking up for them both.

"I'm fine," he responded, "just a little frustrated. Sorry."

"Anything I can do to help?"

"If you could get Harry Pool to answer his phone for me that would be great," he said half-jokingly, a smile of sorts crossing his face. He knew the matter would be resolved, it wasn't the end of the world, but he did feel annoyed at what had happened.

"Not sure I can do that," Michelle responded, "but I can do this." She walked over to him and kissed him on the mouth, her lips parting and her tongue searched for his. He held her tighter to him, he felt the warmth of her body and the curves of her breasts against his chest. They only had a few seconds together, but it felt much longer for both of them. The promise of what could be later that evening.

A cough from Telside, who stood at the open door to the office, made them jump apart. He smiled, Michelle blushed, Cannon nodded.

"Yes, Rich?"

"Sorry to interrupt Mike, but I just wanted to find out if you'd had any luck?" he asked. "With Pool…?"

"As it turns out Rich, no! I tried to call him, but he couldn't hear me. I was just about to try him again," he said, looking at Michelle.

"Okay, well I'll let Peter know that you'll be a few more minutes then?"

"Peter? Oh yes, the driver. Sorry Rich, yes please tell him that I'll just be a few more minutes "

"No worries," Telside replied. "It's just that he wants to be on his way asap. I'll let him know then."

Cannon nodded.

"Well," Michelle said to Cannon after Telside had left the room, "I'd better get on with what I was busy with. See you later," she winked, before giving him a quick peck on the cheek.

He smiled. The frustration he had felt only a few minutes earlier had dissipated. Michelle could do that to him.

He picked up the phone again and rang Pool's number, there was no answer despite him leaving the phone to ring until it rang out. He decided to try Bronton. Again, the phone rang out. After the third attempt without success Cannon replaced the phone in its cradle, his annoyance increasing.

Back outside and having put his coat on again, Cannon stood with Todd under the stable eaves. Rich had gone back into the tack room, conducting a quick review of what the staff had been up to. The two men watched as the steady rain fell, filling the small potholes of the stable yard. It was now much cooler than it had been that morning and Cannon felt the chill.

"I can't expect you to wait any longer Peter, so I think you should get on your way."

Todd seemed relieved. "Thanks, Mr. Cannon," he replied, "I'm not sure what's going on, but I can tell you that the horse in that trailer," he pointed towards the box now glistening in the rain, "is the horse I was told to bring you, the horse I was told you *bought*."

"Well it isn't, I can assure you of that. I even have a couple of photographs of the horse we saw a few days ago, here on my phone," he said, opening up his phone's photo app. "As you can see the markings on the head, of the horse we understand is called *Centaur*, and those on his feet, are much different to the horse you brought with you."

Todd looked at the photographs and conceded the point. He agreed to take the horse in the box back to where he had collected him from. There was no point arguing with Cannon, it wasn't either of their faults. Todd said that he would get paid anyway.

----------------------

He had waved Todd on his way and had briefly met with Rich to update him about where things were at. They had discussed the prospect that

*Centaur* may only arrive the next day once things had been sorted out. Rich let Cannon know that he had told the vet not to wait around after his rounds to inspect *Centaur*, due to the mix-up. He had told him that the correct horse would likely arrive in the next day or so. Cannon thanked Telside for his foresight, he had then left the stable block and headed back to his office to try and call Pool again. He was halfway across the yard when Michelle had called his name from the doorstep as he walked through the rain.

He had answered her immediately, noticing that she held the office phone's receiver in her hand.

"For you," she said, as he reached the door to the house quickly removing his boots and leaving them on a shoe rack just inside the front door.

"Hello?" he said, expecting to hear Pool's voice.

"Hello," came the reply, "who is this please?"

Cannon was confused. If the call was for him as Michelle had said, why was the person asking for his name? He felt a chill along his spine. It was that feeling again. A sense of dread. A sense that never seemed to go away.

He offered his name but no further detail.

"Well Mr. Cannon," the caller said, "this is Detective Inspector Brendan Dockly of the South Yorkshire Police, and I want to talk with you, if I may?"

Cannon had worked with the South Yorkshire team in its various manifestations during the time he served in the Force. He knew quite a number of the members still working there and he appreciated the work they did. They were faced with staff shortages, money, politics, and yet continued to do their jobs. He admired their tenacity. He had seen enough, been through enough, decided he had *had* enough, and had moved on to a new life. Twenty years plus though, had left its mark.

"Certainly Inspector," Cannon replied, wondering what Dockly would want to talk with him about, "please go ahead."

"I think we may have to catch up face to face," Dockly said, "but just for my information, could you tell me how you came to call this number and called it several times today?"

Cannon wasn't sure what this was all about. Dockly was being cryptic.

"I'm sorry," replied Cannon, "but I thought *you* called *me*?" he said.

"I did indeed Mr. Cannon, but I would like to know why you called this number earlier?"

The question was a leading one, to get something out of him, perhaps to be used later. Cannon remained cautious.

"It was about a horse. Harry Pool had arranged to have one delivered to me today. When it arrived ...." he stopped.

"Go on, Mr. Cannon," Dockly encouraged, "when it arrived...?"

Cannon had realized that he was talking to a voice. A disembodied and unknown voice. He had no idea if Dockly was who he said he was. Cannon's internal antenna began to work overtime. Something wasn't right. He needed to find out what.

"I'm sorry Inspector, but before I carry on could you let me know how you got my number? The fact that you called me is interesting in itself and the fact that you know I called Harry is even more so. What's this all about if I may ask?"

Dockly cleared his throat. "Mr. Cannon," he said, "it's quite simple. Using 1471 I was able to establish that yours was the last number to call Harry Pool's phone today."

"Yes, what of it. I was trying to get hold of him," Cannon said.

"About a horse..?"

"Yes."

"Did he answer the phone?"

"No…well not initially."

"Oh?"

"Eventually he did. At least I think he did."

"Think?" asked Dockly.

"He couldn't hear me, and I could only hear him breathing. I intended to try him again later."

Suddenly Cannon realized something, the connections were made. He challenged Dockly.

"Sorry Inspector, something's not right here," he stated. "If you used 1471 on Harry's phone to find my number, why did you need to do that?" he asked. "It must mean you are *in* his house."

"I am, Mr. Cannon."

Cannon had a sense of foreboding. He stayed silent. Dockly knew why.

"It's a crime scene, Mr. Cannon. I'm sorry to say that Mr. Pool and his wife are dead."

"Dead?" Cannon responded instinctively.

"I'm afraid so, Mr. Cannon. I won't share any details with you as I'm sure you will understand why, however, please be aware that I will likely need to speak with you about this matter. As our investigation continues," Dockly said.

Cannon was stunned. Speechless. He nodded in response to Dockly before realizing that the Inspector was not able to see his acceptance of the request.

"I understand Inspector."

"Thank you, Mr. Cannon, I'll be in touch."

They both put down their receivers simultaneously.

---------------------------

Cannon tried to call Bronton. It was an hour after he had finished his call with Dockly.

He hadn't contacted Formrobe yet about the mix up with the horse as he wanted to find out where *Centaur* was. What had happened to the horse? Dockly had said that he was at a *crime scene*. That could be a murder, a suicide, or even a tragic farm accident, Cannon thought, though he doubted it would be anything other than murder. It was a guess, but it was based on experience, and on the way that Dockly had spoken to him, the words he used.

In the interim, while he had waited to contact Bronton, Cannon had shared the details of his conversation with the Inspector with both Michelle and Rich. They, like himself, were confused and shocked. It seemed like the world had been turned upside down. The preparation for the new season had been going well. The new horses that had come into the yard were looking fit and happy. Expectations were high, and now this! They didn't need the disruption. They needed Cannon to be focused.

As with Pool, Bronton's office phone rang continuously. Cannon shook his head. If he couldn't get hold of the agent, what could he tell Formrobe? He had so many questions to which he needed answers. Answers that he could pass on to his client.

Where was *Centaur*? Where was Formrobe's money? How come another horse in place of *Centaur* had been shipped to Cannon's stables? Who had arranged it? The phone rang out.

Cannon tried Bronton's mobile. Like the office phone, it rang out as well.

----------------------------

Bronton had been unable to answer Cannon's call as the mobile lay a foot away from his hand. It was lying on the office carpet, next to Bronton's body, where he had collapsed. His throat cut, Bronton had bled to death. A pool of sticky liquid had soaked his shirt and jacket, a bright red stain had flowered across the chest, down his left-hand side, and had dripped onto the floor. His sightless eyes lay open, staring upwards at the ceiling.

# CHAPTER 18

The man with the dreadlocks made the call. He was sitting alone.

Things were starting to come together well.

"Yes?" a brusque voice said after the call had been answered.

"It's me."

There was a short silence before Clifford Mitchell realized who was calling.

"And to what do I owe the pleasure?" he asked.

"I think we are square now. I just wanted to make sure we are sweet with each other."

"And what makes you think that?" Mitchell asked.

"Because I've done what you asked."

"Really?"

"Yes."

"But did it work?" Mitchell continued.

"Sort of."

"Sort of? Sort of?" Mitchell replied angrily, "Look, I gave you enough time to sort things out and you haven't, have you?" he said. "Nothing's changed. Things are still going ahead as before. Nobody is taking it seriously, are they?"

The man with the dreadlocks didn't need to be lectured to. He was getting annoyed with Mitchell but decided to hold his tongue. Mitchell's time would come, he thought. "Maybe not yet," he replied, "it just takes a little time."

"Well I don't have the time to wait, and *you* don't have either."

"Is that a threat?"

"What do you think?"

"I'm not sure what to think, but I will tell you this, *don't you ever threaten me again.* Do you understand me?!"

Mitchell was taken aback at the audacity of the caller. It wasn't often that he had felt such aggression towards himself, normally it was the other way around.

"Your position is noted," he replied eventually, diplomatically, calmly.

"So, what do you still need me to do?"

In an attempt to still be in control of the conversation and be in control over the caller, Mitchell said. "Do what you did before, but make sure it has *maximum impact.* If you do, then yes, *we are sweet,*" he said sarcastically.

The caller disconnected the phone without offering any response, leaving Mitchell holding his receiver, but with no one to talk to. He slowly put the handset back inside the cradle.

Clifford Mitchell, a cigar-smoking, overweight, sixty-two-year-old, rails bookmaker. He was five foot two in his socks. A small man in height, but a big man on the racecourse. He had made a living for the past forty years, taking bets, laying off the risk, and helping lots of clients *lose* their money. It was lost to *him*, and he was grateful. It helped him live in a huge house in Surrey, just outside Cobham, towards Leatherhead. He had neighbours who were members of the Chelsea football team, their training facilities a mile or so up the road next to the Stoke D'Abernon railway station. Now divorced and his children having flown the nest, he was a man who lived alone and liked it that way. He found people were only useful when it came to making him money. This was attested to by his dealings with his ex-wife. His divorce ten years earlier had cost him nearly half his estate. If it hadn't been for his solicitors and a clever bit of manipulation by his accountant, he would have lost much more than he did. Eventually, the divorce after twenty-seven years of marriage had cost him twenty percent of what he had. Clever people, *lawyers*, he had thought at the time. They had done him proud until he had received their bill then he had deemed them *outrageous*.

He stood for a few seconds thinking about the caller and the agreement they had just made, then he turned and walked towards his drinks cabinet. It was late but there was time for a late-night snifter of whisky. He took out a half-empty bottle of *The Balvenie 21-year-old* and topped up, to halfway, an existing glass sitting on a small table next to a chair. Having put the bottle back, he sat down in the chair and took the glass in his hand. He held it up to the light, inspecting the colour of the liquid. A whisky, neat without water or ice, was his preferred way of drinking the *water of life*. He took a sip enjoying the warmth as it hit the back of his throat then burnt its way down his gullet.

There was one last thing to do before he turned in for the night. He picked up the phone and made a call.

"The arrangements are being made," he said, "it will get done."

A grunt was all he heard in response. He put down the phone.

For a few seconds, he was disturbed by the lack of interaction, the minimal acknowledgement received during the call. He reflected on the fact that it hadn't always been that way.

A grunt! What the fuck did that mean, he thought to himself?

He tried to put things in perspective. It would all be over soon.

Taking another sip of his scotch he allowed himself a few seconds to enjoy the moment. It was one of life's little pleasures.

Closing his eyes, not from tiredness but just taking comfort from his surroundings. He began to relax, the warmth of the room seeping into his bones, his consciousness. He was going to be busy the next day. Raceday always was, especially if you needed to travel hundreds of miles a day to get to a specific track. Fortunately for him, Doncaster and the other Northern meetings only came later in the season. For now, at the end of summer into mid-autumn, most of the meetings he was interested in were in the south of the country or at worst in the Midlands.

A smile creased his face. He replayed the earlier conversation that he had had with the man he always referred to as *dreadlocks*. Those that owed him often tried bravado in an attempt to intimidate him. It was part of the process, but he never took it seriously. He was wealthy enough to arrange the necessary protection. His plan had hit a few hurdles, but it was still on track. He smiled then laughed at the metaphor, before gulping down the rest of his drink. It was time for bed.

# CHAPTER 19

"It was a scam," Brendan Dockly said. "It seems like they have pulled off this type of thing several times before."

Cannon was mute. He had investigated scams in his time in the force, but this one was extremely sophisticated. To sell a horse to a trainer through a third party and to try and pass-off one horse for another, was extremely daring. The use of identification marks, inserted electronic chips under the horse's skin, photo ID, and blood samples made it very difficult to fool people, though from what Dockly had indicated, it seems that some people may have fallen for it.

Dockly had called Cannon back the next day after the police had made enquiries about Pool and his association with Bronton.

"Where is Bronton now then?" asked Cannon.

"I'm sorry to say that Mr. Bronton is dead."

"Dead?" repeated Cannon.

"Yes, Mr. Cannon, and I'm afraid I'm going to have to ask you to come to the station tomorrow so that we can conduct further enquiries."

"Surely Inspector," Cannon asked, "you can't think that I had anything to do with Mr. Bronton's death, can you?"

"At this stage, I'm not at liberty to share what I think," Dockly replied, "I just need you to come and make a statement."

"Can we do it locally?"

"Locally?"

"Yes, down here in Oxfordshire. I would prefer not to have to go up to Doncaster if I can help it. I have my stable to run."

"Is there anyone who you could delegate that too, Mr. Cannon?" Dockly asked politely. "It should only be for a few hours."

Cannon knew that in police terms, a few hours could easily convert into much longer. He had played that game himself many times. After a few seconds pondering the alternative, which was that the issue would not rest until he had made his statement, Cannon agreed to drive up to Doncaster the next day. The matter of Bronton's death, though, was very disconcerting to him. He had no idea as to the cause and Dockly had not indicated how Bronton had died. Cannon knew, however, that coincidence was something he didn't readily accept. There was bound to be something behind it. He knew from experience that someone somewhere had been crossed. Was it another scam that had now gone badly wrong? Someone Pool and Bronton had underestimated? But who would kill like that? Wasn't getting one's money back the best outcome? Murder was taking things to the extreme, surely?

Cannon remembered how smooth Bronton seemed with him and

Formrobe when they had gone to see *Centaur*. In retrospect, Cannon could see how he had been played, but he still couldn't understand how they had hoped to get away with it. It wasn't as if Cannon was new to the game. He knew how to identify a horse. Perhaps there was more to it than first met the eye?

"I'll make arrangements here at the stable for someone to look after things," Cannon said, "but I would like to get back by evening."

"I'm sure that will be fine Mr. Cannon," Dockly replied.

The two men said their goodbyes and ended the call. Cannon had an uncomfortable feeling in his stomach about the interview and statement giving to be conducted the next day, but considered it a remnant of his past. He decided to call Formrobe and fill him in on developments. He hadn't been in touch with his client about the delivery of the *wrong* horse yet, as he wanted to get to the bottom of what was behind it. Dockly's call had begun to add some meat to the bones but there were still many questions to be answered. Cannon anticipated that Formrobe would ask about the money, and if *he* didn't then Jacobsen would. Besides, if Pool and Bronton were dead, Cannon asked himself, where was the horse, *Centaur,* and indeed the ringer horse? What had happened to them? Where was Peter Todd, the driver of the horsebox? Had he taken either or both of the horses anywhere? Had he been a part of the con? Too many questions Cannon thought, and at this stage not enough answers. He picked up the phone again and dialled Formrobe's number.

------------------------------

It was a difficult conversation.

Formrobe was not happy. The money wasn't an issue, but he knew that Jacobsen would make one of it. It was the fact that he had relied on Cannon and now he felt let down. His first foray into horse ownership and he was left with egg on his face.

"Look James, I am extremely sorry about all this," Cannon said apologetically. "I know it's extremely distressing for you and you have every right to be pissed off at me, but I can assure you that what Pool and Bronton pulled off was something quite audacious."

"And they've done it before?" asked Formrobe.

"The police have indicated that they have, yes."

"Are the police going to arrest them?

Cannon had not yet advised Formrobe of the murders of Pool and his wife nor indeed made any suggestion about his own theory concerning Bronton's death. He decided it was time to do so.

"Oh my God!" Formrobe exclaimed once Cannon had relayed the details he had to his client. "All this over a bloody horse?"

Cannon could sense his client's fear growing. Murder wasn't something Formrobe was used to. His business was about protecting data, setting up security systems on IT platforms, not the security of people. The two were incongruent to Formrobe, and Cannon knew it.

He changed the subject slightly.

"The police up in Doncaster have asked me to drive up tomorrow to make a statement about what I know. It will be a long day. I was tempted to ask if you wanted to come up with me, but I think I'll do it alone for now, if that's okay?"

"Are you sure?"

"Yes…at least for now. I will need to fill the police in about the arrangements we made, the visit to Pool's place, and what we discussed. I assume you are okay with that?"

"Of course," Formrobe replied. "If you need me to get involved in any way or need my input, then just let me know."

"Okay, thanks, James. If I need to call you from the station, then I will. Are you going to be around?"

"Yes, I'll be at my office. I'll need to let Jacobsen know what's going on."

"Naturally."

"Plus, Mike, we've had a bit of an issue ourselves over the past week or so."

"Related?"

"Not to me buying the horse, no, but related to the business. Someone has been trying to hack into our systems. Trying to shut down some of our hardware and delete or steal the data of our clients."

"Any ideas?"

"None at this stage, but it has caused us to beef up our own security. Do extra back-ups, strengthen our firewalls, upgrade some of the software bugs that could be used to infiltrate what we do."

"Oh, sounds complicated."

Formrobe smiled. He knew he was talking way above Cannon's head. "It is a bit, but it's what we do. All I can say is that we are trying to find out who is behind it, but it looks like they have covered their tracks pretty well."

Not dissimilar to what happened to *Centaur*, it would appear, Cannon thought. He hoped that resolution would be much easier than what he imagined Formrobe would need to go through.

After a few more minutes discussion about what Cannon's approach to the police interview the next day would be, the facts, the dates, the players, the two men ended the conversation. Both men had concluded that they had nothing to hide, nothing to be concerned about.

In time they would look back and realize how wrong Cannon was.

# CHAPTER 20

The two of them sat in a corner of the Old Swan pub in Market Place, just a half-mile from the Uttoxeter racecourse. It was just after seven in the evening, and the place was almost empty, most of the drinkers having been and gone. The family trade was limited during the week, especially on a Tuesday, so except for a couple of tables being used in the dining area, they had the place to themselves.

They spoke quietly, falling into silence whenever one of the staff passed them on their way to and from the kitchen. They had considered another attack to get their message across but had eventually decided against it. Their initial target before they had abandoned the idea, had been the Newton Abbot racecourse in Devon, but they had eventually decided against it for two reasons. The first was that it was so far away from anywhere and the second was they believed they had made their point. Even though the Doncaster attack had resulted in a failure of sorts, the police and the racing authorities had taken their request seriously by postponing the upcoming meetings at the impacted courses, but had not stopped racing going ahead everywhere. The men knew that a new season was starting soon and had hoped that all National Hunt racing would be put on hold. They had advised the racing authorities that there would be implications, but it appeared that the threat had been laughed off as inconsequential. Despite proving that they could hit a racecourse at any time, the men believed that big money had won the day. It was this arrogance that brought the two men together again.

The shoulder was still hurting, but over the past ten days or so it had improved and was now much more flexible. The man felt much more comfortable now, as he had no pain anymore, just stiffness.

His colleague, the one with the dreadlocks was keen to get an update.

"How did you go?" he asked.

"It's all set."

"Are you sure?"

"Of course," replied the other moving his arm in a circular motion while kneading his shoulder with his other hand.

"Did anyone see you, Kevin?"

"I doubt it," he replied. "The way the track is set out there is a large grassy area in the middle of it, with trees, a few small buildings. I was a long way from any possible CCTV cameras as well. It would have been impossible for anyone to see me from where the stands are. Last night was cloudy and moonless and I managed to get onto the track down the back straight without any problems at all."

"Aren't there two tracks?"

"Technically I guess the answer is yes, but it's really one course with hurdles and steeplechase fences."

The man with the dreadlocks smiled before asking, "They'll be using both tomorrow then?"

"I had a look at the race card they put out a few days ago, it seems they are having more hurdles races than steeplechases, but either way, I've managed to address it."

"Good man," said dreadlocks, giving the other a punch to the arm.

The two men sat in silence for a few seconds, each in thought, both staring at each other, both considering their cause.

Without notice, the man with the dreadlocks let out a sigh, an exclamation, just loud enough for the other to hear.

"Shit!" he said.

"What?" answered Kevin, "what is it?"

"I just realized something…"

"What?"

"About tomorrow! The racing!"

Kevin was perplexed. "What do you mean?" he asked.

The man looked around, bent his head slightly, and drew the other closer to him.

"Tomorrow. Tomorrow," he repeated, "won't the riders and the fence builders….won't they…?"

"Walk the course, you mean?"

"Yes."

"And?" asked Kevin, trying to understand the concern.

"Won't they find out what you've done?"

Kevin sat back in his chair. He was confident in his work. "No," he said, "they'll find nothing."

"How can you be so sure?" dreadlocks asked.

"Because I know what I'm doing," Kevin replied confidently. "I can assure you," he went on, "that they will not be able to find anything at all. No matter how closely they look."

The man with the dreadlocks took his drink and finished what was left in the glass. "Cheers," he said. "Here's to you."

Kevin smiled. He was glad to be part of it. He looked forward to seeing the result of his handywork.

# CHAPTER 21

It had been just over a week since Dockly had advised Cannon of Bronton's murder. Since then, both he and Formrobe had given statements about their meetings with Bronton and with Pool. Where they met, the transaction they had entered into, and why. Dockly had advised Cannon that Bronton had scammed several people, including several horse trainers over many months and that the police were investigating various leads regarding where the monies Bronton had been able to extract from unsuspecting buyers had gone. He also let Cannon know that they were also looking into who had taken things to the extreme and murdered Bronton and Pool. Nobody, including Cannon and Formrobe, were excluded from their investigation.

From what Cannon was able to extract, it had become apparent that over months, possibly years, Bronton and Pool had cheated many people out of tens of thousands of pounds each. The initial police investigation, Cannon surmised, suggested that that the total could run into hundreds of thousands, if not millions. Sadly, those who had been scammed had kept quiet about it.

"Why has there been no publicity about it?" Cannon had asked Dockly *off the record*. Given Cannon's background, which he had shared with the Inspector, Dockly had decided to share a little more about the case than he would with others. While he wanted to keep the integrity of the investigation, he realized that he may need Cannon in the future, so he made a concession.

"We can only surmise that it was the embarrassment that some had felt about the matter," Dockly had replied, "or indeed that some had decided to try and recover their money through legal channels in the first instance. Either way, those that had been stung, we believe, were trying to keep things quiet for one reason or another."

Cannon understood the sentiment of others but was also angry with himself at being caught out. He thought he knew people. In this case, that perception had been proven wrong. His past was something he drew on regularly, as he had seen the best and worst of people. Somehow, however, despite his attempt to keep to the best, the worst always seemed to come out of the woodwork and surround him and those he loved and cared for. At least in Bronton's case, he was only a bit player, on the periphery.

He had to leave the investigation to Dockly, to the authorities. He hoped they would find where Formrobe's money had gone and would be able to recover it for him. Until then, he would remain angry and, in a similar vein to others, embarrassed.

Now he was standing in the middle of the parade ring at the Uttoxeter racecourse, a pale sun trying to push away the low clouds that slung themselves from the west across the Staffordshire countryside. It was still officially early autumn, but the weather gods had decided to send some winter temperatures in advance of the real event. It was clear that *they* didn't care about the calendar. Cannon stood next to his owner, Patrick O'Smullegan, a young, seventy-plus retired merchant seaman who had owned racehorses of different abilities for the past fifteen years. He had been a loyal owner and had been with Cannon for the past six years. They watched their stable' representative, *BKeeper,* jig-jog around the ring in advance of the third race, a two-and-a-half-mile novice chase. Both men hid their hands inside their coats to keep them warm. Cannon was wearing his heavy, black Crombie over a knitted blue jumper and grey corduroys while his guest wore a donkey jacket and jeans. To those in the sparse crowd attending the mid-week meeting and watching at the edges of the ring, it proved that National Hunt racing was not a rich man's sport. It was a sport for the everyman, and long may it continue, Cannon thought as he chatted with O'Smullegan.

"He's looking well," O'Smullegan said, in his soft Irish lilt, "how do you think he will go?" he asked, nodding towards the grey, nearly white horse that passed directly in front of the pair. The horse snorted on cue as if knowing he was being talked about. He was led around by a young apprentice jockey who doubled as the horse's rider during training. When not riding, the lad worked for Cannon as a stable-hand.

"I think he's ripe for this race, Patrick," Cannon replied. "There are only six runners and every one of them are maidens, so there isn't too much opposition."

"What about *Radio Frequency*, the favourite?"

Cannon had studied the form, as he did whenever his horses were racing, and had a clear view of *BKeeper's* chances.

"I think he's still a little bit inexperienced over these fences given he's only had a couple of races so far in his career," Cannon said, "and the best he's done so far is a forth, beaten quite some way, so I'm not too worried about him," he went on. "If our boy can jump as well as he has been at home, I think we are in with a good chance."

"Should I go and put a bet on him, then?"

Cannon laughed. If he had been given a pound every time an owner asked him that question, he would have been rich, he thought.

"That's up to you Pat," he replied. "All I can say is that *he has a chance*, but then don't they all?" He winked at O'Smullegan, letting him know that the decision to gamble on *BKeeper* was that of the owner, but that Cannon had got the horse in the best shape he could to contest the event.

As the men continued watching, a bell clanged and the six jockeys for the race suddenly appeared from the weighing room. The cold wind snagged itself around the brightly coloured outfits of each of the tiny men, blowing their racing silks in various directions, the lightweight coverings hiding the thin bodies beneath. Cannon was always surprised by jockeys. No matter the weather, they hardly ever showed signs of being cold or warm. They just seemed to tolerate the elements. William 'Bill' Circling, a journeyman jockey who Cannon had engaged many times to ride his horses, walked up to Cannon and O'Smullegan and tapped his racing helmet with his whip, holding out his hand to greet them both.

"Hi there, Mike, how's he going?" he asked, nodding towards *BKeeper* who had reached the far apex of the parade ring as he continued to be led around.

"He's well, Bill," replied Cannon, "hopefully this will be a good season for him. He seems to be getting stronger and more willing to tackle the fences now," he stated.

"And today?" asked the jockey, resplendent in his silk top, orange on the left and green on the right, split right down the middle. With the jockey helmet covered with a white silk, the overall effect was the jockey seemingly draped in the Irish flag.

"I think he'll do well," Cannon replied. "Just go easy on him for the first mile and a half, two miles, then if he has it in him, see what he can do over the last 800 yards or so."

"Right you are, Mike."

O'Smullegan who had kept quiet up until now jumped in saying, "And if you do win Bill, remember I'll treat you to a little something."

"Thanks," Circling said, looking at Cannon, who just smiled. Cannon was happy for every owner who trusted him with their horses, but he knew from experience that it was unlikely that every horse he sent out to race would win. He knew it, jockeys knew it, but owners were ever-positive, and thank God for them, Cannon thought.

Another bell sounded and a voice called for the jockeys to mount. It was ten minutes to start time. Circling offered his hand again, then turned and walked away towards *BKeeper*. Cannon followed, leaving his owner to watch as Cannon gave Circling a leg up onto *BKeeper's* back.

The jockey untied his stirrups and settled his feet into them before standing up to check if they were level and comfortable. Cannon said. "Come back safe Bill, both of you," then slapped the horse on the neck and stood back as the horse and jockey were led away towards the course proper.

Cannon and O'Smullegan walked out of the parade ring together. The two men in step as they walked towards the grandstand. As they did so, O'Smullegan said, "I'll meet you in the bar Mike, if that's okay? We can watch the race from there. It'll be warmer than standing outside on the steps of the stand, don't you think?"

Before Cannon could answer, O'Smullegan continued, "I'm just off to put a bet on," he said, turning on his heel and heading towards the betting hall. Cannon sighed and watched his owner's back disappear around the corner of the Grandstand. He made his way to the Owners' Bar.

------------------------

There were only a dozen bookmakers in the betting hall. It was generally quiet around each of their stands. O'Smullegan walked along the line of each looking for the best price for *BKeeper*. Unfortunately, he was the second favourite at two-to-one, *Radio Frequency* was still the favourite at eleven-to-ten. The third horse in the betting, *Tarzan Swing*, was at four-to-one, the rest at ten-to-one and above. From the betting, it was clear that most of the pundits believed it was a two-horse race.

O'Smullegan stopped in front of the bookmaker with whom he wanted to bet. "Four thousand to two grand," he said, to the bookmaker's assistant, "on account!"

The assistant was about to call out the bet to the bookmaker himself to allow the bet to be accepted but was stopped from doing so, a hand placed on his shoulder.

"Are you sure about this Patrick?" Clifford Mitchell said as he chewed on an unlit cigar, staring at the man standing in front of him.

O'Smullegan nodded. He was already *in* to Mitchell for fifteen thousand. He needed a way out, he hoped *BKeeper* would be the start of that process.

Mitchell looked around the hall for a second, business had been a little slow so far, yet he was still winning, both favourites in the first two races having failed.

"Okay," Mitchell said, "but it's time to start paying back, Patrick. If this one fails, then the interest rate starts going up again and the time to repay gets shorter. If it comes in, I'll knock it off the debt you owe, but remember this, thirty days from now is when you need to repay everything in full. If not," he continued with a sneer, "someone will be around to ensure I get what's owed. Do you get my drift?"

O'Smullegan nodded. The assistant issued the ticket, passing it over to the Irishman. "Now piss off!" Mitchell said.

*BKeeper's* owner turned and walked away from Mitchell's stand, placing the ticket inside his wallet and then returning the wallet to the inner pocket of his jacket. He headed towards the Owners' Bar and tried not to show how worried he felt. Cannon was waiting for him, already seated at a table that abutted the floor-to-ceiling glass window of the grandstand, allowing them to watch the races while seated.

"Alright, Patrick?" Cannon asked.

"Yes. A drink?" O'Smullegan enquired, knowing that he needed one to settle his nerves.

"Just a pint for me, thanks," Cannon said, knowing that it would be his only drink for the afternoon. He had one more runner for the day, in race five, and then he would head back home, hopefully, to arrive well before dark.

O'Smullegan went off to get the drinks. Cannon lifted his binoculars to his eyes and searched for his runner. Being the only grey in the race, *BKeeper* was easy to spot as he and jockey Circling walked around with the other horses awaiting the start.

Circling was confident. He had done his homework on the opposition. He had worked out the strengths and weaknesses of the other runners. He also knew the other jockeys very well, too. He knew who was strong in a finish, and who wasn't. He also guessed who was likely to make the running and who was likely to panic when the pressure came on near the end of the race. He had a game plan, now it was all about the execution.

The six horses walked around together in a tight circle. The starting process for National Hunt racing being much more complex than flat racing. There were no starting stalls, just the use of men with flags and a starting tape spread across the track. The jockeys were called by the starter to walk towards the starting tape. They did so without incident, no rushing, which was in line with the rules. As soon as the tape was raised the six runners set off at half pace, slowly increasing the tempo to three-quarter speed when they all cleared the first obstacle. *BKeeper* sat in third place just ahead of *Radio Frequency* in fourth. The running order remained the same for the next half mile until the fifth fence, where the leader *Small Windows* fell, the jockey hit the ground with a dull thud then rolled into a ball, his hands covering his head, his body sore and his mind hoping that he wouldn't be trampled by the horses behind him. Fortunately, the rest of the field cleared the prostrate jockey and continued on their journey towards jump number six. *BKeeper* however had become slightly unbalanced at the fifth due to Circling having to take evasive action to miss the fallen horse and rider as they lay on the ground. The consequence of that decision saved Circling's life, as well as that of *BKeeper*. By taking the action he did, Circling lost ground to the other runners. He was about thirty feet behind the others with only one horse behind him as the field travelled towards jump six. *BKeeper* was making ground on those ahead of him as they charged at the obstacle. The jockeys urged their mounts towards the fence, positioning themselves in the saddle, ready to rise and leave the ground then onward towards the last couple of fences. As the leader was just about to make his leap a massive fireball erupted out of the birch. Flames shot twenty feet into the air. The leader had no chance at all, the horse was in mid-jump when the flames engulfed both horse and rider. The horse's coat and flesh were seared black by the intense heat, the jockey likewise appeared to vapourize, as both fell deep into the flames that licked at the sky and appeared to eat the fence. The second and third horse, including *Radio Frequency*, shied at the explosion, sending one jockey somersaulting over the fence, his silks burning themselves onto his body, the horse twisting and turning in fear but inevitably falling into the raging inferno. *Radio Frequency* disposed of his jockey over the running rail before darting through the wing of the jump and running free on the grassy area on the inside of the track. Circling managed to pull *BKeeper* to the outside of the jump, missing the fireball by metres, the intense heat turning the jockeys face red. He pulled the horse up about thirty metres away from the jump, quickly dismounting, and ran back towards the carnage, hoping to help in whichever way he could.

Cannon couldn't believe what he was seeing. He had been pleased in the way Circling was riding and the easy way that *BKeeper* had been travelling. Cannon was slightly concerned at what had happened at jump five but had been listening to the on-course commentary as the horses had raced towards jump six. *BKeeper* had been going well then suddenly all hell had broken loose. The scream from the commentary box over the course PA had been spine-tingling. No one could believe what they had seen. Death on the course was rare, but it now seemed he had paid another visit. This time it wasn't due to the racing. This time it was something else.

Sitting beside Cannon, O'Smullegan remained motionless, stunned. A series of "what the?" escaped from his lips. There were no answers, just questions.

"Stay here," Cannon said, standing up with urgency.

O'Smullegan just nodded, his eyes fixed on the chaos at fence six. He could see the ambulance that always followed the runners had stopped a short distance away from the fence that still smouldered, the flames slowly reducing in ferocity as the remaining fuel of the fence was consumed. Ambulance men, paramedics, and others appeared to be attending to bodies that lay on the ground. O'Smullegan couldn't see much, but the large screen TV in the bar was now focused on the mess that was the field of runners and the jump itself. He stared at the pictures being shown on the screen. He felt sick. He couldn't help it, he vomited onto the floor.

Cannon ran down the stairs from the bar. He found his young apprentice rider standing at the gate in the outside running rail that was opened and closed as required to allow people to cross the track to get to and from the inside part of the course. It was being marshalled by a course attendant. A crowd of around fifteen people stood together. The gate was closed, the attendant not yet authorized to let people through. There were loose horses on the track, one of them *BKeeper*, and Cannon needed to catch him before he became frightened and ran off, potentially injuring himself.

"We need to get through," Cannon said to the attendant, "my horse is loose."

"Sorry Sir," the attendant said, "I can't let anyone through until I'm told it's safe to do so. Didn't you just see what happened?" he asked incredulously.

"Yes, I did," replied Cannon, 'that's why we need to get through. One of those runners was mine!"

The attendant looked at Cannon, he appeared sympathetic but decided to stick with the rules. "Sorry Sir, but…"

Cannon decided that he had had enough, he grabbed the apprentice by the arm saying, "Come, follow me, let's go."

With that, he ran ten metres away from the attendant then jumped the running rail onto the track.

"Hey!" shouted the attendant. Cannon ignored him, encouraging his apprentice to follow him.

Once on the track, the two men jogged directly towards the ambulance, now only six hundred metres away. It had been joined by a couple of other vehicles. Cannon could hear sirens wailing in the distance, getting louder slowly. A fire engine? Police? More ambulances? Whatever they were, they were needed.

As they got closer Cannon saw the extent of the devastation. He saw *BKeeper* about a hundred metres up the track, standing still, calm, as if nothing had happened.

Pointing, he said to the apprentice, "There he is, please can you go and grab him and take him back to the stables. I'll meet you there later. In the meantime, I'm going to see if I can help."

"Sure, no worries," said the apprentice, branching off away from Cannon, and heading towards the horse.

Cannon arrived at the fence. What he saw was like a battlefield. Several people were running in different directions attempting to get equipment out of the ambulance. Someone was calling for a stretcher, someone else for blankets. Another person, possibly a vet, was calling for a screen to be put around an injured horse. Cannon was stunned, unsure what to do. He had little authority now, he was no longer a policeman. He had powers of persuasion, but not of the law. He stopped a paramedic carrying oxygen and blankets who was heading towards a jockey lying on the ground, another paramedic already rendering assistance.

"Can I help?" he asked.

"I think if you can keep people away from the area for now that would be great," the man said. "We need the professionals to do their job and others to stay away."

"Okay," Cannon replied, "I'll see what I can do." He hesitated just for a second then held the paramedic's arm briefly, before asking. "My jockey, Bill Circling, is he alright?"

"I don't know mate," the man replied. "I don't know the names of the jockeys, but I will tell you that at least one is dead, another is critical, and I don't know about the rest. I think I heard there may be the odd bone broken, but certainly, all those not caught up in the initial blast are suffering from shock."

Cannon let the man go. He was beginning to feel numb. He couldn't believe what he was seeing. All around him people were shouting, some were crying, some were trying to put out the blaze despite flames still edging upwards into the sky. The scene was like one from a nightmare.

Cannon began to pull himself together. It had been a long time since he had been asked to help with crowd and people control, but his training from many years ago slowly kicked in. He began the process. He was a bit player in what had happened, an observer, however, he soon became a participant in organizing and helping to control the solution.

The rest of the day was a blur. Ambulances, the Fire Brigade, the Police, the course Stewards, TV crews, and others all crossed his path during the following few hours. It seemed at times that he had a thousand voices in his ear at the same time. Some told him how he could help, some asked about his observations of what happened, some asked for his opinion, some asked if he was alright.

By the time he made it back to the on-course stables after the ambulances had left the scene, the fire was out and everyone from the race was accounted for, it was dark. Cannon was exhausted and Michelle was at her wit's end. The incident was all over the news channels. He had not called her, despite *her* repeated attempts to contact *him*. He hadn't answered his phone, as he hadn't heard it ring because of all the noise around him.

------------------------------

He had a lot on his mind as he drove back from the course. Who had done this and why? He was angry, he was upset. First Bronton and Pool, now this! What was going on, he thought? As he turned into the short drive of his stables, he saw Michelle come running out of the front door. In the headlights, he could see the relief in her eyes, and he felt the warmth of her tears as she held him close to her the moment he stepped out of the car. As they walked back into the house, Michelle was desperate to hear what had happened. Cannon would tell her everything he knew but would also tell her that he had an obligation to O'Smullegan, to Circling, and to himself to help get to the bottom of the day's events.

------------------------------

Mitchell put the phone down. In the morning he would see if he was free from his obligations.

Dreadlocks had done what he needed to do, and for that Mitchell was pleased.

# CHAPTER 22

They had to recover their systems and data from back-ups. The second attack on *SecureTwo* was sophisticated, and all attempts to trace the source of the attack had proven fruitless so far. Another email had been sent anonymously with another obscure code at the end of the message.
It read:
065/01110011-108/01101111/111/075/01100001/084/074/01110101/089/01100100.

James Formrobe was worried and some of his team were even more concerned. Data security, data sovereignty, the protection of clients' information, were the key tenets of the business. If clients became uncomfortable with what was happening, it could result in them reviewing their contracts and looking to move away.
"How do we stand, legally?" Formrobe asked Jacobsen. They were sitting in Jacobsen's office. It was just after six in the evening. The attack had started around midday. Over the past few hours, a cavalcade of *SecureTwo* team members had been switched from their normal duties into recovery mode. Some services to clients had been put on hold, and in certain cases, the company had been unable to provide them at all. A helpline and a set of marketing messages had been created to keep clients happy, not alarmed.
"Our standard contract is pretty clear," Jacobsen answered, "and we have all the necessary protections in place. Indemnities, limitation of liability, caps on damages, etcetera, *but* some of the termination clauses we have signed up to, which are not the standard, do leave us a little exposed," he continued.
"Christ," Formrobe replied, "we need to get to the bottom of this before it gets any worse and there is a real breach. I've got Paul and Barry focusing on this a hundred percent. In the meantime, I've contacted the police, though I don't expect them to do much."
"Good," Jacobsen replied. He passed a single sheet of paper across his desk to Formrobe.
"It's a letter to our clients advising them of the outage and letting them know about the attack. But also giving them our assurance that no data of theirs was stolen or lost."
Formrobe looked over the wording. As the main shareholder, along with being the CEO, he needed to ensure that anything that went out into the public domain with his name on it, was accurate.
"Seems okay," he said. "What about to our shareholders, Judy, Alan, Artimediant?"
"I've drafted another note to them as well, "Jacobsen replied. "If you are

okay, I'll send it by email. Certified "urgent and personal"."

Jacobsen turned the PC screen on his desk to show his boss the mail message itself. "Yes, that's fine," Formrobe acknowledged.

Turning the PC screen back towards himself, Jacobsen asked, "What about the staff?"

"I've already got HR putting something together. It will be sent out overnight."

Jacobsen nodded. "I think that's all bases covered, then."

"I hope so, but we do need to find out what's going on and more importantly why. The attack today has been much more aggressive than the previous one, much more expansive, more sophisticated."

"Any ideas as to who it could be?" Jacobsen asked.

"Well the obvious answer is that it's a competitor that wants to put us out of business," Formrobe said. "The only problem is that there are so many of them, the market is so wide, that it could be absolutely anyone."

"And there's no one that comes to mind?"

Formrobe considered the question before answering. "None that I can think of," he said. "We have a good product, we provide a good service, and we are successful," he retorted, "but then again, so do many other companies. We are not unique in that regard, lots of companies do well, make money."

Jacobsen agreed, nodding. "What did the police say?"

"They told me they would be at the offices tomorrow at around eleven. They are bringing in some of their people who look into cyber-crime, so with luck, they may be able to help."

"Sounds positive," Jacobsen replied.

"Yes, I hope so. In the meantime," Formrobe said, standing up from his chair, "I'm going to see how Paul and Barry are doing. I'm hoping that some of the tools we have may be able to give us some answers."

Jacobsen nodded. "Well, I have a couple of things to do, such as sending out this mail," he pointed towards his PC screen, "then I'll be off, if that's okay."

"Of course, Samuel, no problem at all. Have a good evening."

# CHAPTER 23

It was two days later. Over the past forty-eight hours' Cannon had tried to get back into a normal routine. It was difficult, as everything he had witnessed just a couple of days ago had emblazoned itself on his mind. He had spent part of the previous day sharing what had happened at Uttoxeter with Telside and Michelle. The stable lads and girls had been given a brief overview of events as well. They had been able to glean what had happened from the TV and newspapers, but a first-hand account had held much more weight.

Fortunately for the stable and O'Smullegan, *BKeeper* had escaped relatively unscathed physically from the incident. He had arrived back at the stable late the same night and had shown no obvious ill effects. Cannon had decided it was best to put him *out* for a while at a local agistment centre to allow the horse to get over any mental scars that may be lingering. An association of such a traumatic event with a fence that the horse was being asked to jump, could easily linger. If it did, a horse could potentially be scared enough never to race again. Cannon had discussed this with O'Smullegan, who was more than happy with Cannon's recommendation. They agreed on a three-month break for the horse before bringing him back into the stable. With luck, and if the horse trained on, he could be ready to run later in the season.

Cannon sat in a high-back chair in the lounge. Michelle was at school, the new term beginning in just a few days. Preparations to welcome the new pupils were well underway. Across the room from Cannon, sitting on the couch, were two policemen. They had come to take his statement about what he had seen at Uttoxeter. Inspector Iain Porter and Sergeant Tim Fox were a little uncomfortable as, after initial introductions, Cannon had established that the police were aware of a threat to the course but only one that suggested that the meeting should be cancelled. The track management having received a letter from an anonymous source.

"And you did nothing?" he asked, anger in his voice.

"It wasn't our decision to make," Porter replied. "We did give the course management and the racing authorities our suggested course of action, a recommendation if you will, but the decision to cancel or postpone the meeting was theirs."

Porter was a big man, about forty-five years old. He was just over six-foot-two tall, but was just as large around the girth, an ideal candidate for type-two diabetes. He had a dark moustache that ran across his top lip and down both sides of his mouth, almost framing it completely. His face was round, with permanently red cheeks. He had green eyes that off-puttingly, seemed to be looking in two directions at once. A *lazy left eye* was the old-fashioned term, the right eye seemingly without problems. Despite sitting inside, he wore a grey mackintosh coat over a well-worn black suit that was shiny on the knees and thighs. His shoes, however, were highly polished and his tie sat neatly in place just under a double chin.

Cannon was not impressed. His own experience told him that the police had the authority to stop the meeting from going ahead if they believed that there was a danger to life or property. He decided not to pursue the matter just yet, but if he felt it necessary, he would. He kept his true feelings locked inside.

"I have to say Inspector, I'm dumbfounded about the whole matter. Whoever decided to go ahead without letting *anyone* know about the potential danger needs their head read. There were people killed yesterday, for God's sake!" he said exasperatedly.

Overnight, the local hospital released the news that a second jockey had died. It was splashed all over the news, TV, radio, the print and the electronic media outlets ran with the story. It was headline news across the country.

"I understand your feelings, Mr. Cannon," Porter said, looking at Fox who seemed just as uncomfortable as the Inspector. Both were aware that Cannon was an ex-policeman and had served the force well. They knew that he could see through any spin they put on the situation.

"Mr. Cannon… Mike," Porter said in his own concerned way, "I know this is difficult and I'm sure your statement, when we take it, will contain nothing but the facts as you saw them, but off the record, do you have any idea why anyone would do what they did at Uttoxeter?"

Cannon was surprised by the immediacy and the openness of Porter's question.

"Why would I?" he replied. Cannon wasn't sure where this was heading. Was he a suspect?

"Well, I just wondered if you had heard anything around the traps? Maybe had wind of anyone who had a grudge with the course management?"

"No, I wasn't aware of anything," he replied.

Porter nodded. While they had told Cannon of the letter, they had not expanded upon it. Cannon sensed something between the two men and decided to push the knife in a little, to see if there was something behind the question. "Should I have been?" he asked.

Porter decided to open-up. He felt that by doing so he would be creating an ally. Someone who he might need to call on in the future.

"Look Mike," he said, "let me level with you." He leaned forward using the classic tactic of speaking in a slightly softer voice that gave the impression of sharing information that was *secret,* information that he shouldn't be offering to share. Cannon knew the process, knew the game. He played along.

"The letter the Uttoxeter management received wasn't the first. Letters have been sent to several courses in recent weeks and each one of them was sent *after* a fence had been set alight, destroyed."

It was the first Cannon had heard of it. It annoyed him, angered him even more. "And the industry wasn't made aware of this?" he asked.

"Obviously not. We think that each of the course's management decided to keep quiet about it, for fear that owners and trainers would stay away and the public likewise."

"That's outrageous," Cannon replied, standing up, unable to keep seated, "is that what this is all about…money? Is that all that matters? Two people were killed!" he repeated, almost spitting out the words.

"Mike, please…please," Porter said, trying to calm Cannon down. "I know this is difficult, but just to be clear," he went on, "the other courses cancelled their meetings, so they didn't put anyone in danger. The issue at Uttoxeter appears much different, they only received the letter yesterday, *after* the event. The other courses received it well before their scheduled meetings so had time to take action."

Cannon sat down. He considered what he had been told. The two policemen sat quietly, giving him time to think about things. Cannon looked from Porter to Fox. Fox, a much younger man than Porter, looked Cannon in the eyes. Neither flinched. Fox by name, fox by nature, Cannon thought. The Sergeant held a notebook in his hand but also had a phone on the arm of the couch on which he and Porter sat. Cannon knew that when they began taking his statement he would be asked if the conversation could be recorded. He looked at Fox again, estimating him to be in his late thirties. He was quite good looking, with light brown hair, offset by green/grey eyes, a strong nose, and a chiselled chin. It appeared to Cannon that the man worked out quite regularly. He had no stomach at all that Cannon could see, unlike Porter. Also, despite being slightly shorter than Porter, he had much broader shoulders that tapered to a narrow waist, almost too thin. He had longish legs that he kept open while seated, legs that seemed proportionate to his body, bulky, powerful, highlighting how serious he seemed to take his fitness regime. Like Porter, he was also dressed in plain clothes. A white shirt, dark red tie, dark blue suit, and brown shoes. He had a light coat that he had draped over the back of the couch. The brown shoes bothered Cannon.

"So do the police have any idea as to who could have done this?" Cannon asked eventually.

"No, we don't Mike. We only have the letters to go on."

"So, no justification? No demands?"

"I'm not at liberty to tell you that," Porter said.

"Oh, come on!" Cannon shouted, "Don't give me that bullshit, Inspector, either you know, or you don't!"

He had forced Porter's hand. If they wanted his help in the future then he wanted them to be more open, more transparent, more honest.

"We don't have any idea just yet."

Cannon slumped in his chair. To hear that people were killed, but there was no known reason as to why, made him extremely angry.

"We have forensics looking into the cause of the blast. We have others looking at the letter received. Believe me, Mike, we are throwing everything we can at this."

"I should bloody well think so," replied Cannon cynically. He knew he was being difficult, but he had every right. It was just luck that had prevented more injuries, possibly more deaths. Cannon had seen the carnage. It was still imprinted on his mind.

Porter acknowledged Cannon's frustration then deferred to the reason they had come to see him at his stables. They took over an hour to take his statement. On paper, the words seemed cold, but in his mind, he relived everything he had experienced two days before. It sparked in him a sense of disgust, injustice, and outrage. He knew the emotions were justified. When added to his feelings about the Bronton matter, the murder of Pool and his wife, it seemed like the world he was living in had gone insane. He needed to find solutions. He couldn't sit back and do nothing. But where to start?

# CHAPTER 24

"What the fuck happened?" he asked.

"What do you mean?" Kevin answered, "It worked exactly as I told you it would."

The man with the dreadlocks was exasperated but needed to hide behind the mask. He tried to keep his tone in line with expectations. Over the phone, he needed to be careful in how it was perceived. "People were killed," he exclaimed, "that wasn't supposed to happen."

"That's true," Kevin replied, sensing a slight softening of position from their leader, "but isn't that just collateral damage? Isn't the cause worth it? Or am I missing something here, Toby?"

Sensing that Kevin could hear a wavering in his voice, the man with the dreadlocks, said, "No, you're right Kev. It's just that I didn't expect it. I thought the charge would go off earlier, during a break between races, so what happened was a surprise," he said. "Strengthens our arm," he added for emphasis. "Good work!"

"Thanks."

"No worries. What we need to do now is lay low for a little while. The cops will be all over this like a rash. It's big news and I'm sure we'll see a lot of crap on the TV and in the media about it. They'll probably be calling us *nutters* or something like that."

"What are *you* going to do?"

Toby had already prepared himself, ready for the question. He didn't believe in their cause, but he had a bunch of people in his hands that did. He was using them, and they were stupid enough to fall for it.

"I'll be sending another letter, but this time with a demand. I'll send you a copy when I've completed it if you like?"

"That would be great," Kevin answered. "I'll share it with Geoff and Sandy."

"The other two recruits I met in the pub the other day?"

"Yes, that's eleven of us now, excluding you," Kevin said.

The ALA, the *Animal Liberation Army* was growing, Toby thought.

"OK. We need to be careful though. We don't want the press or anyone else to become aware of who we are other than through *my* communication," Toby 'Dreadlocks' said. "For now, it's about anonymity. Once I issue the letter to them, they will know that we are serious, and then we can issue our demands!"

"Perfect," Kevin answered.

"Yes, but given what's happened, the police and others will be under pressure to find us. The deaths of the jockeys and injuries to those poor horses will see a lot more focus on us by the police than when a fence was burnt down. It ups the ante quite a lot."

Toby was privately saddened by what had occurred. His objective was just to send a message, he didn't want people or horses killed.

"Well I for one am glad it happened the way it did," replied Kevin. "Remember what you said at our first meeting?"

Toby wasn't sure what Kevin was referring to but played along, "Of course I do," he replied. "It was me that set out our objectives wasn't it?"

"Yes, in the pub, the Angel Inn, in Witney."

"Right."

"You said that if we wanted to free the animals from the tyranny of being used for commercial gain, the best place to attack is the one that makes the most money. The total contribution to the economy from racing, from what we've read, is between 4 and 5 billion pounds a year. This includes betting, training fees, and breeding."

"Right again."

"You also mentioned that it's the second most popular watched sport behind football."

"Yes."

"So where best to start than highlighting this to the general public? Start at the top, rather than silly pranks of letting cows out of paddocks or chickens out of runs."

"Exactly," Toby said, feeling pleased with himself in how he was able to portray a conviction to others that he didn't actually believe in. "And that's why we are doing what we are doing," he went on, "I just want us to be careful that's all. I don't want anyone to give away who we are. As I said earlier, we just need to take things slowly. See how the authorities react. Once things quieten down if we don't see the things being addressed that we've asked for, then we'll take further action."

"Agreed," Kevin replied. "Okay, I'll let you go. Keep in touch, use the Group *Whats-app* if you need to."

"Will do," Toby said, "but only if I need to. I'm wary of any communications app nowadays. You never know who is monitoring them. I prefer face to face meetings in the first instance, or the landline as secondary. Smartphones for communication are a distant third for me. Anyway, I've got to go." He put down the phone's handset and took a deep breath, waiting a couple of seconds with his eyes closed. "What have I started?" he thought to himself. He knew he needed a way out of his dilemma. He had hoped that it wouldn't have been so drastic.

After a few minutes of contemplating where he was at, he picked up the phone and dialled. As soon as it was answered he said. "Mitchell, by now you will have seen what I've done. I can't do anymore so it's over to you now. As far as I'm concerned, my debt is paid!"

Clifford Mitchell didn't like being called by his surname, not by a *shit* like 'Dreadlocks', but he decided to let it go.

"Look," he said, "you've done a good job, but I'd suggest that there is still some way to go. I need at least one course to shut down or at least free up the land for building on. Once that happens, you're home free."

Toby was angry. "That wasn't our deal!" he shouted down the phone line. "What we agreed was for me to give the courses a *reason* to look at closing down. With the revenues dropping, costs increasing and the threat of meetings being cancelled, that should be good enough."

"I agree it should be, but I need to see confirmation that what you've done is working. Not just a perception that it should work."

"You bastard!" Toby said.

Mitchell laughed. "It's still in your hands, boy. But I will admit, you've done well. What happened at Uttoxeter was a good move."

"But not yet enough to wipe the slate clean?"

"Not quite, but close," Mitchell answered smugly.

Toby decided to share with Mitchell, the next steps that the ALA would be taking in their fight. He hoped it would indicate that he had a plan designed to meet their collective objective. However, what he was searching for and wanted were assurances that his debt would be settled soon. He had known that it would be hard to get out of the position that he had found himself in, but he had not been aware of how hard.

"For your information only, Mitchell," Toby said, "the next steps we intend to take will include us issuing some specific demands to several of the race clubs. Hopefully after what happened at Uttoxeter some of them believe that the threat is big enough and they decide to act on our demands."

"Me too," agreed Mitchell.

"Though I doubt some of the larger clubs will," continued Toby. "For example, despite the dire financial straits that Kempton Park has been in for quite a while now, the prospect of shutting it down has been shot down repeatedly at the local council meetings."

"True, but some of the smaller clubs can't survive. Hexham, Fakenham, Market Rasen, Fontwell, and many others are potential opportunities," Mitchell said. "We, I, don't care. It's the land I want. Developers need it. As I told you at the beginning, get a club to seriously consider closing and we are both off the hook."

Toby had realized some time back that there were other players involved, that Mitchell as a bookmaker wasn't the kind of man to want racecourses to disappear that readily. They were his livelihood. He was an old-fashioned bookie, competing with the online giants. He needed his pitch. He needed to be track-side. Toby guessed that Mitchell had got himself into trouble, maybe laid off too many losing bets? Who knew? But was it this that was driving his behaviour, his pressing of Toby to take actions that would result in the freeing up of land? Many of the smaller racecourses were often built in areas with good infrastructure around them and close to existing communities. If any of them closed down, the freeing up of accessible space would potentially allow developers and builders to take advantage and grow their businesses. They could do so without having to invest in infrastructure like roads, drainage systems, lighting, etcetera. This made development costs cheaper and the building of houses much quicker, easier.

"I'll keep you informed," Toby continued somewhat disparagingly, "but after I've issued the note containing the list of demands, I'm giving you four weeks to release me from my obligations…otherwise…"

Mitchell cut Toby off. He was angry. "Is that another one of your threats?" he asked, "You know it's not sensible to threaten me."

"It's not a threat, it's a *promise!*" Toby answered, with more bravado than he felt.

"Now, now," Mitchell answered sarcastically feigning fear. Then softening his voice and through clenched teeth, he responded by saying, "from where I'm sitting, I don't think that you are in any position to be threatening me!"

"Maybe so," Toby replied, "but I've done all that you have asked of me. Doing any more and I could be in more trouble with the authorities than with you."

"Noted," Mitchell agreed, smiling to himself.

"So, if you've *noted* it, then you'll understand that any more actions we take could be putting the whole project at risk. I need to be careful about the next steps, so let's agree on the following, shall we? As a *compromise?*"

"Go on," replied Mitchell, intrigued.

"You agree that what we do over the next four weeks is enough for you to square the ledger between us. If you do, I'll keep your name out of it."

"And if I don't?"

"Well as I said before. What I'll do next, is act on the promise I've just made to you. And that *is* a promise, not a threat"

"Which is?"

"To let the Police know that you were part of what happened at Uttoxeter. That you were directly involved in those jockeys' deaths."

"You wouldn't do that," Mitchell replied, anger boiling within him, but his stomach also beginning to churn.

"Oh, yes I would."

"And what proof do you have?"

"I have….*enough,*" Toby replied, "for example, every conversation we have ever had over the phone has been recorded." The fact was that Toby was lying, but he didn't need Mitchell to know it. He wanted him to *think* that it was true.

Mitchell didn't reply. He stayed quiet, contemplating what he had just heard.

Toby broke into his thoughts. "Four weeks," he said, "after that, I'm free from anything I've ever owed you. If we are not in agreement, then the police will be getting the recordings…*anonymously* and by mail. It will all be done electronically, digitally, from a false email address, and will be untraceable. Once they have all the recordings, I'm sure they will be paying you a visit."

"You fucking bastard!" Mitchell replied eventually.

"Call me whatever you like," Toby replied, "but I'm offering you a compromise. Take it or leave it, it's up to you."

Without waiting for Mitchell to respond, he put down the phone. He felt ill. He had taken a gamble, he hoped it would work. He needed a way out of his dilemma before anyone else knew about it.

# CHAPTER 25

Cannon was still angry, but also saddened.

He had decided to meet Formrobe at his office. The police had let Cannon know that they had been able to trace the sixty-two and a half thousand pounds that Formrobe had paid for the horse. The horse, *Centaur,* that he never received, was never delivered.

They were sitting in Formrobe's office. Cannon wanted to see if his client still wanted him to search for another horse. The events of recent weeks could have turned Formrobe away from the game and Cannon wanted to be sure.

"I've met with the police a few days ago about what happened at Uttoxeter, they took my statement, but I've also been thinking that I need to do something more."

"About what?"

"The investigation."

"But Mike, you're not a cop anymore, you can't get involved, get in the way of what the police do in their investigation."

"That's not my intent," Cannon said, "I just want to see what I can find out. What I saw at Uttoxeter really upset me, so I need to take some time and do some digging. Besides, I also want to see how Dockly is getting on with the murder of Bronton."

"And what about your horses?"

"Don't worry about that, I'll still be involved. But with Rich, my assistant, I have plenty of support to ensure that we are readying our horses for the season, the short and the longer term."

"I guess once a cop…"

"Always a cop," said Cannon, finishing the sentence for Formrobe. "Yes, it's been said to me before, many times," Cannon responded.

"So, you want my view?" asked Formrobe.

Cannon nodded, hoping that he hadn't lost a client before he even had him as one.

As Formrobe opened his mouth to answer, his assistant knocked on the door saying, "Samuel is free now, if you'd both like to go through."

"Thanks, Jackie," he replied. Turning back to Cannon, Formrobe said, "Mike to ease your mind, *yes,* I am still interested in you finding me another horse. As we said at the outset, it's been a dream of mine. So, despite the false start, I would still like you to carry on and find something suitable for me."

Cannon smiled, thankful, but more so, relieved. Formrobe's confidence in him made him feel all the more determined to get to the bottom of what had happened at Uttoxeter.

"Thank you, James, that means a lot to me."

"No worries."

"So, what did your assistant mean about going through to see Samuel?"

"Oh, I thought it would be good for you to be introduced. I know you've spoken to each other on the phone, but seeing as you are here, I thought it would be good to meet face to face. He's very keen to ensure that if we do find another horse, that we do a bit more due diligence than last time."

Cannon wasn't sure if he should take umbrage at what Formrobe was saying, or whether the words were more those of Jacobsen. He decided to keep his thoughts to himself.

"Should we go through?" Formrobe asked.

"Lead the way."

Jacobsen seemed much older than he was. At fifty-three he looked closer to retirement age, thought Cannon. He was tall, spindly with arms that seemed a little too long for his body. He had a firm handshake, yet his key feature was a pair of deep blue eyes, in a long face devoid of sunlight. He had very small ears, flat against the side of his head, bald to the extent of having no hair at all, other than a very small goatee which made his face seem a little longer than it already appeared. He was wearing a suit, including his jacket. Odd, thought Cannon, given the relative warmth of the office. Also, despite the lateness of the afternoon, his crisp white shirt showed no sign of creasing and his smart gold tie sat firmly in place.

He had been sitting behind a large oak desk, highly polished. Along one side of the room were bookshelves filled with legal cases, dictionaries, and textbooks. Directly behind him was a shelf filled with photographs. Family. Jacobsen, his late wife, and two children. They were taken over a period of time. Children below ten with a young wife, individual pictures of kids much older in school uniforms, casual clothes, smiling. Jacobsen and his wife sitting in chairs somewhere where the sea was blue, the sky likewise. One picture caught Cannon's eye, the whole family surrounding a racehorse, taken at some track in the winners' enclosure. The children in their late teens. Jacobsen, mid-forties, his wife roughly about the same age, Cannon guessed.

"Ah, I see you noticed the picture of our best ever racehorse," he said.

"I couldn't miss it," Cannon replied, "it's a lovely picture of you and what I assume is your family?" Cannon recalled their original conversation when Jacobsen had mentioned that he used to own a few racehorses. "Where was the picture taken?"

The lawyer turned and reached for the picture, which was in a silver frame, much like the rest of the photographs on the shelf. He passed it over to Cannon to have a look at.

"It was taken at Sandown. The horse was called *Mystic Force*. He won seven races for us before an injury ended his career. Being a gelding there wasn't much we could do with him so we gave him to a charity to use in one of their programs for children with cerebral palsy."

"A great initiative," Cannon replied. "Well done to you."

Jacobsen smiled at the memory. "The other horses we had weren't very good, but we enjoyed the experience, nonetheless."

"It looks like the whole family did."

"Yes, we did," he said somewhat sadly.

Cannon noticed the change in mood. Trying to keep things light, knowing that he needed Jacobsen on-side should he find Formrobe another galloper.

"Is this your son and daughter, along with your wife?" he asked.

"Yes, my step-daughter from my wife's first marriage and our son, yes."

"I was sorry to hear about your wife's passing," Cannon replied, "she must have been quite young?"

"She was slightly older than me, by a couple of years, but she was only forty-five when she died. Cervical cancer."

"I'm so sorry. I lost my wife to cancer as well," Cannon replied. "Such an insidious disease."

Jacobsen nodded, taking the photograph back from Cannon, who had given it a longing look. It reminded him of Wendy and Cassie. He had a few photographs himself of the two of them together, but they were now put away inside boxes. Pictures from another time. Now that Michelle was in his life, what was in the past of his former personal life needed to stay there.

"They've both grown up now," Jacobsen said somewhat sadly. My daughter has gone off to Israel where she married, no children, as yet. She's a doctor there. My son, on the other hand, is a lecturer in Philosophy and Law down at Southampton University. It's his first academic post. Unfortunately, I don't see much of them now."

Cannon knew how he felt. Cassie was always difficult to get hold of. She was completing her Masters-in-Law in York.

Formrobe, who had stayed quiet until now, decided that the introductions were over. It seemed to him that the trainer and the lawyer had gotten on well, so he was confident to ask Cannon to proceed with looking for another horse.

"Remember, though, that in line with the trust arrangements you'll still need me to sign off on any purchase," Jacobsen said.

"Of course, Samuel," Formrobe answered, "you know me, I always follow the rules." Turning to Cannon with a smile, he said, "You see Mike, Samuel always looks after me."

"That's good, I think it's very sensible."

Jacobsen nodded, looked from Cannon to Formrobe saying, "There you go James, a man who knows what's good for you."

Before Formrobe could answer, Cannon jumped in with a question of his own, addressing it towards Jacobsen.

"I hope you don't mind, Samuel," he asked, "but I wonder if you could do me a favour?"

Jacobsen was a little wary but answered, "What is it? Always happy to help where I can."

"My daughter, Cassie. She's doing her Masters at York University. She's been focused on human rights law and had the opportunity to go to South Africa to see what goes on there first-hand."

"Oh yes,"

"Well she didn't like the environment, too violent she said. So, when she finishes in a few months, she wants to take a bit of time off, do some private travelling, then decide what to do. Would it be an imposition if you could give her some advice, given your experience with the law? Maybe mentor her a bit?"

Cannon could sense a little bit of trepidation from the lawyer, "I'm happy to pay," he added, "if that's an issue."

"No. No. No issue at all. It's just that I've never been asked before, so it's a pleasant surprise," Jacobsen replied.

"If it's going to be too much trouble then…"

"I'm sure it will be fine," Jacobsen said. "Let me give it some thought and then maybe I can have a chat with…."

"Cassie."

"Yes." Jacobsen acknowledged. "Cassie."

"Thank you for just considering it," Cannon stated. "I'm sure she'll be happy just to have a chat with you."

"I'm sure the pleasure will be all mine."

Cannon turned to Formrobe, "Thanks for indulging me," he said, "I think I've taken up more of your time than you expected, so thank you again."

All three men stood up. Cannon shook Jacobsen's hand again, leaving him with the message that he would ask Cassie to give him a call as soon as possible. He and Formrobe then left the office, Formrobe leading the way to the reception area.

They walked through the open-plan office, Cannon noting the huge expanse of infrastructure. Screens, printers, electronic call response and restore time notices. People with their heads down bashing away at keyboards, nearly all wearing headsets.

"Looks busy," he said.

"Well, we've had a bit of a challenge these past few days and weeks," Formrobe said.

"Oh?" Cannon asked.

"Yes, just between you and me, we've had more cyber-attacks against the business. Nothing that we couldn't handle but it's a concern."

"Do you know who has been instigating it?"

"No, whoever it is, has been hiding their tracks well."

"God, what is the world coming to?" Cannon asked. "It seems like a legitimate business like yours, which has done well and provides services to so many other businesses, has become a target. Why? Just because you are successful?"

"I don't know," Formrobe answered, "but whatever the reason, we are trying to ensure that we find out."

"Have you told the police yet?"

"No, we hope to contain it. We'll engage them if it gets any worse."

Cannon understood where Formrobe was coming from. Private companies often kept their issues 'private'.

They continued to walk through the office.

"What's your view about what happened at Uttoxeter?" Formrobe asked.

Cannon was surprised that Formrobe raised the issue. He wasn't sure how much he was aware of what had gone on there. The item had already dropped down the list of noteworthy news items on the TV and radio, but applicable social media posts on Facebook and elsewhere were still keeping the conversation going.

"I'm still thinking about it," he answered. "I was very lucky. I had a horse that was nearly killed and a jockey that likewise just avoided disaster, so it left a very sour taste in my mouth. The police are looking into what happened, but I'm not convinced they'll be putting all the resources required into it."

"Despite two jockeys being killed?" Formrobe responded.

"Yes. I gave my statement to the Inspector responsible for the investigation, but I'm not sure of his complete commitment. I know what it's like being in the police. Too few resources, too many crimes."

"Doesn't sound good."

"No, it's not, but you never know."

"So, what's likely to happen then?"

"Depends what the police find. Nowadays there is so much that they can do forensically. It all depends on what's left behind, after a fire like that."

"Do you think the perpetrators will seek anything else?"

"Like further demands, you mean?" asked Cannon.

"Yes,"

"Very likely. It seems there were other incidents at other courses that have been kept quiet. The police and the racing authorities didn't take it too seriously. They treated it as vandalism."

"My God."

"You can say that again. I guess though, it's a bit like the same issue you just talked about."

"How do you mean?"

"Well at what point do you bring in the police if you can't address it yourself?" Cannon asked.

Formrobe stopped walking. They were at the door leading into the reception area. He dropped his voice to a whisper. "Not everyone in the business is aware of the attack, so we are trying to keep it quiet internally. We don't want anyone outside of the business, especially competitors, picking up on it unnecessarily," he said. "In addition, we don't want our clients spooked either, particularly given it hasn't directly affected them yet. However, we have advised them 'in confidence' about what's been going on at a high level. Just to keep them informed."

"Yet?" Cannon queried.

"Precisely," Formrobe replied. "We are trying to ensure it stays that way. That they are *not* impacted."

"I hope you can get to the bottom of it before it gets too serious."

"Me too," replied Formrobe. "In the meantime," he continued, his tone becoming less intense, "as we agreed earlier I hope you can find me another horse soon. If you pardon my saying, losing *Centaur* was most disappointing."

"That's true," Cannon replied. "That horse was definitely a good prospect. I don't know what's happened to him, but I'll certainly have another look around for you," he said.

They shook hands and Cannon left the building.

As he walked to his car he reviewed in his mind where things were heading. The investigation into what had happened to Bronton, Pool, and Pool's wife was with the North Yorkshire police. However, he was now more determined than ever to find out who was behind the Uttoxeter incident. He couldn't help himself.

# CHAPTER 26

The letter arrived at the Uttoxeter racecourse. It was filled with demands. The management of the course immediately contacted the police. The police had asked for any such correspondence to be passed on immediately, believing they could use it to determine if there was anything they could take away from it. Any residual DNA? Where the paper may have been bought from? The ink and printer type? Anything to try and find out who had sent it.

The *who* had sent it was obvious, as it was stated clearly in the document. The ALA, the *Animal Liberation Army. What* they wanted, was also clear. The end of jumps racing and the closure of racetracks supporting such 'barbaric' practices.

The biggest challenge the police had was determining *who* these people were. The ALA was unknown as a group. They weren't on any database, they weren't notifiable even if they were found to be on one, as they hadn't been put onto any watch list issued by the Home Office.

"Probably a bunch of idealistic nutters," Porter said to Fox. They were sitting in Porter's office. Outside in the incident room, a group had been assembled to try and find out what the ALA was, what were their objectives, and more importantly, who they were as individuals.

The letter lay on Porter's desk. He had already been in contact with the Forensics department. They were expected shortly, to take away the document and the envelope that it had been delivered in, dropped off by hand in the middle of the night by an individual dressed in dark clothing at the entrance to the main administration building. The letter was not postmarked for obvious reasons, and the letter itself was only 1 page in length.

The demands also required a response.

*Ten Days. If there is no progress or acceptance of our demands to be noted by the Racing Industry on the Uttoxeter or BHA websites within that period, then similar action will be undertaken as happened recently. This action, if necessary, will take place at another racecourse of our choosing.*

The letter had been signed, using a printer, 'The ALA'. Everything about the document screamed caution by the authors. It appeared that they had left nothing to chance. At least that is what it seemed. Porter had hoped for a different outcome. A clue of some sort.

Pressure was mounting. The racing public, the other courses. None of them wanted to experience what Uttoxeter had. Ten days! If nothing came from the analysis of the letter and envelope, then Porter was likely to be in serious difficulty. He had nothing else to go on. Just the TV footage of the race and the statements from those on course.

"We're in a bit of strife here, would you agree Tim? The letter is pretty clear, these people are bloody serious!" he said.

"Yes, you are right, Sir," Fox answered, "and I'm worried about the lengths they have gone to already. Two men killed, for what?"

"I agree, but I think the answer to your question seems obvious. They want an end to jumps racing. They see it as cruel."

"But it's not likely, is it? An end to racing?"

"No, I doubt it. It's much too big a sport and very lucrative. Too many players. Too many people whose livelihoods are linked to it. Just look at the Cheltenham Festival and the Grand National."

"So why do you think they targeted Uttoxeter specifically?" Fox asked.

"I don't think they did initially. I think what happened was that they saw traction with the other courses cancelling meetings, but Uttoxeter didn't."

"Because they didn't get the notice in time to change or cancel their meeting,"

"Precisely, and because of that, these…nut-jobs must have thought they were being snubbed, ignored, so decided to teach the course management a lesson."

"Do you think it was deliberate?" asked Fox.

"How do you mean?"

"The fence blowing up just as the horses were jumping it?"

"I don't know," Porter replied. "Either way it caused devastation. Even if it wasn't their intent."

"Umm," Fox replied. "What now?"

"I've been thinking about bringing someone in to help with the investigation."

"Who?"

"Mike Cannon."

"Are you serious?" Fox asked. "Isn't it a bit premature? Surely we can conduct the investigation. Call him in when necessary?"

"That would be ideal, yes, but I've already had a chat with the Chief Constable, who thinks it's a good idea. Cannon has the insight, the background. Looking at this letter. We have ten days to find out who these people are before they attack somewhere else. The Chief Constable also thinks that if we bring Cannon in as a consultant, we can use our budget more wisely. We won't have to classify him as staff, so that will keep our numbers down. As you know we are always under pressure regarding our spending."

"And we only pay him for the work he does," responded Fox, a smile on his face.

"Precisely. With luck, we may even get him for free. Though we don't have too much time. We need to find out who these people are. As I said before, hopefully, someone like Cannon, with his police background and his direct involvement in the sport, may be able to find out somethings that we can't?"

"Have you been in touch with him yet?

"No, I haven't. I only got the go-ahead a short while ago. Plus, now that we have this letter from this ALA mob, at least we can give him something to work with. Without it, we don't have a lot to go on."

"Other than two dead jockeys, a destroyed fence at our local racecourse, and an industry on tenterhooks."

"And the racing public and the press looking for us to find answers," Porter replied.

There was a knock on the open door of the office. While Porter and Fox had been talking, they did not hear the man who was now standing with half his body already inside the room.

"Yes?" Porter asked.

"Winston Caster, from Forensics, Sir. Here to collect the letter you called us about. The one regarding the incident at Uttoxeter?"

"Oh, yes. Here it is." Porter pointed towards the document. "We've tried not to touch it. We've been using surgical gloves when we needed to, but as a heads up we don't know how many people at the course have handled it before they contacted us."

"Have you taken the necessary photos for your own use?" Caster asked.

"Yes, Fox here, and I have taken a few on our phones and then we have printed them out on our printer. We've also sent copies to the team outside for their records, and finally, put them into a shared file on the network."

"Then that should work well, Sir, at least you'll have all the details available so far. Once we've concluded our analysis, I'll send you the report and you can 'bag' the letter as evidence for the ongoing investigation."

Caster walked over to the desk, picked up the letter with a gloved hand, and proceeded to seal it within an A4 sized plastic sheaf which was then put into another larger envelope.

"Thanks again, Sir," Caster replied. "I'll be in touch shortly."

Porter nodded and Caster left the room, holding the envelope to him as if it contained gold bullion.

# CHAPTER 27

The best-laid plans don't always work out. Before Porter was able to make the call, Inspector Brendan Dockly and two of his men came to arrest Cannon.

"For the murder of Henry Bronton, Harry Pool and Mr. Pool's wife Dorothy," Dockly said after cautioning Cannon.

"Are you mad Dockly?" Cannon had responded. "I told you all I know about Bronton and Pool, and how they tried to scam myself and my client, James Formrobe. I'm not sure how you can link that to murder," Cannon said.

"I'm not at liberty to say, Mr. Cannon but all will be revealed in due course as our investigation continues," Dockly replied forthrightly. "In the meantime, unless you have a good lawyer, we can provide you one."

"I know the ropes Inspector," Cannon responded sarcastically, "and yes I will take you up on your offer. The sooner that you realize that I had nothing to do with Harry Pool's death and Bronton's murder, the sooner we can stop this charade and we can both get on with what we need to do."

The drive back to Doncaster seemed to take forever. Cannon was handcuffed and sat between two policemen in the back of a police car while Dockly sat next to the driver. Cannon had let Michelle know what was happening. She in turn advised Rich and James Formrobe.

"That's ridiculous." Formrobe had responded to Michelle's phone call. "Let me see what I can do. I'm sure Samuel will be able to find someone he knows in the justice system that could help. Leave it to me," he had said, promising to let Michelle know what he was able to find out from his own lawyer.

Upon arrival in Doncaster, Cannon was initially placed into a holding cell.

While Cannon waited for representation to arrive, Dockly managed to get him into an interview room where he began to interrogate him. The session began just after six pm. Cannon was grilled for forty minutes before anyone arrived to assist him.

"As I said in my earlier statement," Cannon said. "when I called Pool about the issue with *Centaur* someone else answered the phone. I thought it was Harry, but obviously, it was someone else."

"The killer?" Dockly stated.

"Well it couldn't have been me could it? I was the one calling!" Cannon replied exasperated.

"So you say."

"Of course, *so I say.*"

"You see Mr. Cannon, this is where we have a problem. There is no evidence of anyone having been at Harry Pool's place when you called him."

"So, that may be the case," Cannon replied, "but I know there was someone else there. They answered the phone, and I could hear them breathing, but they didn't say anything when I asked if Harry was there, and by the way, if you hadn't told me about the scam they were pulling I wouldn't have known."

"Ah, but you found out pretty soon, didn't you?"

"Only that the horse that was delivered wasn't *Centaur.*"

"Enough time to act upon the scam? Try and get your money back?"

"No Inspector, I did not have enough time to do anything. The first I knew of anything happening to Pool or Bronton was you advising me!" he replied. "What about Peter Todd? Have you been able to find him?" Cannon persisted.

"Ahh, Peter Todd," Dockly replied, 'the man who delivered the wrong horse?"

"Yes."

"He doesn't exist."

"What!?" screamed Cannon. "You can't be serious, Inspector."

"But I am," Dockly replied. "Nobody we have spoken to so far has ever heard of him."

Cannon was speechless. His mind reeling. What the hell was going on? Eventually, he found his tongue.

"Are you trying to tell me that I made up the whole story, that you think I killed three people just because of a scam?"

"I'm not saying anything about your actions or motivation for killing, I'm just laying out what we think happened."

"So, tell me, Inspector. What *did* happen?"

Dockly sat back in his chair in the interview room, the front two legs lifted off the floor as he did so. He looked at his colleague, a Sergeant, Jeff Cotton, who was seated beside him. "We," he said, emphasizing the single syllable inferring that Cotton agreed with the hypothesis, "believe that as a consequence of being tricked into departing with around sixty odd k of your client's money, to save face, you confronted Bronton and after an argument, you killed him in cold blood. We also think," he said continuing, "that after killing Bronton, you attempted to recover either the money or the horse *Centaur* from Pool, and when you couldn't, you killed him and his wife. How am I doing?" he asked.

Cannon shook his head, smiling to himself. "And you have evidence of this?"

"Better," Dockly replied. "We have a witness." It was a lie, but Dockly tried it as a tactic, to see if Cannon would crumble, confess.

"A witness?"

"Yes…"

"You are lying Inspector," Cannon said. "A witness to what?"

Dockly stayed quiet. Cannon knew the game, however. It appeared that the Inspector had almost forgotten Cannon's background. They stared at each other for a few seconds.

Cannon spoke first. Not the normal way of doing things. *He who broke the silence first normally lost the game*, Cannon recalled from his training, but he felt he was in the best position.

"If you do have a witness, then I suggest you ask him or her how it's possible for me to do what you are insinuating. It would have been impossible for me to do what you are suggesting. Travel up from Oxfordshire to Doncaster, murder three people, and then get back to my stables in what, less than a day?"

"Well you claimed that you were back at your stables," Dockly said.

"I was," interjected Cannon, "In fact, I never left the place."

"So, you say."

"It's true," replied Cannon. "Rich Telside and my partner Michelle can testify to that. Rich was with me when Peter Todd arrived driving the horsebox."

"Oh yes, the mysterious Peter Todd again. The elusive driver."

"Not so much elusive, Inspector. He was, is, real."

"Maybe," Dockly said cynically.

Cannon threw up his hands in disgust at the line of questioning and of the comments made.

Dockly carried on probing. "So you are telling me that after this man, Peter Todd, left your stables with the wrong horse, the one you had paid for using James Formrobe's money, you spent the rest of the day at home from where you continuously tried to call Pool and Bronton?"

"Yes."

"Without a reply?"

"Yes. I tried several times, calling both men. I thought I had eventually got hold of Pool when I thought he had answered the phone."

"And you are suggesting it wasn't Mr. Pool but someone else? Someone, who may have had something to do with Pool's murder?"

"Yes."

"How convenient," Dockly replied, turning again to the Sergeant who sat quietly, immobile, listening and learning.

"It's not convenient Inspector, it's the truth."

"Yet you have no idea who this person was?"

"How could I? They never said a word."

"Yet you think it was a man?"

"It's just a guess Inspector."

As Cannon uttered the last few words, there was a knock on the door to the interview room. Cotton nodded to a Constable who was standing statue still at the entrance, intimating that the door should be opened.

A woman, in her mid-thirties, with pale white skin walked through the entrance. She was extremely confident, power dressed despite the lateness of the hour. Her long blond hair was cut severely but suited her face and had no curl. It was straight and was long enough to lie across her shoulders. She had green eyes, a pointed nose, and a severe mouth. Her jacket matched her skirt, black. A pin sat in the lapel buttonhole. It indicated the RSPCA and looked like a silver cat. In addition, she wore high heel black leather shoes and black stockings. The contrast between her outfit and white skin was quite stark. This was someone you didn't easily argue with.

"Xandra Ambleton," she said holding out her hand, "from *Phonic and Cope*. I'm here to represent Mr. Cannon."

Dockly was surprised, but not as much as Cannon was. Who had organized this woman, he thought to himself?

"I've been sent by Mr. Samuel Jacobsen," she continued, "to assist…"

Cannon suddenly felt relieved. He wanted out of the situation and was glad that he had someone on his side. It dawned on him that James Formrobe may have been able to pull some strings. That he had been able to leverage his relationship with Jacobsen.

"Well then please sit down and join the party, Ms. Ambleton" Dockly said somewhat sarcastically.

"Mrs. Married and happily so," Ambleton said, showing two rings on her left hand. "Now can we get on with it?" she continued, determined to get the job done.

Dockly and Cotton were no match for Ambleton and despite the situation, Cannon was amused at how she handled the discussion. She was polite but firm and had immediately advised Cannon that she would speak on his behalf and that he should allow her to do so.

Cannon acquiesced and within thirty minutes was a free man again, at least until the police were able to charge him properly. It was clear from the *evidence* they had that the case against him was circumstantial. It was almost as if they needed to find someone to place in the crosshairs, to show the community that they were doing their job and that the murders of the Pools and Bronton had been solved. Having someone in custody seemed to provide the right optics. It seemed to Cannon that this was more important to the police than finding the real culprit. The question needed answering still, who was Peter Todd? Did he have anything to do with the murders and if so, why?

Outside the police station, Bryon House on Maid Marion Way, Cannon thanked Ambleton for her help. He was looking up Derby Road trying to orient himself to where he believed the Nottingham railway station was. It had been a long time since he had spent any time in the city.

Ambleton could sense his distress. "I'll get you an Uber," she said, "to take you to the station. Samuel asked me to do whatever we could to help."

"Thank you," Cannon replied, "that's very kind."

"It's no problem," she answered, opening the Uber app on her smartphone and ordering the ride.

They stood silently while Ambleton completed the transaction. Payment for the taxi was being made by the local lawyers.

After the heat of the interview room, Cannon was feeling the cold autumn air as they stood waiting outside. He pulled his coat around himself to stay warm, while leaving the buttons undone, his habit of a lifetime not changing.

"I think there is a train shortly, to take you back to Oxford," Ambleton advised. "I guess it's another taxi after that, once you get to the other end?" she asked.

"I'll get my partner or one of my staff to pick me up at Oxford station," Cannon answered, "though looking at the time, it's going to be around eleven o'clock when I get home."

"Yes, I'm sorry about that. If only Samuel had called me a little earlier," she answered, "then hopefully you would have been well on your way by now."

He nodded but accepted the circumstances. At least he was out.

As they waited, Cannon asked Ambleton how she knew Jacobsen.

"I don't really," she replied. "I've never met him formally, but we have spoken on the phone and we have *Skyped* each other as necessary, but that's been infrequent. He's an old boy of the firm. He did his articles here and so has a long association. Apparently, he could have become the Managing Partner years ago but decided to go into the wider world of commerce instead."

"Interesting," Cannon said, rubbing a hand across his chin. "Are you a firm that does more criminal than civil and commercial work?"

She smiled at him. "We do everything, Mr. Cannon," she said, "including tax work, fraud investigations, whatever is necessary."

"Well I'm glad that you do," he replied, "and I'll be sure to thank Mr. Jacobsen for engaging you to help me."

Ambleton looked him up and down. "It was no problem at all," she answered her mouth in a smile, lips slightly apart, a glint in her eye. It appeared to Cannon that she was flirting with him, but he realized that being nice was just part of the job and she was doing it well.

The Uber arrived and he thanked her again. He was free…. for now. As the car drove off to the railway station, he knew that to get closure, to clear his name, he needed to find Peter Todd.

Who was he and where could Cannon find him?

They arrived back at the stables and he was absolutely exhausted. Michelle had collected him at Oxford railway station, and it had taken them over an hour to drive to Woodstock.

During the drive, Cannon had filled her in about the interview. He also told her about Jacobsen's help in getting Ambleton to assist him and getting the police to release him.

"It looks like you've made a friend," Michelle had said, "with Jacobsen…"

"I guess so," he answered. "He seems a nice guy, and he's been involved in the game before. He has a family photograph on his desk taken quite a few years ago ofhimself, his wife, and their kids, along with a horse called *Mystic Force*. A bit sad really, she died of cancer, quite young," he continued.

"That is sad."

He had put his hand on her knee, a sign of empathy. She had felt the warmth of his touch and smiled in the darkness at how lucky she was, how lucky they both were to be able to share their lives together.

# CHAPTER 28

Finding an abattoir had been relatively easy. It had taken a little longer than he would have liked but he hadn't worried about it, he just needed to get everything lined up. He wanted to find a place that wasn't too paranoid or desperate enough with regards to animal welfare or one that surrounded its facilities with security cameras, guards, and steel gates. Also, he didn't want to be noticed. He had changed his appearance for each visit to ensure that whichever facility he eventually chose would not be able to verify him visiting any other if the police ever asked.

There were several options in the Midlands and while questions *were* asked, as expected, he was able to provide all the necessary details and provide all the answers. The fact that every piece of paper he presented was faked, didn't deter him.

Individual horses being sent to a knackery was quite unusual, especially a thoroughbred that appeared to be sound and well. He knew that he may face some resistance, some pushback and he tried to limit any risk of being remembered. He knew that the story he was giving would have credence, would make sense, as long as they didn't dig too deeply.

Eventually, once they had agreed on the fee, the process was quite simple. The evidence was disposed of…

# CHAPTER 29

Porter and Fox sat at the table in the boardroom of the Uttoxeter racecourse. Through the window, they could see the remnants of the jump that had been destroyed, where the two jockeys had died. The obstacle had not been replaced yet, due to the Forensics teams still analyzing the charred remains.

The meeting had been called by Porter and it was unusual because he had specifically requested that both the Chairman and the CEO of the BHA attend. They had agreed and had travelled up from London. There were two additional attendees, the General Manager of the Uttoxeter course and a lady PR representative engaged by the BHA.

After thanking everyone for attending and highlighting the need for quick decisions and clear actions from the meeting, Porter stood up from his chair and pointed out of the window.

"Lady and Gentlemen," he said, "we have a crisis on our hands, and I need your help to resolve it." He looked around the table at the severe faces looking back at him. "Over there," he said, pointing across the course, "two men, two jockeys died, not from injuries resulting directly from their sport, but *because* of their sport and as a consequence *we* have an obligation to find out what happened, who was responsible and why they did it."

"Don't we know the "who" already?" asked the course GM.

"You are referring to the letter the course received?"

"Yes, the one signed by the ALA."

Porter shook his head. "What we know is that the Organization has indicated that they did this," he nodded towards the window, "but we have no idea who they are and whether or not the letter itself, or indeed the ALA, is genuine."

"Surely Inspector," the PR representative, Georgina Lipton added, "the letter itself and the threat it contains reflect a genuine intent?"

"Maybe, but our investigation needs to prove it beyond *any* doubt before we can consider making any arrests."

"And where are you at this stage, Inspector?" asked the Chair of the BHA, Peter De Misgeny.

'To be honest with you Sir, not very far at all. It's for this reason that I requested you all attend this meeting."

"We are all ears Inspector. How can we help?"

Porter sensed that despite the atrocity, the BHA wasn't taking the incident as seriously as he believed it should be. He got the feeling the BHA Chair was speaking down to him. He felt the authorities were being condescending, almost as if they resented having to leave London to travel to the country. He had *summoned them* and despite the fact they had appeared, fronted up, *and* were saying the right things, Porter wasn't convinced about their sincerity. It was as if it was an acceptable or inevitable outcome that jockeys in jumps racing died at various times, at various courses, and that it was just part of the game. He sensed a lack of compassion. It surprised him.

"Firstly, you can help by suspending all future race meetings *until* we have found or apprehended those responsible for the murder of the two jockeys who died here the other day."

"The ALA?" repeated the BHA CEO, Andy Phillips.

"Possibly," Porter replied.

"Well if not them, then who?"

"We don't know yet, Sir," Porter responded. "Our investigation will hopefully verify the theory that the ALA was behind it, but until it does, we need to keep an open mind."

The BHA Chair was getting annoyed. He and his colleague had travelled for hours to be at the meeting, only now to be told that what he thought was a simple case regarding the perpetrators of the jockey deaths at Uttoxeter, may not be the case. He asked for clarity.

"I'm not sure I follow, Inspector. You are saying you are not sure that this group, the…the…ALA is responsible for the recent attacks, but you don't know who else it could be?"

"I'm just saying, it's not a done deal, Sir. We don't even know what the ALA is. Whether it's nothing more than a group of nutters or a group that is focused on wider issues, such as animal rights, climate change, green policies. At this stage, we have no idea. What we do know is that they have gone way too far regarding their cause. We have two people dead, Sir, and that's why we need to suspend all racing across all courses."

"And how long will this suspension last, Inspector?"

"Until we've found the culprits."

"And how long is that?"

Porter sighed. He knew what was coming, but he needed to say his piece.

"It will take as long as it takes, Sir. That could be days, weeks, months, or even much longer."

"My God, man!" exclaimed De Misgeny, "we *can't* stop racing for months or possibly longer, it would be unthinkable, disastrous. It's an industry, people's livelihoods depend upon it."

"Well Sir, I'm sorry to have to advise you that…"

"Not a hope in hell, man," De Misgeny interrupted, "it's out of the question. What other options do we have?"

The room went quiet, Porter realized that he was right. The focus of the BHA was on the industry, while his focus was on solving a crime and preventing another. Two different perspectives of the same problem.

He looked at Fox who had sat quietly during the discussion, observing, keeping notes. Finally, Porter said, "*We* have *no* other options, but we do have a way forward, a plan that we believe will limit any damage to your industry and will hopefully save lives."

"Go on Inspector," Andy Phillips requested, "let's hear it."

"Okay," Porter began. "Firstly, what we are dealing with is a criminal matter. As such there are some key protocols and processes that we, I, need to operate within in order to get a conviction. Because of this, I am asking you all to accept the fact that despite the need for a speedy resolution, certain limitations within the legal process may prevent that from occurring. Secondly, if we look at the letter we have received from the ALA, it is clear that they, or he or she, have taken great care in ensuring that there is very little evidence, fingerprints, DNA etcetera on it. What this means is that whoever created the document, knows what they are doing. They have even used a printer that is either old, no longer available, or only found now in one of the few remaining Internet Cafés around the country."

"I understand the sentiment Inspector," Phillips replied, "but what of it?"

"What it means is that if they went to these lengths to remain undetected, we need to accept that they must be serious with regards to their threats, especially given their actions of the other day."

"And on that basis, you want us to shut down the entire industry?"

"Yes!"

Phillips looked towards De Misgeny. "I can't believe it, Inspector, I'm sorry but I just can't. To shut down everything doesn't make sense to me," he went on.

"Well Sir," Porter said, "sadly it's not my call to make. Unfortunately, it's *yours*," he stated, emphasizing the matter by pointing at the two BHA men. "I can only recommend that you do, but I also strongly advise it."

"Or at least give the impression that you have?" Georgina Lipton asked.

"How do you mean?" Phillips said, confused.

The PR representative smiled at Porter, who returned the favour. "I think the Inspector is right, we need to respond to the demands of this, this…group, but we need to ensure that we all understand that what we are doing is giving the Police more time to find out who these people are."

"By closing down the industry?" Philips asked again.

"No, by keeping the industry advised of where things are at. I think from what the Inspector said, we should be able to close things down for a few days but give the ALA the impression that we have stopped racing and that we are willing to work with them in understanding their issues."

"But won't they see through our charade? I mean if we only stop racing for a short while, the moment we start up again, they'll be on the warpath, surely? Maybe they'll be even worse than they've been so far. You can never tell with fanatics!" he answered.

"This is where I come in, I guess," Lipton stated. "It's my job as PR to get the right message out, but with a little bit of smoke and mirrors we can confuse these people, isn't that right Inspector?"

"It would certainly help," Porter said. "It would give us time to take the necessary actions we hope may bring this to a resolution."

"And they are?"

"I've been permitted by the Chief Constable to hire a consultant who is directly involved in the business to do some digging for us and to try and find out who is behind all this," he said, picking up a copy of the ALA letter then somewhat laconically letting it fall back onto the table.

"And who is this person?" De Misgeny asked.

"I don't wish to say at this stage, Sir," Porter responded, "however, I can say that he is an ex-policeman who has links to the industry and is someone who we can rely on."

The room went quiet. The BHA members considering what they had just heard.

"In the meantime," Porter continued, "can we please decide how we are going to respond to these demands? We only have a short time in which to advise these people of our actions. Also," he stated, "we need to get something out to the industry. I see from the BHA calendar that there are three jumps meetings scheduled for the coming week, so what we need to do is advise the courses about the threat we have received and ask them to agree to a suspension of their meetings. If we can do that, it buys us time."

After further discussion, consensus was ultimately achieved. A response to the threat would be put on the Uttoxeter website, the relevant media would be advised, and a request made to postpone the coming week's meetings. In a separate communication to the relevant racecourses, they were to be advised that the postponed meetings could be rescheduled.

Porter was happy with the outcome, though not happy with the personalities he had to deal with. Now he had to get Cannon over the line, get him involved. He needed a win, and he hoped his plan would bring one.

# CHAPTER 30

Ralph Tolman had been with the Racing Post newspaper for the past thirty years. Now a Senior Journalist on the paper, he knew a story when he saw one. He sat in a chair in his apartment in East Dulwich and looked at the *Press Release*. It was a single page, issued on behalf of the BHA, and had been issued at exactly five pm with a blackout requested until nine pm.

The Racing Post would be unable to change the front page of the next day's edition that was currently being printed and therefore would only be able to include the announcement under a banner headline the day after.

Tolman didn't much like the electronic media but he knew something would be put on the *Post's* website overnight.

The notice in front of him was quite clear. *All jumps racing at all courses had been suspended until further notice.* The decision had been made due to the incident at Uttoxeter.

No mention was made of any police investigation. Given the amount of media coverage the jockeys' deaths had received, the upcoming funerals and the industry outcry, plus the social media posts in tribute to the jockeys, and the statements regarding the horse deaths from some radical animal rights groups, it didn't sit well with Tolman. Surely the police weren't sitting back and doing nothing? There must be some investigation underway, he thought.

He needed to find out.

# CHAPTER 31

Mitchell called again, his previous attempt having not been answered. He had done all he needed to, as far as he was concerned. They had an agreement and now was the time to honour it.

The phone rang another few times before it was picked up.

"I think I've done enough," he said.

There was silence at the end of the line for a few seconds.

"Almost, I'd say. I accept that we have mutually benefited so far, don't you?" the voice said eventually. "So, if I need any more favours, then I will call *you*. Don't ever call me again."

The line was disconnected. Mitchell looked at the receiver still in his hand. He wasn't sure why, but he was shaking.

At last, it was over!

He replaced the handset on the cradle and poured himself a whisky.

He drank the scotch in one mouthful.

# CHAPTER 32

"Some of our clients are getting a little concerned," Formrobe said.

He and Jacobsen had arranged a special teleconference with the board members. The second attack had been contained and the team dedicated to looking into the matter was still trying to work out who was behind it. So far, they had not had much luck. Whoever was involved had been able to cover their tracks well.

*SecureTwo* had likewise been able to maintain the integrity of their clients' data. However, they had been unable to stop the rumour mill. Systems were easier to contain, staff, talking out of turn, no matter how innocently, were much more difficult to contain.

"In what way, James?" Tom Birtles and Judy Smerdon asked almost simultaneously.

Formrobe took a deep breath. He needed to ensure that neither of them panicked in any way. The last thing he needed was for either of these important shareholders to start thinking that they needed to pull out of the business. It could cause the value of the business to fall, plus if clients began to feel nervous, it could cause them to look at other options to provide the services they acquired from *SecureTwo*. If there was a run on them, then very soon the business could look much different and face even more challenges.

"We've had enquiries from a couple of them, who heard *rumours*," he said emphasizing the word, "that our systems were compromised, and their data had been stolen. This, despite the letter that we put out advising them that there was nothing to be concerned about."

"And is it true? Should they be worried?" Judy Smerdon asked.

"Of course not," Formrobe stated dogmatically, "no one has had their data or information compromised at all."

"That's good to hear," she responded, "*my* investment is safe, then?"

"Of course it is, Judy," he replied, his eyes rolling in his head. Jacobsen was sitting across the boardroom table from Formrobe, both sitting forwards as they spoke into the telephone, Jacobsen smiled at Formrobe's facial expression.

"So what is the plan, the next step?" asked Birtles.

"I'm glad you asked, Tom," Formrobe said. "Samuel and I have already drafted further correspondence, which, in addition to our recent letter, will spell out the status of things to our clients. It's designed to ease their concern even more, but also make it clear that the threat has not gone away, and we are working through the issues raised."

"Can we see it?"

"Of course Tom," Jacobsen interjected, "I'll be sending each member of the Board a copy of the correspondence, but I am happy to read out the contents now on the phone to everyone, if you wish?"

"That sounds reasonable," Birtles replied.

Over the next ten minutes, the wording of the correspondence to be issued to *SecureTwo*'s clients was debated and amended slightly until everyone was satisfied.

The details of the letter were clear, concise, and accurate. No one had experienced any loss or breach of their data, but it was clear that whoever was involved appeared not to be deterred. The management made it clear that they were doing everything they could to find out who was behind the attacks and were convinced that their systems were robust enough to counter any further attacks.

"What about calling in the police?" Birtles asked, "I would be much happier if they were aware of this."

Jacobsen concurred, but suggested that until *SecureTwo* had more information about who could be behind the attacks, it was unlikely the police would get involved so early. They needed suspects and proof, stealing data was common nowadays and the police were limited in terms of their capability concerning cyber-crime. It was happening every day and they also didn't have the resources to focus on every single company or individual that was subject to fraudulent behaviour.

"I agree with Samuel," Formrobe said, "but we will bring the police in when we think we have some detail that they could use. At the moment, all we know is that there is an attempt to break into our systems. What we don't know is by whom or indeed why."

"Do you have *any* idea at all who could be responsible?" Judy Smerdon asked.

"None whatsoever."

"And no one comes to mind? No disgruntled ex-employee?"

"No. Anyone who has left our employ appears to have left on good terms."

"Isn't that a little naïve?" Birtles stated, "surely not every person who left the business was happy to do so?"

Wendy Richards the CFO had been quiet up until now. She decided to add her two-pennies worth.

"As CFO with responsibility for Finance and HR, I've instructed the team to do an audit of those people who have left us over the past couple of years and to look at the exit interview paperwork. While we know it won't be conclusive, I've asked them to pull out any names and any other details they may have of anyone who appeared aggressive, unhappy, or even *docile* at the time of their leaving us, especially at the exit interview itself," she said. "It just might give us some clues, something to look at. It's nothing scientific, it's just a long shot."

The board acknowledged Wendy Richards' attempt to find out more information about the ex-employees was a good move, but also understood the limitations. After a brief statement by Formrobe about keeping everyone up to date, the meeting closed.

"At least that went reasonably well," Formrobe said, letting out a sigh of relief.

"Agreed," Jacobsen said, "let's hope whoever is behind this doesn't have the capability to get through the firewalls and other levels of protection we have in place."

Formrobe and Richards nodded in agreement. Formrobe, however, had a very uncomfortable feeling in the pit of his stomach. He hoped, though he felt he was hoping against hope, that there would be no further incidents. Expecting something to happen, he subsequently proved himself correct.

# CHAPTER 33

Cannon and Telside stood side by side. The area set aside on the common a half-mile walk from the stables where they trained their horses, was filled with the sound of hooves pounding upon the grass. A mist had settled across the plains where the tracks that the horses followed merged into each other. The sun had barely raised its head above the eastern horizon and the horses and their riders appeared like ghosts as they chased each other in single file, clearing the hurdles or steeplechase fences with a curse or a grunt of encouragement from each rider as they did so.

"Some good signs," Cannon said, "we've got a chance to improve on the past few seasons, looking at some of the new horses we've picked up."

"Aye," Telside agreed. "In addition to this first *lot*, we've got a couple of others who may do well in some of the better races later in the year."

"Exactly, Rich," Cannon said, "I really like *The Politician* for The Tingle Creek."

"I tend to agree, and as a five-year-old, he's going to be a lot stronger than he was previously when he was trained by Fred Kiplock. I think it was a bit silly for Fred to try to get him into the race last year, it was a bit of a long shot, anyway. Now that he's five I think he'll be able to do well. As a weight for age race, he would have struggled in the Tingle Creek so I'm glad he didn't get in. I think it would have ruined him."

Cannon knew that Rich was the consummate horseman. He knew what he was talking about and Cannon took his advice seriously.

"Exactly. Thank God for sensible owners."

"And for moving the horse to us," Telside laughed.

They continued watching as the horses came out of the mist, their exertions reflected by the steam that exited their nostrils and the burr of their snorts as they leapt across the training barriers. A series of five pairs now ran along together, training partners, jumping the barriers as they came to each, paired based on experience and age. Cannon and Telside began walking alongside the track to get a better view of every horse as it galloped along under the urgings of its rider. Cannon looked at the running actions of every horse. Noticing one horse in the third pair, a horse named *NorrisMcWherter* running in an ungainly fashion, Cannon called out to the rider to jump off the animal so that he and Telside could inspect its legs. Allowing the others to continue with their exercises, Telside took hold of the reins from the jockey and walked the horse in a large circle while Cannon watched the way the horse moved.

"He seems a bit short to me," Cannon said. Turning to the jockey he asked, "how did he feel?"

"He seemed okay, Guv'nor," the jockey, Sy Talbot stated, "though, after the first pass, he did seem a little hesitant to be going on with things."

"Umm," Cannon responded, removing his cap before scratching his head, thinking. He asked Telside to walk the horse away from him, then turn around and walk back in Cannon's direction. Telside did as requested. As the horse walked away, Cannon could see that it was walking awkwardly.

Telside felt it as well, calling out to Cannon. "Mike, I think you're right. He does seem a bit hesitant to stretch out. Something's not right. Could be a tendon or could be in the back. Either way, it's not good. We'll need to get the vet in to see him."

Cannon agreed. "Okay Sy, take him home. We'll see you back there in about half an hour. Just make him comfortable and I'll get the vet over asap."

"No worries, boss," Talbot replied.

They watched as the horse was led away. Both horse and rider disappeared into the mist, which had lifted slightly, but still meant visibility was limited to about a hundred metres.

"Damn," Cannon said, 'just when the horse was starting to show us something. I had entered him into a two-and-a-half-mile hurdle race in about three weeks. If the horse is badly injured, he could be out of action for a good while. I'll need to let the owner know asap."

"Yes," Telside agreed, "I think he was one to watch. The owner won't be too happy I'm sure, but until the vet gives us a diagnosis, the positive is that it could be just a few weeks."

"And the negative is," interjected Cannon, "that he could be out for the entire season."

Telside turned away, the injury to *NorrisMcWherter* was sad, but part of racing. He had seen horses come and go. Some he had become attached to early in his career, however eventually he had learned to distance himself from disappointment. Life carried on and he believed that no matter what happened there was always next week, next month, next year. A new season always brought a feeling of positivity into the stable, and a new season was about to begin.

They watched the rest of the *lot* complete their work then they headed back to the stables for breakfast. They would watch the work of the second and third *lots* later. By then they hoped the mist would have fully lifted. The forecast was for a breezy day.

As they arrived back in the yard, Telside told Cannon that he just needed to check something in the tack room and he left Cannon to walk back into the house, saying he would join him in a few minutes.

It was now close to seven-thirty am. Michelle had made breakfast, leaving it in a warming drawer in the kitchen for them. She had then gone off to shower, before leaving for school. Cannon put his cap on the dining room table. The kitchen felt warm and inviting, the smell of bacon permeated the air. He took out a couple of plates from the cupboard and was just about to put some scrambled eggs onto a plate when the house phone rang.

He looked at the clock on the wall and despite knowing it was very early for someone to call, he decided to answer it rather than let it ring out for a message to be left.

"Hello?" he said.

"Mr. Cannon? Mike Cannon," a voice, a man's voice, one he didn't recognize.

Cannon was reluctant to confirm anything to an unknown caller, especially given what had ultimately happened with Henry Bronton. He wasn't in the mood to talk with any potential scammer. It seemed that dodgy calls were becoming more and more frequent now and someone calling so early in the morning was likely to be another one, he thought. Over the past few days, the house had been inundated with phone calls from unknown people who tried to tell him that they had heard he had been involved in a car accident and that they could help him make a legal claim. The spate of calls had begun to irritate him.

"No, I haven't been involved in any car accident…." he said, trying to put off the person at the other end of the line before they started their patter.

There was a short silence before he heard the caller laugh. He waited for the voice to speak again.

"I'm sorry?" said the man.

"Look, who is this?" Cannon asked, "and what do you want?"

"I'm looking for Mike Cannon," the voice said, "my name is Tolman, Ralph Tolman, from the Racing Post. I would like to speak with Mike Cannon please."

Cannon knew of Tolman, but they have never met. Cannon read the *Post* regularly and was aware of where Tolman stood in the hierarchy of the paper. He was on his guard straight away. Why would he want to talk with him? Tolman had never sought him out when Cannon's horse, *RockGod* almost won the Grand National, so why now?

"Hello Mr. Tolman," Cannon said, "it's Mike Cannon here, how can I help?" he asked politely but cautiously.

"I was wondering if I could come and have a chat with you about the news that all jumps racing is to be suspended, almost indefinitely as a consequence of the incident at Uttoxeter," Tolman replied. "It can be *off the record* except for when you'd like your comments to be published, but given you were at the meeting and saw what happened, I think your input would be valuable as to why the decision has been made."

Cannon thought about what he was being asked. Before he could respond Tolman continued with, "I'm also interested in how the suspension will hit stables like yours. Financially, plus physically, the horses, the staff, even yourself, and the planning that goes into setting targets for the animals under your care. Not to mention how the owners feel."

The added comments gave Cannon an idea. "Okay," he replied, "when are you wanting to meet and where?"

"I would like to meet as soon as possible, to get the story into the paper sooner rather than later. The suspension is very topical, as are the deaths of the two jockeys. I think a story linking what happened at Uttoxeter to the upcoming funerals of those poor jockeys, the total suspension of jumps racing, and how it is affecting the industry would be useful for our readers."

He deliberately didn't mention his view of any police investigation into the events at the Uttoxeter meeting and Cannon didn't talk about it either, nor indeed his arrest and subsequent release without charge up in Doncaster for what had happened to Bronton and the Pools. He felt that knowing he was innocent there was no need to raise the issue with the journalist.

"How about tomorrow then?' Cannon asked. "I assume you will come to me? After all, I have a stable to manage."

"Of course," Tolman advised. "Name the time and place," he said.

"How about the *Black Prince* pub, on Manor Road say twelve-thirty? It opens at around midday, so that will give me time to manage my lots for training, do some admin, and meet you there in time for lunch?" Cannon asked. "I assume you are paying?" he added with a smile in his voice.

"Ahh, the days of long lunches, big expense allowances have all gone, but I'm sure I can spare a few pounds to get a story of sorts, so yes that will work for me."

"Good," Cannon replied, "oh how will I recognize you? Your picture never appears in the *Post*."

"Don't worry Mr. Cannon. I'll recognize you."

Cannon wasn't sure if that was a good or bad sign but took it as a positive. He hoped that by talking to Tolman, the idea that was brewing in his mind would be able to help the police in their investigations. He was as yet unaware of Porter's thoughts about engaging him.

# CHAPTER 34

The call to Cannon was made in the late morning. Porter asked to catch up with him later in the day if that was possible. Cannon advised him that it was and made the necessary arrangements with Rich to ensure that all the work needed around the stable would continue as normal.

Porter agreed to come to the yard, so while Cannon waited for Porter to arrive, he worked in his office. While doing so he wondered about Tolman's real intention and readied himself for the conversation the next day.

Porter arrived around two pm, it would be a few more hours before Michelle got home from school, so he and Porter would have plenty of time to chat. Cannon noted, as he went outside to greet the policeman as he parked his car, that he was alone. No Sergeant Fox today, it seemed. Cannon thought it may be the case that Porter had decided to come alone so as not to intimidate him. If it was, Porter was wrong. Cannon was not intimidated at all. He knew the police tactics, they were ever imprinted on his mind. He had played the game many times himself.

The last time they had met, it was to take Cannon's statement after the Uttoxeter tragedy. Today Cannon was unsure of the reason, Porter had been somewhat vague on the call. He had indicated that he needed Cannon's help. Cannon in turn had held his tongue. He himself had been planning to find out what had happened and needed to find a way to do so. Maybe Porter could be the gateway?

Before they settled down, knowing Porter was on duty, Cannon offered his guest some tea, but the policeman declined. Cannon decided to give things a miss as well, so the two men settled themselves down in the lounge. A fire cracked and spluttered in the fireplace. The days were shortening and cooling, outside a wind had picked up and what was originally a fine day, had begun to cloud over. Rain was expected the following day, along with a strong wind. A good day to meet a journalist in a pub, Cannon thought.

"Well Inspector, what can I do for you? Any news, any progress in your investigation?"

"To be honest Mike, not a lot so far. Whoever is behind this, has been exceedingly clever. There are very few clues in what we have been able to gather so far. The letters, which I told you about last time, have been so sanitized that it has been almost impossible to get anything off them. No DNA, fingerprints, saliva, even printer and ink type. I expect the forensic boys will likely be able to tell us about the printing, but that will be about all. It doesn't give us much to go on."

"So what brings you here then?"

Porter looked at his hands. Being a big man, the fingers on both hands seemed like little sausages. Cannon noticed how the policeman's open suit jacket strained, the buttons almost leaving the safety of their holes. He didn't say anything else, he waited for Porter to continue, to answer his question.

"I, we, need your help," he said.

"In what way Inspector?" Cannon replied. He was beginning to feel that the request was the ticket he'd been looking for himself. His own personal drivers, after the carnage he had seen, needed no kickstart, he just needed a way in. He hoped this was it.

"I've been given permission by the Chief Inspector, and I have met with the senior leadership of the BHA and the Uttoxeter racecourse, to hire a consultant, someone with racing experience such as yourself, to see if we can find out who is actually behind the attacks on the various racecourses. We need to get to the bottom of it as quickly as possible."

"Before anyone else dies," interrupted Cannon.

"Exactly, Mike. Also, before the industry dies! We are aware that some of the courses are on a knife's edge with regards to their financial survival. If the industry is shut down indefinitely some of them will go to the wall."

"To whose benefit?" Cannon asked."

"We're not sure if it's genuine but we expect to the benefit of an animal rights activist group called the *ALA*. Though it could be another reason."

"Such as?"

"Housing developers, Green activists, who knows…could even be someone from inside the industry who now has a grudge."

Cannon replied saying, "It's a bit of a long bow to draw about a begrudged employee don't you think? I mean people getting killed is not ideal for their cause."

"I'm not sure the intent was for anyone to die," Porter replied, "and that's why I need your help."

"Do you think it was a coincidence? An error in judgement by the perpetrators?"

"I think so, yes," the policeman replied. "All the other letters and threats received, as we discussed when we spoke last time, indicated a voluntary shut down, not a forced one. The fence exploding during the race at Uttoxeter seemed to be highly unusual. Most of the other attacks were at night where no one was likely to be injured, hurt or worse, killed."

"And therefore, the requests for action would be more around vandalism, with less involvement by the police."

"Yes, the focus would be looking at extortion claims rather than murder. And even with extortion, there has been no request for monies, just purely a question of stopping the racing. This ALA mob, seem to be sending a message about animal cruelty as far as we can see, not one about seeking money or anything else…"

"So what do you want from me? Cannon asked.

"We'd like to ask that, given your knowledge of the industry and your background as a former policeman, you consider working with us in trying to find out who the ALA are, their motives, their membership, what they are planning next, and whether the actions the BHA have taken in suspending racing are enough for them to stop what they are doing…at least for now."

"Go on," Cannon said.

"We hope the suspension will buy us time, but I must warn you that the industry body is not happy. When I met with them, they reluctantly compromised with me, to give us a short amount of time to try and find the culprits, hence the recently issued industry-wide correspondence about meeting suspensions until further notice. However, I guess you will have seen that they have indicated that the meetings can be re-scheduled, where possible, to a later date."

"I saw that," Cannon replied, thinking back to a couple of emails he had read earlier in the day from the BHA. "Wouldn't the idea of rescheduling meetings be like a red rag to a bull?" he asked.

"Yes, I think it would be," Porter replied. "If that message surfaces, then it's likely the ALA would see the messages on the various course websites as the industry just paying lip service to the issue. They may see that the demands they have made haven't been taken that seriously and who knows what steps they would take next."

Cannon contemplated what Porter had said before replying. "How much time do we have?"

"I'd suggest ten days, maybe two weeks at most. All the letters received from the ALA seem to suggest that if nothing of a permanent nature is done and they are advised of it, then they will take further action."

"Resulting in more deaths?"

"Maybe, but what we can see is that should they start with their campaign again, it's likely that the industry and several courses will naturally suffer."

"Because the public will stay away, the fields of horses running per race will get smaller, turnover for both on course and off course bookmakers will reduce and finally as you said before, some places and businesses will not survive."

"Exactly, just think of the job losses, the staff at the courses, the complementary and supplementary industries, for example, horse transport, catering, and distribution. All of them will be impacted."

Cannon didn't want to contemplate what would happen to his own stables, his own business that he and others had worked so hard to build, to grow.

"Okay," he said eventually, "what do you want me to do?"

Porter didn't have much to offer but agreed to Cannon's suggestion to leave it with him. Cannon would advise Porter what he found out as and when he could. They both agreed that time was of the essence and that Cannon would need to move as quickly as he could. He asked Porter to arrange for the BHA as the highest industry body, to insert onto their website a request for a face to face meeting with the ALA. That it was to be conducted at a neutral venue and that a representative of the industry would attend the meeting, without police involvement, in order to see how their demands could be met. The meeting to take place within the next seven days at the latest.

"What if they don't agree to meet?" asked Porter.

"If they don't, well I'll need to consider something else," Cannon responded. "But if they are serious about their cause, they should see the meeting as a win for them. They need to be seen to be getting a response, otherwise, all they will see ultimately is increased security around courses, and meetings beginning again. Plus, they will be looking over their shoulders to see if the police would be closing in, given the death of those jockeys."

"Won't they be seeking immunity for that? The jockeys being killed?"

"They might," Cannon said, "but until I meet with them, I don't know. I guess we can speculate, but you never know."

"True," replied Porter.

"Oh, and I need to advise you of something else," Cannon said. "something which I hope *you* can help *me* with."

"What's that?" replied Porter, intrigued.

"My arrest."

"Arrest?"

"Yes,"

"For what? When? By whom?"

"For murder. Of three people."

"You've got to be joking," Porter said, sitting up in his chair. "When did this happen?"

"A couple of days ago," Cannon replied. "It relates to a horse I was buying on behalf of a client. It seems it was a scam."

He went on to explain what had happened, the delivery of a horse that *looked* like *Centaur,* and the conversation he had with the mysterious Peter Todd.

"Don't you have any CCTV around here that you could use to corroborate your story? I would have thought it essential."

"Well we do have a system, but we've had a problem recently that we hadn't picked up on until just the other day. The system has been working, that is you can see live pictures, but apparently, the box wasn't recording anything. So on the day leading up to Peter Todd delivering the horse and the subsequent days, we have no recordings at all. Consequently, we only have our own, that is mine and my assistant trainer, Rich's, vague description of this guy. Personally, I'm not even sure if he was wearing a wig or not. It's something I would normally notice, but because of the horse situation I was more focused on that."

"So, what happened? How come you were arrested?"

"After Todd left, I tried to contact the agent who found the horse for us as well as the trainer who was acting on behalf of the seller."

"And?"

"It seems like they had been killed and somehow the Notts police put me in the frame for the murders."

"And how did they manage to link you to the deaths of these people?"

"Incredibly they noticed that I had called several times to the home phone of the trainer, Harry Pool, and they used the 1471 number to call me back. I believe they assumed that I was another disgruntled buyer and due to the scam they had been pulling, that I had taken the law into my own hands."

"Without proof?" replied Porter, incredulously.

"I guess they needed a quick arrest and I was the only one they could find to possibly pin something on."

"Ummm…"

"Anyway," Cannon continued, "they arrested me under false pretenses, and I ended up being taken to Nottingham. Fortunately, a lawyer known by my client's legal advisor was able to get me out of police custody, without charge and without any bail needed."

"Seems like they were clutching at straws," Porter said.

"I think so too. I even explained to them that I talked with someone on Pool's phone who had answered it when I tried to call him about the wrong horse being delivered."

"And what did they say?"

"I don't think they believed me to be honest. I'm guessing they think I made it up."

"Do you have any idea who the person was?"

"No. None whatsoever. I'm guessing it could be the killer, but that's just my view. Anyway, if the police, an Inspector named Dockly, did his job properly he would have been able to see that it was impossible for me to get from here to Doncaster in the time they think Pool and the agent, was killed from when I tried to call them and when Peter Todd left here."

Porter considered his options. He needed Cannon free to do the job they wanted him to do. He didn't need anything hanging over him.

"Okay, leave it with me," Porter said. "I'll make some enquiries and see how we can resolve it for you."

"Thanks, Inspector," Cannon said. "I know I've been out of the Force for a while but there are certain things that I'm sure haven't changed. One of them is gathering evidence and building a case against a suspect, not charging someone based on some flimsy excuse just because you want to solve a murder. Surely the Crown Prosecution Service needs to be satisfied that enough evidence exists before any court proceedings would ever take place?"

"Yes, that's right Mike. I'm not sure what's been going on, but I will look into it."

"Thank you again, Inspector."

Cannon felt relieved. He knew he didn't yet have a cast-iron guarantee that Porter would be able to resolve the issue with Dockly, but he did understand that at least in the short term he would be able to concentrate on the ALA issue and have the support of the BHA, notwithstanding his previous experience with them a few years back when they accused him of race-fixing.

The two men discussed the content of the message Cannon wanted to send to be put onto the BHA website. How it should look and sound, so that the ALA would understand its contents, but the general public, including the industry members, could not. Once they had completed their discussion, Porter got up to leave. Cannon looked at his watch, he expected Michelle home shortly. He would just have enough time to do his evening rounds of the stables.

"Just before you go Inspector, a quick one, if I may?"

"Yes?"

"I got a call this morning from a journalist, Ralph Tolman from the Racing Post. He wanted to meet with me tomorrow."

"What about?"

"Well, he says he wants to get my view of the indefinite suspension of racing seeing as I was there at Uttoxeter. He tried to couch it as if it was a humanitarian story, the impact on stables, financially and otherwise, but I think he's after something else."

"Like what?"

"An exclusive I'd suggest. Journalists always have angles, don't they? I think he has got an inkling of a story in his head. Maybe he's heard something about what you want me to do? Maybe he knows about my background and is putting two and two together? I don't know, but it's curious, coincidental don't you think?"

"Perhaps," Porter replied. "Either way, I think you will need to be careful when you meet with him. We wouldn't want the ALA to know your background, especially if he goes and publishes a story of sorts. If they find out you are ex-Police and are working for us, they may break off the conversation."

"If we ever start one," said Cannon.

"True. Hopefully, they take up the offer so we can find out what's really going on. The last thing we want is anyone else killed. We need to find out who these people are before they do anything more," he continued. "Either way, I think I will have a chat with the newspaper's Editor, just to be sure." Cannon thanked Porter for his support and the two men shook hands before walking outside to Porter's car. Cannon watched as the policeman drove away, then turned back into his house and headed towards his office. He still had some doubts in his mind about what he was being asked to do.

# CHAPTER 35

Cannon smiled at his longtime assistant. Much older than Cannon, Telside had been with him ever since Cannon had started out on his own after obtaining his training license. Telside took over the running of the stables whenever Cannon asked. They seldom argued and Cannon could rely on Rich to be discreet, but also honest. He would say what he thought and leave it at that, whether people agreed with him or not. Rich didn't hold grudges against anyone. His focus was on the horses in their keep and by doing so, he enjoyed each day. It was his life and he didn't see it as a job.

During the previous evening, after Michelle had returned from work and they had finished with dinner, Cannon had let her know about his discussion with Porter. Michelle was apprehensive but reluctantly accepted that it was something he needed to do. It wasn't the first time, she realized. It seemed to go with the territory. That night they had made love, quietly, gently as if something was bringing them even closer. A sense of belonging, a sense that nothing would ever come between them, no matter the dangers. As they lay together before sleep came, both with their own thoughts, they shared them as if they were confessing something to each other. Cannon realized that the bond between them was getting stronger each day, he needed to ensure that nothing happened to either of them that would break it.

Standing together with Rich, he repeated what he shared with Michelle the previous evening about Porter's request for help. Rich nodded, he knew what it meant.

The two men stayed quiet for a few seconds. "I think we should plan to run *SparkleDust* in the Persian War Novices Hurdle at Chepstow in October," Cannon said, watching as the horse smashed the tops off the jump closest to where he and Telside stood at the side on the hurdles training track.

"Do you think we will be racing by then Mike?"

"I should hope so Rich, it's still a couple of months away. Let's hope that the weather plays ball by then, too," Cannon replied, zipping up his parka jacket. The day had dawned with a red sky, the sign of things to come. Rain was on its way, but before it arrived the breeze would strengthen. Gusts occasionally whipped up the grass that had been torn from the bridleway that Cannon's horses used to get from the stables to the training track. "I'm hoping that racing will resume quickly, especially if I have anything to do with it," he continued.

"Me too, Mike," Telside replied, "me too. You just need to be careful though. Don't go and do anything silly. Michelle, Cassie, and I all need you to be around."

The mentioning of Cannon's daughter reminded him that he needed to give her a call. After the meeting he had with Jacobsen and agreeing with him to have a chat with her, he hadn't yet got around to suggesting it to Cassie. He would give her a call that evening.

"What about *Redjet Jones*?" Rich asked, jumping in on Cannon's thoughts, "I think another *bumper* race, maybe two, would be useful before we take the mare over the sticks." They watched as the horse took an ungainly leap over a small steeplechase fence. Training of the horse was coming along. She was too slow for flat racing and a little hesitant in jumping, so it had been decided to bring her along slowly. Fortunately, the owner agreed. The hope was that near the end of the season, the horse would be ready for a run in a Conditions race. Maybe the next season, if the horse improved, they would look for a handicap race and take it from there.

"I think you are right Rich, let's see where we can place her. Maybe sometime late September?"

They watched the rest of the lot complete their exercise then Cannon excused himself, asking Rich to take over and handle the second lot of the day. Cannon wanted to prepare himself for his meeting with Tolman. It was going to be a long day. Cannon hoped that he would hear from Porter in the next few days about the possible meeting with the ALA. In the meantime, he needed to clarify in his own mind his specific plan of action.

# CHAPTER 36

The 16th Century *Black Prince* pub was quiet. When Cannon arrived, he walked straight into the bar area. The low dark beams and the subtle lighting inside contrasted with the sandstone building and the warm invitation to visitors that the hanging flower boxes outside facing the road conveyed. He was only a few minutes late and the place had been open around thirty minutes, just enough time for a young couple to find a seat alone in the corner of the restaurant area, the garden overlooking the river which ran along the back of the pub being closed due to the cooler weather. He took a couple of seconds for his eyes to adjust to the low light, and as his sight improved, he noticed a man sitting on a bar-stool waving towards him.

He realized it was Ralph Tolman. He was dressed in a light, tan-coloured coat over a dark blue cardigan and light blue shirt. He wore casual slacks and shiny black shoes. Cannon guessed the man was in his early sixties, grey wisps of hair tempted fate just above the ears. Large bushy eyebrows above green eyes and a drinking man's skin, spread across a Roman nose, almost completed the picture. Tufts of grey hair protruded from the man's ears and nose like tiny weeds in a desert garden.

Holding out his hand, Tolman introduced himself. Cannon returned the favour.

"What can I get you?" Tolman asked, picking up a pint glass of Trelawny Pale Ale that was already half empty. Cannon guessed that it was just an appetizer as far as Tolman was concerned. The heavier stuff would come later.

"Just a half-pint of cider will do for me," Cannon replied, "I'm driving."

"No problem," Tolman said. "Maybe a glass of wine though? With lunch?"

"I'm sure I can stretch to that."

"Good to hear," the journalist replied. Turning to a young girl behind the bar, Tolman ordered Cannon's drink. He was an old-fashioned scribe who needed someone to drink with, and Cannon's acceptance of another with lunch made him feel more comfortable. Tolman didn't like the modern trend of conducting interviews with men who only drank bottled water.

"Cheers" Cannon said, touching his glass with that of his host, "to your good health."

Tolman reciprocated, thanking him for agreeing to meet.

"So, what can I do for you?" Cannon asked. He was intrigued but also on his guard as to why Tolman wanted to meet with him. While Tolman had made out during their phone call that he was looking into the likely effect that a suspension of racing would have on Cannon directly, and the industry more broadly, he knew that Tolman was much more astute than he first appeared and that there likely was another angle. Another reason. A story, an investigation, that he could claim an *exclusive* on, particularly the happenings at Uttoxeter.

Cannon wanted to use Tolman. He guessed Tolman wanted to use him. A *quid-pro-quo.*

"Firstly Mike, thank you for agreeing to meet with me. I know it's a busy time for you and one that must be frustrating given the suspension of racing?"

"It is frustrating yes," Cannon replied, "but I think the safety of everyone, the public, the jockeys, as well as the horses themselves, when there is a group of people at large willing to cause injury and mayhem, is paramount. I think the suspension of all jumps racing until the problem is resolved is a good one."

"Can I quote you on that?"

"Of course," Cannon replied. "However, I'd like this conversation to be off the record if you don't mind? I'm happy to share my thoughts, but they should remain private at this stage."

Tolman nodded. He was disappointed that he wouldn't be able to name Cannon as a *source* for a story that he was hoping to be able to gather from the conversation, but the use of the word *attributable* wasn't something Tolman would shy away from if he needed to add credence to a story. He had done some research on Cannon, looked into his background, knew he was a former Detective Inspector. Call it experience, a gut feeling, Tolman believed that with Cannon's police background, and having been at the meeting itself, seeing the carnage and nearly losing his own horse and jockey, he was the ideal person for the BHA to approach, to act on their behalf, to try and find the group or person behind the attacks. His gut feeling was seldom wrong, it was why Tolman wanted more from Cannon. He wasn't sure if he would get it.

He would try anyway.

"Do you know who is behind the attacks?" Tolman asked directly. A question without warning. No subtlety here, Cannon thought.

"No, I don't," he lied.

"If you were asked to assist the police or the BHA in finding out who was, would you?"

"Naturally I would. Wouldn't anyone?"

"I'd suspect only if they have the necessary experience."

"Like me?" Cannon asked, realizing that Tolman knew a bit more about him than he would like.

"Well you are an ex-copper, right?"

"Yes."

"So with that background and your industry insight, if a group wanted to use violence to disrupt or even stop racing, you'd be someone who the BHA may approach to act on their behalf?"

"To do what?"

"Act as a go-between, maybe?"

"And what about the police themselves? They've got all the tools, people, and processes they need. They don't need me."

"But that's the point isn't it Mike?"

"What is?"

"The fact that they *are* the police," Tolman continued. "If I was someone looking for an outcome, I wouldn't want the police involved. I wouldn't want them to know *who* I am. I'd just want those controlling the industry to give me *what* I want."

"True," Cannon replied, "but it's highly unlikely for that to happen, isn't it?"

"What won't happen?" Tolman asked.

Cannon realized he had said something that he shouldn't have and Tolman had seized upon it. Trying to recover Cannon said, "An industry shutdown. Permanently. Highly unlikely. Whoever the people are who ended up killing those two jockeys and their mounts, they'll get caught eventually."

"So, you have been asked to help then?" Tolman persisted, sensing the passion Cannon reflected in the response to his questions. Something behind the words, the way he spoke told Tolman that Cannon was getting involved but was not letting on in what way.

"As I said before, Ralph," Cannon used the journalist's Christian name for the first time, "I've not been approached by anyone. I'm not involved in any attempt to find these people, *but* what I can say is that *if* I was, I'd hope you would help as well. Play your part?"

He wasn't sure if the hook had been baited properly, but Cannon hoped that this last comment would be noticed by Tolman. It was Cannon's way of offering something to the journalist without saying it.

"What do you mean?" Tolman asked, suspiciously.

"Are we still off the record?"

Holding up three fingers on his right hand, and almost saluting, the journalist smiled and said, "of course we are. Scout's honour."

Not sure whether to believe him completely, Cannon said, "If I can give you an exclusive, what would you give to me?"

"An exclusive on what?"

"The shutdown."

"I thought you haven't been approached on the matter?" Tolman enquired again.

"As I said, I haven't. But I'm happy to give you the exclusive details of anything I do get involved with, should it happen."

Tolman laughed. "Mike you are offering me nothing. How do you expect me to do something for you, when from what you have told me there has been no request made to you to get involved, and there is no possibility of you being approached by the BHA or anyone else, either?"

Cannon smiled. "Maybe it's because I have another story for you, something else."

"Better than finding out who is behind the attacks?"

"I think so."

"Why do you say that?"

Cannon hesitated. He wanted Tolman to think that what he had to offer would warrant meeting what he would ask for in return.

"Let's just say that it has legs. It's a story that could run for a while."

Tolman was intrigued, but he wasn't sure he should give away anything just yet to get the story.

"What do you want from me then?" he asked. "Remember, whatever it is will need to go via the Ed."

"I'm sure you can convince your editor without any problems," Cannon replied. Flattery will get you somewhere, sometimes, he thought, but he doubted it would work that easily on Tolman.

"Okay, shoot."

Cannon let Tolman know what he wanted from him. In return, he agreed that he would give Tolman complete and ongoing access to any and all detail that Cannon could provide concerning the police investigation into the attack *if* he was asked to get involved. In addition, Cannon provided a snippet of information about his second story, the Bronton murder, and his thoughts on the subject. Again, they agreed their conversation was off the record, so Cannon felt a little more comfortable about sharing his view on the subject. He kept aside the majority of what he knew, he just needed to ensure that Tolman had enough. It was. The hook had been taken. Lunch was so much more palatable once they sat down and ate.

# CHAPTER 37

"What do you think, Toby?" Kevin asked.

The two men and three girls were sitting in Kevin's flat, allocated to him by his college in Oxford. Except for Toby, the rest were graduates, all members of Jesus College, and all passionate about animal rights.

They had read the request on the BHA website for a meeting. It had been cleverly done. An obtuse message that only members of the ALA would be able to understand, had been inserted into the text of a special page on the site. It was a page set up to advise the general public about the temporary halt to racing. A link to a portal within the body of the page had been created which required an account number to open another page. To do that another SMS would be sent to an encrypted app. The SMS would be sent, allowing the ALA to open up the page, from which they could reply to the BHA, providing the necessary details of where and when the industry representative would be allowed to meet with them.

"I think it's a start," Toby said in response to Kevin. "It looks like they have started to take things seriously."

Kevin smiled, the girls giggled. Toby felt uncomfortable but needed to keep his true feelings under control.

"So, what next?" asked one of the girls. Her name was Tracey. She was tall, lithesome, her long dark hair falling halfway down her back. Seated on the floor, her knees touched Toby's. He was so much older than she was, but sitting so close, smelling her perfume, it excited him. She touched his dreadlocks then cheekily kissed him on the cheek. The other girls laughed. It was Friday night, pizza boxes and beer bottles were strewn around the room, reflecting an atmosphere that Toby himself didn't really feel comfortable with. They saw him as their de facto leader, but he wanted out. He had done his bit.

The deaths of the two jockeys and their upcoming funerals was playing on his mind. Their bodies would be released by the Coroner after the necessary inquiry into what had happened was concluded,. He tried to focus on the issue at hand.

"I think we need to get the meeting set up with the BHA rep. and give them our demands. After that, we'll see how they react."

"And how will we do that?" one of the other girls asked.

"I think we need to play the game very carefully, Sarah," Toby replied. "We need to be as invisible as possible. We don't want them to know who we are. We just want them to accede to our demands."

"Do you think they will?" Sarah asked.

"If they don't," Kevin jumped in, "then we go again. Harder this time!"

The girls all reacted with a cheer. Toby remained silent.

"What's up, Toby?" Tracey asked, turning her head slightly towards him, coquettishly. She wasn't only flirting, she was offering herself.

"I think we need to get serious," he replied. "We need to respond to the offer the BHA have made. We need to make a plan about where and when we will meet with them and as I mentioned before, we need to be careful. Two men died for God's sake…"

"Collateral damage," said the third girl, Tina. "It's made the racing industry focus on what we know is a cruel sport."

"It's also got the police and the public involved. Mostly supportive of the industry. To get them to stop fully is a big ask."

"Well if they don't stop, then we won't," Kevin replied, full of bravado.

Once again, the girls whooped. Toby could see that things were getting out of hand. His own weaknesses had got him here. He could see that if he wasn't careful, he could end up getting himself into further problems. He believed that what he had done to date with regards to the *cause* had helped pay off his debt, that he was now free from any further obligation. He had to find a way to extract himself from Kevin and the girls, to put some distance between them.

They spent the next couple of hours working on their response to the BHA. Where they would meet, who would be there and what the ALA's expectations were from the meeting. Between additional beer and wine, the group managed to put a list of demands together. There was nothing particularly new or clever, just a rehash of previous requests. The only additional consideration was the implied threat of additional violence, of further disruptions, and the likelihood of more animals or jockeys being hurt.

"Isn't it somewhat contradictory," Toby asked, "to say that we could cause injury or death to the jockeys *and* horses?"

"Unfortunately, that's true," Kevin replied. "But we need to get them to understand that we are serious. That we don't want to hurt the very animals we want to be freed, but if the means justify the end, then so be it."

Toby nodded. It was getting late. Tina and Sarah had already left. Tracey was now sleeping on the couch.

"Okay," he said. "I'll arrange for the details of where we intend to meet to get to the BHA asap. I would like to get our demands agreed to within forty -eight hours of proposing them."

"In the meantime, I'll be providing them another surprise," Kevin said.

Toby wasn't sure what he meant. "Sorry?" he asked.

"To keep them on the back-foot, to show them we are serious, I want to give them something to think about."

"Such as…?"

"You'll see, Toby," Kevin replied.

"I'm not sure I'm happy with this," Toby said. "We can't operate in bad faith. If we hold a gun to their heads, it could come back to haunt us. We need to be seen to be genuine."

"Ah, but we are, it's just that I want to remind them that not only are we serious but also that we are in the right."

Toby was beginning to think that it was the alcohol talking but when he looked into Kevin's eyes he could see how serious he was. It unnerved him a little. He already knew that things had gone much further than he wanted them to when he had started the process. Now it looked like it was going way beyond his comfort zone. He decided not to respond to Kevin's comments.

# CHAPTER 38

"So you are still serious about getting a horse?" Cannon asked

"Yes, of course, Mike," Formrobe replied. "What happened with *Centaur* was a big disappointment, but it hasn't changed my desire."

It was Saturday afternoon, Cannon was waiting for the BHA to be notified about where and when the ALA would meet with him. Formrobe had contacted him and asked if they could have another look at what may be available for Formrobe to buy.

"Is the money burning a hole in your pocket?" Cannon had said when Formrobe had contacted him early Friday afternoon.

He hadn't expected a reply but Formrobe was open, willing to share his thoughts with Cannon.

"You could say that Mike. I think the whole *Centaur* issue made me want to get involved even more."

"Despite the recent attacks?" Cannon had said.

"Yes, despite all that. I think the industry needs all the support it can get. Whatever I can do, no matter how much, I hope will be useful. I'm not very altruistic nor much of a philanthropist, I'm a businessman, but for some reason what happened to those jockeys and horses has set off something inside me that wants to help."

"That's very noble, James," Cannon replied, "but as a businessman, you'll know that sometimes you don't get any return for your investment. Be it time, money, or your own labour."

"I understand, Mike."

Cannon nodded.

Seated in Cannon's office, looking at the computer screen, tea and biscuits provided by Michelle on the desk, the two men looked through several websites offering horses for sale that were *ready to run*. The season start was only a short time away, *subject* to resolution of the ALA matter. Cannon had not mentioned his involvement to Formrobe but did advise him that until the matter was resolved, it was unlikely that racing would start again soon.

Formrobe indicated that he was aware of the issue and the implications, however, he insisted that they continue the search.

After an hour they had compiled a list of four horses that they felt could be of interest. Being led by Cannon, Formrobe accepted the rationale behind each of the four. Age, sex, races run, wins, previous trainers…and potential, were the key criteria Cannon had indicated were necessary to consider. Formrobe was surprised that the horses' breeding was less of an issue to Cannon.

"Doesn't it play a part in a horse's potential success? he asked.

"To some degree, yes," Cannon replied, "but it's not like flat racing, where there is much more money to be made through the stud barn. National Hunt racing is all about courage. A horse can be quick when running on flat ground but lack the guts to leave it," he said. "So we need to know if the horse that you get has the will to win by jumping over hurdles or the bigger fences, or whether it is really just a show pony."

"Sounds a bit harsh Mike, a show pony!"

"Well, it's true, sadly. Some horses look the part but never deliver. What we need to find is a horse that has a heart, a great constitution, and a will to be first past the post. And all for less than one hundred k."

"It could be more," Formrobe replied with a smile.

"Don't let Jacobsen hear you say that" Cannon responded.

The two men laughed. Cannon was enjoying the company. They continued to review the various sites. After a further ten minutes of looking, they had still not found anything else of interest but as they continued their search, Cannon's phone rang. It was Porter.

"They've been in touch," he said without introduction.

# CHAPTER 39

Dockly called Cannon later in the day. Porter had been in touch and had filled him in on what Cannon had been asked to do. Dockly wasn't happy, he felt that he was being used. He was angry and he let Cannon know in no uncertain terms.

"I don't care how much Porter believes in you," he said, "until we have concluded our investigation, I have you in the frame," he said.

Cannon didn't want to embarrass Dockly any further, acknowledging where Dockly was coming from but re-emphasizing his innocence.

"I know it may be hard to accept," he said into his phone, "but I can assure you that I had nothing to do with Bronton's or the Pools' murders."

"So, you keep telling me."

Cannon kept quiet, not wanting to respond any further, antagonizing Dockly would be counter-productive. He wondered if Tolman had made any progress? Eventually, Dockly said, "I've been approached by a journalist from the RP, the Racing Post, about the murders. Do you know anything about it?" he asked.

"Should I?"

"Don't get smart with me, Mr. Cannon," Dockly replied. "If I find out you have been sharing information pertinent to the case with a journalist in an attempt to disrupt my investigation, I'll come down on you like a ton of bricks."

"That's very reassuring, Inspector," Cannon said sarcastically, 'but I have no idea what you are talking about."

Dockly grunted back down the line. Cannon saw a gap.

"Tell me, Inspector, how are you going looking for Peter Todd?"

"Ahh, the disappearing horsebox driver?"

"Yes,"

"You'll be pleased to know, Mr. Cannon that the answer to your question is *nowhere*! We don't think he exists. We ...."

"Of course he exists," Cannon interrupted, "he was the one who brought the wrong horse. Rich saw him too."

Dockly chuckled. "And coincidentally on the day he did, your CCTV had stopped working!"

"Yes, coincidentally."

"Well until we find him, or he ends up dead somewhere, as far as I am concerned, he doesn't exist, never has done."

Cannon wasn't impressed. He had known lots of policemen during his time in the Force. He felt that Dockly wasn't one of the better ones. He thought him lazy, someone who would likely take the easy route to any investigation. He had more faith in Tolman.

# CHAPTER 40

It had been necessary for them to work through the night to recover from another attack. To put things back to normal, checking to see if anything had been lost. The attack on *SecureTwo* was the most sophisticated so far. Formrobe had received a call from Barry Sincaid, just before ten pm.

"We've been attacked again," Sincaid had said as soon as Formrobe answered his phone. Sitting in his flat, an empty cup of coffee lying on a small side-table next to the couch, he had just finished a strong expresso and was about to get another. He had been looking at the previous attack details on his laptop, having downloaded the code while he was in the office, and was about to start a program the team had just written to try and decrypt the hack that they had found.

*SecureTwo* had some of the best software developers and engineers in the country, especially in relation to IT security. It was what they did, and they did it well. It was for that reason that Formrobe found the attacks on his business so compelling.

What had happened to date almost seemed like a precursor to something else, but what was it? He and his team had looked at the data since the initial threat had raised its head. The messages and data within them implied that the following attacks would be more thorough and that the business would be brought to its knees. The question needing to be answered though, was who was behind it, and why?

Why would anyone want to destroy the business? Did someone, a competitor perhaps see *SecureTwo* as a threat to themselves and wanted to bring them down first? To Formrobe it didn't make sense. He had his suspicions and he needed to follow them up. The problem was that he had no proof, though he *had* detected something. He knew that he had more IT firepower inside the business than the police would have, and as far as he was concerned, they would persevere with the various steps needed to try and uncover who was behind the attacks. They would continue to address the issue without external police influence. He was contemplating the next steps when the call from Sincaid had come through.

"What's happened?" Formrobe said, standing bolt upright almost dropping his laptop to the floor as he did so.

"A huge DoS, *Denial of Service,* attack on our communications platform,"

"What!" replied Formrobe, knowing full well the implication.

"Yes, a mass spamming of our systems. Whoever is behind this, they know what they are doing."

"Have you been able to find out where it's coming from?"

"Not yet," Sincaid said, "but it is inside the UK."

"Shit."

"You can say that again," the Team Leader said. "I'll need to get some of the boys in now to work through the night using our *recovery* processes, to make sure our clients are not impacted."

"And what about data loss?"

"We can't see any as yet, but we need to investigate further."

"Do you need me to come into the office?" Formrobe asked, "I can be there in twenty minutes."

Sincaid knew that his boss was relying on him and the team. "James, don't worry. If I need you, I'll give you a call. Leave it with me, I'm sure we can get through this."

"Okay Barry, but it's getting serious now. We need to find out who is behind this, it's no joke. The business could be put at risk and the implications are very serious. I'm going have to let Jacobsen know what's going on as well."

Formrobe terminated the call.

--------------------

"How did you go?" he asked.

They were sitting in the boardroom of *SecureTwo,* Jacobsen alongside Formrobe. On the other side of the table were Wendy Richards and Sincaid, with Judy Smerdon and Tom Birtles sitting in on the meeting via teleconference, their images projected on a screen.

Barry Sincaid looked around the table before answering.

"We think we're okay," he said, answering Formrobe's question, "though we are doing a check on our meta-data DB and also verifying the integrity of the clients' DBs ."

"Because?" asked Jacobsen.

"Just to make sure that nothing was changed, amended, or extracted."

"And what if it was?" Judy Smerdon said.

"Well it could cause us some significant problems, especially those of our clients," answered Formrobe. "The first issue is their data, the second is access to it. If the clients' information has been compromised, then we are in a whole world of pain."

"That's right," interrupted Sincaid, "attacking our systems, bringing down hardware and software is not the real issue. It's data. Data access and abuse. If anyone was able to penetrate our systems, we would be dead meat."

"And did they?" Birtles enquired over the phone.

Sincaid, looked at the screen, at Birtles image.

"No," he said finally.

"Thank God," Jacobsen stated, relief in his voice.

"I won't go into all the technical details, but the tactics the hacker or hackers used were very clever. A DoS attack, followed by a sophisticated piece of software, almost like the old worm-ware, to try and get through our 'walls. Smart!"

"But they failed?" Birtles asked again.

"Yes, but they could try again."

Jacobsen turned to Formrobe. "We need to get the police in James, as soon as we can. This could cost the company its future if we are not careful."

The others echoed the lawyer's view.

"No," Formrobe said. "Not yet."

"Sorry?" said Birtles. "Why would we not get them involved? This is serious James. I must insist on behalf of...."

"No!" Formrobe repeated, interrupting Birtles' flow, "there is something that I need to investigate first."

"What do mean?" Jacobsen asked.

Formrobe turned to Sincaid. "Barry, did we get any warning before the attack took place? Anything at all?"

"You mean like a threatening email or something similar?"

"Yes."

"Not that I can recall, but I can ask the team, specifically Paul Alblom. He will know if anyone does. At the start of the attack, I was so concerned with the error warnings in connection with the comms that I didn't even ask about anything else."

"That's okay," Formrobe replied, "If you can check with Paul asap and let me know, that would be very useful."

The rest of the room was quiet, not sure what Formrobe was thinking. Sincaid excused himself and left the room to follow up with Alblom.

"It seems like we have dodged a bullet on this one," he said, "fortunately we've been able to fend off whoever is behind this."

"For now," Birtles said, feeling very uncomfortable.

"Yes, for now, Tom," he replied firmly. Jacobsen noticed how Birtles responded to Formrobe's put down. He looked at the other board members' faces as well. They were all decidedly unhappy.

"I've been thinking about the previous attacks," Formrobe said, a milder tone to his voice. He was trying to placate the room. "There is something about the messages. They were sent before the attacks but this time, it seems there wasn't any advance warning."

"Would you expect any? If someone is trying to ruin your business?" Smerdon asked.

"No, I wouldn't."

"So, what's so interesting about this latest attack then?" she asked. "Maybe it was a ploy? From what you've told us it seems like whoever is behind it is getting closer to breaking into the...the....D-bases. Isn't that right?"

"Yes it is," he responded, "but that's the issue."

"What is?" Smerdon asked, she was confused.

"The fact that we *were* given advance warning. It tells me something…"

Before any further questions could be asked, Sincaid re-entered the room.

"There *was* another message," he said, passing Formrobe a printed page.

# CHAPTER 41

He was sitting in his office, the darkness outside allowing him to see his reflection in the window. The patchy rain had stopped, leaving small fingers on the windowpane. He watched as little lines of water ran from the top to the bottom of the pane, each starting slowly as the building was caressed occasionally by a gentle breeze. He had a lot on his mind. His stable, his *false* arrest, Tolman, the meeting with the ALA. Also, Formrobe was wanting Cannon to find him another horse, fortunately, he knew that his client was happy to wait. He had his own problems to deal with.

Cannon had the weight of the world on his shoulders, and he was beginning to feel guilty. Particularly guilty about his relationship with Michelle. He needed her now more than ever, but he was finding himself being dragged away from her due to what was going on around him. Somehow he had allowed it to happen. He needed to find a solution. He knew that they needed more time together, as when they were, it was special. He didn't want to take her for granted and he didn't want to lose her.

And now there was Cassie. He hadn't spoken with his daughter for a couple of months, He had planned to phone her once he had agreed with Jacobsen that the lawyer would act as her mentor, but he had forgotten. He decided that despite it being late he would give her a call.

The mobile continued to ring for a good twenty seconds but wasn't answered. He was using a headset so that he could continue working on the plans he had for his runners once the suspension of racing was over. He looked at his smartphone, waiting for it to be answered. He heard a voice. It was Cassie. Voice mail. He felt guilty, so he left her a long message with Jacobsen's details and suggesting that she call the lawyer when she could. He talked until a notice came on the line saying that the limit had been reached regarding message recording and he could send the message if he wanted to or he could delete it. He sent it. Less than a couple of minutes later an SMS message came through on his phone.

*Can't talk. Out for the evening.*

*Will call soon*

*Love Cassie xxxxx*

He could imagine what she was up to. He sighed. She had her own life to lead now. She was her own woman. He knew he had to let her go completely, but she was still his daughter and like all fathers, he wasn't sure how. He didn't want to contemplate it, so he got up from his chair and walked to the dining room where Michelle was busy creating test papers for her various school classes. He walked up behind her and kissed her head, a habit that she enjoyed.

"Tea?" he asked.

"Yes please," she answered, stretching her arms skywards and arching her back. "I think I've done enough for tonight."

Cannon stood immobile for a second. Michelle was his life now, their bond solid. He looked at her as she began collating the papers into a single pile on the table. She didn't notice how she made him smile.

He held the picture of her in his mind, like a photograph. Then without warning, he began to think about the coming days, when all thoughts of domesticity would be put on hold. The meeting with the ALA would be his main focus. It was funny how his past was coming back to taunt him. It was as if it could never let go. He was no longer a Constable, a Detective, a DI, or DCI, he was a horse trainer yet somehow death was never far away from him. The death of a horse, the deaths of jockeys, and even the deaths of people he didn't know, Bronton and Pool. Death had a way of revealing itself, slowly, slyly. Death often revealed itself by stealth. He needed Death to stay away.

# CHAPTER 42

They had shared their stories. It was as if they needed to. A friendship, something beyond owner and trainer, had developed. Formrobe had let Cannon know about the attacks, the messages, and his view about them, his suspicions. In return, Cannon had partially shared with Formrobe the request of Porter to help with the industry shutdown.

The entire issue was now news across the country. It was reported on in the TV, press, and social media. Speculation about what was happening was rife, however nobody seemed to have an answer. The BHA had issued the necessary press releases about *'ongoing investigations'* and the involvement of the *'Police and other Authorities'* but there was a blackout with regards to any further comments. Cannon's role acting as an intermediary was ignored.

Cannon used Formrobe as a sounding board. While still young, the latter had built a business based around security, and Cannon believed sharing some aspects of his own thinking was justified. In sharing what they did, the two men found that it provided them a way of clarifying their thoughts.

They were standing together outside Cannon's house, a cool breeze was blowing from the west, but the sun was shining, casting shadows of the horses as they walked around some twenty yards away. They were cooling down after their exertions. The second lot of the day.

Rich stood in the middle of the eight horses, watching each as the circle continued in an almost endless loop. He called to each of the riders in turn, asking how they felt their mounts had gone. If their training regime had shown up anything such as an uncomfortable gait, or the horse not stretching out as it ran or jumped. The responses were soft, barely audible at times. The riders were respecting their mounts. There was no need to shout. Rich and Cannon liked things to be kept calm.

"Let's walk over," Cannon said, taking a stride towards where Rich continued to chat with the group.

Steam was rising from the animals' bodies, a sight that Cannon had imprinted on his mind. He enjoyed every aspect of the game but there were certain things he loved more, like seeing horses enjoy their work, be it at training or on the racecourse. These magnificent animals gave him so much pleasure and they gave so much more to millions of others. Throughout the world, thoroughbreds were revered, looked after, pampered. Yes, there were those that mistreated some in their care, but they were the minority. Still, you found them in all societies, just like many who mistreated human beings. It was sad, unnecessary. However, it wasn't right for anyone to try and stop the world from continuing. To stop an entire industry wasn't justified at all. Even the coronavirus, covid-19, couldn't stop the industry forever. So, the ALA, no matter how passionate, needed to understand this,

Cannon thought as he and Formrobe stopped a few metres from the horses encircling Telside.

"That's a lovely looking horse," Formrobe said, pointing at *The Politician*. "Look at the way he holds his head. He looks almost *regal* as if he knows he's good."

Smiling, Cannon responded. "To be honest James, the horse *does* know that he is good. Remember they are herd animals, and they know which is a leader and which isn't. It's the reason why we train them together. They are sociable but they also have a hierarchy and as trainers and owners we should respect that. We hope to run him in the Tingle Creek at Sandown later in the year, but we need to give him a couple of races before then."

"That's quite a philosophical view, Mike. One of respect, understanding the social structure."

"Agreed, but it's one I subscribe to."

"Is he for sale?" asked Formrobe.

"Who?"

"*The Politician*," Formrobe replied. "I'd like to buy him."

Cannon was taken slightly aback. The two men had compiled a list of four potential horses when they had sat together just a day or so ago. They hadn't even considered what was in Cannon's stables.

"I'm not sure if the current owner will sell," Cannon replied, "the horse looks to have a reasonable career ahead of him, certainly over the next couple of seasons, if he stays sound, and I'm sure the owner is looking forward to racing him soon."

"If racing goes ahead,"

"I'm sure it will," replied Cannon remembering his meeting with the ALA would be happening shortly. Inside his mind, he was quietly confident of the future of racing, but he knew that there were a few gates to get through before things could revert to normal. He hoped his positivity wasn't misplaced.

"Can you ask?" Formrobe's question found its way into Cannon's thoughts, bringing him back to the present.

"Sorry?" he asked.

"Can you ask," repeated his client, "whether the horse is for sale?"

Cannon contemplated the request, thinking of the current owner. "Yes, of course, I will ask him if you'd like."

"I'd like," Formrobe stated. "He looks a lovely horse," he continued, pointing towards the animal as it walked in front of them.

Suddenly Rich called out to the group, making Formrobe jump.

"Okay everyone, that's it. Time for *stables*," he called.

Within seconds the circle disintegrated as the horses were turned around haphazardly, the jockeys dismounting then leading their charges away to the stables by the rein. The routine of washing, grooming, then bedding down the horses for the rest of the day was to come.

Cannon and Formrobe turned away, walking back towards the house, the sounds of the horses' hooves on stone slowly receding as the two men continued to talk.

"Does that mean you are no longer interested in the others we've shortlisted?" asked Cannon continuing the conversation.

"Not at all Mike. If anything, seeing *The Politician* has increased my desire to buy a horse."

"Okay," Cannon responded, looking at Formrobe quizzically. He was unsure if the man's disappointment about *Centaur* was driving his desire to buy *The Politician* or if it was something else. "But let's be clear," he continued, "if it's a no sale, then you still want to go ahead looking at the other four?"

"Yes, of course," he replied, "but it it *is* for sale, then I still may want to see the others as well."

"Money still burning that hole?" Cannon asked cheekily.

"I guess so Mike, but after everything I've worked for over the past few years, having someone trying to destroy it has made me realize that there are other things in life other than just work. Things that I'm missing out on, things that I've always wanted to do, like own a racehorse."

Cannon remembered the first time that he met Formrobe, how passionate he was about *RedRum,* and his desire to buy a horse ever since something about the 1973 Grand National sparked a desire within him. The confession now, however, was quite unexpected, especially from such a young man.

"But you're still so young James," Cannon said, "you've got all the time in the world."

"Maybe," he replied, "but I guess it's not about the money Mike. I've got enough of that, I'm pretty well off now. It's about… *living.*"

Cannon looked Formrobe in the eye. He understood what he meant.

It *was* about living. Cannon had changed from a Policeman, a Detective, to where he was now, and he couldn't be happier. He let Formrobe continue.

"All my life, I've been developing my skills, building my career, building a business, but not looking after myself…it's my time now," he said, "time to enjoy myself."

"Through the purchase of a horse?"

"Maybe more than one!"

They had reached the front door of the house now, Formrobe's car was just a few metres away, parked at an angle, an Audi S7. He leaned against it for a second, then pushed himself away and held out his hand.

"Thanks for your time Mike, I'd better be on my way."

"No worries," Cannon replied. "I've enjoyed it. Are you off to the office now?"

"Unfortunately, yes, the team needs me. As we discussed before, I have an idea who is behind the attacks but I'm not sure why. I just have my suspicions."

Cannon wished him well. "I'll follow up about *The Politician* for you and let you know as soon as I can"

The men shook hands a second time and Formrobe climbed into his car. Cannon watched as Formrobe drove through the yard gates, the car's engine making a low rumble as it did so. The car turned right onto the road and headed towards Woodstock.

Cannon went into the house and headed for his office. He decided to call *The Politician's* owner straight away.

# CHAPTER 43

Tolman was making enquiries. He knew a lot of people in the area, contacts he had made over the years, from stories he had worked on. Many from his time as a racing journalist, but some, those still alive, who he had known from his time working on the red mastheads, the Sun and the Daily Mirror. He knew the police wouldn't be happy, so he was careful with his questions. He didn't want his contacts to start speculating and for them to start a rumour. If they did, the story may come out. He needed to keep it buried for now. He wasn't getting very far but he would persevere, it was his profession. He needed a breakthrough. He would keep trying, pushing, probing. He needed to find Peter Todd.

------------------------------

The attacks on *SecureTwo* had gone well. The necessary messages had been sent. The attacker considered the next steps.

------------------------------

Judy Smerdon lay on the bed. She was fully clothed.

The expensive chintz curtains of her bedroom were closed. A sliver of light from the dull day outside slid through the tiny crack between the two edges which didn't quite meet. She had her eyes open, but they were sightless. Her tongue, now black and raw lolled to one side of her mouth. Her nose, lips, chin, and ears were also swollen. The empty kettle that had been used to boil the water which was then poured directly into her mouth as she had struggled to escape from the ties binding her legs and arms, was on the bedroom floor. A bright pink and grey silk scarf, one of her favourites, had been used to complete the killing. Wrapped around her neck as she suffered the pain from the boiling water, it had been tightened progressively until her airways were crushed and she was asphyxiated. Flies now buzzed around her open mouth, landing on her forehead, crawling towards her nose. She had been dead for less than a day, it would be another few more before her body would be found.

# CHAPTER 44

They were very clever.

They had agreed to the meeting with Cannon after discussions they had had with Porter. It was to be held at a 15th Century country pub, the *White Hart of Wytham* just off the A34 not far from the small village church. He was surprised that they would choose something so upmarket but was quick to understand why. Firstly, it was quite remote. Secondly, it had an outside garden that could be used to hide someone if they wanted to, and thirdly it was on a day guaranteed to be quiet. A day where the pub with lots of nooks and crannies would ensure people could have private conversations and not be seen or heard by others.

Arriving ten minutes before the agreed time, Cannon walked into the building and asked for the table number that the ALA had given Porter. He had no idea who he was going to meet or how any contact would be made. The details provided to Porter had been vague. Cannon and Porter had agreed that the police should stay away from the pub. They would remain about a mile away on Godstow Road where they would set up roadblocks. The road was the only one that ran in a north-south direction from the pub towards the A34. They suspected that this would be the likely escape route to be taken by the ALA members, they could not see any other option.

The police would have everything in place within thirty minutes of Cannon entering the pub. They believed they needed this time to do a scan of the road to make sure no one was watching them, ready to alert the ALA of their presence. During their planning for the meeting, Cannon had advised Porter that he refused to wear any form of police communications device as he knew that they would likely check him for one. He hoped therefore that the police would be ready when the ALA tried to make their getaway. He didn't tell Michelle or Porter that he wouldn't be taking his mobile phone into the pub either. Being practical had some downsides, but he knew that it would likely be taken off him and he didn't want to lose it.

He was shown the table, which was a table for six, a bench on either side would seat three people each. One end of the table sat against a dividing wall, a stained-glass window with a motif of Saint George and the Dragon built into it. He had been seated for less than thirty seconds when three young women each wearing baseball caps walked from the ladies' toilets and as they passed his table they suddenly dropped into the seats, two on his side and the other sitting opposite him. Immediately they each put on a pair of large dark sunglasses hiding their eyes and most of their faces. The two on his side of the table pushed him towards the wall.

"If you say anything I'll scream," the girl next to him said, "*Paedo* is such an easy adjective to use don't you think?" He stayed quiet, taking everything in that he could. He felt a hand run under his jacket and then inside his pockets. The woman next to him was searching for a *wire* or transmitting device. She looked at the woman on the opposite side of the table, then shook her head almost imperceptibly.

They had been clever, but he tried to use the limited time he had to take in all he could. He noticed little things about each of them as they placed chiffon scarves around their necks to add to the subterfuge and hide most of the bottom of their faces. He looked at them in turn, trying to assess each. While they could hide their faces, they could not hide their height or their physical size. He estimated that they were all in their early twenties and he knew that he would be able to physically extricate himself from them if he wanted to, but at what cost? He waited, staying silent.

The woman opposite had long black hair under her cap. It fell below her shoulders. Cannon tried to assess if it was a wig or not. He concluded that it wasn't. He thought that she looked too thin for her height, somewhat emaciated, but of the three of them, he guessed that she had taken up the mantle of leadership.

"My name is T," she said, speaking through the thin material in front of her mouth and pulling out a mobile phone from a pocket of her jeans, placing it on the table.

Cannon tried to make light of the situation, "Hello T, I'm Mike. Quite a performance," he went on, indicating the disguises they had adopted. "A little over the top for inside, don't you think?" They ignored his banter. He held out his hand in a mock gesture for her to take but she didn't rise to the gibe. "And who may these ladies be?" he asked nodding towards the two women hemming him in.

Like T, they also ignored him.

"I want you to listen carefully," she said. "We represent the Animal Liberation Army, the ALA. You are about to get a set of demands from us. They will be relayed to you through this phone," she continued, pointing at the device still sitting on the table. "You will *not* get anything from us in writing, so you will need to listen carefully. Also," she went on, "in the cubicle behind you there are two men who are with us and they will act as our eyes once we have finished here. Should you try to follow us they have been told to stop you in any way possible. Do you understand?"

Cannon nodded, he could hear the men's voices. "I understand," he said. He looked at the girl who was pushed up against him, then he looked at the others. They all appeared similar, perhaps it was age and the fashion, however, what he could retain, he did. What he could see concerning their ears and hands, their voices, was imprinted on his mind. His police training and his experience within the Force was still useful. Whether the detail he was collating would prove valuable, time would tell.

*T* took out an earpiece from a small handbag she was carrying and passed it across the table. A blue light flashed repeatedly on the side of it. She nodded and then she and the other women took similar devices from their own pockets and each put it onto one of their ears. Bluetooth connections Cannon surmised. T then took the mobile phone and began dialling the number. As she pressed each button Cannon could hear the individual *beep*. Eventually, she stopped and the phone began to ring. It was answered within seconds.

"We have him here," T said.

"Good," replied the voice, "very good. Can you all hear me?"

"Yes," the women said in unison.

T nodded towards Cannon, a gesture for him to confirm that he likewise could hear the person on the other end of the line. "Yes," he relayed, to the unknown person. He noted it was a man's voice.

"Okay Mr. Cannon, before I begin," the voice said, "just so you understand how serious we are, we agreed to this meeting knowing who we are meeting with. We know who you are, we know you're background and we know where you live and everything about your family."

Cannon had been in similar situations before during his time in the Force. Criminals often tried to use threats against a family member and pretend that they knew more than they did in order to get him to do what they asked. Most times it was a ruse. Given what he had seen to date, he believed that it was the same now. He didn't take the threats lightly, but based on what he knew of the ALA from Porter, and his own assessment of them, they were all about Animal Rights, not about killing people. He was aware that his view could be wrong, but he doubted it. The deaths of the horses and jockeys at Uttoxeter he believed were an aberration. A contradiction. Something had gone wrong. It seemed illogical that such a group would want horses to be killed, as was the case there.

He played along with the narrative. "Leave my family out of this," he said. "they have nothing to do with why I am here."

Without any consideration to what Cannon had said, the voice at the end of the phone cut him off saying,

"We have three demands. Meet these in full otherwise jumps racing tracks conducting National Hunt, Point-to-Point and any other kind of jumps racing activity across the country will continue to be firebombed until they are met," the voice said. "One, the BHA to issue a notice to every owner and trainer that all jumps racing will cease permanently. Such notice to be issued and confirmed on the BHA website within seven days. Two, that all horses in every stable in England, Scotland, and elsewhere being trained for racing over jumps, steeplechases, or hurdles, be released immediately from such hardship and allowed to live the rest of their lives in paddocks where they can be looked after properly. Three, any racecourse solely used for jumps racing to be closed down within thirty days, and the land is to be used for the development of social housing. That is housing for the poor and the disadvantaged, not housing for private consumption."

The line went quiet. Cannon noticed the women all facing him. He couldn't see their facial expressions, but their body language indicated that they were excited about what they had heard.

"Am I supposed to respond to these demands?" he asked.

"No," the voice from the mobile, "just remember and relay them."

"You know it won't happen don't you?" Cannon said, trying to extend the conversation, hear more. Listening for background noise, anything that could be used later, "the industry is too big, you can't stop it, you know." He was trying to antagonize the man. He was hoping that he could buy time, that Porter and his team would be in place by now. He wasn't so sure, the whole meeting with the ALA had been over in less than five minutes. Way too quick for the police to be in place.

There was silence on the end of the line, then a click. The phone had been disconnected.

The woman on Cannon's side of the table furthest from the wall stood up and began walking towards a back exit. Once away from where the rest were sitting, her back to them, she lowered the scarf from her face and walked out of the building.

"Stay where you are Mr. Cannon," T said, picking up the phone from the table. She nodded towards the other woman, who immediately stood and left the table. She likewise walked away but headed in the direction of the front door of the pub, removing her cap and scarf as she exited.

T shuffled towards the edge of her seat. "Goodbye," she said sarcastically, walking away from the table. Cannon felt helpless. He listened for the voices of the men behind him, but it was quiet. He tried to hear if they were still there. He was concerned that if he turned around, they would see him do so. It was now thirty seconds since T had left the table. He decided to chance a look. There was nobody there. He jumped up from the table as quickly as he could. He needed to make a decision. The back or the front? He decided to go to the front door, it was where T and one of the other women went. He ran as quickly as he could, as he did so a man came through the door, they bumped into each other, the man's shoulder cracking into Cannon, knocking him to the ground. "Sorry mate," the man said, "are you okay?"

Cannon picked himself up and rubbed a hand across his chest. "Yes, I'm fine," he replied, looking into the man's face then looking anxiously towards the front door. He noticed a couple of motorbikes ride off in the direction of a back road, towards the B4044 - Oxford Road.

"Are you alright yourself?" Cannon asked the man, resigned to the fact that the women had got away.

"Yes, I'm alright. Should have been more careful though. At least we didn't spill anything," the man answered.

"That's true," Cannon said, "I guess we both should be a bit more wary next time."

"No worries then," the man said, moving to Cannon's left then walking past him and heading towards the men's toilets. Cannon watched him go, the man's dreadlocks swinging half-way down the man's back, as he walked away.

# CHAPTER 45

Under the cover of darkness, the figure bent double, and crouching, ran across the track to the hurdle. Taking out the liquid from a rucksack that he carried, he poured half of the contents onto the obstacle. Once satisfied, the figure placed the device into the body of the hurdle, then moved up the track towards the steeplechase fence. Repeating the process, the figure had completed his objective much more speedily than expected. The figure drew himself up to full height. Dressed in black, shiny droplets of rain sparkled on his jacket and jeans. It was very quiet, the silence deep. There was no moon and no one around. Even the night sky was quiet. There was an absence of birds and bats. Away to the right, at least six to seven hundred metres away, the small Grandstand stood like a large square animal, silhouetted against the sky. They had chosen wisely. For the second time, the Southwell racecourse was the target. This time two fences were burnt to ash and twisted plastic.

The ALA were serious in their demands. This was the evidence that the figure hoped the BHA would be taking seriously.

# CHAPTER 46

"Fuck it!" Toby said, "Fuck! Fuck! Fuck!!"

"I didn't think," the woman stated, "I just needed to get out of there!"

They were concerned about the Bluetooth headset. She had forgotten to take it back from Cannon before she had left. It had been Tracey's responsibility.

She was sitting along with Toby and Kevin in Kevin's flat at the college. The other girls had left after a few beers.

They had conducted the entire meeting with Cannon with military precision and they had celebrated.

Five minutes was all that they had needed. They had all made an easy getaway. When they had left the pub, it was easy to get back to Oxford. They had done their reconnaissance well. They had guessed correctly where the police were likely planning to set up roadblocks, so they had ridden across fields adjacent to Godstow Road then along the bank of the Thames where the fields dropped into a series of river bank tracks. After about a quarter of a mile, they then left through another field, bypassing any other police roadblock that may have been in place. While the girls were busy with Cannon, Kevin had driven along Godstow Road and had seen the police setting things up. He had arrived at the pub, waited outside, and let the girls know which direction to go when they came out. Each had jumped on their respective motorbikes and had ridden off before Cannon had been able to follow any of them. Cannon's car had been parked in front of the building, but Toby's intervention had given the girls time to get away. They now realized that their celebrations could now be premature.

He had asked for the headsets back and it was then that she realized that she had left it on Cannon's ear.

"Fingerprints," Toby said, "or DNA! Who knows what they could get from it."

"But they may not," Tracey pleaded, "he took it from me and handled it himself. If they do find anything on it, it would likely include his DNA, his fingerprints as well as mine," she continued. "Plus, even if they did find anything, I'm not sure if they could match it to me. I don't think I'm on any database. I've never been arrested or had my fingerprints taken that I can recall."

"Never?" he asked.

"Not that I can remember," she said, "....except when I went to the US, last year."

Toby looked towards Kevin. His initial anger was beginning to wane, "With luck, we may be okay, but it's heightened our risk. We need to stay calm now and see what response we get to our demands."

"Well, I hope they realize that we are serious and that my trip to Southwell was a reminder. I hope it wasn't in vain," Kevin replied.

Toby laughed. Relief flooded through Karen.

"I need to be getting back to work," he said, standing up from the floor where he and the others had been sitting. "It's a bit of a drive and it's getting late. I'd best be on my way."

The others nodded. He said his farewells, leaving Kevin and Tracey together. As he walked towards his car, he was thinking that things were beginning to get a little loose. People were starting to get just that tiny bit sloppy. It was this type of behaviour that concerned him. After all, he didn't believe in the *cause*. As he climbed into his car, he decided that he needed to get out as soon as he could. He needed to let the ALA live on without him before they were caught. He had done all that was necessary, all that was asked of him, for the ALA *and* Mitchell. The last time he had spoken with the bookmaker he had taken a risk, pretended that he would give the police details of Mitchell's involvement in the incident at Uttoxeter and elsewhere. He had lied, telling him that he had recordings of their conversations. He had also given Mitchell four weeks to solve his own problems, after that Toby would be free. Time was moving on. There were now just over three weeks left since he gave Mitchell his ultimatum about the issues between them. It should mean that there was enough time to see if the demands made by the ALA would be responded to *or not.*

Kevin asked Tracey about her commitment to the cause. She had replied that she was with Kevin, with Toby, with the others, one-hundred-percent. The two of them continued to talk well into the night, eventually, the issue of the lost headset dissipated, dissolving in their dialogue such that they believed it would not be an issue. "No one can trace it to you," he had said.

At around 1 a.m., Kevin asked her to stay. She did.

# CHAPTER 47

He had come straight back to the stables after the meeting at the *White Hart*. He had called Porter straight away but had only gotten voice mail. Cannon had left a message guessing that Porter was working through what had happened with the roadblocks, knowing that Porter had needed the help of members from the local Force. After the event, he knew that Porter would need to relay back to the commanding officer the results of the operation. The hierarchy would not be pleased about the lack of success and would likely let the Inspector know in no uncertain terms. Despite a thorough search of the area, there had been no sign of the motorbikes. If they had been dumped, Porter and his team had no idea where. There was consensus that the Police had underestimated what was now deemed a genuine threat to the community. The ALA was not yet considered a domestic terrorist group, but they were considered very dangerous.

"I don't know how they did it, but they did," Porter said. He was now on the phone to Cannon, having managed to get back to his own station and had listened to Cannon's earlier message. He would not be able to physically get to Cannon during the rest of the day, so he made the call. "They were bloody clever. Don't you think?"

"Yes, they were," Cannon said, "though not as clever as they perhaps think."

He was in his office, seated on his chair facing the window, pushing it backwards, leaving the front legs of the chair a few centimetres off the floor. He could see his car through the window, parked slightly to the right of his vision, the sun's last rays just catching the back wheel.

His computer was in screensaver mode, displaying various photographs that he had taken over the years. They included images of Cassie, Michelle, himself, various places they had visited locally, in Europe, and Australia. The pictures merged and melted into each other like an easy melody, one photo disappearing in various ways, various patterns, to reveal another picture. Something about them stirred an idea. He looked at the headset, it was in a plastic bag that he had found in the kitchen the moment he had arrived home. He picked up the bag to look at the contents through the clear plastic just as Porter asked, "What do mean, Mike?"

"A couple of reasons actually."

"Oh?"

"Yes."

"What are they?" Porter asked, his voice indicating that he was intrigued.

"Firstly, they left something behind. Something that I hope you can use."

"What is it?"

"A headset. Bluetooth connectivity. I'm assuming there are fingerprints on it. Maybe only partially. It will include mine as well, though."

He explained what had happened in the pub and the rush of the girls to leave, resulting in them forgetting about the headset.

"That could be very useful indeed," Porter said. "And the other one?" he asked.

"It was what one of them said."

"What do you mean?"

"The language she used. It suggested to me that they could be students or academics. It certainly indicated something like that to me."

"What did she say?"

"She used the word *adjective*."

"Adjective?" repeated Porter as if to ask Cannon to verify that he had heard correctly.

"Yes. When they forced me into a corner and sat beside me on the bench at the table, she said, *"Paedo is such an easy adjective to use don't you think?"* That's an odd word to use. Most people would say something much simpler than that."

Having heard what Cannon was referring to, he wasn't so sure if it was likely to be useful in their investigations., but he conceded that the phrase did indicate that the girl who had said it was likely to be educated. "I guess so, but how does it help?"

"Perhaps we need to think outside the box?"

"How so?"

"Well, if you think about where we are, where we are living and the fact that they chose the pub that they did, it means to me that they wouldn't live too far away from here."

"Not necessarily," replied Porter, "surely they could have just looked on the internet and found the place?"

"True, but given the escape route they took suggests that they do know the area. Using motorbikes, but not using the roads in order to avoid your roadblocks would also indicate some local knowledge."

"Umm…"

"Add that to the way the girls spoke, they definitely seemed educated."

"And the closest Academic institution around here…"

"Is…*Oxford*," Cannon interrupted.

"Exactly."

They were bouncing their thoughts off each other, testing each other's propositions.

"If you take into consideration the actual issue, an extremist view of horse racing, where do most *causes* develop?" Cannon asked.

"At Uni, Porter replied, acknowledging that Cannon could be right. "I think the headset may come in handy Mike. If we can get some *prints* or some DNA from it, and we begin our search at the University, then we may just get lucky."

Cannon agreed. "I have tried to limit touching the device. I have it here with me in a bag. Come and collect it as soon as you can," he said.

"I'll send someone around straight away," Porter said. "The sooner we can get it to the lab boys the better."

"Fine with me," Cannon replied.

"I guess you didn't get much of a look at their faces, did you?"

"No, they were too quick, putting on the dark glasses and twisting scarves around their necks. It must have seemed strange to the few people that were there, but they were so quick, the waiters or waitresses didn't even have time to come back to the table after I sat down to take an order before it was all over."

"Perhaps another thing to add to your theory?"

Cannon considered what Porter had said. "Yes," he replied eventually. "It seems to me that not only did they have the opportunity to get me there, but the way they handled it when I was there, was very slick. How they cornered me and used a mobile phone to maintain a vacuum, a physical gap, between the man on the phone, their leader, I guess, and me, was very clever. If you add the fact that each of them was wearing a headset, all *paired* together to be able to hear the conversation, and the motorbike getaway afterwards, it tells me that a lot of thought went into it. I'm more and more convinced that these are people with a *cause, intellect, and money...* Without being prejudicial to anyone, I'd guess most, if not all, are students, and wealthy ones at that. If not, then they could be academics."

"If you add the way they have attacked the various racecourses over the past few weeks, I think you're right. They would need someone who could design and build a device of the sort that exploded at Uttoxeter."

"Who also believes in their cause," Cannon stated. "You don't farm that out to anybody. If you are trying to keep things secret, you would need to have someone close to you who agrees with what you are doing."

The two men continued talking, ultimately convincing each other that they were on the right track. The problem, however, was how to find the parties responsible? They knew that the police needed to be careful. There was always the fear of groups like the ALA splitting up, dissolving for a while, going *underground*.

It was the right time now to share the three demands that the ALA had requested.

"Are they mad?" Porter stated. What was being asked for was ridiculous, in his mind.

"I don't think so," Cannon replied, "if anything I think they are more serious than ever."

"But it's never going to happen, is it?"

"Not in the long-term, no. These ideologues come and go and ultimately life moves on, but while they are around, they can cause all sorts of mayhem, certainly in the short-to-medium-term. Look at where things are at now. There is no racing, everyone is wondering what is going on, and those courses without any punters or meetings are losing more and more money. I'm sure some of them won't survive if this goes on much longer, the ALA will have their wish about courses closing and the land being sold pretty soon, if you ask me."

"Have you spoken with the BHA yet?"

"No, I've drafted them an email so that they have a record of the demands. I had intended to get in touch with them earlier, but I wanted to speak with you first. That's why I left you a message."

"Okay."

"What I'm going to suggest, and I'd like your opinion on, is to meet with them face to face. Ideally the day after tomorrow. If I send them the email later tonight, they'll have the whole of tomorrow to digest it. I'll make some recommendations as well. It will be short and sweet but given we don't have much time we need to act, and act quickly." Cannon suggested.

"That's fine with me, Mike. Once I get that headset we'll start working on whatever we can get from it."

"And what about the mobile they used, I guess that will never turn up?" asked Cannon.

"I doubt it. It's likely to be in pieces by now. Maybe even in the river."

Cannon imagined a hammer being used to smash the device to pieces and the bits scattered in bins or even in the Thames, as Porter suggested.

"You are probably right," he replied.

"Okay Mike, I'd better get on with things. I'll make sure someone gets around to you in the next couple of hours."

"No worries. Oh, just before you go, any word back from Dockly? Do you know how the investigation is going? I don't want him back down here again, if it can be helped."

"To be honest Mike, I don't know. I haven't heard from him, but I wouldn't worry. We had a chat. That's all you need to know."

Cannon knew what that meant in *police speak*. He thanked Porter accordingly but wasn't convinced about Dockly and his methods. He had seen many similar Detectives during his time. They were often lazy, they cut corners and often they ended up causing more pain than reducing it. He decided to give Tolman a call.

# CHAPTER 48

Her's was the second car of the night, the first had been the police who had come to collect the headset to be taken back to Porter. They had departed thirty minutes before she arrived. Cassie drove into the stable driveway, parking her car next to Cannon's. It was just after ten-thirty in the evening when she took out a small suitcase from the boot. It had stopped raining. A short shower just lasting long enough to dirty his car a little more than it already was. She noticed the blue lights of the security cameras attached to the hay barn, the stables, and the main house flash on and off. She waved playfully at one of them, not knowing that the recording device was still not working. Cannon had forgotten to call the supplier to get it repaired.

Her feet crunched on the short crushed-rock stone pathway that led to the front door. She was about to ring the bell when the door flew open.

"Cassie!" Cannon shouted, his arms wide before he hugged his daughter to him. "We saw the car lights shine through the curtains," he said, explaining how he was able to answer the door before she had rung the bell. "Why didn't you call and tell us you were coming?"

"I wanted to surprise you," she replied, "can't a daughter do that to her Dad?"

He laughed and took the suitcase from her, then they both went inside.

"Hi Cassie," Michelle said, before embracing her, "I thought I heard your voice at the door. What a surprise!"

"The exact words I just said to Dad," Cassie replied.

They walked collectively into the lounge, Cannon leaving the suitcase in the hall.

"Let me look at you," he said, holding her steady by the waist as if she was a mannequin. "Somethings different since I last saw you," he continued, looking her up and down. She was wearing jeans, black boots, and a beige jumper under a brown corduroy Sherpa jacket. Standing at around five foot six, she had a slender build and a fair complexion. Her hair was cut in a *bob* style, but one that wasn't severe, it was more soft and tousled and had been lightened slightly since he had last seen her. Michelle had noticed it immediately.

"It's the hair!" he said, laughing. "I knew there was something."

He hugged her again. Despite just the three of them, she felt embarrassed. They went to sit down, Michelle offering to make some tea as they did so. Cassie accepted and Michelle went off into the kitchen, leaving Cannon alone with his daughter. He turned the TV off. They had been watching the 10 pm news. Nothing had been said about the incident at Uttoxeter. It was now old news. The media cycle had moved on.

"So, to what do we owe the pleasure?" he asked.

"That message you left."

He was unsure what he meant until it came back to him.

"Oh," he said.

"Yes. Mr. Jacobsen."

"Did you give him a call?"

"I did," she replied, "though I must admit I was a little wary. Your message was a *little* vague, but I called him anyway, and he told me what you had said."

"About getting some advice from him, maybe him acting as a mentor for you?"

"Yes," she replied. "though I must admit, it was perhaps a bit forward on your part, Dad. After all, we hadn't discussed it in any detail."

"I know," he said apologetically, "I was probably a bit enthusiastic. I'm sorry if that's the case."

"That's okay," she replied. "Anyway, he seems like a nice guy, so I've agreed to meet with him tomorrow. To have a chat and get some perspective about different strands of the law and how they work in practice."

"Well he *was* quite senior apparently in the practice he worked at. As I understand it, I believe he could have been its head if he wanted it."

"Yes, that's what he told me when he spoke. Though…." she hesitated.

"Though?"

"Though… he seemed a little reluctant initially, to act as a mentor," she said, "but he clarified it by saying he'd never been asked before, so he just wanted to let me know that."

"He told me the same thing. I just said that he shouldn't worry. That it was a great favour he would be doing for us. Sorry, for you," he continued, "and he seemed to be happy with that."

They continued speaking for a short while, Michelle joining them with the tea she had made, and a few biscuits. Cannon devoured a disproportionate amount. It was just before midnight before they realised the time and decided that it was time for bed. Cassie went off to her old bedroom. Cannon needed to be up by five am, the first lot of eight horses were due on the heath by six. Cannon needed to check with Rich that he was okay to take training and run the stables while he was away. It wasn't the first time and unlikely to be the last. Cannon had faith in Telside, he never doubted him.

# CHAPTER 49

They had decided to meet at the offices of *SecureTwo*. Before Cassie had arrived the previous evening, Cannon had spoken with Formrobe to give him the good news about the owner of *The Politician* agreeing to sell a half share in the horse. Formrobe had been delighted, so given how his client had reacted, Cannon had taken the chance to recommend another horse that he had found. The horse that he had come across was for sale in the small village of Chilson, at the stables of a local trainer called Walter Finch, just off Pudlicote Lane, about seven miles from Cannon's stables in Stonesfield,. The owner had decided to cash in on his horse called *Happy Gilmour*. He had bought it for five thousand pounds about eighteen months prior. Now it was a five-year-old, a grey gelding. It was from the same family line as the great *Desert Orchid*. The horse had won twice in five outings so far, but Cannon felt that it had a lot of potential. He had watched the two wins on YouTube and noticed the attitude of the horse when it won. The animal seemed to know it was good. While keeping perspective and wanting to see the horse in the flesh, he had a good feeling about it. At thirty thousand pounds he still felt it would be a bargain buy.

Cassie and Cannon entered the *SecureTwo* building, having driven from the farm together. Cassie had suggested that they travel in her car. She had been lucky in being able to afford one. She had worked part-time, doing various jobs during her years at Uni, and had managed to save much of what she had earned. The second-hand Nissan Altima was her first real purchase.

They waited together in the Reception area, each sitting in a red *bucket*-style visitor's chair that surrounded one of two low, white square tables.

Eventually, Formrobe arrived, holding out his hand for Cassie to take after Cannon had introduced them.

"Lovely to meet you," he said.

"Likewise," Cassie replied.

They walked along a short corridor before Formrobe stopped at a solid door. He used a security tag from around his neck, holding it to a reader to open the door. They were in another part of the open-plan office area that Cannon had not seen before. People sat hunched over laptop computers at various desks, in pods with names like *Agile Team, Security One, Service Desk, Level 2, Level 3*. Computer screens dominated everywhere. There was a lot of activity. Formrobe explained at a superficial level what each area did, but most of it was above their heads.

He took them into an empty meeting room, a wall to ceiling glass window next to the door allowed them to see what was going on outside.

"Once Samuel is ready, I'll take you through, Cassie. After that, your dad and I can have a chat."

"I hear you are looking at buying into a horse?" she said.

"Yes that's right, we've been looking to buy something for a little while, but we haven't been able to find anything suitable, until now," he replied looking at Cannon hopefully.

"That's right, until now," repeated Cannon, nodding in agreement. "Though our luck may have just changed," he said, "at least I hope so."

"Me too," Formrobe echoed. He excused himself, 'for a minute' leaving the two of them together.

"A pretty impressive setup," she said.

"Yes, it is. Not bad for a thirty-something is it?"

"Is that how old he is?"

"Yes, and very wealthy he is his, too."

"And not bad looking," she said.

"Hey!" he replied, slightly taken aback. "He's a bit old for you."

"Only by about ten or twelve years," she replied jokingly.

They could see Formrobe coming back towards the room, then opening the door.

"Cassie, if you'd like to follow me?" he asked, "I'll take you through to Jacob's Assistant who can arrange something to drink for you. Apparently, he's going to be a little while longer than expected."

"Okay," she replied, "no problem. Bye Dad, see you later."

"Bye, Cass. Enjoy," he replied.

------------------------

"I think *Happy Gilmour* is going to be a good acquisition," Cannon suggested. "I think at thirty grand he's a bargain."

"Why do you think they want to sell?" Formrobe asked.

"I'm not sure, but it may be just a case of cashing in. I understand they bought him cheaply, they've recovered more than they paid for him and they want to move on."

"And your view, Mike, is that he's a good one?"

"Yes. I've done my research, looked at the races he's run and won in, and I think he'll make a great steeplechaser going forward. He's from a good bloodline and he seems to have all the things we want in a 'chaser, as we discussed previously."

"Sounds good. Maybe we can aim for something long term with him? Like the *National* or the *Gold Cup?*" Wouldn't that be great?" he said enthusiastically.

"Hey," Cannon replied, "let's not get ahead of ourselves. They are great ambitions but even *Desert Orchid* never did the National.*"*

"But he did win the Gold Cup.*"*

"Several times," Cannon concurred, "but in this game, there are no guarantees as I've said before. Plus, we are not even racing currently, so we need to solve that problem first."

Formrobe considered Cannon's comments for a second. "Yes, I understand, but it's still worth investing in the horse?"

Noting an element of doubt, Cannon responded as positively as he could. "Well, we need to be sensible. No matter what, racing *will* start again. It may be in a week, maybe longer, but it will get back to normal. Who knows how it will get resolved? I certainly don't, but I'm sure it will."

"I understand you are helping the BHA and the police?" Formrobe said, somewhat out of the blue. Cannon waited for a second, not sure if he should reply or not. He thought that his involvement was between him, the police, and the racing authorities. Clearly, the ALA knew, but they likewise hopefully would keep his involvement quiet? Eventually, he asked the obvious question.

"I'm not sure how you are getting your information, James? I know you are the head of a security company, but some secrets should be left at that, a secret," he said lightheartedly, trying to deflect where the conversation could go. He did not want to reveal any more than Formobe may already know.

"To answer your question, Mike, it's quite easy. I was talking to Cassie as we went through to Samuel's office and she told me all about it. She said it was good that the police had chosen someone to work with them and the authorities to act as a go-between."

"Did she now," Cannon replied.

"I hope I haven't gotten her into trouble?" Formrobe replied, noticing Cannon's face. The trainer's face was a combination of anger and disappointment.

"To be fair, James, I didn't say to her that she shouldn't discuss it with anyone, so to some degree, it's my fault. I just didn't think she would mention it to anyone that quickly."

"If it's any consolation she didn't go into detail, she just mentioned that you were helping, so she didn't reveal too much."

On hearing this Cannon was relieved. He was satisfied that Cassie hadn't spoken about anything other than at a high level or cursory overview of Cannon's role in the ALA matter. He hadn't mentioned to her the meeting with the ALA or the follow up with Porter. The next few days would be crucial, though. The meeting with the BHA and the police was scheduled for the next day down in London.

"That's okay James, no problem," he replied. "Let's get back to *Happy Gilmour*. If you are still keen, I will try and set up a time in the next few days to go and see him, but in the meantime, I'll contact the trainer, Walter Finch, and give him the news that we are keen to buy so that he can tell his owner."

"You said he was for sale at thirty thousand, do you think we should offer less?"

"I can try, but I think that's the lowest the seller is prepared to go. We can offer two-and-a-half grand less, maybe offer twenty-five, but I doubt they will accept any of the offers. At thirty-k I still think he's a good buy."

"Okay, I trust your judgement Mike, despite what happened with *Centaur*," he said gently and playfully punching Cannon on the shoulder.

"That's still a touchy subject, but it looks like several people were taken in," Cannon replied, ignoring the subtle goading. "We haven't talked about *The Politician* yet," he continued, "you seemed to be happy to buy just a half share, as we discussed previously. Are you still interested?"

"Absolutely," Formrobe replied. "what are the sellers asking for?"

"They want twenty-five thousand."

"Done!" Formrobe replied without hesitation. "I would have offered more, to be honest."

"Well, he is a good prospect. As I've said before, I'd like to aim him at the Tingle Creek at Sandown in December. After that, we'll see where we can take him. The race itself is a Grade 1 over two miles, so a bit short of his best. We will need to get a few races in before then and see if he is ready for such a strong event. If not, we can look at something else."

"Either way, I'm very excited," Formrobe answered. "It's been a bit of a journey, but I hope we get there soon. I can't wait."

It was always good to have a positive relationship with an owner or a potential owner, as in Fomrobe's case. Cannon said, "I'll let the owner know that you are okay with buying into *The Politician*. They are very nice people as well. I'll arrange a meeting for you at some point, ideally before all the paperwork is completed. It would be good for you to meet them, considering you will be partners."

"Who are they?" Formrobe asked.

"Well, the family owns a small butchery near me actually, in Stonesfield. It's been there for almost as long as I can remember. It's been passed down for generations I believe since the late nineteenth century."

"Okay, I look forward to meeting with them,"

"Sounds good," Cannon said. "If we are done here, I guess we can and see how Cassie is getting on?"

"Oh, one other thing," Formrobe said, "Going back a bit to the earlier part of our conversation, I don't like the name *Happy Gilmour*, can we change it?"

"Yes, that can be arranged," Cannon replied. "There is a formal procedure, but yes it can be done."

"Excellent,"

Intrigued, Cannon asked. "Do you have an alternate name?"

"Not just yet, but I'll think of one."

"Let me know as soon as you can so that I can get the paperwork in. Once the ownership is transferred, we can get the name change done quickly."

Formrobe smiled, before saying "Excellent. I'll take you through to Samuel now, I'm sure they will be close to finishing."

Cannon nodded in agreement. The two men stood and walked out into the open-plan office. As they did so, Barry Sincaid stood up from his chair and walked towards them.

"Sorry to bother you James, but I need to talk with you urgently."

"What's it about Barry?" Formrobe replied, looking at Cannon, hoping it wasn't something that Cannon shouldn't hear. It was.

"Another attack."

Formrobe looked at Cannon again.

"We've been having a few issues, which I mentioned to you previously. Things that you would expect from time to time in our business," he said, trying to play it down.

Cannon was sharp enough to notice. The body language between Formrobe and the team leader gave the issue away. There was concern between them.

"Do you know who is behind it?" he asked. "I know nothing about your game, but in my time in the Force, I experienced this type of thing. I know it's been a few years and I guess it's a lot more sophisticated now, but the principles and reasons behind such things are still the same."

"You may be right Mike. I have an idea, but I can't say for sure if I'm right. There are some clues, I think, in what has gone on to date, but I need to do some more work." He turned to Sincaid. "Okay Barry let's meet in my office in five minutes, I'm just taking Mike through to Samuel."

Sincaid nodded and went back to his desk.

Formrobe led the way. At Jacobsen's office, he walked past the assistant, acknowledging her with a subtle nod of his head, and then knocked on the partially open door of the lawyer.

"Can we come in?" he asked.

"Of course," Jacobsen said, raising a hand in a gesture of welcome. Cassie was sitting opposite him, her back to the door. She turned around to see who it was. Noticing her father entering just behind Formrobe, she gave him a huge grin before turning back again to face Jacobsen.

"Well, I'll leave you three together," Formrobe said. "Jacob, we've had another event occur, I'm just going to meet with Barry. I'll come back to you once I know more." With that, he turned and left the room.

"Okay, please sit down, Mr. Cannon, Cassie and I have just finished and I do have another appointment to attend to, but given what James has just said, it may mess up my day a little."

"Yes, he did say there were a few issues that the business was facing."

The lawyer contemplated what Cannon had said. He was unaware of Cannon's involvement with the ALA and the industry bodies, as Cassie had not mentioned it to him during their conversation, but if he was made aware he would have kept it to himself. Likewise, he wanted to ensure that nothing was leaked about this new attack on *SecureTwo* so he ignored Cannon's utterance. They were keeping clients informed as necessary about the services the business supplied, but the attacks themselves he deemed were internal matters.

"We've had a good chat, Cassie and I," he said, deciding that he need say no more about Formrobe's comments. "She's a bright girl and I think she'll go far."

Cassie smiled.

"That's good to hear," Cannon replied, looking with proud eyes at his daughter.

"Mr. Jacobsen has agreed to act as a mentor to me," Cassie said.

"That's great news," Cannon replied. "Thank you," he continued, expressing his delight to Jacobsen.

"No problem at all," the lawyer responded. "I'm happy to help Cassie where I can. Once I knew what was expected of me, then I was more than happy to give it a go."

"Yes," Cassie added. "Mr.Jacobsen has given me an insight into the real world of the law, not just the theoretical. I think I've found what I want to do next."

"And that is?" Cannon asked a little dubiously, knowing his daughter had been focusing on Human Rights Law in the recent past, even having travelled to South Africa along with another student who had invited her to see the environment there.

"Criminal Law," she said. "Not commercial, environmental, or even I.P. Law."

Cannon looked at her quizzically.

"Intellectual Property," Jacobsen said, "Copyright disputes, that type of thing."

Cannon nodded his understanding.

Cassie thanked Jacobsen again.

"It's been a pleasure meeting you Cassie. I'm sure we'll have many conversations in the coming months. I'm looking forward to it."

"Me too," she responded.

"I'd like to thank you again, Mr. Jacobsen," Cannon said, "with you being so close, maybe I'll get to see my daughter here a little more."

"Dad," she replied, "I still need to finish my studies up in York, after that I'll see."

"I did ask Cassie if she intended to do a Doctorate next or go into practice and get some experience while she studied, but it's something she is going to have to think about."

"Well whatever she does, it would be nice if she was closer to us."

"I mentioned to her the program that they have down at Southampton where my son lectures, which may be suitable for her in the next step of her journey."

"Well, it's much closer than York is. About half the distance," Cannon replied.

Cassie not willing to be embarrassed by her father said, "Dad, things can be done remotely nowadays. With Doctorates you just need a mentor inside the Uni who can guide you through the process, help you with your dissertation."

"Like my son," Jacobsen said, taking one of the photographs from his shelf and passing it to Cassie. She looked at it fleetingly before passing it to Cannon. "I'll introduce Cassie later if she would like me to?" Jacobsen continued. Cannon passed the photograph back. He had seen what he wanted to.

Jacobsen's assistant put her head around the still partially opened door.

"Samuel, your next meeting is due now. Just a reminder," she said sweetly.

Cassie and Cannon stood up, shook hands with the lawyer and they thanked him for the third time. It had been a useful meeting for both of them.

# CHAPTER 50

She left for York early the next morning. It was a drive of just over three hours. It suited Cannon, as he needed to catch a train down to London to meet with the BHA. She had dropped him off at Oxford station from where they said their goodbyes. It had still been dark when he watched the tail-lights of the car disappear out of sight, turning out of the railway carpark and on her way back North. He missed her a lot.

During the train journey, he watched the rain come down, showering for a few minutes, then stopping to leave a pale blue sky above. The sun tried its best to offer some warmth but then the rain would start again ten minutes later. As they headed further south towards the capital, the wind in the trees seemed to ease. He hoped that the forecast was right, cold, and blustery but no rain.

Cannon and Porter met in the foyer of the BHA building. They had a few minutes to discuss their approach with the BHA and then they were invited and escorted into the boardroom. Cannon had been here before. Then it was to defend himself against charges of race-fixing, now the very body that he had been charged by was the hopeful recipient of his help. He could see the irony.

They were kept waiting for a few minutes before they were joined by the BHA Chair, Peter De Misgeny, and its CEO Andy Philips. Cannon had met neither, his previous run-in with the BHA had others in the roles now occupied by those he was introduced to by Porter.

"Okay gentleman," De Misgeny said once they were all seated, "let's get down to business, shall we? Tell us what you have learnt and what you are recommending that we should do, Mr. Cannon. We can't keep the industry closed down for much longer, and I am hoping that the police are making progress with their enquiries," he continued, looking at Porter.

"I'm happy to share everything I know," Cannon said, "besides, we have some news about the investigation which I am sure the Inspector here will be able to fill you in on. After that, we can discuss our recommendations."

"Thank you, Mr. Cannon." De Misgeny replied, "but before you do that I'm not sure if you have heard but post your discussion with these people, the ALA, they attacked Southwell again, burning down two fences this time. The management of the course are on the verge of deciding whether to shut the course permanently. The cost of repairs, and no income from betting and other sources is putting them in a precarious position."

"I can imagine," Cannon replied.

"Yes," Andy Philips jumped in. "A few days ago, they also received a letter from a developer to buy the property. It seems like someone knows something about what's going on."

"Well that would seem to tie in with the third demand of the ALA," Cannon said. He went through the three demands the ALA had put on the table.

"Are these people mad?" asked De Misgeny, a point that he had said before, Cannon suspected. "Don't they know it's impossible to meet their demands?"

Turning to Porter, he asked, "Inspector are you making any progress with your investigations?"

"We have had some luck, yes, Mr. De Misgeny. When Mr. Cannon met with the ALA he was able to obtain some vital information that we are following up."

"Are you able to share such information?"

"To be honest Sir, I would prefer not to say, other than it has enabled us to narrow down a search area which is allowing us to focus on a targeted set of the community in the area we are looking at."

"So nothing concrete?" Philips asked cynically.

"I wouldn't say that Mr. Philips. Mr. Cannon here managed to obtain something additional that we are looking at that may provide us some DNA evidence, and which may, I stress *may*, lead us to a specific person. If we can do that, then we have a good chance of finding these people."

Philips and De Misgeny looked at each other, seemingly satisfied with what they had just heard.

"Okay Mr. Cannon," De Misgeny said, "now we know where the investigation is at, and we know the demands requested by the ALA, let's hear what you recommend we do."

Cannon cleared his throat. "Well, my first recommendation is that given there is only a couple of days left before the ALA want to see confirmation of acceptance that racing will be shut down permanently, I think that we should issue a notice to all clubs and owners and trainers, that racing will recommence in ten days from now."

"Goodness," Philips said, "I expected you to say the opposite. Could you tell us why you have taken this view?"

"Certainly. We need to flush these people out. If we sit back and let them dictate the agenda, then who knows what they will do next?" Cannon responded. "We have a police investigation underway, let them do their job and let the racing authorities do theirs. I can help the police as much as possible. We can work together to catch these people, by stealth if need be."

"Okay," the Chairman responded, not exactly sure what Cannon was referring to in his last comment, but letting it go. "And the other demands?"

"Again, we can't be asking all owners to *free* their animals to go off into some field and let them roam in a paddock for the rest of their days. The industry is not just the racehorse, but the owners, the trainers, the work riders, the jockeys, suppliers, the courses themselves, horse transporters, feed suppliers. I could go on forever as you would know already, so my recommendation is that we say nothing in any correspondence with the ALA. We don't say anything on the website either, despite what they may be expecting."

"Won't this provoke them?" De Misgeny asked.

"I guess it will," Cannon replied, "but as I said, we need to flush these people out. With luck, we can be ready for them the next time they attack a course."

"Isn't that a long bow to draw Mr. Cannon? How would you know where to protect or where to focus?"

"Well, I'd like to think that they will try to stop racing at the first opportunity, so if we let the industry know where in ten days or less the next meeting will be held, I think they may focus on that course. If we put police resources into the area, especially after-hours and particularly overnight on the evening before the meeting, then maybe we'll be able to catch them."

"Do you have a preference for where the first meeting should be?"

"Maybe Huntingdon? We can bring forward their season opener by a few weeks and because of where it is situated, it is well suited to having the police flood the area a couple of days in advance of the event, in fact as soon as the announcement is made."

The BHA men contemplated Cannon's proposal, both nodding in agreement with each other before accepting Cannon's proposition.

"If the police are willing to do what you have suggested, then we agree Mr. Cannon."

"Yes, we are," Porter said, "I can confirm that."

"Thank you, Inspector. Please continue Mr. Cannon," De Misgeny requested.

"Finally," Cannon continued, "in relation to the closing down of those courses that conduct jumps racing only, well that's up to each club. I know many of them are struggling with attendance given the racing coverage on TV, on betting apps, and other forms of gambling options nowadays, but I don't think we can advise them one way or the other. It's up to them, but I wouldn't like to see any of them close up shop just because the ALA wants to have developers buy the land for social housing. To me it seems like there is something else behind that request," he said, "Can I have a look at the copy of the letter that was sent to Southwell?"

Philips found the necessary correspondence and passed it to Cannon. He read the letter then saw something that he hadn't expected to see. He made a mental note to follow it up.

"Thank you, Mr. Philips," he said, "that's been very useful." He gave the letter back to the CEO who promptly filed it away.

Over the next hour, the four men discussed the next steps, including the announcement to be put on the BHA website and a request to be made that all clubs were to be asked to insert the same detail on their own sites. Racing would commence again at Huntingdon, ideally in just less than a week. The club would be advised separately by the police of the plans they were working on to keep those attending the meeting safe, as well as what steps the police would like to take in and around the course before the meeting. Porter would coordinate that.

Once the discussions were concluded and everyone was in agreement, Cannon and Porter left the BHA office, deciding to pop into a coffee shop that Porter had passed on his walk from the station to the building in High Holborn.

Over coffee, Cannon and Porter talked about the investigation. Cannon shared with the Inspector what he had noticed on the letter he read from the Developer. "I'll need to look into that a little more," Cannon said. "If I find out anything worthwhile, I'll let you know."

Porter nodded, adding, "Likewise, Mike. I haven't got any news yet about the headset, but I know the lab has managed to get some DNA from it. It appears as if it could be from any of three different people, of which one will be you. They are looking into databases that they and we have to see if they can find a match. It may be a long shot, but you never know."

"I understand," Cannon replied, drinking the last of his coffee. He looked at his watch. "I think it's time to go," he said. "My train is due in about forty minutes."

"Mine's a little later," Porter said, "but happy to walk with you, despite the crappy weather."

The two men left the cafe and made their way to the station, braving the elements, hoping the rain would hold off long enough.

# CHAPTER 51

"They've completely ignored us!" he said, the anger in his voice palpable.
Kevin was on the phone with Toby. He had been the one in the group responsible to read any news that the authorities were to insert onto websites. Before he had the chance to do that, the National news agencies, the BBC, Sky, ITV, and other outlets, had already reported that racing was to begin again at Huntingdon. It was to be a kick-start to the new season, almost ignoring earlier meetings.
"The meeting with Cannon was a complete waste of time," he repeated, "even my attack on Southwell doesn't seem to have bothered them. I'm not sure what else we need to do, Toby? It seems we are not getting through to those bastards."
Toby had also had a look at the BHA website and the links to the other courses' communications. What he noticed was that they only talked about the first demand that the ALA had wanted. They had ignored the second and third demand. Given his own view on things, and his real motivation, he was quite non-plussed about what he had uncovered. Frankly, it was only the third demand that interested him. In his view, *silence meant acquiescence,* and the fact that nothing had been said, meant to him that the BHA was shifting, or at least placing the responsibility of deciding whether the individual courses would continue in business on the individual clubs themselves. He had guessed that the BHA would support them where possible, but would not dictate to them if their viability was untenable. Many courses had closed over the years. One had been opened, Ffos Las, but that was the exception. Some had survived by introducing all-weather tracks, but that was predominantly those with existing flat racing tracks, which was already part of their business model. Very few courses with only jumps circuits were likely to have the money or willingness to introduce similar solutions, the competition for meetings was already fierce. Going further into debt wasn't viable, selling out, closing down, had some merit but National Hunt racing needed to survive, the associated communities needed to survive. It couldn't do so by closing down clubs and courses. Even the recent debate about closing down the Kempton Park course had ultimately failed and that was a course with both Flat and National Hunt events.
Toby would be making one last call to Mitchell after their last conversation and then as far as he was concerned, he was definitely out! He had done all he could now. He had engaged with those who were more radical than he had expected. His engagement with students on campus and his failings had gotten him into trouble. People, jockeys, had died. His career could be destroyed if things came out and he was exposed beyond the few who knew

of his role in the ALA.

"What do you think we should do?" Kevin asked, breaking into Toby's thoughts.

"I think for now we should keep our powder dry, Kev. Hold our fire. The police will be looking for a reaction from us, and we need to be careful. Perhaps go underground for a while?" He was hoping to buy himself some time to get out of the situation as soon as he could. He needed to persuade them that the cause may not be worth them putting themselves, their liberty at risk. Perhaps they needed to find another way to achieve their goals? He knew that if one of the girls or Kevin were arrested, they would readily bring him into it and then he would be finished.

Kevin was livid. It wasn't the reaction that he had expected from their 'leader'. "Are you serious Toby? Do you really want us to give up now?" he asked. "That everything we are fighting for, everything we have done so far is a waste? I can't believe it!"

"I'm not saying that Kev. I'm just saying we need to be careful. We need to be sensible, practical, otherwise, if anyone in the group is caught, we won't achieve anything."

He hoped that Kevin could see the sense in his argument, but he wasn't convinced.

"Let me think about it, Toby," Kevin replied. "I'm not saying I agree with you, but I'll consider it."

"Well don't do anything silly, Kev. Let's see what happens after Huntingdon. I suspect the best thing for us to do is to do what we have done before."

"What's that?"

"We'll advise the BHA by our anonymous letter process that they have ignored our warning by going ahead with recommencing racing and that they will now be subject to further random attacks until they listen to our demands."

"But they'll just ignore us again Toby, I know they will."

"Look Kev, trust me. The element of surprise is in our favour. If we lay low, then after a while they'll let their guard down. Once they do, we can hit them again."

"I'm not so sure, I think we should hit them now. Let them know that we are serious."

Toby sighed inwardly. His way of escape was to let things cool off. People changed as time passed and being up for the fight often decreased as other things in their lives became more important. He was buying himself time, as much as anything. He tried one last time.

"Look Kevin," he said, "just give it until after Huntingdon, then we can get together and decide our next move. I can't get up there anyway for a week or so, we have mid-term examinations coming up soon and I need to prepare papers."

The line went quiet for a few seconds. "Okay Toby, have it your way," Kevin replied eventually. "I'll let the girls know."

"Thanks Kev. Stay safe, stay calm. We will win this war even if we don't win every battle." Toby said, trying to leverage some philosophical thinking on his fellow conspirator. He wasn't convinced the bait would be taken, however.

"You too," Kevin replied. The tone in his voice giving away more than he intended.

When Toby put down the phone, he had a bad feeling in his stomach.

# CHAPTER 52

James Formrobe looked at the message again. He had been studying it ever since it had been sent at the same time as the recent attack on *SecureTwo's* systems. The previous email messages were very clear, and he was surprised that he hadn't seen what they meant initially. The latest message made things clearer. The attacks were just a way of getting him to focus on an issue that he was not aware of until now. He realized that the warnings were not about destroying the business but were about something else, something much more personal. He also knew who was behind the attacks. On an A4 page printed out from the HP laser printer situated on a small desk in his office, was the latest email that had arrived just as the attack began. The sophistication behind this latest event made it evident that it was someone who knew what they were doing. They were slowly revealing themselves, but in doing so were giving reasons as to why.

To: *SecureTwo*
From: *097/01010011*

Message: *Highlighting the real security breach is the aim.*
*Destruction of SecureTwo is not the game.*

065/01110011/01001011/115/106/01010010/069/01001010/117/011001 00/121/01110011

He couldn't believe what was being suggested, but he had worked out what had been going on. The clues were in the message and had been all along. The use of the ASCII – Binary Character Table was very clever. Although he should have realized what was contained in the messages sent, he hadn't. The use of the strands within the coded emails each reflected a letter, and it was something he should have noticed. However, between the attacks, the discussions with the board members, and his obsession with buying a horse, he had relied on others in the business to work out what was going on. Also, he had made the mistake of thinking that the attacks were from unfriendly fire. He now knew otherwise.
He looked at the three messages in sequence, he had decoded each of them.

097/01010011/116/01100101/083/0101011

A    S    T   E    S    T

L    O    O   K   A    T   J   U    D   Y
108/01101111/111/075/01100001/084/074/01110101/089/01100100.

A    S    K    S  J   R    E   J    U
065/01110011/01001011/115/106/01010010/069/01001010/117/
01100100/121/01110011
   D   Y   S

The first one was just sent as a test, along with a warning about server and systems shutdowns, in order to get the message to be looked at seriously.

The second was a specific message and the third was one that had been used to corroborate the second. The highlighted first and last digits worked in two ways. One to clarify who had sent the message, AS (Alan Smerdon), and secondly who the focus on the message was on, SJ. He was the individual who could provide the answers. SJ, Samuel Jacobsen.

Formrobe couldn't believe was he was reading. He picked up his phone and made a call. He needed support when he met with Jacobsen.

# CHAPTER 53

Toby made the call to Mitchell. It was still within the timeframe that he had given the bookmaker to release him from his *obligations*, but he was getting desperate now. He needed certainty.

"We issued the necessary ultimatums. The BHA hasn't responded but I think it's because they don't want to push too hard on the clubs. There is enough doubt about a few of them, so I think we've done enough now for some to consider closing."

"I guess we'll see about that," Mitchell replied. "I see racing at Huntingdon is being used as the next venue. Kick-starting the season, was what I read in the press and on the websites."

"That's right. I think the police want to use it as a trap to catch the group."

"So what are you intending to do?"

"Nothing," Toby replied.

"Nothing?"

"Yes. If we fall for it, then I think we're finished. I've told the group to lay low. We've already made one mistake…." he stopped not wishing to go into it any further. Letting Mitchell know what had happened with the headset that was left behind would not work in his favour. He needed to focus on getting off Mitchell's hook. He had played the card about dragging Mitchell into the ALA's agenda. He wanted the bookmaker to realize that they would go down together if he was caught.

"So, what's next?"

"By staying below the radar we can make our presence felt at any time in the future. It will keep the pressure on the courses and clubs and for some, we think it will be enough strain for them to close. If we don't do anything stupid, the fear of the unknown will hopefully take one or two to the wall."

"Do you believe the group is willing to follow that strategy?"

"I'm not sure about one of them, but I don't want to speculate. If some of them do go off the rails and act independently, then it could endanger both of us. On the one hand, if caught they could drag me into it, and that would mean you as well…"

Mitchell was about the interrupt, but Toby beat him to the punch. "On the other hand," he said, "it could hasten a course shutdown, which is what you wanted, isn't it?"

"Assuming no one is caught."

"Exactly," Toby replied. "And on that note, this is the last time I am going to contact you. My work is done. We are square. I can't do it anymore. I have the recordings," he perpetuated the lie again, "they are my security."

Mitchell knew he was beaten. He had been sloppy. Throwing his weight around during previous conversations without acting on it, showing aggression. He had been caught in the middle. He tried one last time, he needed Toby to be left with some doubt.

"If I'm free from mine, then you are free from yours," he said. "If you don't hear from me again in the next three weeks, you are off the hook."

"Well remember what I told you," Toby replied. "We both go down if I do."

Mitchell didn't reply. He put the phone down.

Toby knew that he was free. It was almost over for him too. He had one more thing to clear.

---------------

Mitchell called the number again. There was no answer. It was three days since he had last called. They had agreed that he should never make contact again, but he needed to get his own story right, he didn't want to have the past brought up when it should have been well and truly buried. What had happened, had occurred in a very different time.

# CHAPTER 54

"I need your help," he said.

Cannon and Formrobe were sitting in the Woodstock Arms on Market Street. It was just after seven in the evening. After Cannon had received the call from Formrobe, he agreed to meet with him straight away. The pub was lively and from where they sat, pints of pale ale and lager on their table, they hoped they would seem innocuous to the other patrons, that no one would hear their conversation.

"I'm not sure what to do, how to approach the next steps, so I wanted to bounce it off you, Mike. I hope that's okay?"

"Sure," Cannon replied, pleased that Formrobe had seen in him somebody who could help, that he was more than just a racehorse trainer, even though ideally, he would prefer to be seen as one. He had reflected many times why the past never wanted to leave. Maybe it never would?

"Well the first thing is that I know who has been attacking the business. However, the second and most important issue is what they were trying to say."

"I'm not sure I'm with you," Cannon replied, "what do you mean?"

"Well, firstly the attacks were intended to warn not to destroy. Secondly, the warning was against someone who I have trusted for years. Someone who I never thought possible would betray me or the business."

"Who is that?" Cannon asked.

Formrobe looked embarrassed. Cannon waited for him to speak.

"Samuel," he said.

"Jacobsen? Your Legal adviser, your lawyer?"

"Yes."

Cannon thought back to the meetings he had had with Jacobsen. How he had asked him to mentor Cassie. Had he got it wrong? Was Jacobsen really someone who would undermine Formrobe? There was something he remembered about the meeting, something shared, something that was stirring in his memory. What was it? He took a drink of his pint hoping it would jar his thoughts.

Formrobe cut into them.

"I've been able to decipher the messages we got with the attacks. It's these that I wanted to share with you."

He placed each one in sequence in front of Cannon. The numbers didn't mean anything to him, but he read the simple letters above and below the lines. The highlighted letters were what attracted him.

"What do these letters mean?" he asked. "The ones highlighted in the last message? I see they are on the first line as well."

"AS?"

"Yes."

"Alan Smerdon," Formrobe replied.

"Your partner, or should I say ex-partner, the one with whom you set up the business?"

"Yes, Judy Smerdon's son."

"And this JUDY referred to in both the second and third message is the lady who caused the split between you? Yet she is still a board member and a shareholder in your business?" Cannon asked.

"Yes."

"So why would she want to destroy it?"

"I don't know," Formrobe replied. "I'm not even sure that's what the message is trying to suggest. Maybe it means something else and that's why I need your help."

"With Jacobsen?"

"Yes."

"What about asking her directly. Why Jacobsen first?"

"I have tried calling her already. In fact, I tried calling straight away, once I had deciphered the coded emails, but I've got no answer from her. I've left a couple of messages hoping that she would call me back, but so far no luck."

"And what about Alan Smerdon himself?" Cannon asked. "Have you tried to contact him?"

"No, I haven't. As I told you some time back, we haven't spoken in ages. I don't even have his number, mobile or otherwise."

"Judy would have it?"

"I'd assume so," Formrobe said.

"Okay, well I guess there is nothing you can do on that front until she calls you back?"

"That's right."

"Let's talk about Jacobsen then. We need to make sure we don't scare him off or even put him in a difficult position. From what I've read from these messages, they are not suggesting he has done anything against your business, they are just recommending that you have a conversation with him about Judy." Cannon went on. "He may be totally innocent, and it may be that he knows something about her that Alan wants you to check on. It could be as simple as that."

"It could be, but I think there may be more to it."

"What makes you think that?" Cannon asked.

"I know Alan, he's a good man. I should have realized something right from the start of the attacks."

"What's that?"

Formrobe tried to keep things reasonably simple in his explanation. He told

Cannon about how Smerdon was the better student, the better programmer of the two of them. That if Smerdon wanted to damage the business he could have done so. While their relationship had soured, it had been because of Judy, not because of disagreements about the business. They had built it together. They had become wealthy together. Judy was a beneficiary of that and from all accounts, she wanted more.

Cannon understood. He had seen greed destroy families, tear them apart. He had seen money corrupt. It looked to him that Alan Smerdon had not lost his soul, he was somehow trying to put a wrong right. How he was doing it was something Cannon saw as noble but was it the only action Smerdon was taking?

The two men agreed to try and meet with Jacobsen within 48 hours. It was too late to expect anything to happen the following day however. They needed to ensure they were ready for the conversation. Cannon knew that for Formrobe, it was going to be tough, so he agreed he would take the lead in the meeting with Jacobsen. Cannon would try and use his skills to eek-out the truth behind the messages without the process being too onerous or challenging for Formrobe.

Knowing that he had a potential client who had much on his mind, Cannon changed the subject, tried to lighten the conversation.

"I've made contact with the owners of both the horses we discussed the other day," he said, "and both have agreed with what I offered them."

"Which was, Mike? Remind me, please. With all that's been going on, I've completely forgotten."

Cannon smiled, pleased to be able to talk about racing rather than about corporate politics and the internal machinations thereof.

"The people who own *The Politician*, the family that owns the butchery just around the corner from here, still want the twenty-five-k for the half share, and as far as *Happy Gilmour* is concerned, and I know you don't like the name," he said, "they are willing to sell him at twenty-seven-five. Two-and-a-half thousand below the original price."

"That's great, Mike. Let's do it." Formrobe replied enthusiastically. "I can't wait to see my colours on the track."

"If we can get back to racing, yes," Cannon replied, "that *would* be good. We'll need to register your colours as well. As far as *The Politician* is concerned, I'm afraid he'll need to run in his current colours."

"When can we see them, the horses?"

"I think we should try for two or three days from now, after we have met with Jacobsen. We don't know what the fallout could be, and if we need to cancel the stable visits then that would be easier to rearrange."

"I understand racing is starting again soon. At Huntingdon," Formrobe stated.

Cannon was surprised that Formrobe was aware of this. "Yes, you're right," he responded smiling. "It seems like you are already getting into the swing of things."

"Not really, I just happen to see it on the TV news."

Cannon nodded. He was looking forward to racing starting again, especially having the better horses in his stable run as soon as possible. He was very keen to run *The Politician* in a couple of races before the Tingle Creek, but he needed the go-ahead from both of the owners, current, and future. As far as *Happy Gilmour* was concerned, he was a longer-term prospect. Once racing started again, he would recommend that *The Politician* race as soon as possible, perhaps even at Huntingdon. He also had several other horses that he was keen to get onto the track as soon as he could. He and Rich had worked hard. The horses deserved to be back doing what they loved to do, to run, race, and show their courage over fences.

# CHAPTER 55

Kevin had heard enough. He had met with the girls. They were disappointed about Toby's comments. He decided he would act alone. He knew that Huntingdon was going to be the first meeting to be held after the suspension of racing and he felt that he had done most of the work helping the ALA with its cause. While he was sad that a couple of horses and jockeys had been victims of his work, he still believed in the bigger goal, to free the animals that brought riches and power to some, while being abused themselves. The thought of pushing animals to their physical limits and putting them in danger by jumping fences was anathema to him. If nothing else, he would do his very best, as an individual, to stop the practice.

When he and the girls had discussed what Toby had said, it was clear that they were starting to see *him*, rather than Toby, as the leader of the ALA. They agreed that actions spoke louder than words and they encouraged him to carry on with what he planned. He was happy to get the go-ahead, particularly from Tracey.

He knew the risks he might face with the focus being on the Huntingdon course, but given the actions he had taken at previous courses over recent weeks and months and the success thereof, he believed he knew what was required. He was determined to make a statement.

# CHAPTER 56

Porter had good news.

"We've managed to get a couple of prints from the headset," he said. "We are seeing if we can find a match on any of our databases."

He was calling Cannon on the mobile, while he and Rich were watching the first string from the stables exercising on the heath. Both men were wearing their heavy parka coats. The cloud from the previous evening had disappeared overnight, leaving the sky clear. A light frost had settled, leaving the ground firm and with a dusting of white. Cannon never liked this time of year, early autumn. He always worried about the horses' legs, the hardness of the ground, and the jarring they could take after jumping fences. He preferred soft and wet going. Sadly, not every horse did. Some liked the hard, dry surfaces. Wet and muddy racetracks made many a race a long slog and Cannon was acutely aware of this. He liked to place his horses in races in which he knew they could complete. That they could run the distance. Fatigued horses, tired horses, were more likely to fall. He always tried to prevent that, however, he was not always successful. No trainer could guarantee a horse would never fall. Sometimes other things happened in races, things unforeseen, but he tried his best. He was careful. The horses were his to train, he did not own them.

"Did you get my prints as well?" he asked, nodding at Telside as a pair of horses passed directly in front of them heading towards a set of hurdles. The two men watched as the hurdlers *cleared* the jump at speed, knocking back the flights with their front legs. In hurdling, the aim was to jump low and just touch the tops of the jumps. By keeping low and being speedy through the air, there was an advantage gained over those horses that did not jump that way. Cannon and Rich, along with the track riders, had to work together to get the horses to learn how to do it.

Despite the thunder of the hooves from the second pair of hurdlers passing them by, Cannon heard Porter say they had eliminated his prints from those that they had been able to recover. "We found yours on our DB from your time in the Force, so it was easy to ignore them. We've got a partial print in one case and two good prints of someone else, at least that's what it seems. The lab boys are now running them through the various machines."

"And DNA extracts?" Cannon asked.

"We did get some yes. The specimens included a piece of hair that was stuck on the unit, plus some saliva. Obviously, we don't know yet if this is yours or someone else's but within the next twenty-four or forty-eight hours maximum, we'll know."

"And I assume you'll let me know too?" Cannon asked, watching the third pair of hurdlers make their way over their jumps.

"Of course, Mike."

"Thanks, Iain," Cannon replied. It was the first time he had used the Inspector's christian name. He realized that the relationship had grown substantially. He just hoped that Dockly was going to be more reasonable in the future as well.

Once the first lot of horses had completed their work, Cannon sent the riders and horses back to the stables to do their warm downs. At the stables themselves, the horses walked around in circles, their hooves clattering on the stones in the yard. Soon they would be washed, fed, and bedded down for the day. A short walk later in the day would be taken to loosen their joints, check for any heat in the legs before they would be locked up for the night.

Cannon watched them walk around, the riders' soft chatter filling the silence of the morning. The sun had now risen higher. The feel of autumn, which would soon turn to winter, reflected in the sky-blue colour of the day. It was still cold, but it was expected that the morning would change into a reasonable afternoon with more sun. Cloud and rain were only due in a couple of days. Cannon hoped that by the time the Huntingdon meeting started, the weather would have changed. He was confident that the police would be ready, but he hoped they would never be needed. If the weather deteriorated then it was possible, just possible, that the ALA would abandon any prospect of conducting an attack on the course. Wet and cloudy weather may provide some form of cover and camouflage, especially at night, but it also allowed footprints to be left in the grass, in the dirt, and in the mud that would naturally develop given what the course and surrounds was made from. With the previous attacks, there had been no police around. By the time anyone had looked at the area around the fences sabotaged or destroyed, covered in burnt plastic and birch, no one had considered looking for footprints. Even if they had, they would have not been noticed or even easy to extract, as too many people had been in the area of the fence, removing the debris, looking at the damage, or even trying to repair it well before the police ever arrived at the scene. This time with the police expected to patrol around the track a few nights before the meeting and to be on-site during the actual race day as well, Cannon was quietly confident that any incident could be avoided. At least he hoped so.

He watched the horses clip-clop and jig-jog for a further minute before inviting Telside in the house for their usual breakfast. The track-riders saw this as the cue to leap off their mounts and begin the cleanup. They would take the second string out for training once Cannon and Telside had eaten. The riders themselves would have breakfast together in and around the tack room, then be ready in forty-five minutes or so, for the next part of their day.

# CHAPTER 57

It was going to be a difficult meeting. It was something that neither Formrobe nor Cannon were looking forward to. They had set it up for six pm, Formrobe having asked Jacobsen's assistant to put the meeting in the lawyer's diary. A late meeting wasn't unusual, it wasn't really out of working hours. The business ran twenty-four-seven, however, the after-hours staff was generally the technical teams, the operational part of the business, not the accountants, HR, lawyers, and others.

Formrobe tapped on the door before he and Cannon entered, Jacobsen was looking downwards reading a document that lay flat on his desk. He looked up, surprised to see Cannon. His face, however, quickly reverted to one reflecting stoicism. He wasn't sure what the meeting was about, Formrobe had been deliberately vague when he had asked for it to be arranged.

"Come in gentleman," he said offering his hand to Cannon. "Take a seat, what can I do for you? I see there is no subject in my calendar, just a meeting with James here." He pointed at the younger man, his boss.

"Yes, I'm sorry Samuel to be so evasive, but I needed…we needed," he pointed at Cannon, "to have a chat with you, about these ongoing attacks on the business."

The lawyer looked quite startled. "You don't think I had anything to do with it do you?" he asked.

"No, I don't Samuel," Formrobe replied, "but we do need to talk to you about them."

"What do you mean? I have no idea who is behind them. Why would I?"

"That's a good question, but we think we do know now who is."

"Who?"

"It's Alan," Formrobe said.

"Alan Smerdon?"

"Yes. Judy's son. My former partner and still a shareholder in the business." Jacobsen was taken aback. He sat stunned for a second, his face froze. "But why?" he asked.

"We're not sure yet," Cannon jumped in. He had been sitting watching Jacobsen. His facial features, his body language. The man seemed genuinely shocked. "We do however think that it has something to do with yourself and Mrs. Smerdon. It's the reason why we are here."

"Go on," Jacobsen said, "I can assure you that it has nothing to do with me."

"We'll see," Cannon said looking over the man's shoulder.

Jacobsen noticed. He seemed uncomfortable.

Formrobe took out the A4 pages that he had printed and worked on, to reveal the hidden messages that he believed Alan Smerdon had sent him. He placed them on the desk, the text, the coding, the meanings. They were facing the lawyer. While Jacobsen assessed what was in front of him Cannon reflected on what he had ruminated on overnight. He had thought about what Formrobe had told him at their very first meeting. Alan Smerdon had started a new venture, but Formrobe wasn't sure what it was. Cannon now assumed it was still in the IT Security game and that what Smerdon had done was to test *SecureTwo* without hurting it. It was a guess, but he felt that he wasn't far off the mark. Perhaps what Alan Smerdon was doing would be complementary to what *SecureTwo* did? He hoped that Formrobe and Smerdon would be able to get back together again once the issue surrounding the messages had been addressed, but that would be up to them. He had no reason to interfere. It seemed that Judy had been the reason for the breakup of the friendship. Once the matter was resolved, the issue that hopefully Jacobsen could help with, then maybe the split could be mended. It was perhaps fanciful on Cannon's part. He had nothing to gain either way, but he liked Formrobe.

"So, what does this mean, James? **Ask JS re Judy S?**"

"I was hoping you were going to tell me."

"I'm not sure what you want me to say," Jacobsen replied.

There was a tense pause between them. Cannon noticed Formrobe biting his lip. Jacobsen looked to be staring into his boss's eyes, waiting for him to blink. There didn't appear to be any malice, just disappointment. Cannon wasn't yet sure if Jacobsen was disappointed in his boss or in himself.

"Tell me about your son," Cannon said, addressing Jacobsen. The question seemed irrelevant and it caught Jacobsen off guard.

"What about him?"

"Well, I think in a roundabout way this message has got some relevance to him," Cannon said.

"I'm not sure what you are talking about, Mr. Cannon."

"I think you do," Cannon replied. "And before you suggest otherwise. I'd just like you to know that I've met him."

"Who?"

"Your son."

"When? Where? I haven't seen him for ages myself," the lawyer said.

Cannon smiled. "Lets' just say *recently*."

Formrobe had not heard this before. He looked at Cannon for an explanation. Cannon ignored him and continued talking to Jacobsen.

"I'll explain what I mean shortly. Let's get back to the messages," he said, pointing at the desk.

Jacobsen looked again at the page. He wasn't sure where to start, nor what to say.

"I, I…I have never been lost for words, but…"

Cannon's mobile rang suddenly. He looked at the number, the caller. It was Ralph Tolman. Cannon excused himself and answered the phone. Formrobe and Jacobsen waited, looking at each other slightly embarrassed.

"Hi Ralph, how are you?"

Straight to the point, Tolman answered, "I'm well Mike, but you'll never guess who isn't."

"Who?" Cannon asked.

"Someone who may be pertinent to your investigation," he replied.

"Go on."

Tolman filled Cannon in on what he had uncovered. Cannon listened intently, occasionally stopping Tolman and seeking clarity about anything that didn't make sense. Once Tolman had indicated that he had provided everything he could, he said, "Oh, by the way, Mike, I still haven't found Peter Todd. My contacts, though, are still working several angles and so am I."

"Thanks, Ralph," Cannon replied, "keep it up. I have the utmost faith in you," he continued. *Flattery and an exclusive would get you anywhere*, he thought.

"Any news from your side?" Tolman asked.

"I think we're making progress, but I'll fill you in later," Cannon responded, inferring that he had some detail he wanted to share with the journalist, but was not wanting to do so publicly. Tolman understood the subtlety of Cannon's response, reading between the lines, as a good journo like him should.

Fomrobe and Jacobsen continued sitting silently waiting for Cannon to finish his conversation. Cannon could sense their impatience, ending the call with a promise to call Tolman later.

"Sorry about that," Cannon said after he had put the phone back inside his inner jacket pocket, "I do apologize, but I have some news for you both."

Both men asked Cannon to continue.

"It's Judy Smerdon."

"What about her?" Formrobe said, keen to get back to the reason they were meeting with Jacobsen.

"That call I just took. It was from a journalist. I've asked him to do some digging for me while we are unable to race," he said. "He's just advised me that Judy Smerdon has been found dead."

"Dead?!" repeated Jacobsen.

"Yes. It seems that she was murdered. A few days ago," Cannon added.

Jacobsen went white, his skin pallor rapidly losing its colour. "Oh my God!" he said. "I can't believe it!" He pushed his chair back and stood up, his hand rubbing his forehead vigorously, showing the reaction that Cannon had suspected would happen once he relayed the news. Formrobe also looked at Cannon, his mouth agape.

Cannon's instinct was right. He needed to ask Jacobsen the obvious question, although he suspected he knew the answer already.

"You were having an affair, weren't you? You and Judy Smerdon," Cannon asked.

Formrobe appeared stunned, lost. He looked at Cannon as they both waited to hear a response to the question.

"No!" Jacobsen replied. His denial was emphatic.

"No?" queried Cannon.

Jacobsen denied the accusation again, he walked to the window of his office, looking out through the glass. He had his back to them. Cannon had no doubt in his mind and asked the question differently. He pointed to the page still lying on the desk.

"This note," he said, "isn't it referring to your affair? Is that why it asks to check with you about Judy Smerdon?"

"I don't know," Jacobsen said, his back still turned. "What do you think?"

Cannon was beginning to get annoyed. He knew at some point he would have to complicate the issue if necessary but hoped that the truth would come out before he needed to. While he understood the lawyer's reaction to the news about Judy, Cannon still needed to find the truth.

"Okay, let me tell you what I think, Samuel," Cannon responded, deliberately using Jacobsen's christian name. "I think you've been having an affair with Judy for quite some time. Somehow, and I'm not sure in what way it happened, something went wrong, something you said, perhaps?" Cannon speculated. "Whatever it was, it resulted in a split, a fallout and since then there has been an ongoing issue, hasn't there?" he stated.

Formrobe who had been listening intently jumped into the conversation. He addressed Jacobsen who had returned to his chair, slumping into it like a defeated man.

"Is it true, Samuel? You and Judy?"

Jacobsen could hear the disappointment in Formrobe's question. He noted Cannon was about to continue with his questioning. He put his hand up indicating Cannon need not ask.

"It's been over for quite a while," he said. "Our affair." It seemed like a tacky thing for Jacobsen to say, to admit to.

"Go on," Formrobe said, nodding towards Cannon, giving him free rein to ask what he needed.

"There's not much to say, really. Judy and I did indeed have a relationship, but it ended nearly two years ago now," he said, "and since then I've only ever dealt with her as a shareholder and board member."

"How long had the relationship lasted?" Cannon asked.

"I'm not going to answer that, Mr. Cannon. It's none of your business."

Cannon acknowledged the response with a slight nodding of the head and a wry smile. "Okay, so let me ask you this. *Why* did the relationship end?"

"Why does any relationship end? It just does."

"Without any reason?

"Nothing of relevance to you."

"Then why do you think Alan needed to go through all this subterfuge just to get us to talk to you about Judy?" Formrobe asked.

"As I said before, I don't know."

"Come on, Samuel, please don't treat us like fools," Cannon said, "if you are not prepared to tell us, then perhaps I should tell *you*?"

The pressure was beginning to tell on Jacobsen, but he invited Cannon to continue.

"Firstly Samuel, let me say that your reaction to the news about Judy's murder appears genuine, and for that despite what comes out, I just need to say that I'm sorry that you had to hear it from me. I know it's devastating news."

"Thank you, Mr. Cannon."

"However, having said that, I also think that the news will come as welcome relief to you, will it not? Because of the problem that you have been living with, the problem that's inferred in Alan Smerdon's warning. It should go away now with Judy's death, shouldn't it?"

"Please Mr. Cannon, could you get to the point you are trying to make? I've already admitted to my affair with Judy. I'm not sure what else you want me to say."

"The truth," Cannon said, "the rest of it…."

Cannon stopped talking. He allowed the silence to build. There were no takers, so he decided to fill it. "The reason why Alan was sending a warning was that he knew what she was up to."

"And what was that?"

"She was blackmailing your son, wasn't she?"

"I beg your pardon?"

"Your son," Cannon said, "in the picture behind you."

Formrobe was lost, seeking an explanation from Cannon with his eyes. Jacobsen stayed calm. Stoic. Cannon knew he was right, the lack of response from the lawyer gave it away. Confirmed his theory. He pointed towards the photographs that he had seen previously. He had recalled the face when he had tried to follow the girls out of the pub. When he had met the ALA. The man he had bumped into, the man with the dreadlocks.

"As I mentioned before, I've met your son, though I should rather have said that *'I ran into him',*" he added humourlessly. "Was Judy aware of his involvement with an extremist group?" he asked.

"I'm not following you, Mr. Cannon."

Cannon decided to press on but not to reveal where he had met Jacobsen's son. He would eek-out the true story piece by piece, if necessary.

"I'll ask the question again," he said, "and I think it would be wise if we could get to the truth," he added provocatively. "I'm sure the police and the board would be interested to know if Judy Smerdon and yourself were engaged in anything that would be detrimental to the business."

Cannon knew that Jacobsen would react to the inference.

"How dare you," he said, "I would never put this business at risk. It's my life."

Cannon held up his hands in mock surrender. He had heard what he needed to. He knew the lawyer was an honest and reasonable man. He looked towards Formrobe who was looking decidedly uncomfortable with the conversation.

Unfortunately, being honest could not be said of Judy Smerdon. She had taken advantage of Jacobsen and he was now paying the price. Cannon pointed again to the photographs that sat on the shelf behind the lawyer, the ones so proudly passed amongst them just a short while ago. Cannon decided he needed to bring things to a head.

"A couple of days ago, I ran into your son," he stated matter-of-factly. "Initially the face didn't mean anything, but overnight it came to me where I had seen him before, and it got me thinking as to why your son would be involved in something so dangerous, so extreme."

"This extremist group you referred to earlier?"

"Yes," Cannon said, "and it was a puzzle at first."

"Well, all I can say is that I know nothing about it," Jacobsen indicated.

"And I believe you."

The lawyer appeared relieved.

"So I started to wonder why? After all, you said your son was a lecturer in Philosophy and Law at Southampton University, correct?"

"That's right."

"So, I asked my journalist friend to make some enquiries and he told me that your son was under some form of *provisional* suspension, due to some allegations having been made."

"That's news to me," Jacobsen replied. Shock evident on his face.

"Yes, it seems someone has suggested that your son has been passing some of his students in their courses even though they haven't written exams or done the course work they should have."

"And who has made these allegations?"

"Apparently some *unknown source*, but I would guess it was Judy Smerdon."

"But why?"

"For her own purposes, her benefit."

"But I only ever mentioned the..." Jacobsen blurted out, then stopped, suddenly realizing he had almost let something slip.

Cannon had been waiting for the slip-up. His probing and inferences were used to draw out the truth, the skill he had learnt while in the Force. He latched onto what Jacobsen had revealed.

"So, what was it you let slip to Judy? What did you reveal?" he asked. "Whatever it was, it was used against your son and I'm not sure if it's directly linked, but somehow as a consequence, he's ended up in a very dangerous situation," Cannon said, thinking about the current hold on racing, the deaths of jockeys and horses, the risk to the livelihoods of thousands of people, and the ongoing investigation into the ALA.

Jacobsen crumbled. The secret was out. He felt humiliated, downcast.

"I accidentally let slip that Toby, my son, was in debt to a bookmaker and that he was in danger of being expelled from his post."

"How?"

"The bookmaker, a guy called Clifford Mitchell, had threatened him. Told him that he needed to pay up otherwise he, the bookmaker, would advise the University that Toby had been sleeping with some of his students and had passed them in their course, just to keep his affairs quiet."

"And it wasn't true."

"No it wasn't, but the fact that he owed money was."

This didn't quite fit the narrative Cannon had formed in his head. He needed to establish a few more facts.

"So why didn't you try and help him with his debt?"

"Mr. Cannon, I've been able to do so several times over the years, but it got to a point where I couldn't do it anymore. I gave Toby the opportunity to stop gambling by paying off several of his debts in the past, but I had to bring a stop to it. I couldn't keep doing it. He needed to take responsibility for himself. I pleaded with him to stop."

"What happened?"

"Simple. He didn't."

"And he asked you to bail him out again."

"Yes, and I refused."

"But you let it slip to Judy Smerdon, his circumstances?"

"I didn't think anything of it. It was just a passing comment."

"I'm sure you didn't expect it to be used against him, Samuel," Cannon said, taking a sympathetic approach, "but what I can tell you is that Judy used that information to get what she wanted from him. I'm not sure what it is yet, but whatever it is, she's now paid the ultimate price for it."

"You don't think my son killed her, do you?"

"I have no idea, that's something the police will need to find out. In the meantime, however, your son could have a price on his head. He's involved in something extremely serious, something that could jeopardize his career and his life."

"My God," Jacobsen said, "what have I done?"

# CHAPTER 58

He was back in his office. Cannon made a few phone calls, leaving a lengthy voicemail on the BHA's messaging service. He also called Cassie and left a message. *Does nobody answer phones anymore*, he thought?

He had left Jacobsen and Formrobe together. He expected that they would resolve the issues between them. It was evident that Jacobsen had not put *SecureTwo* at risk at any point and that his only crime was being a lonely widower, a man in his later years, who had been duped, conned, by Judy Smerdon. What he had thought was a genuine relationship, was nothing of the sort. He wasn't the first man that this had happened to and he wouldn't be the last.

What had surprised Cannon was who Jacobsen's son had been indebted to, Clifford Mitchell. When Cannon had asked the amount of the debt, he had whistled when Jacobsen told him. When previous debts had been added to the amount that Jacobsen himself had settled, the sum-total of what Toby Jacobsen owed was more than seventy thousand pounds. Cannon could scarcely believe it was possible to get oneself into such a position, especially someone so well educated as Toby Jacobsen. However, he knew that it could happen to anyone, no one was immune.

He called Porter and filled him in on what he had learnt during his conversation with Jacobsen and Formrobe. He suggested that they, the police, should have a chat with Mitchell. Being in debt to a bookmaker wasn't illegal, but doing something illegal to benefit a bookmaker was. He offered to sit in if it would help. Porter advised him that it would be impossible but said that he would relay anything pertinent back to Cannon.

The issue of the upcoming Huntingdon meeting still played on Cannon's mind. The linkage of Toby Jacobsen to the ALA was still tenuous. It wasn't yet proven. Cannon had drawn some conclusions, but they were based on gut feeling, circumstance, and coincidence, not solid evidence. Cannon believed that he was right in his thinking and suggested to Porter that he get a DNA extract and fingerprints from the lecturer and check to see if they matched anything from the headset. It was an educated guess on Cannon's part, as he was convinced Jacobsen's son was one of the leaders of the group, however, he still couldn't work out why. The linkage was still unclear.

-----------------------

Kevin sat in his rented lockup. It was just off the Banbury road almost halfway between Summertown and Central Oxford. A single globe lit the inside of the room, casting shadows as he moved from his chair to a series of shelves standing along one side of the interior wall. A small table lamp powered by battery added a little more light onto the desk surface that he worked on.

He used a soldering iron to attach small components to a green, two-inch by three-inch circuit board. The silver tracks glinted slightly in the light as Kevin populated it with various diodes, fuses, and resistors. The work was delicate and complicated. He had already completed three other boards. This one would be the last. Every one of them would be used at the upcoming meeting at Huntingdon. They would be linked to various explosive devices. He hadn't used Bluetooth or wi-fi to send signals to his previous *bombs*, he had relied on old-fashioned timers. It was the timer that caused the carnage at Uttoxeter. The race being run late had resulted in the deaths. Timers were fine but he wanted to make a statement. No, he thought, *the ALA wants to make a statement*. The plan he had created, however, without input from the others, was his own to carry out.

He continued with his project, all the time thinking about how he was going to insert the devices and the accelerant into the 'chase fences and the hurdles. He knew the course would be watched and the jumps inspected before the meeting began. He had a basic idea of what he was going to do and how, but he needed to be careful. He only had two more days to wait.

------------------------------------

Cannon called Dockly. It was after nine in the evening. Michelle had gone to bed already. He would join her shortly.

"Any news?" he asked.

"Nothing as yet, Mr. Cannon, however, our investigations are continuing. In the meantime, please do not try to leave the country."

Cannon found the comment unnecessary.

"I'm not likely to do that, am I?" he responded, somewhat tersely. Dockly was becoming a bit of a pain.

"I don't know Mr. Cannon. Where you go, I can't control, can I?"

"Well let me reassure you, Inspector. I have a stable to run and along with that, many other things to do, including helping you to solve your case."

"That's very kind of you, Mr Cannon," Dockly said sarcastically, "but I don't need your help, thank you very much. I'd advise you to stay away."

"Always happy to comply with the law," Cannon retorted, "but also always happy to help rectify *your* mistakes," he added, enjoying the provocation.

Dockly huffed down the line, letting Cannon know that he was still on the *suspect watch list*. "If you *are* guilty, I'll find out," the Inspector concluded.

Cannon didn't rise to the bait batted back to him. He knew that Tolman was on the case, trying to find Peter Todd as well as trying to find out where Dockly had gotten to as far as the explanation behind Bronton's and the Pools' deaths.

Having poked the bear enough, Cannon put down the phone. He hadn't learnt much but he knew that until the killer or killers had been found, he was still going to be a *person of interest*. He needed the issue to be sorted. He looked at his watch, Michelle would be fast asleep by now. He needed to join her. He was tired yet felt that he may not sleep easily. His mind was running ahead.

# CHAPTER 59

"It would be good to support the Huntingdon meeting," Cannon said. "What do you think, Rich?"

"I suppose so, Mike. Who do think we should run?"

"There are a couple I think could do with a race. I'd like to give *The Politician* a go, if possible."

"Well there is a three-mile chase on the card, but he'll carry quite a bit of weight compared to the others."

"That's true. I'll ask the owners, including the new one, James Formrobe, to see if they are willing to give it a go," he said. "As long as they realize that the run is to get him race-fit rather than to try and win at all costs, then that should be okay. We don't want to mess up the horse, we want to save him for the Tingle Creek."

Telside agreed.

They were standing together watching the first lot continue with their morning exercises, occasionally requesting a rider to ask a horse to *stride out* or take the hurdle again. As they did so, the light improved from the east as the sun made an appearance above the horizon. Clouds still scudded low over the gallops and beyond. There was no red sky, just a dull greyness. There was no sign of rain, but a cruel wind whipped the grass that was thrown up by the horses' hooves as they thundered along the tracks cut into the field. Shouts of the riders filled the air as each horse rose from the ground clearing the steeplechase jumps, their bellies scraping the birch as they did so. The hurdlers' jockeys likewise encouraged their mounts along, as each horse in turn smashed down their respective hurdle with their front legs. Cannon wasn't pleased. The technique would eventually cause injury. He called the riders together, reading them the *riot act*.

He wanted low and speedy jumping, but he wanted the legs of each animal tucked under their bellies as each hurdle was cleared. He re-emphasized the point, making each rider complete the hurdle circuit twice before being satisfied. Once exercise was over, Cannon made his way back to the stables. Rich would take the second lot. Cannon had more thinking to do.

# CHAPTER 60

Porter had managed to contact Mitchell.

He had insisted that the bookmaker meet with him the following day in Oxford. As there was no racing on, Mitchell agreed he would drive up from Cobham, before realizing that he forgot to ask what the meeting was all about.

The Inspector had been vague. He had said enough, suggesting that their meeting was to help police with an enquiry. Mitchell knew what that meant but wasn't sure which enquiry the Inspector was referring to. "Always happy to assist the police," Mitchell had said.

-----------------------

Mitchell had tried the number again, it must have been the twentieth attempt, but he still had no response. He had been told it was all over and that he need not call again, but he wasn't yet convinced he was off the hook, nor was he sure that the issue wouldn't be raised again sometime in the future.

He had been unnerved by Porter's call.

He made a few more calls to see if his contacts were aware of where *she* was.

Later that evening he got the news. She was dead. Was that why Inspector Porter had called him? What did they know? When he had heard about her, he had breathed a sigh of relief. It *was* over, as she had indicated a few days before.

Now, however, he wasn't so sure.

He sat in his chair. The whisky in his glass didn't taste as good as usual. The taste left in his mouth wasn't as clean nor as smooth as normal. He got up and poured it down the kitchen sink.

# CHAPTER 61

Formrobe received the email and he passed it onto Cannon immediately. It was from Alan Smerdon. Formrobe had tried to call Alan, but his call had not been answered. He left a message on Smerdon's message bank. He then contacted Cannon. It was the first time, thirty hours after the meeting in Jacobsen's office, that he had tried to speak with Cannon. He was frustrated to get Cannon's voicemail. The trainer was unavailable. He left a message about the email that he had forwarded on to him.

"It's an email from Alan," he had said. "It says the police should ask Mitchell about his, Alan's, dad. I'm not sure what it means but he does provide some details that perhaps the police can use. Anyway, I'm not sure where Alan is or why he hasn't contacted the police himself, but it seems he wants to work through me," he had continued, "just like he's done with regards to Judy."

---------------------------------------

Cannon listened to Formrobe's voicemail once he had parked in a side street just off University Road and before walking through the Highfield campus of Southampton University. He was looking to find building number four, the Law Building. Through a simple search on the University's website, he had been able to find Toby Jacobsen's details. He had decided to take a chance. He had called the University administration and managed to establish that Jacobsen would be in his office the next day and had made an appointment with him through the Law School's office assistant. He had lied as to the nature of the meeting by saying he was a mature student looking to conduct further postgraduate studies and wanted to discuss some options with the lecturer. He wanted to meet Jacobsen before Porter did, as he believed he would get more from the man than the Inspector would. His rationale being that, as a law lecturer, Jacobsen would know how best to manage his conversation with the police compared to a casual conversation with a normal civilian. When Cannon arrived at the building and found the correct floor for Jacobsen's office, he was shown to a small room by the office assistant where he was asked to wait.

At ten minutes past the agreed time for the meeting, two pm, Jacobsen opened the door and entered the room.

"I'm sorry, Mr……." he stopped talking the moment he recognized Cannon who was seated on a chair that he had moved to directly face the doorway.

"Nice to see you again, Mr. Jacobsen. Toby!" Cannon replied, standing up and holding out his hand. "Different circumstances to our first meeting, aren't they?"

Jacobsen wasn't sure what to do. He did a quick double-take then closed the door. Cannon noted the dichotomy in the lecturer's appearance. On the one hand, he was dressed in a dark blue suit with a crisp white shirt, tieless, and he wore expensive leather shoes that were extremely well polished. Comparing that to his long dreadlock hairstyle that flowed and bounced as if dancing to its own reggae beat, it seemed somewhat surreal. Under one arm he carried a mottled grey and black box file, which Cannon surmised contained documents and papers and possible lecture notes. Jacobsen put the box down on the ground.

"What do you want?" he asked in a hushed tone, a sense of disbelief in his voice.

Cannon sat down again, looking the man up and down before responding. He knew that the information he wanted could take a while to obtain if the man was difficult, alternately if there was some form of cooperation, the meeting could be short and sweet. He wasn't sure which way it would go yet.

"Let's start with some answers."

"About what?"

Cannon was immediately annoyed by the obfuscation that he had expected would play out. He was right. "Look, Mr. Jacobsen, this can take as long or as short as it will, but if you are smart you will work with me and I can be out of your hair inside ten minutes." Cannon almost smiled at his own joke, but Jacobsen hadn't seen the funny side.

"I'm still not clear what you want answers about," the lecturer said, "and by the way, you got me here under false pretenses s….."

"There is nothing illegal in what I've done, *Mister* Jacobsen, but from what I've been able to deduce I can't say the same applies to you."

"That's outrageous!"

"Is it?" asked Cannon, "I'm not sure it is. In fact, I'm sure what I am going to be relaying shortly is the truth. It's something the police are soon to question you about as well, I believe?"

For a few seconds Jacobsen stood silently, staring at Cannon, then without notice he seemed to deflate like a balloon losing its air. In an instant, his bravado seemed to dissipate from his body, and he crumpled down into a second chair that had been behind the door.

He rubbed his face with one hand and tossed some of his dreadlocks back over his head with the other.

"What do you need from me, then?" he asked.

"The truth."

"About?"

"About your role in the ALA. About why you've put your father through hell? About what the ALA is planning to do next?" Cannon felt he could go on but decided that he had made his point.

Jacobsen's response surprised Cannon. "What's it to you about my father?" he asked.

He had expected this question and had a ready-made answer, one that he truly believed. "He's a good man, and I want to help him."

"How do you know him, anyway?"

"All you need to know is that he works with someone I respect, and as I said, I want to help him. He's agreed to help me with something personal and I wanted to repay him by keeping his son out of prison."

"You want to help me?" Jacobsen asked.

"Yes. If I can."

Jacobsen went silent. Cannon could sense the man thinking about his options, thinking about the alternative to not cooperating. Finally, he responded. "Okay, what do you need?"

"I need everything. The whole story."

The lecturer sighed, "I'm not sure where to start."

"How about at the beginning?" Cannon proposed.

The weight of confession being lifted, Jacobsen gushed all he dared to Cannon. He told him of his gambling problem and how his father had helped him out of a hole on several occasions. He relayed the fact that eventually his father had refused to help any further and he got to a point where he owed so much money that his life was threatened.

"Threatened by Cliff Mitchell?"

"Yes...how do you know that?"

"Never mind," Cannon replied, ignoring the question. "What else?"

Jacobsen thought for a second, then shivered, the memory of the recent past bringing things into stark reality.

"He threatened my position at the university if I didn't pay up."

"By spreading rumours about you and some female students?"

Open-mouthed and wide-eyed, Jacobsen looked stunned. "Yes..." he said finally, "but it wasn't true."

"So, what else did he do and how did you end up getting involved with the ALA?"

"He gave me a deadline to settle my debts and if I couldn't pay by then, then he would *come and collect*."

"Which you took to mean...?"

"That he would beat me up, expose me by starting another rumour...possibly kill me. I don't know..."

Tears began to well up in Jacobsen's eyes, he knew he was still not yet in the clear. The ALA linkage alone would not sit well with the University.

"So, what happened next?"

The lecturer wiped away a tear that had run down his cheek. "Out of the blue, without any warning, Mitchell offered me a way out. It was weird, it was as if something had come over him."

"What was it?"

"He asked me to take the lead with a group of people who wanted to stop jumps racing because they felt it is cruel."

"Is that all?"

"No. He wanted a campaign launched that would result in the long term shutting down of racing and the ultimate closure of some racecourses."

"The third demand of the ALA," Cannon said out-loud, remembering what he had been told when he was in the pub with the three girls. As Cannon listened to Toby talk, he recognized that it was his voice on the other end of the phone from that very conversation. He stayed quiet.

"Yes, the third demand of the ALA," Jacobsen repeated.

"And is that how you got involved with them?"

"He introduced them to me. He set up a meeting, up in Oxford."

"And?"

"Well I'm not sure how he found them, I can only suspect that one of the group owed him money as well, but I don't know. We never spoke about it. Mitchell arranged the time, and I joined the group."

"What did you do?"

"Let's just say they are a group of idealistic people who are easily led. They have a cause, and they believe in it. I was able to magnify the cause, take it beyond freeing animals or using whips in a race and take it up a few levels to stop all jumps racing and close down jumps courses."

"Do you believe in the cause, then?"

The reply came back quickly, without hesitation, "No! Of course not. I don't believe in their cause at all. It was just a means to an end."

"To pay off your debt?"

"Yes."

"Which resulted in some people *and* some horses getting killed."

"Which should never have happened."

"But it did!" replied Cannon angrily.

"Yes, you're right. It did, and for that, I am eternally saddened. It was a mistake."

Cannon watched Jacobsen's shoulders begin to shudder. The man began to weep again. Cannon waited until the lecturer had stopped crying and had wiped away the tears from his eyes before asking, "Is it all over now, then?"

"How do you mean?"

"Well the BHA has decided to go ahead with the meeting at Huntingdon in the next few days and have ignored the other demands made, so what has the ALA decided to do in response?"

"To be honest I don't know."

"You don't know?" Cannon asked incredulously. "How come you don't know? And anyway, how big is this group?"

Jacobsen laughed sardonically. "That's the whole point. The whole group excluding me is no more than a dozen people, and the main group who did all the work, all the planning, was only me and four others."

Cannon couldn't get his head around the fact that a small group could cause so much damage to such a large industry. Most people were generally aware from the TV news and Hollywood movies about small *cells* affiliated to larger organizations that often worked alone. Even individuals, *lone wolves,* did that, but to think that such a small group of people were nearly killing the racing industry beggared belief, in Cannon's eyes.

"Surely you've been in touch with the group since the Huntingdon announcement was made?" Cannon asked.

"Yes, and I told them to lay low. To do nothing."

Cannon suddenly had a thought. "Wait a minute," he said, "what about Mitchell? If the BHA have ignored the threats of the ALA and racing is continuing again, aren't you still on the hook to him?"

"No, I'm not anymore."

"Why not? From what you have told me I would have thought he would be calling in his money by now?"

Jacobsen gave Cannon a sad smile. "I managed to negotiate an out," he said. "I let him know that I'd done enough. I'd done all he asked of me and that I wasn't prepared to do anymore for him."

"A bold move, I'd say."

"Perhaps, but after what happened at Uttoxeter I made it clear to him that I thought we were even. That I had met all my obligations."

"How did he take it?"

"Not well, but I also told him that I had recordings of our conversations and that if I went down, so would he."

"And do you? Have the recordings?" he asked. "They could be useful, you know."

"What do you think?" Jacobsen asked.

Cannon said nothing. He drew his own conclusions.

"Okay," he said eventually. "If you give me the details of the other members of the ALA, names, addresses, etcetera, then I'll do the best I can to keep you out of sight of the police."

Jacobsen looked at Cannon cynically. He thought about things for a second knowing that he had nothing to lose and everything to gain. He wasn't sure about Cannon's motives but eventually accepted that his cooperation could only be for the better.

He provided Cannon will all the detail he could. All he knew.

---------------------------

On the drive back to Oxfordshire, Cannon called Porter and told him about

Formrobe's voicemail and of his own meeting with Toby Jacobsen. He gave Porter the address where Jacobsen and the others of the ALA had met within the university precinct but left out some of the detail of the conversation. Porter was furious with Cannon. He castigated him for getting directly involved, telling him that he should have left well alone, that it was the police's responsibility to question Jacobsen. Cannon tried to change the subject, suggesting Porter should arrange a swoop of the premises where the ALA as a group met. Cannon knew now that it was someone called Kevin who was a student at the University who rented the apartment and that he should be arrested along with the other members of the ALA. He provided Porter with all the applicable detail that he felt was appropriate to share from that he had gleaned from Jacobsen. He hoped it was enough. He told Porter that he had established that Jacobsen was only a bit player. He held his tongue and fought his conscience as he lied. It went against the grain, but in the end, he believed that Jacobsen had never really intended to take the ALA beyond the use of words, had never intended for them to act upon them. Time and further questioning would confirm that conclusion.

Before he had left the campus, he had asked Jacobsen to provide him with a hair sample for DNA purposes and a few fingerprints. When Cannon told Porter that he had managed to obtain these, Porter was again less than pleased and talked about clever lawyers and loopholes in connection with how the samples were collected. Cannon was aware of all the arguments, having heard them many times in the past when he was in the Force. Cannon accepted the criticism but hoped that the game he was playing would keep Jacobsen out of court, out of jail. It was a gamble, as he knew Porter was still likely to question Jacobsen, anyway.

# CHAPTER 62

Clifford Mitchell sat alone in the interview room. He was extremely nervous but tried not to show it. He had driven up to the Cannock Police station on Wolverhampton Road and had arrived just before eleven-thirty. By the time his details were taken, it was just after midday when he was seated. He had thought a lot about what to expect, but still had some doubts in his mind as to the real reason for being asked to meet with Porter.

The door to the room opened, Porter, Sergeant Fox, and a Constable who took a position by the door, entered.

"Don't get up, Mr. Mitchell," Porter said jovially, suggesting nothing untoward, "please stay seated, and thank you for coming."

Mitchell nodded, "No problem at all Inspector, I enjoyed the drive."

Porter introduced Fox and explained the reason why he had asked Mitchell to meet with them.

"We are investigating what's been going on around the country with regards to the attacks on several racecourses, and you will have seen what happened at Uttoxeter."

"Yes."

"Well we think you can help us," he lied, "and we'd like your input or your insight into a couple of issues."

Mitchell took the words literally. Subtlety and reading between the lines were not his forte. Porter was relying on it.

"Mr. Mitchell," Porter continued, "we are going to record the meeting and as no one is under arrest or is to be charged, there is no need for anyone to be represented. Are you in agreement?"

Mitchell nodded acceptance and the recording device was switched on by Fox.

"Excellent," Porter said.

Mitchell began to relax, he wanted to sit back but being seated in a straight-backed chair he was unable to do so. Mentally he was more settled but physically he was uncomfortable. Formalities over, Porter began.

"Mr. Mitchell, if I may could you please tell me your occupation?"

"Sure, I'm a bookmaker. A licensed bookmaker, a private one. I'm not part of any large corporation and don't intend to be. I've been in this game for over forty years now and I'm happy being my own boss," he answered.

"And you have a *rails* stand or patch at several courses?"

"Yes, I do. Some patches I've had ever since I started."

"Including Uttoxeter?"

"Well yes, nearly. I've been there for well on thirty years."

"A long time," Porter acknowledged.

"Yes."

"So, what happened the other week at the course, and the shutdown of racing ever since, must be a big blow to you?"

"Absolutely. It's costing me money."

"Do you have any idea who would have carried out such a thing?"

"The bombing? No, why should I?" Mitchell replied. He was curious as to the question and he eyed Porter accordingly. Suspicion was slowly creeping in.

"Well we are looking at all angles and given your presence at the various courses we wondered if you had heard or seen anything? Anything unusual? Talk in the bar perhaps?"

"No," Mitchell repeated. "I may be on course a lot but I'm normally too busy to sit or stand around and listen to other people's conversations. I have my business to run. I don't worry about anybody else's."

Porter saw the opportunity. "Does your *business* extend to other things?"

"What do mean, Inspector?" Mitchell replied, hiding a nagging feeling that was beginning to form in his stomach.

"Well, you know."

"No, I *don't* know."

Porter knew he would need to spell things out. "If people don't pay up. Your customers or clients, what do you do?"

"My clients *always* pay." An emphatic reply.

"Umm…well, we've had a couple of complaints and we wanted to check their validity," Porter replied. He was bending the truth a little. O'Smullegan had mentioned his concern to Cannon about the bet he had placed with Mitchell on the day of the bombing and how Mitchell was not likely to refund the full amount of what he considered a *null and void* bet. It seemed that Mitchell bent the rules of bookmaking at times. Cannon had mentioned this to Porter, and additionally, he had been able to obtain how much O'Smullegan owed Mitchell. There was a pattern emerging.

"Complaints? By whom?" Mitchell asked, his ire beginning to rise.

It was what Porter wanted. He needed Mitchell in a space where he was not thinking clearly.

"It's not necessary to discuss it yet, Mr. Mitchell, we are just trying to establish the efficacy of the complaint first. If we think it's worthwhile pursuing, we will come back to you."

"Fine," Mitchell responded, still seething.

Porter played his first card from under the table. It was time. "Tell me about Toby Jacobsen," he asked.

"I'm sorry, who?"

"Oh, come now Mr. Mitchell," Porter reacted disbelievingly, "are you telling me you don't know the name? One of your customers?"

"Never heard of him."

Porter turned towards Fox. He raised an eyebrow and then turned back to face Mitchell. "Never heard of him, you say?"

"That's right."

"Really?"

"Yes. Really."

Porter's face showed the incredulity he felt. "Are you telling me that the man who has lost more than fifty thousand pounds to you alone over several years is someone you *don't* know?"

Mitchell was beginning to feel uncomfortable inside. He wasn't sure if it was showing on his face or through his body language, but he was unhappy as to where the conversation appeared to be going. He needed to find a way out.

"I'm sorry Inspector, but not every client I have uses their real name when they place bets with me. Some use non-de-plumes, some use false names, I don't care which, as long as they honour their obligations."

"And if they don't?"

"They generally do."

Porter thought about this. "So, you are saying that the man we know as Toby Jacobsen, is known by you under another name?"

"On the face of it, yes."

"I'm not sure I believe you, Mr. Mitchell."

The bookmaker didn't respond. He felt inside his jacket pocket and pulled out a cigar case. He was playing for time. Time to think. What had that bastard Jacobsen said, he thought? Did he really have taped recordings of their conversations? He opened the case before seeing that both policemen were looking at him with disdain. Smoking inside the room was banned. A large no-smoking sign sat on one of the walls.

He closed the case, returning it to the jacket pocket.

"Do you know that Toby Jacobsen may have been involved in what happened at Uttoxeter?"

"I keep telling you Inspector that I don't know him."

Porter leaned forward on the desk that they were sitting at. He lowered his head so that his eye line was level with that of Mitchell, and responded by saying very quietly, so softly that Mitchell had to strain to hear what was said.

"And I'm telling *you*, Mr. Mitchell, that I think you are lying."

Before Mitchell could react, Porter shot upright, pushing his chair back with his legs sending it clattering to the floor. The Constable jumped with fright. Mitchell did the same. It was a tactic Fox had seen before. He didn't move, however, a grin crossed his face, the entire episode designed to unsettle a possible suspect. Mitchell's heart hammered in his chest. At sixty-two he felt that he was close to a heart attack.

Porter turned around and picked up the chair as if nothing had happened, casually sitting down upon it saying, "I'm sorry about that Mr. Mitchell, what were you saying?"

Mitchell waited for his heart to slow, the thumping to ease.

"What about this Jacobsen fella? What does it have to do with me, anyway?" he asked.

"Ah, so you *do* know him?" jumped in Fox.

"I'm not saying that. I'm just wondering why you think I do."

"Because we believe he was acting on your behalf."

A quizzical look crossed Mitchell's face. "Really?"

"Yes. Really."

"To do what?"

"To pay off his debt."

"I told you before, I…."

"Yes, we heard. You don't know him…" Fox jumped in.

Mitchell crossed his arms. Things were getting uncomfortable. He was trying to work out what Porter knew and what was guesswork or conjecture. By holding the line, Mitchell believed that he was safe. He would deal with Jacobsen once he was able to get away and was back to Surrey.

"Tell me, Inspector, I came here of my own free will and as I understand things, I believe I can leave at any time on the same basis. Is that correct?"

"Yes, Sir that's right. Until we charge you with anything, you are free to come and go as you please."

"Okay, so do you intend to charge me, then?"

"With what?"

"You tell me."

Porter always loved these games. Sometimes they lasted weeks or even months before results were achieved. Given his commitment to the BHA and the need to resolve the ALA issue, this one wasn't as much fun. He played his second card.

"Do you know a Judy Smerdon?"

Mitchell felt like he had been punched in the stomach. It was as if he was suddenly winded. He couldn't breathe. He tried not to react, but he had an involuntary spasm, a coughing fit. There were jugs of water on a side table. Fox got up and poured half a glass, offering it to Mitchell who took it with both hands, sipping at the cool liquid.

They waited until Mitchell appeared ready to continue.

"I'll repeat the question, Mr. Mitchell. Do you know a Judy Smerdon?"

Mitchell nodded. "Barely," he said.

Porter went for the jugular.

"Did you kill her?"

"What?" replied Mitchell. "What is this? What's going on here?" he complained. "I think I need a lawyer," he said somewhat dramatically, almost theatrically.

"Okay, let me put it another way. Did you *arrange* for her to be killed?"

Mitchell was both scared and outraged, the accusations getting too close to the bone.

"Look Inspector, I don't know what your game is, but I've had enough of this. You asked me here to help you with your enquiries, not be subject to this…this…abuse."

"It's not abusing *you* if it's true, Mr. Mitchell," Porter replied, knowing that he was walking a fine line given he hadn't yet charged the bookmaker. If he was going to, he needed to read him his rights first. He decided to try another tack.

"Mrs. Smerdon was found dead a day or so ago at her home. She had been deceased for a few days and it wasn't a pretty sight. The autopsy will confirm the cause, but we believe that she was strangled to death."

"Murdered?" Mitchell asked, noting in his head that in terms of timing it was probably the reason why she hadn't returned his calls. He felt much better now. It *was* over.

Porter's comments broke into his thoughts. "Yes. She was murdered."

"Well I can assure you, Inspector, I had nothing to do with it."

"So, you say."

"Yes, I do."

"So can you explain to me then why, if you only *barely* knew her, you tried to call her mobile phone nearly twenty times in just a few days including some calls made around the time we think she was killed? It seems very strange to call someone so often, someone you hardly know, doesn't it?" he said. Continuing, Porter added, "We have already accessed her call history and we have been able to establish the owners of the numbers who tried to contact her. Your number pops up quite a lot it seems, *including* Mrs. Smerdon contacting you. It seems very strange for people to do that if they hardly know one another."

Mitchell stayed quiet, thinking. Eventually, he said, "Okay, yes I do know her, barely, but I also called her *after* the time you said she was likely killed, including yesterday. Why would I do that if I knew she was already dead?"

"To give the impression that you didn't know she was."

"I keep telling you Inspector, I didn't know. I didn't kill her! How many times must I tell you?"

"So why did you keep trying to contact her then, Mr Mitchell? What was so important that you needed to speak with her so urgently?"

"It's private."

"Private!?" Porter laughed out loud, unsettling Mitchell even more. "Something so private and so urgent that required you to call her phone so many times?"

"Yes."

"I don't believe you."

"I don't care what you think, Inspector. I had nothing to do with her death."

The game was on. Porter realized that Mitchell had forgotten that he could walk out at any time. He was too busy defending himself to realize it. Keeping the conversation going allowed Porter to lead Mitchell to where he wanted him to go.

"So, you don't know Toby Jacobsen, you barely know Judy Smerdon, so tell me, did you know *Lesley* Smerdon?"

Mitchell's insides turned to water. His face drained of colour. He felt dizzy. He reached for the glass of water again.

"Have we hit a nerve, Mr. Mitchell? It seems like we have," Fox said somewhat sarcastically. He had been playing the quiet one of the pair so far, it was how the game was played. They waited again for Mitchell to compose himself, then Fox read him his rights.

"What am I being charged for?" he asked.

"The murder of Judy Smerdon *and* her husband Lesley Smerdon."

"But I told you I had nothing to do with Judy Smerdon's death."

"And Lesley Smerdon?"

"I know nothing about that either," he said.

Porter smiled cynically. "Well we have evidence to the contrary, Mr. Mitchell," he said. The email from Alan Smerdon forwarded to Porter wasn't enough to convict anyone, indeed it just inferred Mitchell's role in Alan's fathers' death, but was enough to be used against Mitchell to try and get him to crack. Porter hoped he would. The game of cat and mouse was still to be played out.

"I want a lawyer before I answer any more of your questions," Mitchell said. He didn't know what the police knew. He guessed that they had no evidence of any of the crimes that they were accusing him of. He believed that what had happened years ago had remained buried. He thought the police were bluffing. In his mind, he couldn't see how they would know about what had happened that night. How could they?

"You can have a lawyer, your own, or if you like we can provide one as I have just indicated. It is your right. In the meantime, Mr. Mitchell you are under arrest."

Mitchell reacted, pushing back the chair he was sitting on with a loud scraping noise. He shouted objections and obscenities, but Porter and Fox let it wash over them. They had seen the like many times before.

Porter slowly stood up and nodded to the Constable at the door. Mitchell was placed in handcuffs, while repeating his demand for his lawyer, and was eventually taken from the room to a holding cell. He was left overnight. Fox contacted Mitchell's lawyer as required. The man agreed to drive up the next morning from Dorking and would be available before midday.

# CHAPTER 63

The raid on Kevin's flat was arranged for three am. It was two days before racing would start again at Huntingdon. A dozen policemen, in addition to Fox and Porter, were used to take positions around the building and a small contingent from that number were to break through the door if Kevin did not answer. The Forensic team was to remain outside until requested to enter.

The clear sky had resulted in a temperature drop, it was heading down towards freezing. The previous few days showers had made the garden soil and grass, soft and soggy. Plants and shrubs in the garden around the building were trampled on as the police got into position.

When everyone was in place Porter gave the signal and suddenly a cacophony of noise pierced the air. Banging on the flat door and shouting, the police signalled their presence and intent. Within forty seconds of starting it was all over. The door was smashed in, lights turned on, rooms and cupboards searched. What was originally a neat, ground floor student flat had been turned into a ragged mess. Muddy boots left a trail from the front door, across the carpets, and into the kitchen and bedroom. There was nobody in the flat. It was empty. There was no sign of anyone having stayed there for a few days. Nothing in the fridge, no food in the cupboards. The place had been made spotless. Even the bed had been stripped of sheets and pillowcases. The place had been vacuumed completely and there were no clothes, towels, or even a toothbrush. It was clear that any attempt to obtain DNA evidence had been made much more difficult than it would normally be.

Porter looked for any sign of a computer, a laptop, but there was no sign of one. If there had been, Kevin had taken it with him. But where? Even the wifi Router had been removed, along with all remote-control devices. Porter called in Forensics to conduct a sweep of the premises, looking for traces of explosive residue and drugs.

They had hoped that the raid would mean that the worst was over. Now it was clear that it wasn't.

Two hundred yards down the street from the flat, a figure dressed in black had braved the cold. He crouched low, staying in the shadows formed by a privet hedge at the end of a small garden. He had watched them take their positions, heard them shout, but he had been a couple of steps ahead of them. Watching what was happening he realized in that instant that *he* was the real leader of the ALA. He concluded that Toby wasn't really one of them. He was just an interloper. The police could only have found where he lived if Toby had given them his details. It was a shock in one way, but when he thought about Toby's insistence that they wait to see what the authorities would do in response to their demands, it all made sense now. All the pieces fitted together. He was angry. Once he had finished his work at Huntingdon, he would finish Toby. It was a promise to himself that he intended to keep. Toby Jacobsen was dead!

Having seen enough he slowly crept away down the street, turning left at the next road, and soon he was out of sight of the flat. He could never go back. He never intended to.

He arrived at Tracey's flat just before four am. He used the key that she had given him. Once inside he undressed and quickly climbed into her bed. His body was cold, and she complained as he put his arm around her naked body. She awoke briefly as he snuggled closer to her. She felt him getting aroused. "No," she said.

He didn't fight her. He lay for a few minutes thinking about what *they* had started and how *he* wanted to finish things. The cause was important. It was now up to him to show *them* how seriously he was taking it.

# CHAPTER 64

Cannon had sent in his nominations for the Huntingdon races as soon as the meeting had been announced. He had two runners, *Western Bay* and *The Politician.*

"If we want to get him into the *Tingle Creek* then he needs to get a few runs under his belt," Cannon explained to Formrobe and Simon Lithgow. Telside stood to the right of *The Politician's* original owner and Cannon stood to the left of Formrobe. Lithgow had not met his new 50% partner before getting together on the gallops, but Cannon had now introduced them. They clicked easily. Lithgow, a 4th generation butcher was easy going and Formrobe was extremely grateful to him and the family for allowing him to buy into the horse. All four watched as the gelding undertook his work. The horse was relishing the task at hand, ears flicking with each jump that he took, landing ahead of his training partner, and expanding the gap between them at every obstacle they cleared.

"He's jumping out of his skin," Telside said, "even with the big weight tomorrow, he'll do well."

"Do you expect him to win?" Lithgow asked, "I wouldn't mind putting a bet on."

"We're not taking him there to win," Cannon advised, "we just want to give him a good run to blow out a few cobwebs after the halt in racing, but the way he is going currently, he'll certainly give a good account of himself."

"I'll take that as a yes then, Mike?"

"I didn't say that Simon," Cannon replied with a smile.

"You never do, Mike. You always hedge your bets."

The four of them laughed. What Lithgow said was true about Cannon. He was always cautious. There were never any guarantees in the sport no matter how well things seemed to be with the horse. Sometimes luck or fate could play a hand.

--------------------

Cannon was back in his office when Porter called him. The two owners of *The Politician* had earlier left to go to work and while Telside made sure the normal stable routine continued, Cannon had used the time to arrange everything needed for the meeting at Huntingdon the next day. He had been reading a press release issued jointly by the BHA and the Huntingdon course management when the phone had rung. The meeting was going to be bigger than usual due to the number of runners in each of the seven races on the card, and the expectation of a massive crowd. The course had arranged a celebration as well, to show its appreciation. A *Welcome Back to Racing* gift bag for the first three thousand patrons through the turnstiles was on offer. Normally, the average the course had for each race meeting was about eighteen hundred attendees. The hope for this meeting was for four thousand. This would be a big boost to the club, and they had been rewarded with an above-average field size of twelve runners per race. To add to the festivities, and despite the cool weather forecast, the course had also organized various types of entertainment to keep punters happy. Bands, food, and other specialty stalls would be set up on the inside of the track. It was going to be more of a celebration than just a normal race meeting.

"We've charged Clifford Mitchell with the murder of Judy Smerdon and her husband, Lesley," Porter had said.

"How did he react?"

"He said he had nothing to do with Judy's murder, and didn't say anything about the husband. After that, he asked for his lawyer. The man is due up here in the next couple of hours."

Porter then shared more detail about his discussion with Mitchell, both agreeing that what was said between them was *unofficial, off the record.*

Cannon listened carefully. Things seemed to fit when he took on board the clues left by Alan and what he and Formrobe had discussed earlier once they were alone, after the training gallops. Lithgow had said his goodbyes and Rich had returned to the stables leaving Cannon and Formrobe alone on the heath allowing the latter an opportunity to give Cannon further insight into Alan and Judy Smerdon. Judy had brought-up Alan more-or-less alone. He was raised in Wolverhampton and had remained living there most of his life, except while attending University. Judy had never moved very far away from where she had been born, despite being very wealthy. She had lived in the same house for the past twelve years, until her murder. Alan had originally lived just a few streets away from his mother, but since he had sold most of his share in *SecureTwo* he had moved up north to live in a small village called Church Wallsop, near Mansfield. This was the last information that Formrobe had.

"Something is still bothering me about all this," Cannon indicated to the policeman, "something I should have remembered, but I can't recall what it was."

"About what?" Porter asked.

"I don't know and that's the whole point. I can't recall but I'm sure it's important. God what is it?!" he admonished himself.

"Is it related to Mitchell?"

"No, but now that you've said it, I don't think Mitchell killed Judy Smerdon."

"Why not?"

"Why would he?"

"That's what we need to find out," Porter said. "They clearly had some form of relationship otherwise why would he keep trying to contact her?"

"Could they have been lovers?"

Porter hadn't considered this. "I guess anything's possible," he replied, "but I'm not sure Mitchell will own up to it. We know he's lied about knowing anyone so far, including Toby Jacobsen."

"Well, it's clear from the email that Formrobe received from Alan, which he passed on to us, that something was going on. He specifically said to ask Mitchell about Alan's father."

"I'll be doing that soon, once Mitchell's lawyer arrives. In the meantime, I've requested that the Nottingham police try and contact Alan Smerdon."

"Oh shit, no. Not Dockly?"

"No, not Dockly," Porter replied, putting Cannon at ease. "Anyway, what I need them to do is below his pay grade. I've been in touch with local command and asked that they pay a visit to Smerdon's house. I'd like to get him in here for a chat, see what he really knows about Mitchell, not just what he has been inferring in his email. The problem is though, that it seems he's not answering his phones, either the landline or his mobile."

"Doesn't that seem strange to you?"

"It does, yes," Porter said, his voice expressing frustration. "I'm not even sure he knows yet that his mother is dead. As next of kin, we need to advise him."

Cannon sought a favour. He knew it was pushing the barrow out a little, but he requested that Porter allow him to sit in on any conversation Porter would be having with Smerdon.

"I'm not sure I can, Mike," Porter said, "maybe you can watch through a monitor outside the room, I'll need to see. But," he added, "I'll only advise you once we've been able to track him down."

Cannon couldn't argue. It was a favour and he knew he had no right to ask. There being nothing else to discuss, the two men said their goodbyes and ended the call.

Cannon sat for a minute trying to recall what he knew was in the back of his mind. It was important. He knew it was. What was it, he thought?

Unable to recall, he turned back to his computer and continued to look at upcoming race meetings, nominating horses within his stable where appropriate.

After a while, his mind still unsettled, he looked again at Alan Smerdon's email passed on to him by Formrobe. It was clear that Alan was hinting at something between Mitchell and his own father. As he looked at the words, a linkage formed in his mind. A chain. He picked up the phone again and called Porter.

---------------

After speaking with Porter, Cannon called Ralph Tolman.

"Any luck with Dockly and the Pool and Bronton murders?" Cannon asked.

"Not yet," Tolman said, "but I think some progress has been made."

"What are your contacts in the police saying?"

"Well those that don't like Dockly have told me how incompetent he is at times and so they have leaked some information to me, but as far as making an arrest is concerned, it seems they are not yet close."

"Umm," Cannon replied. "To be fair to Dockly, I don't think he's useless. I just think he's a bit lazy at times. Tries to cut corners, perhaps. He wouldn't be an Inspector if he was unable to do the job."

"I guess you're right, Mike but…up here they call him a *Dudley do nothing*," he laughed.

"Well keep me informed, will you? I don't want him coming to arrest me again."

"I'm sure it won't come to that," the journalist continued. "Oh, by the way…"

"Yes?"

"I need to tell you that I've run up a bit of a bar bill, Mike," Tolman continued, "despite the cold weather, it's thirsty work keeping my contacts happy."

Cannon laughed out loud. "No problem," he said. "I didn't expect anything less," he continued. He needed some light relief and Tolman had just given him some. "Send me the bill when you can."

Tolman chuckled himself before adding. "Oh, and as far as Peter Todd is concerned, no sign, I'm sorry to say, Mike. Nothing. Whoever he is, he's just disappeared."

"Okay," Cannon replied, disappointed. "Well, just keep looking, if you wouldn't mind? Maybe your contacts in the Force may still be able to help?"

"I doubt it, Mike, they are too busy with other duties. Searching for someone like Todd, who has not been reported as missing, is not critical. I'll just keep poking around anyway and see what comes up."

"Thank you, Ralph, I appreciate your help. I hope you're still able to do what you need for the paper?"

"Actually, yes I can. It's been easy so far with nothing happening on the track. I haven't needed to worry about the lead story over the past week or so either. It's the *Ed* who has been struggling, as he's needed to fill the front pages with what's going on. I think the BHA have been providing most of the news for him, you know, *the way forward*, etcetera? I've been relegated to the inside pages for now. Once racing is up and running again properly, then I'll need to get back to it seriously. I'll need to let go of your stuff."

"I understand."

"I'm assuming the story you have for me is nearly there?"

"Yes. I'm sure it's going to be sensational. We just need to…."

Cannon suddenly stopped talking. Tolman thought the line had dropped out.

"Hello, hello. Mike? Are you still there?"

"Yes, sorry Ralph," he apologized. "I just realized something."

"Anything I can help with?"

"No, not just yet, but I think you've given me the answer I was looking for."

"Really?"

"Yes, really!" Cannon replied. "I think you've just solved the Peter Todd conundrum."

Tolman was surprised and curious but Cannon kept his thoughts to himself.

He thanked Tolman for his continued help and they disconnected. Immediately he made another call.

# CHAPTER 65

He was used to it now. He knew how to evade most of the security that they had put in place. His only concern was the dogs. It seemed like the Huntingdon course management had been advised that it was possible an attack could be made on them, so the number of security guards had been increased in the hope of warding off anyone stupid enough to want to try. The police may know a little about the ALA, but as far as he was concerned, they didn't know everything, Kevin thought.

Since the raid on his flat, he had stayed with Tracey, not bothering to go back. He knew that there was nothing of significance that he had left behind and so far, the police had not attempted to raid Tracey's place or that of Sara and Tina who shared an accommodation unit. Of the others, the hangers-on, those on the periphery, Kevin knew their names and their phone numbers but he had never shared their detail with anyone, even with Toby. He believed that his *need to know* policy had worked. It had stopped any leakage of information and at worst the only real detail the police would have been able to glean from Toby was Kevin's name and address. If the police worked quickly enough he knew that by contacting the University they would get his personal details and maybe those of some of his associates, like Tracey. He hoped that privacy considerations and red tape would hold the process up for a couple of days. By then he would be long gone. He had completed his studies in the spring, only remaining in the city to see if he would be offered a tutorship. It was still pending. He would have been happy if it came off, but he was no longer committed to it. What he *was* committed to was the ALA cause, or at least the principles. He was driven by his view on animal cruelty and he saw jumps racing as a cruel sport. To him, it wasn't a sport, it was something akin to fox hunting. At times he thought he was the only one who took the cause seriously, and it was this reasoning that was driving him to make a statement at Huntingdon. "Fuck everyone," he said to himself, thinking of Toby, the girls the racing establishment, "Fuck them all!." After tomorrow, he may be a fugitive, but he had a plan. As soon as he had completed what he had to do, he would be off to Ireland and from there it was across to the Far East. In his mind, the cause was more important than anything now, and it drove him to the exclusion of all else. He even had the next item on his list, the stopping of dolphin massacres in and around the waters of Japan.

Having left his car in a dark corner of the Holiday Inn car park near the racecourse, he had doubled back, and keeping to the shadows, had found Alconbury Brook that flowed around the perimeter of the track. He followed it until he was furthest away from the racecourse stands. Dressed all in black, including wearing a balaclava to hide his face, he crossed the field until he came to the perimeter fence, and using wire cutters carefully cut a gap through which he could climb. Taking his time, he then carefully linked the wire fence back together, leaving a small piece of orange tape on the lowest section of the fence so that he could find the way out when he had finished his work.

He crouched down on his haunches staying absolutely still, listening for any movement. The closest sound he could hear was an owl hooting in the distance and the soft whistling of the wind through the trees around the edge of the course. In the far distance, there was a faint hum of traffic on the A141 and the A14, the traffic heading south-east to Cambridge, north to Peterborough, and west to Kettering. Once satisfied that he couldn't hear anyone in the immediate vicinity and he was happy with his night vision, he crossed the remaining gap between his position and the outside running rail of the track. He quickly ducked beneath the horizontal posts making up the rail and ran across to the closest steeplechase jump. It was the second jump down the back straight. He pushed himself flat against the *wing*, breathing heavily as he stood stock still for at least a minute. Heart beating like the pistons in a formula one race car, he tried to calm himself down. What was sixty seconds seemed like an hour as he waited for his pulse to steady. He looked across towards the stands. To the left, he could just make out some figures moving. Lights set on telescopic arms created silhouettes as men carried boxes and what looked like pipes. He realized it was those setting up the carnival rides and various other stalls. He could imagine how busy they would be, needing to be ready for the next day, race day. With so many people moving around he hoped that it would keep others away from where he was. One thing he suddenly realized was the total lack of police anywhere. He hadn't brought any binoculars that would have helped him scan the activity near the stands, for fear that light would glint off the lenses, giving him away, so he relied on his own vision, making an evaluation as best he could. He had expected that there would be some additional security around the course, protecting it. If so where was it? Maybe they were there, maybe they weren't? The thoughts in his head began to affect him. He wasn't sure if his assessment was correct. Could he really be assured that no one was watching him? Despite the cold, sweat began to trickle down his neck and his back. He felt clammy, uncomfortable, and the cold was beginning to seep through his clothes. He needed to move, to act quickly. He had four devices he needed to plant. Having made a study of the course from details he had been able to gather from the racing club's website, google maps, and other sources, he knew where he needed to go. He dropped down onto the grass and he began leopard crawling along the jump side of the fence. Once he reached the middle he got to his knees and took off the backpack that he had been carrying. Taking out a small torch that was covered with red plastic he had glued over the reflector and lens, he turned it on allowing him to find what he was looking for in the bag. It was one of the four circuit-boards that he had populated in the lock-up. He took it out of the bag, unwrapping it quickly from several sheets of carefully wrapped used newspaper. He then turned towards the jump. At the base of the jump was a wooden trough where the birch and bristles were inserted, and which held the material together forming the 5-foot barriers that the horses needed to clear. He reached into the birch, pushing his arm towards the base of the trough and placing the board at the bottom of it. Removing his arm, he used the torch to check if there was any sign of the birch having been tampered with. On the face of it, there was no sign at all. He was pleased with his work. Unless you knew where to look, no one would ever know that an electronic device, at least an ignition source, was present. Next, he took a one-litre plastic bottle of bio-ethanol fuel from the backpack. The fuel was easily obtainable from outdoor camping shops and indoor heater suppliers. He didn't need much of the highly flammable liquid. All he needed was enough to ignite, and then the flames would quickly spread to the birch. He had chosen the fuel because it was within the spirit of the *green activist* philosophy he was drawn to, and more importantly, the liquid had *no* smell, no odour. Being so benign anyone who came looking to find something unusual within or on the jump would be unable to do so.

He was pleased with his decisions. He had done his research well. Quickly pouring half the contents in the area immediately surrounding his ignition device, he closed the cap on the bottle and re-inserted it into his backpack. He took a few minutes break to see if there was any movement in the immediate vicinity then noticing all was quiet other than the area away in the distance, he ducked under the inside running rail making his way in the shadows towards a hurdle jump near the corner of the track. It was the final jump before the horses entered the straight. It took more time than he had hoped before he managed to reach the hurdle. He had stopped regularly, listening for any noise or looking for any movement that he thought may be unusually close. There was nothing obvious. If the police were around, he could not see them. His confidence grew as he completed a similar task on the second hurdle. He then moved towards the final steeplechase jump, which was in the racecourse straight, about 400m before the finish line. It was only a relatively short distance from the Grandstand, but he took great comfort from the noise of the workers constructing the kiosks in readiness for the meeting. He noticed there were several types. Food, merchandise, and several carnival-style tents, with their red and white candy stripe coverings. Staying low he crawled from the inside of the track, deciding to put his incendiary device just inside the jump, right next to the inside wing, rather than in the midsection like the others. It wasn't ideal but it was easier than exposing himself to the workers. As he was pouring the last of his fuel onto the obstacle a bright spotlight lit up the darkness. He dropped to the track, tasting the long grass in his mouth. He pushed himself as low as he could go. He hoped the dark clothes he was wearing would save him from being seen. The light moved in an arc along the track and over onto the inside of the course, before completing a circle, 360 degrees, finally lighting up the stands and the course entrances. Kevin was about to move, to finish his job when the light began to return and travel in the opposite direction. He couldn't see who was controlling it but as it skimmed his back while he lay as low and as flat as he could, a shout broke out. He thought he had been seen. His heart began racing. He raised his head slightly to see where he could run. He needed to find an escape route. A voice, a man's voice rang out. The light stopped. The beam was still, static, about ten feet to Kevin's right.

"What the hell are you doing?" the voice called.

Kevin braced himself to run. A few more seconds he thought, then I need to go!

Suddenly a second voice called out. Kevin rose to his knees.

"What do you think I'm doing?" the second voice replied. "Doing my bloody job, that's what."

"Well try and keep it out of my bloody eyes," exclaimed the first voice, "it's blinding me every time you swing past."

"Okay," shouted the second voice before muttering an oath, "will do!"

The spotlight began to move, traversing the track and away from Kevin. It moved slowly over the tents, before finally being extinguished. Kevin began to breathe easier, taking five minutes to allow his eyes to become accustomed to the dark again. He looked at his watch, the luminous figures showing him that it was just after one a.m. Aware of the spotlight and the workers putting up the tents, he quickly completed his work on the jump before deciding where he would place the fourth and final device. He hadn't considered a specific spot, but when he saw it, he knew it was perfect. The place to cause maximum damage and chaos. The pop-up food court. He noticed a group of five tents, already constructed. They were placed on the lawns to the left of the stands, close to the parade ring, and stood on three sides of a square. The fourth side was a bandstand and in the middle of the square were tables and chairs where people would be eating and drinking the next day. Because the area was already completed, nearly all the workers were busy in other parts of the course. He crawled across the track and under the outside rail, noticing that he was concealed from the workers by the tents themselves. Standing up into a crouch he worked his way around the back of the tents until he found what he was looking for. It was a tree, a large oak tree in the middle of the grassy area. In the darkness, it stood out in silhouette, light from the stands caressing one side of its frame. He visualized its leaves now turning brown and red as the summer months faded away. If he could get it to ignite, there would be mass panic. It was perfect. As he was going to attend the meeting himself to be able to set off the devices when he wanted to, he knew that he would be able to maximize the casualties if he was able to see for himself the number of people in the immediate area of the tree at the time his device ignited. He cursed himself that he hadn't made five of them, as another one under the bandstand or behind a food tent which would have resulted in the structures catching fire, would have been even better than just the four *bombs* he had brought. Despite the potential to be seen, he ran across to the tree, and using a chair to stand on, he reached upwards. He lifted himself up and from there he climbed another five feet into the body of the tree, attaching the last of the devices to a larger branch using black cable ties. Then cupping his hand, he poured some of the ethanol into it from his last bottle before rubbing it onto the trunk of the tree and along several branches. He worked as quickly as he could. He wasn't sure all the leaves would readily burn, as he could make out that some of them were still green, but he knew that the branches would ignite despite the early morning dampness that he felt along their length. Once he had satisfied himself that he had done all he needed to, he checked his surroundings before dropping back onto the chair. He placed it back into position. He made his way back behind the tents, crossing the track before searching for then finding the hole he had made in the outside fence. After climbing through and restoring the wire the best way he could, he made his way to his car. By the time he found it again, it had taken him nearly an hour and a quarter from the point he had left the tree until he had reached the car park. He was elated and exhausted.

He had decided not to go back to Tracey's place for fear that she could be raided. She wasn't aware of his thinking but he didn't know how much the police were aware of her, so as a precaution, he had booked into the Old Bridge Hotel on Castle Moat Road, barely ten-minutes' drive from the racecourse. He needed to remain invisible.
He would be back on course just before midday. His pockets would be emptied at the entrance. All the security guards would find would be keys, a wallet, and his mobile phone. The most important thing was the last item.
He felt slightly ashamed that Tracey hadn't noticed, when he moved from his flat into her's, that he hadn't unpacked his suitcases. He had also left his laptop in the boot of his car. When she had gone out the previous day to the university library and subsequently the local convenience store for some groceries, he had taken all his belongings and put them in the car. He had told her that it was precautionary, "just in case" he had said.
His thinking was that once he had finished executing his plans at

Huntingdon the next day, he would drive down to Heathrow, approximately ninety minutes away, and catch his flight to Dublin.

He had been able to dispose of the backpack and the empty bottles of fuel in a nearby Tesco parking lot, taking advantage of some charity bins that he had noticed when he had reconnoitered the area. He had pushed them deep inside, burying them under clothes, bits of metal, and various cardboard boxes that had also been illegally dropped through the bin lids. He expected that they would only be emptied every few weeks. By then he would be long gone. He anticipated that whoever found them would curse him and have them destroyed along with the other pieces of junk.

Entering his hotel room, he made his way to the bathroom to thoroughly wash his hands and face. All traces of the bio-ethanol fuel he had come into contact with would be washed from his body, particularly his hands. Once he had showered in the morning there would be no trace at all. He would dump the clothes he was wearing when he could find a convenient spot. His main concern was to ensure that there was no trace of any explosive residue on his bags or his person when checks were made at the airport. He was leaving nothing to chance.

He climbed into bed, setting an alarm on his phone for seven-thirty. He wanted to be at breakfast by eight, allowing him to take his time getting to the racecourse. He was excited.

# CHAPTER 66

It had been a busy morning already.

Rich had taken the first and second lots for training while Cannon saw off his runners for the day. The float left his yard just after seven. The weather was playing ball, it was cool but dry and the sun was expected to breach the remaining cloud before the first race of the day at one pm. His best chance, *The Politician* was in a very good mood. Cannon could tell the horse was ready to run, and run well, and he was happy for Formrobe, as a new part-owner. He hoped it would a good start for him. While the horse wasn't running for him as a full owner and was still racing in the currently registered colours, Cannon hoped Formrobe would enjoy the experience. They had planned to meet up at the track later in the day. If they were unable to catch up before their race, they had agreed to see each other in the parade ring.

Cannon looked at the photograph for the umpteenth time. He should have asked for it earlier, a single picture from Formrobe. He had passed it on to Porter in the interim after he had spoken to him earlier. He now knew the identity of Peter Todd. Tolman's comment the previous night had sparked a memory, a thought. It was the voice, the one he had heard on the phone when he had tried to contact Pool about the wrong horse having being delivered. The call he had made to find out what was going on. His follow up as to why the horse delivered wasn't *Centaur*. He remembered the voice had said very little. As he tossed and turned overnight to Michelle's chagrin, he recalled what Formrobe had told him about where Judy Smerdon lived, where Alan was raised. Wolverhampton. The Black country! It was the accent. Peter Todd equalled Alan Smerdon. The photograph from Formrobe of the two of them together now proved it.

Cannon had hoped that Porter could find him quickly, however, the Inspector had been more concerned with the immediacy of what could happen at Huntingdon. Porter had contacted the BHA and advised them of the information the police had been able to obtain. He told them of his concern about the meeting, given his team had been unable to find some of the ALA members, particularly Kevin. The police now thought of him as the leader of the group and the most radical. Cannon had agreed and had a sick feeling in his stomach. The fact that the police had been unable to find Kevin was a major concern.

During their conversation, Cannon and Porter had discussed what they knew about Alan Smerdon. Something had happened to set off a series of killings. Cannon wanted to help. It was he, Cannon, that had found the linkage that Smerdon had been trying to warn Formrobe about. Alan's clues had linked Samuel Jacobsen in a chain that led to his son, the ALA, to

Mitchell and then to Judy Smerdon. The question was why?

He hoped that Porter would allow him to observe the initial interview with Alan once they were able to find him. Porter advised him that a request had gone out across the country to all police stations to have him arrested. Cannon knew the drill.

As he was about to leave for Huntingdon, he realized that he should call Dockly and fill him in. He told the policeman his theory about who Peter Todd was, only to receive a sceptical response. Cannon told him that Porter was now chasing Smerdon, was trying to find him, and bring him in for questioning. Dockly objected to what was happening saying that the case was his. Cannon deflected the objection by asking Dockly to liaise with Porter. He sensed that Dockly was not particularly keen to do so, but he left it to the two of them to resolve. He also called Tolman quickly telling him his theory about Peter Todd, which was now confirmed, the photograph that was still sitting on the desk in his office providing all the necessary evidence. He let the journalist know that, as agreed, he could have the full story once the final pieces were put together. Tolman was happy to stand-down telling Cannon that he was already on his way to Huntingdon. He hoped that they could meet up during the day if Cannon was free at any point. Cannon agreed.

# CHAPTER 67

Alan Smerdon/Peter Todd was arrested at a Services stop on the M42 just south of Birmingham airport and a few miles north of Solihull. He was heading back to Wolverhampton. He did not put up any resistance and the few onlookers at the petrol station where he had stopped to buy fuel barely noticed him being taken into custody. He had been somewhat unlucky to be caught. The policemen who had recognized his car had stopped a short while earlier to buy themselves a late breakfast and had pulled up in the car park near the petrol station pumps to eat.

The drive to Cannock police station, where he would be charged and interviewed by Porter, took about forty-five minutes. He was placed in a cell pending Porter being available. The Inspector, however, would not be able to conduct an initial interview until the following day. Porter's focus was on Mitchell, but once he had the news about Smerdon's arrest, he called Cannon out of courtesy and told him the news.

---------------------------

Mitchells' lawyer, John Howton had arrived. He had been allowed an hour with his client before they began the interview. They started just before one in the afternoon. Porter was focused on the interview with Mitchell, however, in the back of his mind, he was half expecting someone to rush in and tell him that some drama was happening at the Huntingdon meeting. He had a team of people at the track, led by Fox, and he had his phone next to him on the table that sat between himself, Mitchell, and Howton. He was ready to take a call should anything happen in Cambridgeshire.

After all the formalities had been concluded, Porter began his questioning.

"Mr. Mitchell," he said leaning forward, both hands together as if he was praying, "yesterday you said that you didn't know Judy Smerdon, Toby Jacobsen, or Lesley Smerdon. Is that still correct?"

Mitchell looked at his lawyer. Horton replied on Mitchell's behalf. "My client now recalls that he did have some slight engagement with Mrs. Smerdon and with a Mr.Toby Jacobsen, yes."

"Slight!" Porter responded.

"Yes."

"So little that he called Judy Smerdon nearly twenty times in what was a very short period of time?"

Howton smiled. "My client's phone was on auto-dial. It wasn't a manual attempt to call Mrs. Smerdon."

"Ummm," Porter responded.

Howton and Mitchell stayed quiet.

"You know that we've charged your client with murder. The murder of Judy Smerdon?"

"Yes, I know that Inspector," Howton responded. "It's a charge that we strenuously deny."

"I didn't expect anything else, Mr. Howton."

"And we will be applying for bail the moment this interview is concluded," Howton continued. "I haven't seen any evidence yet that suggests my client had anything to do with Mrs. Smerdon's death, so I don't think we will have any problem with our application."

Porter knew from his earlier conversation with Cannon that Mitchell was not involved in Judy Smerdon's death, but he wanted to scare the man. He knew from his questioning the previous day that Mitchell had something to do with Lesley Smerdon's death, but the only evidence he had on that matter was the information that Cannon had provided, Alan Smerdon's email.

Porter turned to face Mitchell, who had remained completely silent so far. "I asked you yesterday about Mr. Lesley Smerdon and you said you didn't know him either. Is that still true or has your memory improved overnight?" he said sarcastically.

"As I said …" Mitchell began before being interrupted by Howton.

"Inspector, I'm not sure where these ludicrous charges are emanating from, but as with Mrs. Judy Smerdon, my client does not know what you are referring to."

"The murder of Judy Smerdon's husband, is what I am referring to, Mr. Howton," Porter replied.

"Another piece of fiction, Inspector?"

Porter sat back. He rubbed his chin, thinking. What he was about to say was a gamble. He watched and waited as Mitchell and Howton conversed quietly. Mitchell smiled at his lawyer. It seemed that he was comfortable with the process so far, his demeanour radiating confidence that he would soon be released and would be on his way home. Porter decided to wipe the smile off Mitchell's face.

"We have evidence of your client's involvement in the murder of Lesley Smerdon," he said.

The gamble caused a stir, getting the reaction he wanted. Howton turned swiftly to his client, whispering in his ear.

"What evidence is that, Inspector?"

"A witness," he said. "An eye-witness."

"That's impossible!" Mitchell blurted out, "There was no one els…."

He stopped suddenly, realizing his error. Howton was quick to jump in. "My client retracts his outburst," he said, "and denies any knowledge of what you are inferring, Inspector."

Porter smiled. Neither Mitchell nor Howton was aware of what Porter knew or didn't know about Lesley Smerdon. He kept them guessing but hoped like hell that Alan Smerdon was going to provide everything that Porter needed to convict Mitchell. He still didn't know what Cannon knew either, but he had faith that there would be enough to put Mitchell behind bars. He suspended the interview.

Tomorrow would be an interesting day.

# CHAPTER 68

The management of the course were ecstatic. Over three thousand people at the meeting. It was a huge coup for Huntingdon. To be the first track in use after the halt in racing was special. The crowd was in good spirits. The organization of the parking facilities, improved course access, and the giving out of the *Back to Racing* gift bags had been well received. They had met in the board room earlier that morning and were now watching from the glass-enclosed restaurant that overlooked the course. Congratulating themselves, they observed the crowds moving around from the various food stalls, the bookmaker stands, the parade ring, and the stable area. The sun had come out from behind some low-level cloud that still threatened to ruin the day, but for now, it left the entire area bathed in a dull but warming light.

Kevin had been at the track just after the gates opened. He had been required to queue for at least twenty minutes before the crowd had begun to move forward and he found himself through the turnstiles. He took a walk to the grandstand and found himself a seat on the top row. To maintain his anonymity, he sat next to a group of three men and two women who had already claimed their spot. To the casual observer, he appeared to be with the group. He wore dark blue jeans, black trainers, a white polo shirt under a heavy parka coat. He also wore a dark beanie to reduce the possibility of being recognized. He didn't wear sunglasses. It wasn't bright enough, despite the improvement in the weather from the morning. He kept his left hand inside the side pocket of his coat, holding onto his mobile phone. When the time was right he would use it to send signals to the devices planted within the various jumps. They would react instantly, responding to his request to fire, to ignite the fuel surrounding them. He had originally planned to set the devices off at different times but had decided to create more chaos by having multiple explosions at the same time. By doing so, he hoped it would aid his escape.

-----------------------

Cannon was in the stables. His two runners were in stalls next to one another. *Western Bay* was to run in race two at ten-past-two, and *The Politician* in race five, at four-thirty-five. The last race was scheduled for five-thirty, a bumper, a National Hunt race where horses ran on the flat, without any jumps involved.

Cannon hoped that the day would go off without a hitch, that the ALA had

228

stayed away, but he was doubtful. He had walked the course on arrival along with his jockey for the day, Bill Circling. The jockey had recovered from what had happened at Uttoxeter and over the past week had been racing again in Ireland where meetings were still being held. His confidence had returned, and Cannon was happy to have him back aboard his two runners. Like all those who checked the jump and hurdle circuits, they could find no trace of any tampering with any of the flights or steeplechase fences. The track was given the all-clear and it was after the *sign-off,* the approval to go ahead, that the gates to the track had been opened.

----------------------------

Race one went off without a hitch. The increased field meant that the jumping was more spectacular than usual. Kevin watched from his seat as the crowd roared the winner home. His fingers nervously caressed his phone as he considered when best to set off his devices. He hoped that the bio-ethanol fuel would not evaporate in the drying sun. He knew there would be some loss due to the warmth of the day, but he only needed a small fire to start the birch burning rapidly.

------------------------------------

Cannon was ready to saddle up *Western Bay* for his race. He had the horse walk around for a few minutes in the saddling enclosure to stretch the animal's legs. *Western Bay* was entered in a two-mile hurdle race and was safely held in the betting, sitting around fifth in a field of eleven. Cannon wasn't overly confident. He just hoped that the horse would get around safely. He would improve as the season progressed. Having saddled the horse and attached the necessary racing gear, including a set of half cupped blinkers to keep the horse focused on his work, he told the stable hand to take the horse to the parade ring. He watched the horse being led away before taking out his phone and calling Porter.

"Any luck about me sitting in on the Alan Smerdon interview?" he asked. The reply was muted as Porter had just finished the interview with Mitchell, but the response was in the affirmative. He thanked the Inspector. With Smerdon having been brought into the police station, things were likely to move quickly, he thought. Things were coming to a head at last. Porter had agreed to allow Cannon to watch the interview via a CCTV link to an adjacent room. Cannon requested that he be allowed to pass questions to Porter which could be asked of Smerdon. Porter acknowledged and accepted the request.

--------------------

Cannon had worked out how everything now fitted together but was keeping his thoughts to himself. All he needed was Smerdon's cooperation. It wasn't going to be easy. There was a story that needed to be unpacked.

------------------------------

Kevin was getting bored and agitated. He had watched the first race, almost flinching every time he looked at the screen in the centre of the track near the winning post. He could see tired horses near the end of the event being whipped to keep going. It bothered him. He didn't care that the whips did not hurt the horses. He didn't care that the horses were trained for the events they raced in. He didn't care that the animals were looked after, like precious pieces of jewellery. He just saw cruelty. He intended to stop it. He left his seat and walked down the steps of the stand before heading in the direction of the food court. He was stopped for a few minutes, along with many others of the crowd as the runners for the second race walked to the parade ring. The horses walked along a special walkway that had gates that could be opened to allow spectators to cross when there were no horses around. At the gates, he watched the runners for the race walk by, led by their handlers. The horses looked magnificent to him. He wasn't going to impact this race. He was waiting for later when the police would be off their guard a little. If nothing had happened by the start of the fifth race, he believed that their attention would have slackened off. The only concern he had was that he needed to allow four races to go ahead, knowing all the while that some of the horses would fall, some would be pulled up due to exhaustion and others would be encouraged to run faster despite being tired. To add insult to injury, they would be hit with a whip. He felt sick. While he contemplated the cruelty he felt the horses were subjected to, the gate was opened once all the runners had passed by. He continued walking towards the food court area. As he did so, he noticed several police walking in pairs around the area. He didn't notice Mike Cannon walk right past him as he made his way to the parade ring. Cannon likewise did not see Kevin, despite having studied a photograph of the man. A photo that Toby Jacobsen had provided. It was a missed opportunity. Cannon had his head down looking at the racecard, looking at the runners in his upcoming race. One of them had just been scratched from the race. It was the outsider of the field, so it was unlikely to impact the success, or otherwise, of his horse.

------------------------------

Kevin wandered through the grounds of the course. Things looked differently in the daylight. He saw people sitting at tables in the weak sun, and others standing under canvas at small bar-type counter-tops that were affixed around central poles. He suspected many never moved far from their seat or moved away from the tables near the bar areas. Those *inside* the stand watched the races on TV monitors. Those in the food courts hardly watched anything to do with the races at all. It was a day out for them. The racing was secondary. He felt them complicit in the cruelty of the sport, their focus was on having a good time. It sickened him.

---------------------------------

Race two turned out to be a bit of an anti-climax. The race was won by the favourite, beating the second and third favourites to the line in that order. There were no fallers in the race, no horses were pulled up. All got around safely, *Western Bay* finishing fourth, running into a small amount of prize money that the owners would be happy with. The horse was brought back to the stall by the stable hand. Cannon looked over the animal checking for any injuries. There were none. The horse was sound, but blowing hard, indicating that he still had some way to go before reaching peak fitness. Cannon sent the lad off to wash the horse down after its exertions, then ensure he was dry before putting him away in the horsebox ready for the trip home. After *The Politician's* race, they would leave as soon as they could, hoping to arrive home before dark. Cannon would drive home separately, ideally reaching his stables in Woodstock well before the horsebox. His phone rang, it was Tolman. They agreed to catch up immediately for a quick drink in the owners' bar where they would swap details of what they had each been able to uncover in their investigations.

Cannon bought the drinks. *Journalists,* he thought, *always wanting someone else to pick up the tab.* They spent a half hour together before Tolman advised that he needed to go off in search of a couple of owners to discuss the chances of their horses that were running on the day's program. The two men decided that it was necessary to expand upon their conversation the next day. There was so much to discuss and not enough time. Both had jobs to do. Cannon agreed to take a call from Tolman and said that he would provide him with more detail about what had happened at Uttoxeter and subsequently. In the short time they were able to talk, their discussion had moved on to the rest of the racecard and the chances of Cannon's runner in race five. Tolman observed that the horse needed to do well if Cannon wanted him to run in the *Tingle Creek* later in the season. Cannon agreed.

------------------------

Kevin bought himself a coke and a burger. He was hungry at the end of the third race. It was later than he normally ate lunch. His stomach was telling him that he needed to eat. Having paid for the food, he pushed his way through the crowd towards the stand and sat down close to where he had been sitting previously. He consumed his meal ravenously. As the day had worn on, more people had arrived at the course and the seating in the stand had become more crowded. As he was near the top of the stand he noticed a number of people at the back, standing against the railings that separated the seating areas below from the restaurant windows, and the owners and trainers viewing area at the top of the stand. It was an open area sitting like no man's land. At one point he turned around during the lull between the third and fourth races and he saw a man looking down at the crowd. Kevin quickly turned back to face the track. However, the sudden movement had caught Cannon's eye.

-----------------------------

Cannon looked at the back of the head of the person who had turned so rapidly away from him. He wasn't sure if it was just another punter who was wishing they were in the restaurant, or someone who felt sheepish having been caught staring at those with a slight privilege for the day?

He wasn't sure, *but* he was on his guard. So far nothing had happened, but he sensed something was in the offing. Porter had been explicit and Toby Jacobsen had hinted that something big could happen. As time had passed Cannon's nerves were on edge. He knew that the police had flooded the grounds of the course but apart from those in uniform you obviously wouldn't notice those in plain clothes. If there were any? He had been told that there were at least twenty, but was that true?

He focused his attention on the individual who had stared at him for a brief second. Cannon had the advantage of knowing what Kevin looked like from the photograph that Toby had provided. Kevin, however, had no such information. He was relying on instinct. Everyone he saw could be a policeman in plain clothes.

Cannon took out his phone and checked the photograph of Kevin stored digitally in the photo section then looked again at the crowd. It was like looking for a needle in a haystack. Gut feel made him focus on the individual he had seen staring at him, but he couldn't do it alone. He was due to go back to the stall to saddle up *The Politician* after the fourth race. He looked around to see if he could see anyone in uniform, but he had no luck. He tried to call Porter but for some reason, Porter didn't answer. Cannon's call went to voicemail. He became frustrated as Porter had promised to answer if Cannon called again. Unbeknownst to both men, Porter's phone battery had died, he had forgotten to charge it.

Cannon continued to watch the man. He didn't have much time. Occasionally the spectator would half turn around to check if anyone was watching him, staring at him. Finally, as the fourth race began and the crowd's focus turned to what was happening on the track, Cannon ducked under the railings and walked casually down the steps pushing his way past the few individuals who were standing where they were not officially allowed to. As he descended the steps and past the row where the individual sat, Cannon took a quick glance at the man's face. He wasn't one hundred percent sure, but he felt that the person sitting in the stand, in the row he had just passed was indeed Kevin. The thought filled him with horror. If it was him then he knew something big was going to happen and soon.

In an attempt to be sure, Cannon pushed his way into the crowd standing at the bottom of the stand, moving ten feet into the mass of people watching the race on the big screen as the horses continued to chase around the track. He turned one hundred and eighty degrees and faced the stand, he took his binoculars that he wore around his neck and focused on the man sitting in a seat near the top of the stand. He was looking for the face in the photograph. The face of the man he knew as Kevin. He had been right. It *was* him, it *was* Kevin!

--------------------------

He had followed Cannon's progress as he walked down the grandstand steps. He watched as the trainer moved into the crowd then turned and raised a pair of binoculars looking in his direction. The whole process unsettled him. It was clear that Cannon had spotted him. He needed to find a way to lose himself in the crowd. His plans could not be disrupted. As the horses on the track entered the final straight, the crowd roared and most in the stand stood up from their seats. It was the opportunity he had been waiting for. Those on their feet in front of him created a human shield. He ducked low, left his seat, and went upwards towards the top of the stand. He had noticed a glass door that those inside the restaurant used to come onto the balcony, from where they could watch the races. He climbed under the railing and went into the restaurant. He wasn't challenged by anyone. Most of the spectators were watching the end of the race. Even those looking to check tickets on the door, allowing an individual entry into the facility, had eyes on the TV screens. Within seconds Kevin was through the door and headed downstairs into the back of the stand. He would be safe there. Anonymous.

--------------------------

"Shit!" Cannon exclaimed.

The race was over, and an opening occurred in the crowd that occupied the rows of grandstand seats. Some people sat down while others made their way down the steps. Some headed upwards back into the restaurant. Cannon could see that Kevin had gone. Disappeared. All around Cannon, gaps occurred as the crowd dispersed to collect their winnings, move to the bars to share thoughts on the race, or seek commiserations for their losses. Others left for the unsaddling enclosures to see the winning horse or just go off for food. The milling crowds meant that it would very difficult for anyone to be found.

"Fuck!" Cannon said under his breath.

He was in two minds now. He needed to go to see his horse, saddle him up for the race, meet Formrobe, and the other owners in the parade ring, but he also needed to alert the police to Kevin's presence.

He decided his first port of call was the police tent set up midway between the food court and the main entrance to the course. He staggered his way through the crowds who were heading in different directions. The swirl of humanity on the course made it difficult for him and he was subject to verbal abuse as pushed and shoved his way through the masses.

Arriving almost breathless at the police tent, he found a Sergeant and a Constable in deep conversation. Interrupting them, he told them who he was, his relationship with Porter, and what he had observed regarding Kevin. Cannon was aware that the police had been briefed about the ALA and what could happen at the meeting and they were quick to respond to what Cannon explained to them. The Sergeant issued a verbal advice notice across the police radio network, a warning to all members that Kevin was on course and that if they saw him, he should be apprehended immediately using due care. In the course control room, two specialist police team members took over a series of cameras that were used to scan the crowd. No one on course knew that they could be watched, but the security of the type used had long been in place, similar to that used at football matches to catch hooligans.

Once he was satisfied that he had done all he could, Cannon left the tent and went to the saddling enclosure. He looked over *The Politician,* feeling the horse's legs for any heat. There was none. The horse had travelled well. He was still showing, indicating through his actions, that he was ready to run. That he couldn't wait to get out on the track and do his job. Cannon smiled. The horse was being overlooked in the betting. He was at twelve-to-one, the big weight was likely the reason why. He didn't do it often, but Cannon would suggest to the owners that they back the horse each-way. If the horse ran up to expectations even finishing in a place, the first three would give them a return on the investment.

Leaving the stable hand to walk the horse around the saddling enclosure before bringing him to the parade ring, Cannon left to meet the owners in the parade ring. As he walked through the crowd he kept scanning faces, looking at what people were wearing to see if he could spot Kevin. He had no luck. He hoped the police were more successful.

---------------------------

Kevin stayed under the stand. He would wait there until the fifth race was being run. He wasn't sure now if he should set off the devices during or after the race. If he did so during the race, there was a possibility of horses being injured or killed. He had fewer worries for the jockeys, it was the animals he wanted to protect. He decided to set off the devices immediately after the race finished. It would mean the jumps fences destroyed, people near the oak tree possibly killed, certainly burned and the rest of the meeting abandoned. It would also send a message that the ALA was still active, their demands still real, and that they could strike again at any time. Kevin didn't need Toby Jacobsen anymore. He was the ALA leader and Toby had sold out. Kevin's promise to himself to go after Jacobsen still stood. No matter how long it took, he would be back to seek revenge.

"How are you both?" Cannon asked, firstly shaking the hand of Lithgow then that of Formrobe.
"Fine. Excited," Formrobe answered. "I can't wait to see the horse."
"Well, he's looking well, and I think he should give a good account of himself."
"Despite being top weight?" Lithgow asked. He was a man of stocky build, just the right size to be a butcher. Strong arms from carrying half carcasses from the freezer hooks to the cutting table. He was dressed immaculately in a suit and tie. A beige overcoat slung across one arm. Cannon had only met him at the track once before as the man had not normally been able to leave his business to travel to the races during a busy working day. It was especially true if the race was a good drive away from Woodstock. Formrobe was dressed more casually, in line with *his* normal business attire. Blue jeans, boots, and a light blue shirt under a dark grey jersey. He kept his jacket on, a grey/blue windbreaker.
"Yes, despite being top-weight," Cannon finally answered Lithgow.
"So you are saying that we should have a go, Mike?" Formrobe asked. "Put some money on?"
Cannon smiled inwardly. He had expected Formrobe to ask the question.
"If I was you, I'd go each-way."
"Not going for the win?"
"James, it's your first runner. Anything can happen in this game," Cannon replied, his mind turning to Kevin. "We just want him to get around safely this time. If he runs up to expectations, we could see him do better than the

bookies expect, but you never know…"

Lithgow and Formrobe looked at each other. Both were optimists. Both had businesses that were doing well. A small gamble was something they were willing to take.

"Okay two hundred pounds each way," Lithgow said.

Cannon shrugged. It was their money. Two hundred wasn't a lot for Formrobe to spend. He was a very wealthy man, but Cannon wasn't sure if Lithgow was in the same big money league. He wasn't going to interfere, it was up to them. At twelve to one, if the horse won they would share over 4000 pounds or around 800 pounds if the horse placed.

Slowly the runners entered the parade ring. Around the edges of the ring, punters stood three-deep in places, watching as the horses walked slowly around the perimeter. Eventually, all the runners were in the ring being led by their handlers. Formrobe watched excitedly as *The Politician* paraded. Suddenly a bell chimed and the jockeys for the race entered the ring, their bright silks dampened by the sun's limited rays, as it slowly started to head towards the horizon. The few clouds hanging around in the sky left shadows on the ground. There was little breeze, so the temperature hadn't yet begun to fall. At around eighteen degrees centigrade, it was still quite pleasant.

Cannon introduced their jockey, Circling, to Formrobe and Lithgow. The owners were aware of the man, after what had happened at Uttoxeter. They knew he was very lucky, that he could have been severely injured or worse, killed. Given what had happened there, both men wished him well for the race.

Circling thanked them and touched his racing cap with his whip. Suddenly, another bell rang and a call to mount was made. Cannon gave Circling a leg up onto *The Politician* who immediately began to jig-jog on his toes. Circling was able to calm the horse down with a pat, and the two of them continued to parade around the ring. Cannon looked at the opposition for the race. From what he saw, including the first and second favourites, he was quietly confident. The outcome now lay with Circling and the horse itself.

----------------------

Kevin made his way to the fence at the side of the track. He didn't want to expose himself to the prospect of Cannon watching him while he sat in the stands again. Taking up position alongside the outer rail with other spectators as the horses for the race cantered by him heading towards the start, he felt safe. The horses on the track were introduced to the crowd as they each ran past the winning post in the opposite direction to that they would race.

Kevin thought that he was safe where he was, that he blended in with the others around him. He was wrong. The cameras focused on the crowds. Those at the rails were more in the open. They stayed static, so by not moving they were easier to focus on. Eventually just before race five began, the police spotted him. A message was sent to each police resource. Not knowing if Kevin had any weapon, explosive, or another device upon his person, they were told where he was, but that they needed to proceed with caution. There were many members of the public around him. It could be disastrous if he let off a bomb. They needed to be careful. Isolate him somehow.

------------------------------

The starting flag dropped and the race started. Cannon and his owners watched from the balcony at the back of the stand, the owners' excitement palpable. *The Politician* ran most of the race in midfield, jumping superbly. The instructions were to stay out of trouble and attack the front in the last quarter of the race. As the race unfolded, two of the leaders fell during the first lap. One horse that was badly tailed off was pulled up less than a third of the way into the race. Circling was riding the horse well. He was judging the pace perfectly. As the horses entered the last bend with three jumps to take, the favourite made his move. The horse had been sitting in third place about four lengths ahead of Circling and a couple of lengths behind the leader. The jockey pushed the horse forward, accelerating towards the leader. The commentator on track noticed the swift move and excitedly broadcast it to the crowd. Another roar went up. Circling stayed still on *The Politician,* it was still too early to go for it. The remainder of the field cleared the third last jump in various ways, some more smoothly than others. Circling's better handling of his mount moved him up to fourth just by getting the horse to jump low and at speed. Now, with only two fences to go, the horses charged into the straight. Gaps began to appear between the runners. Tired legs were beginning to cause some of the runners to drop away. The favourite continued to extend its lead. Circling asked his mount for a final effort. The horse responded swiftly, leaving the second and third horse in his wake. Circling whacked *The Politician* on the left side of the horse.

Kevin watched on the big screen as the crowd roared louder. A sense of disgust rose in his chest. He took out his phone. The crowd around him looked away from the big screen in front of them and peered down the track, craning necks and looking to see the horses come into view as they jumped the penultimate fence. Cannon's owners began to scream as *The Politician* closed up to the flanks of the favourite. There was one jump to go. Kevin began to make a call on his phone.

The vision from the course camera in front of the police specialist showed

Kevin looking at his mobile phone screen. He wasn't interested in the race, it was clear. The police specialist radioed to the Sergeant who relayed a message to those near and around Kevin. It was time to move.

On the track, the favourite jumped the last fence just ahead of *The Politician* and a battle ensued over the last three hundred metres towards the finish line. Neither horse nor jockey gave an inch. The crowd noise became a cacophony when mixed with the on-course commentary. Over the last fifty yards of the race, it looked like the favourite was weakening. Circling gave it all that he had, driving his mount towards the finish. However, despite gaining late, *The Politician* was beaten by a head. It was a great race. The two owners turned to each other shaking hands and hugging each other, celebrating what their horse had done. As the sound around them died, the crowd having seen the race conclude, a huge boom was heard from across the track, and then a wall of flame reached skywards at two of the fences. At the last fence in the straight, a further whoosh was heard before it too began to burn. Screams from those standing near the obstacle, photographers in particular, could be heard. A couple of them had caught on fire from the initial rush of the explosion. Pieces of birch and wood had spilt into thousands of pieces sending arrows of flame towards them. The crowd went silent, there was an almost eerie sound of nothingness. Then suddenly the last of the devices ignited in the tree in the food court area on the course lawn. Pieces of a branch, already alight, fell on two tables of revellers sitting in the shade directly below the tree. Fortunately, most just received glancing blows as branches fell, but the tree was engulfed in flame. The blast wasn't strong enough to knock people over, but the flames caused panic. People rushed to get away, knocking over tables, and each other. Kevin could not see what damage he had done but he heard the chaos. People around him scattered, some for exits, others towards the sounds of screaming. Others crossed towards the inside of the track to get away from everything.

------------------------------

Cannon had just finished telling his owners how pleased he was with their horse's run. He was about to go and take them to the winners' enclosure for a quick photo opportunity with the horse when the blasts happened. He looked towards the sound. From up high he had a good view of the last fence as it burnt, smoke drifting upwards, flames licking along the whole width of the jump.

"Not again!" he screamed under his breath. He had expected something to transpire given Kevin's presence, but he had hoped otherwise. At least the race was over. At least the horses and jockeys should be safe, he thought.

He looked towards the big screen that showed the fences on fire, the vision jumping from one fence to another. An announcement came over the course public address system asking people to remain calm and not panic. Formrobe asked Cannon what they should do. He advised them to stay where they were. He believed it was best for now.

As he looked at the screen, he noticed a scuffle at the rail about thirty yards beyond the base of the stand. A gap had opened up. Three policemen had someone on the ground, kneeling on top of him. They had managed to handcuff the person, pulling his arms behind their back. Cannon watched as they lifted the person off the ground. Muddied and bloodied from the scuffle, he was turned around and led away. It was Kevin.

---------------------------

The rest of the day was a blur. The last two races were abandoned. Cannon dealt with the impact, managing to get away from the track through the mass of traffic that had congregated in the car parks, the formal and the informal. His horses would arrive back in Woodstock when they could.

He left Formrobe and Lithgow to a muted celebration and to enjoy the fruits of their horse's run. It wasn't easy to celebrate, indeed with all the police, ambulance, and fire brigade activity, it would be callous to do so. The amount that they had won on their bets and in prize money was small, and after all that had happened, Formrobe suggested that they give the money to charity. Lithgow agreed wholeheartedly. As the on-course confusion still reigned around them, they had nowhere to go, so they sat in the restaurant watching cleaners and the waiting staff slowly clear the area. The day had ended traumatically and there was an air of sadness felt by all those that attended the meeting. While they waited for the police to allow them to leave the track, they sat together, silently considering what they had experienced. They ignored the drinks that still sat on the table between them, ultimately deciding to donate their winnings to the injured jockeys' fund.

The arrival of ambulances and fire trucks had made the escape from the track all the more of a challenge. However, Cannon had wanted to get back to his stables as soon as he could, so he had braved the traffic chaos. He also wanted to find out the status of Kevin's arrest and believed that he would be best able to do that once he got home. He didn't want to call Porter from his car. He knew it would take a little time for Kevin to be taken to the police station at Cannock. Even if Cannon had tried to call Porter's phone, it was still dead.

As he listened to the car radio, he heard the news broadcast details about the events of the day and the ongoing happenings at the course. Huntingdon was big news. It seems that seven people were badly injured from the initial blasts and three more from the panic that ensued. Two photographers were believed to have significant burns, as were three people from a single family who were caught by falling debris, raining fire, from the oak tree in the food court area. A journalist from the Racing Post, believed to be Ralph Tolman, was injured along with the two photographers.

"Christ!" Cannon said out-loud.

"Another person, believed to be one of the track maintenance workers was injured when flames erupted at one of the steeplechase fences just as the fifth race concluded," said the reporter on the radio. "The man's condition is not known but it has been reported that his clothes were ablaze for a short while before others were able to put the fire out. It is expected that the man, along with the others injured, will require treatment in the burns unit at the Nottingham University Hospital where they are all being taken. Three other people have been treated on-site before being sent off to the hospital. It has been reported that they have suffered broken bones and shock."

"What a mess," Cannon said to himself. "What a bloody mess!"

The reporter on the radio continued. "A man has been arrested in connection with the blasts and has been taken into custody at the Cannock police station in Nottingham. The meeting at Huntingdon was the first after recent problems at other racecourses which had resulted in jumps racing being put on hold. It was seen as a test and was given the go-ahead by the BHA after the group that had previously attacked other courses were believed to have been largely discredited and had been broken up. This was not..."

Cannon turned the radio off. He didn't yet know the fallout. He didn't want to think about it just yet. Inside, he felt that he had failed people, but had he? He had done all he could. With Kevin in custody, he hoped that it would be the end of it, the end of the ALA. They had promised destruction, Cannon had expected worse. Death. Death by stealth. It had happened, not only on the racecourse but elsewhere too. Once he was able to speak with Porter, he hoped that tomorrow he would be able to fit all the pieces together. He still planned to go and be part of the interrogation of Alan Smerdon and nothing was going to prevent him from doing so. If he was right, he knew exactly what had gone on. He had worked it out. He just needed Porter to play his part.

------------------------------

When he finally reached the stables, it was just about dark. He walked into the kitchen straight from his car. Michelle put her arms around him. She sobbed into his shoulder. Her worry now eased. He hadn't called her on the way back from the course, but she had heard on the radio after she had arrived home from school all about the happenings at Huntingdon. She admonished him for not calling, then held him tight to her again. As was his habit, he kissed her head. Once she relaxed her grip, he wiped away her tears. He told her that he loved her and that he knew that she had been worried but that she hadn't needed to be. She made some tea and they sat at the dining room table while he told her what had happened. He let her know that he would be going to Nottingham the next day.

---------------------------

After dinner, Cannon had a brief chat with Rich Telside telling him about the events at Huntingdon and asking him to run the stables the next day. As they talked they watched as the horsebox float containing *The Politician* and *Western Bay* finally arrive back from Huntingdon. It was an hour later than expected. Unloading the horses, they noticed that both had taken the delays in their strides. Neither horse seemed stressed. They were taken to their own stalls where they each received a special feed. Carrots were added to their normal dry food. Both horses ate up fully. It was a good sign. Cannon was still pleased with the runs of both.

----------------------------------

Once back inside the house, Cannon knowing that Tolman did not have any immediate family called the hospital at Nottingham University from his study, pretending to be his employer After a short discussion with a nurse about patient privacy, he was able to convince her to provide him with a brief update of Tolman's condition. He got the good news that the journalist was not too badly hurt. He had burns on his arms and legs but not on his face. He was being treated and tolerating it well. The nurse advised him that Tolman could be lucky and escape the need for skin grafts, but it was too early to tell. Cannon hoped that it was the case.

After he concluded the conversation with the hospital he tried to call Porter again. The policeman answered the phone eventually. He was at home. His phone was charging while he spoke.

"I think we have him," Porter said, "Mitchell, I mean."

"And what about Smerdon?" Cannon asked.

"He's in custody, he hasn't said anything yet, and I haven't spoken with him, either."

"Well when you meet with him tomorrow, you said I could sit in," Cannon said. "Is that still okay?"

"Yes, it's fine, though a bit unconventional," Porter replied. "Lucky you're an ex-cop. I'm not sure I should be doing it, but I'll take the risk."

Cannon thanked him again.

Porter carried on, "We'll have you in another room. You should be able to talk to me via earpiece, but I won't be able to talk with you. I'll just relay any questions you have."

"That will work for me."

"Do you want to share what you know?" Porter asked, hoping that the favour he had shown Cannon, would be immediately repaid.

"No," Cannon replied emphatically. "That's for tomorrow."

"Okay, Mike. I hope you have it worked out. I would hate to look a fool."

"You won't," Cannon promised. "Oh, by the way, what's happened to Kevin?"

"We've got him here as well. The bloody place is like Waterloo station. We've never had so many people locked up in connection with one case," he said.

Cannon smiled at the thought.

The two men then agreed on a time for Cannon to arrive at the station the next day. They would meet beforehand to work out their final approach with Smerdon. Kevin would be left in his cell until Porter was ready to interview him. Mitchell likewise.

The conduit to both was Smerdon.

Cannon put down the phone. He noticed it was nearly eleven pm. He yawned. He heard Michelle turn off the TV, the news was still dominated by the events at Huntingdon. She walked down the passage telling him she was off to bed. He said he would join her in two minutes.

By the time he got into bed, she was already out for the count.

He put his head on his pillow, turned to hold her in his arms, and was asleep within seconds.

# CHAPTER 69

Cannon had never met Alan Smerdon, but he felt that he knew him. On the trip up to the Cannock police station, he called Formrobe and told him that Alan had been arrested. Formrobe responded that he understood why but that he was saddened. Cannon painted a quick synopsis about what would happen to Alan, especially once all the details came out. Cannon explained that he had put all the pieces together and was hoping that when he shared them with Porter it would bring the whole sorry mess to an end. He also advised the *SecureTwo* man that perhaps Formrobe would be required to give evidence in mitigation once the case got to court, as it inevitably would. Formrobe agreed. He didn't know all the detail as yet and he was sure Cannon would fill him in once he was able to do so, but he felt that without Alan's input the case may never have been resolved. Cannon accepted that it was a distinct possibility, noting that once Smerdon was interviewed, more detail would emerge that would confirm his views of what had transpired recently, driven by things from the past.

Upon arrival at the police station, Porter was waiting. He took Cannon into his office and closed the door.

"I've been able to get you clearance to sit in on the interview with Smerdon," he said, a matter of factly. "Fox and I will take the session. You will be able to watch on a monitor in the room next door and be able to hear what's going on. You will have communication with me, one way only though, through an earpiece I'll be wearing. Anything you want me to ask, you can just say, and I'll repeat it as if it's coming from me."

"Will Smerdon have representation?" Cannon asked.

"Yes, we've provided him with a solicitor who arrived a short while ago and is currently with his client."

"Okay. Well, I am ready when you are," Cannon said.

"Give me fifteen minutes before we get going," Porter said, looking at his watch. It was just after ten-thirty. "Let's get you set up," he continued, "I've got a technician already in the room to ensure we have no glitches so let me introduce you, then I'll get Fox and we'll get going."

Cannon nodded, they left the office and Porter led him to the observation room, where Cannon was met by a Constable, Bill Whittingham, who would manage the communications between Cannon and Porter. Cannon had been through a similar process several times in his former life, but technology and equipment had moved on since then and he was given a quick overview of the necessary clicks to make with a mouse and the use of the applicable software.

Before too long he watched on the monitor as Smerdon, his lawyer, Fox and Porter entered the interview room. Another policeman, dressed in uniform entered last, closing the door and taking up his obligatory position, at attention, in front of the door. A silent witness.

Cannon recognized Smerdon immediately. He *was* Peter Todd. He looked different from when they had met previously. He kept looking downwards, his head barely raised, his chin just above his chest. Downcast, he seemed exhausted, not the vibrant man that Cannon could recall when he tried to drop off the horse at Cannon's stables, the replacement for *Centaur*. Cannon could guess what the man had gone through but was shocked to see the difference in him. What was about to be revealed would explain the change.

Porter invited everyone to sit down at a table affixed on one side to one of the walls of the room. Six inches above the tabletop, a tape machine stood on a small ledge. Fox turned the machine on to begin recording what was said.

For the record, Porter cautioned Smerdon.

"You have been arrested on suspicion of the murder of Mrs. Judy Smerdon. You do not have to say anything, but it may harm your defence if you do not mention, when questioned, something which you later rely on in court. Anything you do say may be given in evidence. Do you understand, Mr. Smerdon?"

Alan nodded. Porter asked him to verbalize his understanding. "For the record."

"Yes, I understand," Smerdon said.

The Inspector opened a file, looked at a couple of pages then closed it again. He was buying time, making Smerdon uncomfortable. It wasn't really necessary. Cannon knew the tactic but believed that Alan would cooperate without any games being played.

"Mr. Smerdon," Porter asked, "do you know why you have been arrested?"

"Yes."

"And do you know what you are being charged with?"

"Yes. The murder of my mother."

"And…?"

"Don't answer that, Mr. Smerdon," the Solictor, Sol Emmaus, said. "It's for the police to decide what to charge you with. So far, it is one count only. If they have anything else against you, they need to put it to you directly, not try and get you to admit to something you haven't done."

Emmaus looked at Porter, then Fox. "Do you have anything to add, Inspector?"

Cannon watching the screen in front of him spoke into the microphone, interrupting Porter's thought process. The Inspector touched his ear indicating that Cannon was talking a little louder than necessary, Whittingham turned down the volume, apologizing to Cannon as he did so.

"Ask Alan about Bronton and the Pools," Cannon continued. "Find out about them. I think he killed them first. I think I know why, but I'd like to hear it from him."

Porter gave a slight nod of his head indicating he understood the question. It was not what Emmaus was expecting in response to his own.

"Tell me about Henry Bronton and Harry Pool. Did you kill them as well?"

Again, Emmaus tried to interrupt, but Smerdon stopped him by moving his hand suggesting that he was willing to answer.

"Yes, I did."

Watching, Cannon steepled his hands together. He looked closer at the monitor of those in the room. While he was right, he didn't find any satisfaction in the confession, he just felt a deep sense of sadness.

"Can you tell me why you killed them?" Porter asked.

"Because she was in league with them."

"She…being your mother?"

"Yes."

"And why was that do you think?"

Smerdon looked up into Porter's face, the pain he felt inside evident.

"Because she hated James."

"James Formrobe? Your ex-partner, in *SecureTwo*? The company you both founded together?"

"Yes."

"Can you explain why?"

"She believed that James had stolen the company from me," he continued, "that he had benefited more than I did when I sold out, and she wanted to get back at him."

"But wasn't she a shareholder as well? Didn't she benefit from the growth of the business?"

"Yes, she was, and she did," Smerdon said, "but she was extremely money-conscious, and she wanted to get back at him. When I sold my shares to the Artimediant Investment Company, she believed that I should have kept hold of them, or at least sold them to her."

"Why didn't you?"

"Because she didn't have the money," Cannon said into Porter's earpiece before Smerdon could reply. "This was why she started blackmailing Mitchell."

Porter was a little confused. He knew that Cannon had the big picture in his head. It just needed to come out.

"I'm sorry, but maybe I misunderstood," Porter said. "If your mother didn't have the money to buy your share, why did you sell?"

"Because I wanted out. I wanted to start something new. James and I had a great relationship but my mother was always interfering. She was in my ear all the time and I couldn't take it anymore. James and I thought it best to go our separate ways, while remaining friends, but my mother wouldn't let it go. She insisted on staying in the business. *To keep an eye on James* she would say, *to see what he had stolen from me and to try and get back what was rightfully mine at some point.*"

"Which wasn't true?"

"That's right Inspector. James and I set up the business as a fifty, fifty partnership originally. We both worked hard and we both shared equally in the results."

Cannon listened carefully as the conversation continued. So far, the reason for the killing of the Pools and Bronton was not yet clear. Cannon suggested to Porter that he went back to the matter and find out the real reason.

"You said earlier, Mr. Smerdon, that your mother was in league with the equine agent, Bronton, and the trainer, Harry Pool. What did you mean by that?"

Emmaus nodded, suggesting Smerdon could answer the question. Emmaus made notes as Smerdon responded.

"As I said before, my mother hated James. She would do anything to see him suffer, lose money, whatever. She arranged with Bronton to contact the trainer Mike Cannon once she heard that James was going to buy a horse."

"And how did she learn that?"

"From Samuel Jacobsen."

"The company lawyer?"

"Yes. He needed to sign any documents that required a spend over a certain amount that James was to make. He was managing a trust set up to protect James."

Cannon realized the significance of the comment. The scam that had been set up was Judy's idea, in conjunction with Bronton. Smerdon had found out about it and had eventually taken things into his own hands. If he hadn't brought the wrong horse to Cannon's stable, no one would have been the wiser. He had done it deliberately. It was his way of leaving a clue to what was going on. He asked Porter to question why Jacobsen would tell Judy about what James was doing buying himself a horse.

Smerdon seemed embarrassed. He looked down onto the table before lifting his eyes again to look into Porter's face.

"Because they were lovers."

"Judy, your mother, and Jacobsen?"

"Yes, at least some years earlier they were."

Porter took a step back. "I'm sorry Mr. Smerdon but I'm losing you here. Are you pulling my chain, because if you are, I am *not* impressed?"

Emmaus leaned over to Smerdon and whispered in his ear. After they had spoken, the lawyer asked for a ten-minute break.

"We've only just started," Porter said.

"I know Inspector, but I'd like a few minutes with my client, please. I need to clear up something and I'd like to get some more detail from him. In private if you wouldn't mind?"

Porter nodded. As the men stood up to leave, the Inspector decided to seek permission for Cannon to join them in the interview room when everyone returned. While it was deemed unusual, Smerdon did not object, despite Emmaus' protestations.

Porter advised Emmaus of Cannon's former police background and the relationship with James Formrobe and Samuel Jacobsen. He also mentioned how Cannon had been involved with the BHA in trying to resolve the recent problems experienced with the shutdown of racing and how he would be instrumental in helping address the matters arising from the incidents at Huntingdon the previous day.

Having established Cannon's *bona fides* Emmaus dropped his concerns.

An hour later, Cannon had joined the other four men seated at the same table. The same Constable as before remained stoic at his post, standing on the inside of the door. Whittingham continued to watch proceedings through the monitor.

Porter was about to continue his questioning of Smerdon. Cannon had filled him in on what to ask and when. In return, Porter invited him to comment as necessary during the interview. Just before he was able to speak, Emmaus said to Porter that his client wanted to cooperate fully and was willing to fill in any blanks that the police needed. Porter nodded. "Very wise," he said, "though I suspect we know most of what has been going on. Mr. Cannon here believes he has been able to establish a number of links, but we will get to that shortly," he said.

Emmaus nodded.

"I'd like to get back to what happened to Bronton and Pool," Porter asked. "Why was it necessary to kill them?"

"They were in league with my mother. They had conned many people and would have carried on doing it if they could."

"But again, why kill them?" Porter asked.

"Because it was the only way to bring attention to what was going on, wasn't it?" Cannon interjected softly. "It was as if you needed to find a way to tell your story and it was a way of bringing things to a head."

Porter and Emmaus looked at each other. It seemed both were about to say something before Smerdon responded.

"Yes, that's right."

"Let me get this straight," Porter asked. "How did your mother get involved with the two of them. What was the rationale?"

"As she did with many people in her life," Smerdon replied, "she took advantage. *Abused* and bullied them."

"As she did with you?" Cannon asked.

Smerdon looked at his hands. He had tried to hide them under the table. Constantly rubbing them together, twisting them over each other. A sign of stress but also nervousness and fear. While they waited for a response and more details, Cannon looked at Emmaus. They saw in each other's eyes an understanding of what was going on, what had been motivating Smerdon to do what he had done. They were saddened by what they were seeing and hearing, however, the rest of the detail needed to be obtained, clarified.

"She broke up the relationship with my best mate. She hated him so much, that I couldn't even mention his name. She was obsessed with getting back something she believed was rightfully hers."

"Which was?" Porter asked.

"That's the whole point, Inspector. There *was nothing* owed. It was all in her head."

There was a pause, a silence in the room. Porter was hoping for clarity but the focus on Judy Smerdon and her obsession with revenge against James Formrobe didn't make anything clearer to him. The questions and answers were going around and around.

Cannon decided that it was time to try and pull all the pieces together, to act as the circuit breaker. He and Porter had agreed to a course of action if things weren't working out as hoped.

He wasn't sure if he had all the facts and expected that he could be potentially embarrassing himself, but it seemed that somehow, he had unwittingly become a central player in the whole matter. He asked Emmaus and Porter if it was acceptable to them to share his thoughts, to test his theory. They agreed.

Smerdon likewise did not object. It seemed like someone else pulling the strands, the pieces of the puzzle together, would be cathartic to him. A confession from another man potentially expunging the dark thoughts from his soul.

"As far as I can tell," Cannon began, "your mother, Judy, had a relationship with Samuel Jacobsen at some point?"

"Yes."

"But she also had a relationship with Clifford Mitchell?"

"Yes."

"And you tried to tell us through your email to James, which he passed on to me? To ask Mitchell about that relationship?"

"Yes," Smerdon admitted.

"Why weren't you specific about it?" Cannon asked. "What did you mean by it? Surely the relationship was her business?"

"It was her business. But it was also the catalyst to everything that has happened," Smerdon replied., "to everything I've done."

Tears began to well up in Alan's eyes. All the memories and thoughts in his head were affecting him badly. His left leg began to shake almost uncontrollably. Emmaus highlighted his concern for his client to Porter, but Smerdon told him that he was okay. The lawyer nodded and Cannon carried on with his theory.

"I'll come back to Mitchell in a second," he said. "Let's see if I've got this right regarding your mother and her obsession with money."

"Okay."

"Sometime after you and James start in business together your mother has a relationship with Samuel Jacobsen?"

"Yes. I think it began a little while after he was appointed our Chief Legal Officer. He's a good man, he was a widower and someone she felt she could take advantage of, manipulate."

"You didn't approve?"

"Of course not. By the time I found out, she already had what she wanted."

"Which was?"

"Influence over him."

"In what way?" Cannon asked.

There was a pause for a second. Porter and Fox looked at Cannon, not sure where the discussion was going.

Smerdon took a deep breath. "She found out that Samuel's son, Toby, had a gambling problem. I'm not sure how she did it, but I assume Samuel told her, because Samuel was always bailing Toby out."

"And what did she do?"

"She made it work in her favour."

"How?" Porter asked.

"She introduced Toby to Mitchell after telling Samuel not to help Toby anymore."

"And what happened?" Porter continued.

"Toby began losing even more money. Money he didn't have."

"Which resulted in...?"

"Toby being compromised. He ended up being at Mitchell's mercy. When he couldn't pay up, Mitchell made him an offer he couldn't turn down."

"Which was?" asked Porter.

"To establish a group of activists," Cannon jumped in. "A group that would be able to recruit enough resources, particularly in a University setting, based on a flawed premise."

"I guess so," Smerdon replied. "I didn't pay much attention to it initially. I didn't realise that my mother was behind it until much later."

"After she started the rumour about Toby sleeping with some of his students?"

"Yes. But it wasn't true."

"No, it wasn't," Cannon replied. He was still hoping to keep Toby out of the mess.

"I didn't know initially what occurred after Mitchell began putting pressure on Toby, but I know my mother was livid with Mitchell at various times. I heard her on several occasions screaming at him on the phone. She wanted results. I found out what she wanted later."

"For the ALA to deliver?" Cannon asked.

"Yes."

"And that meant?"

"That Toby would pay off his debt to Mitchell by getting the ALA to create mayhem. If he delivered, his debt would be wiped clean, and his reputation would be restored. I know he didn't believe in the ALA cause, but he was given no choice. Anyway, all he needed was for the actions that the ALA took to cause some courses to be closed down and my mother would profit from that. "

"How?" asked the Inspector.

"By being the main investor in a development company," Cannon said. "Making millions from the land. The sale and the building of housing, social or otherwise. I saw her name on the letterhead that was sent to the Southwell racecourse, the one that the BHA let me read. I only released the significance later."

"That's right," Smerdon responded.

"So, let me get this straight," Porter said. "Your mother's greed forced Clifford Mitchell to blackmail Toby Jacobsen. Jacobsen, who did not believe in a cause but had a gambling problem, established the ALA and out of that *madness* hoped to pay off his debt to Mitchell?"

"Yes."

"So why the murder of Bronton, the Pools, and ultimately your mother?" Porter asked.

"Because they were part of it. Bronton and Pool had worked with Mitchell over several years. They conned people out of thousands, tens of thousands," Alan said. "They were going to do the same to James. I couldn't allow it."

"So, you killed them, to get back at your mother?" Cannon said.

"Yes. I deliberately brought the wrong horse to your stable, so that James would be able to get his money back."

"You killed them after you had returned the horse? After I had tried to call them?"

"Before you called."

Cannon was surprised at Smerdon's admission. It was bold. He remembered the breathing at end of the phone when he had tried to call Pool. It obviously wasn't Smerdon, yet he was saying that Pool and Bronton were already dead by then.

"So who answered the phone," he asked, "if you were down here delivering the horse?"

"It was my mother," Smerdon said.

"I'm lost," he replied, his face reflecting his confusion. "If she was in league with them, why would she be at the Pools' house. Surely, if they were dead, she would have reported it?

"She was there because I told her she needed to go and see Pool. I told her that they were ripping her off, that James was paying more for *Centaur* than they had told *her* he was paying and that they were skimming money off the top."

"And?"

"She believed me. As I said, greed is a big motivator."

"So she went there, and what happened?"

"As I said, they were already dead."

"Because you had killed them?"

"Yes. I wanted her to see their bodies. I wanted her to see what she was involved in."

"And then I phoned," Cannon said.

"Yes, but she told me she didn't say anything."

"That's right. She just said *hello* and put the phone down. It was only later that I recognized the accent. Yours and hers. The Black Country. It was the connection."

Smerdon remained silent.

"What happened to the horse?" Cannon asked eventually. "The one you brought?"

Smerdon suddenly appears sheepish. Childlike. "I took him to an abattoir."

Cannon and the others knew what that meant. Nothing else needed to be said about the animal's fate.

Cannon asked, "What about your mother. Why kill her?"

Smerdon squirmed in his chair. He didn't appear to be a monster, but he *was* one. He had become what he was due to a parent obsessed with something other than the love of a child. It was the love of money.

"I couldn't let my mother get away with what she was doing. She had destroyed so many things, so many *good* things and she was on the way to destroying other people's livelihoods, potentially their lives, forever," he said. "She was not only greedy, but she was uncaring, money-obsessed, and would do anything she could to make herself more wealthy, richer. She didn't care about anything except how much she had in the bank!"

Alan suddenly stopped. His anger was evident. He began to sob uncontrollably. Cannon, Porter, and Fox looked at each other. Emmaus sat quietly. He slowly closed a folder of papers on which he had been writing notes.

It seemed like they had the answers they needed. Smerdon had confessed to the killings of Bronton, the Pools, and his mother so in that regard, there were no loose ends. Mitchell was in custody and would be charged with blackmail and possibly extortion, and Kevin would be charged for the deaths at Uttoxeter. Toby Jacobsen would probably also face disciplinary action at Southampton University, including some relating to being part of the ALA, despite his objection that he didn't agree with the ALA cause.

Cannon and Porter waited for Smerdon to stop sobbing. Fox left the room to find water for Alan. Emmaus began to pack away his bag. The tape still running, Cannon made an observation. Something was missing.

"Alan?" he asked quietly, attracting Smerdon's attention.

Alan looked up, his eyes red, puffy.

Porter wasn't sure what Cannon was doing. The interview hadn't been stated as having ended, but to all intents and purposes, it was. Porter felt that he had all he needed. A confession, to three murders.

"Tell me, Alan," Cannon said. "Something is bothering me. Something that I may have missed. It's the thing that I've been trying to understand for quite some time."

"Go on," Alan responded softly. He knew the question that was coming, he had been waiting for someone to ask it.

"How was your mother able to get Mitchell to do what he did? To get him to force anyone, particularly Toby Jacobsen, to set up the ALA and cause so much destruction?"

Smerdon smiled a wry smile. "He murdered my father," he replied.

Porter almost fell off his chair. The question and response were totally unexpected.

"Why? When?" Cannon asked.

"About fifteen years ago. His body was never found."

"So how do you know this?" Cannon asked.

"I overheard Mitchell and my mother talking. It was a few years ago now, just before I left the company."

"What happened?" Cannon asked again.

Smerdon seemed to look inside himself, to drag out a painful memory. Something he had heard, had been carrying. Eating away at him.

"This all occurred before James and I got together at Uni. Before we became successful, made money," he said. "If she had only waited, none of this would have happened," he continued. "Like Toby, my father got into debt with Mitchell. He couldn't pay. Mitchell was going to take everything he had from him. My father didn't have much anyway, but my mother wasn't going to let what she had go anywhere."

"So, what did she do?" Cannon asked.

"She started an affair with Mitchell. She convinced him to kill my father."

"Why?"

"Why do you think? Insurance money."

Cannon was skeptical. "If it was for insurance, surely your father's body would need to be found?. To prove he was dead?"

"Possibly. But he *never was* found. After several years and an extensive investigation, he was *declared* dead and my mother was paid out."

"How did she survive in the interim?"

"Through Mitchell. He sponsored her. She told him she would pay him back when she got the money."

"And did she?"

"Did she?" Smerdon repeated. "Yes, she did. In spades."

"How?"

"By letting him know that she would tell the police that he was part of the scam to defraud the insurance company and that he had killed my father."

"So, she blackmailed him, too?" Cannon said.

"Yes, and what's worse, she was *there* when my father was murdered"

In an instant, the air seemed to leave the room. A silence descended upon each of them. What Smerdon had said, stunned them all. They sat immobile.

Eventually, Porter asked the obvious question. "How do you know she was there?"

"As I said before, I heard them arguing. It was after their affair ended. By then she had started another with Samuel Jacobsen, but she still remained in contact with Mitchell. I worked out what had happened when I overheard how she threatened to expose him as a killer if he didn't do what she wanted. She told him that she had a video of him firing the shot. She said that she had taken it on her phone while he wasn't looking and that she had stashed it away in a safe place."

"And did she?" asked Cannon. "Have a video?"

"I don't know, but even if she didn't, she certainly scared him."

"And as a consequence of you finding this out...?"

"I began to put a plan together....to get back at her. It took me a while. I told you she was callous. She didn't care for anything other than money. She felt that she deserved to be rich, not poor and she didn't want anyone to take anything from her."

"Or take anything from you?" Cannon responded. "Like James."

"She hated him with a passion. She wanted him to lose everything. She would do anything to spite him. In her mind, he had taken our company and she had lost out. Lost out because I was no longer there. This, even though James had improved the business. He had grown it after we split, yet she couldn't get it into her head that she was a beneficiary of what he was doing."

Cannon shook his head. Fox re-entered the room just as Porter terminated the interview. The police had all they needed. They had heard similar stories in the past during other investigations but each time they did, it always surprised them how low some people could go. How base desires could drive mothers to ignore their children. Cannon likewise had experienced similar cases while he was in the Force. He was always glad to look back at the good things but the bad was never far away. It seemed that despite time passing, that despite humanity's goodness, and most people trying to get ahead as best they could, nothing had changed.

He drove home alone with his thoughts.

# Epilogue

Cannon stood on the steps of the grandstand. The early winter sun shone weakly. As he looked out at the mass of people walking around, talking, laughing, he turned to Formrobe with a smile.

"How are you feeling?" he asked.

"Nervous," Formrobe responded.

Since the confession of Alan Smerdon, they had both been on a roller coaster ride. Formrobe because of the impact on his relationship with Samuel Jacobsen, and the restructuring of the company due to Judy's death and Alan being convicted. Cannon, because of him being a witness at both Alan's and Kevin's trial.

Mitchell's court case was due to start in the new year after more evidence was collected. The charges being murder, corruption, and extortion.

Cannon still felt sorry for Toby, but ultimately admitted to himself that the lecturer had gone too far. While not believing in a cause, he still participated in something duplicitous and that involvement had resulted in jockeys and horses being killed.

As they waited, the crowd around them became more animated. In the distance across the expanse of the Sandown racecourse, the green grass of the track partially in shadow, the field for the *Tingle Creek* came into line.

Since the second at Huntingdon, *The Politician* had easily won its next race. It was only two weeks after the drama at the Cambridgeshire course when the horse ran, winning by fifteen lengths. Today he had a much lighter weight and was starting the race as the third favourite at eight-to-one.

Cannon smiled. Inside he felt nervous as well. He always was, no matter which horse of his was running. They were all precious to him. He just wanted them to reach their potential, but always come back safely. He hated it when a horse fell or was dragged down, interfered with. It happened in racing. It was part of the game. Like life, things could happen that you could not control.

The starter raised the tape, and the race began. A journey of two miles and thirteen fences. A roar leapt up from the crowd and Cannon watched through his binoculars as a mass of racing silks merged together. The noise around them was incessant. As each jump was cleared those watching the large screen near the finish line, oohed and aahed as the on-course commentary became more animated.

"He's doing well," Formrobe said to Cannon, elbowing him the side as the trainer focused on the horse. Cannon nodded. They were racing as he had hoped. The track had dried somewhat from the overnight rain. It was no longer a mud pit, as some had hoped for, but a track that gave everyone a chance. Jumping well was one thing, but stamina and courage over the last half mile up the long Sandown straight, the hill, was necessary to win the race.

The field entered the straight, the curve of the track, and the sun making it difficult to see which of the runners was ahead. Of the thirteen starters, there were still eleven in the race. Six were tailed off in various positions, they appeared to be racing in single file. The other five, including Cannon's horse, were line abreast as they leapt over the second last fence. Landing together the favourite pecked, his front legs bending, his nose nearly touching the ground. The jockey pulled hard on the reins, lifting the horse's head and somehow managing to stay on its back. Unfortunately, he had lost momentum and the other four runners moved ahead of him. The jockey tried to drive the horse to go faster but his chance was gone.

Up ahead, the remaining runners vied for the lead.

Formrobe began to shout, scream. The crowd grew even louder, urging their favourites on. The race was close, any one of the four could win.

The colours the jockey was wearing were still those of Lithgow. Formrobe didn't care that the horse wasn't racing in the silks that Cannon had registered for him. He had what he always wanted, *The Politician*.

The two men watched as the race concluded. Over the last two hundred yards, one of the four horses fell away, the jockey realizing that his mount was tired and could not win. He went easy on the horse, making sure that it could race another day.

Of the remaining three horses in the running, the jockeys urged their mounts towards the line. Whips cracked, the crowd screamed, photographers readied themselves to take the picture of the winning horse crossing the line ahead of the others.

The race began to take its toll, the last fifty yards saw the lead change three times as the horses raced neck and neck towards the finish. The commentator's voice was lost to the crowd as he reached fever pitch. The horses flashed across the line, a short half-head and a nose separating the three of them. Some of the crowd punched the air, others looked at the large screen, desperate to see if their choice had got up on the line. *What did the photograph say?*

Third! *The Politician* had been beaten by less than eight inches.

Cannon turned to Formrobe, satisfied, not disappointed. He was happy for his part-owner.

"I'll let you lead him in," he said.

# ABOUT THE AUTHOR

Other books in the Mike Cannon series:

- *Death on the Course*
- *After the Fire*
- *Death always Follows*

An ex Accountant with a lifelong love of horseracing. He has lived on three continents and has been passionate about the sport wherever he resided. Having grown up in England he was educated in South Africa where he played soccer professionally. Moving to Australia, he expanded his love for racing by becoming a syndicate member in several racehorses.

In addition, he began a hobby that quickly became extremely successful, that of making award-winning red wine with a close friend.

In mid-2014 he moved with his employer to England for just over four years, during which time he became a member of the British Racing Club (BRC).

He has now moved back to Australia, where he continues to write, and also presents a regular music show on local community radio.

He shares his life with his beautiful wife Rebecca.

He has two sons, one who lives in the UK and one who lives in Australia. This is his fourth novel.

www.erichorridge.com

Printed in Great Britain
by Amazon

12400521R10149